"This stunning evocation of ... to give solipsism a good na...

"Kimhi's vibrant writing, ex... by Dalya Bilu, is rich in m... ...raises the narrative and characterisation to new levels. The scope and variety are endlessly satisfying".

EMMA KLEIN, *Hampstead and Highgate Express*

"Kimhi has a bold original voice and in Susannah she has created an extraordinary and memorable heroine"

ANNE SEBBA, *Jewish Chronicle*

"*Weeping Susannah* is about how encounters transform not only our perceptions of people, but also people themselves"

ELAINE GLASSER, *Times Literary Supplement*

ALONA KIMHI was born in the Ukraine in 1966 and emigrated to Israel with her family at the age of six. She studied drama, and has worked as an actress, journalist, playwright and theatre director. A volume of her short stories, *Lunar Eclipse*, was published in 1996.

DALYA BILU has been awarded a number of prizes for her translations of Hebrew literature, including the Israel Culture and Education Ministry Prize for Translation, and the *Times Literary Supplement* and Jewish Book Council Award for Hebrew English Translation.

Alona Kimhi

WEEPING SUSANNAH

Translated from the Hebrew by
Dalya Bilu

THE HARVILL PRESS
LONDON

First published with the title *Susannah Ha-Bochiah* by Keter Publishing House, 1999

First published in Great Britain in 2001 by The Harvill Press

This paperback edition of the English translation first published in 2002 by The Harvill Press

www.harvill.com

1 3 5 7 9 8 6 4 2

© Alona Kimhi and Keter Publishing House, 1999
Worldwide Translation © The Institute for the Translation of Hebrew Literature, 1999

Alona Kimhi asserts the moral right to be identified as the author of this work

A CIP catalogue record is available from the British Library

ISBN 1 86046 630 3

Designed and typeset in Quadraat by Libanus Press, Marlborough, Wiltshire

Printed and bound in Great Britain by Bookmarque Ltd, Croydon, Surrey

CONDITIONS OF SALE

To Inbal, to her bright memory

No Relation To

Everyone's used to my name being Susannah Rabin, and they don't ask me any more if I'm any relation to. Since my life isn't exactly bursting at the seams with a surplus of new acquaintances, the need for clarifications hardly ever comes up. Sometimes there are exceptions, of course, and then I'm obliged to go into the story of my name in all its vicissitudes and metamorphoses, and the reasons for the latter. But for the most part the burden of explanation rests on my mother's sturdy shoulders, and she bears it with the quiet pride of a person doing her duty. I should point out that we're dealing with an exhausting process here, and my admiration for my mother at such moments knows no bounds. In certain cases she tends to exaggerate, both in dramatic intensity and in piling on the details, leading her audience to regret their initial polite interest. So, to sum up the subject, I can say that my name, despite its national glory, is mainly an inexhaustible source of misunderstanding and embarrassment.

There are, of course, exceptions to the rule, and although in the end they only serve to underline the general principle, they may even produce certain benefits. For example: some time ago the pianist Radu Lupu arrived in the country. He was due to give a recital at the Mann Auditorium and Nehama, my mother's best friend, suggested that the three of us go to hear him. Naturally we invited Armand to come along, but he said he hated Chopin because he was Polish schmaltz. Armand is a good friend of my mother's too, and they usually undertake all their cultural activities together, but Armand – give him Satie, Debussy, even give him Schoenberg – composers whose sophistication sticks out a mile – otherwise – ha ha – don't waste your time.

In any case, after Armand refused, we took the number 61 bus to Tel Aviv to the "Encore" ticket office, but when we arrived and my mother began groping in her bag for her purse it turned out that the recital was already sold out. The woman behind the counter suggested that we leave our name and telephone number – if there were any cancellations she would call us, although she couldn't believe there would be because people in Israel were crazy about Radu. And then, when my mother gave her name, Ada Rabin, the woman asked her immediately if she was any relation to, but even before my mother could get started on her usual explanations, Nehama butted in and said: That shouldn't make any difference, what if she is a relation of the family? Will tickets suddenly grow on trees? A country of cronies! A Third World state! And she pulled us outside.

And, wonder of wonders, the very next morning the ticket office called to inform us that we had three seats in the middle of the third row. Three and three. I myself am thirty-three. So that must mean something.

I always pay attention to coincidences like this, even though Nehama and my mother say that only benighted primitives do so and, what's worse, paranoids, who think they're being sent signs from outer space or somewhere. But I don't stop it, I couldn't even if I wanted to, because I have an urge to understand the order behind things, even in strange ways.

By the way, my mother tried to argue with Nehama that we'd obtained the tickets under false pretences because we weren't really related to, but Nehama pursed her lips and said: Ada, do me a favour, the end justifies the means. My mother yelled at her, of course, like she always does: Nehama! That's a Nazi slogan! But Nehama said you could learn from anyone, let alone the Germans, who were after all a cultured and enlightened people. My mother, as a Holocaust survivor, couldn't agree with these dubious claims put forward by Nehama, who was a Holocaust survivor herself, and gave her what for with a lecture on the banality of evil, until in the end Nehama nearly cried and said that my mother never understood her, or else she understood her incorrectly, and it was all because she was paranoid from the Holocaust, and if that was what she wanted, let her go ahead and return the tickets and we would all be stuck in front of the television instead of listening to Chopin. This was a really silly thing to say to my mother because the one who was clinically paranoid from the Holocaust was actually Nehama herself, who suspected everyone of harbouring murderous, criminal and evil intentions. A violent argument broke out, with claims and counter-claims illustrated by examples of the paranoia exhibited by each of the friends in the past, until in the end they were obliged to make up because it was late. They never went to sleep on bad terms with each other so that they wouldn't have nightmares and wake up in a bad mood the next morning. In spite of the enforced reconciliation, the incident did quite a lot to spoil the atmosphere, but when we actually went to the concert, all dressed up and smelling of scent, we enjoyed it and how we'd obtained the tickets didn't really make any difference, especially as ideological arguments with Nehama are rhetorical anyway and nothing to get upset about.

In the past few weeks the matter of our name has come up twice, filling me with a sense of flux and eventfulness. Sometimes months pass without this happening, and my peculiar name – Susannah Rabin – exists quietly and unsurprisingly, taken for granted by me, by everyone around me and apparently also by the God of names himself. Be that as it may, the first time was when we received a notice informing us of the arrival of an item of registered mail. When I arrived at our local post office with my mother we discovered that there was a new postal clerk there. I liked the look of her even though she had a plump, unpleasant face, because when she opened her mouth to remove a little lump of greyish gum she smiled at us apologetically and exposed a wide gap between her two front teeth. This immediately gave her a cute expression and caused me and my mother to exchange a quick glance of shared appreciation at this amusing discovery, as if to say to each other in our secret language: Isn't she adorable? The new clerk looked at our notification and went to search through the registered parcels and letters, wearily waggling her broad, low-slung hips. When she returned and handed the letter to my mother she exposed the cute gap again: Here you are, Rabin, sign. And then, in a sudden flash of suspicion, she knitted her brows and examined us with new interest: You're not related to? My mother, who regarded putting the record straight as a vital mission in life, immediately began explaining that our Rabin wasn't a Hebraization of some trivial Rabinowitz as anyone might think, but the shortening of an exotic name, Rabinyan, which was my father's surname. He was born in the Thirties, in Odessa, to a Jewish family with a rare history: his grandfather had gone there on business from Persia, fallen in love with his grandmother and remained in Russia, where he immediately caused a stir with his unusual family name.

My mother shifted her weight from one foot to the other, preparing herself for the enjoyable experience which had become increasingly rare with the passage of the years – the recital of our life history. She motioned me with her chin to take the cigarettes out of my bag, and before she had finished taking her first puff she was already continuing her story, blowing the smoke out of her nostrils like a dragon: when Avram – in other words, my father – emigrated to Israel and joined the army, Rabin was his commanding officer. And he shortened his name to Rabin, both out of admiration for his commander, and so it wouldn't smack too much of the Diaspora, which was the fashion then. With the passage of the years my father joined Mapai, the Israeli labour party, and once he even visited Rabin at his home, but he himself never aspired to a political career because it didn't suit his personality. He was too soft and he had a weak character. At this stage the new postal clerk yawned and looked to see if there was anyone behind us to save her from the rest of the story, but the post office was empty, and my mother ignored this display of rudeness on her part and went on. Her – in other words, my – father, she said, always thought for some reason that he was an artist. Not that it did him much good. Being an artist isn't only enjoying yourself, drinking and, pardon the expression, fucking. It isn't easy. You need character for that too. So in the end he became a book-keeper for the Chamber Theatre and stuffed the child's – in other words, my – head with all kinds of Greek myths and poems. I myself – in other words, my mother – grew up in Kibbutz Ben-Shemen and received a decent Zionist, agricultural education without all kinds of bees in my bonnet. Even though my – in other words, her, my mother's – life wasn't a bed of roses either, my parents sent me out on the last train from Germany and they themselves perished in Buchenwald together with my big brother Theo and my little brother Aharon. The one with the short leg.

At this stage the postal clerk lost all shame and began reading the women's magazine lying on the counter in front of her, which made no difference to my mother, who was already deep in the thickets of the plot. She leant on the counter, made herself comfortable, and went on with her story. Luckily for him – in other words, my father – she said, he died exactly one day before the elections of 1977 and he didn't have to witness the debacle. She remembered how she and Susannah – in other words, me – went to visit him a few days before he died in the Tel Hashomer Hospital and he stroked my hair and said: Susannahleh, this is our country, it belongs to working people, it always has and it always will. So don't worry, we'll beat the Revisionists this time too.

Here she was obliged to stop, because a little old man in a hat came in and stood behind us, puffing and panting asthmatically, his aggrieved expression threatening that every gasp might be his last unless we got a move on.

When we left the post office I said to my mother: You didn't have to tell her the whole story, it was obvious she wasn't interested, and my mother tried to argue with me and said that it was an interesting story because it had historical implications, and anyway the postal clerk had asked, she herself had asked explicitly: Are you related to or aren't you. I maintained a sullen silence because she knew that I was right and I wanted her to admit it, and in the end she gave in and said: You're right, Susannah, sometimes I just can't resist the temptation to talk about your father in a detached way, like an outside observer. To tell people about him. And how many new people do I already meet? I said: You can always talk about him to me, you can tell me, or Nehama or Armand, and she laughed and said: Oh come on, I've already told you everything there is to tell a million times. Then she gave me a look and asked: What is it, are you ashamed of your old mother? And I said: Of course not, I love you more than anyone in the world. And I sensed the smell, which in spite of her cleanliness was the mouldy smell of old age, and I also sensed a faint smell of frying and of egg shampoo against dandruff from her hair, and I was proud of myself for overcoming my disgust.

One of the things that makes me suffer most is the disgust and hate I feel for people I love. For Nehama or Armand, but especially for my mother. Sometimes, when I hate something about her movements, the way she removes her false teeth before she goes to bed, or when she goes to the bathroom in her night-gown and her breasts, huge and floppy without the support of her bra, dangle above her fat belly, I appal myself but I can't stop staring, as if there's something about this disgust that I need, that I'm addicted to, which prevents me from averting my critical gaze. I think that the main fear in my life is of her finding out about these feelings which overcome me so frequently, and I therefore invest major efforts and develop sophisticated methods of disguise and deception to avoid distressing her and hurting her feelings. And now too, as soon as I felt disgusted, I hugged her tighter and tighter, smacking my lips in exaggerated kissing noises over her ear, until she said: Stop it, that's enough, what are you getting so excited about? and began tearing open the envelope of the registered letter. What a brilliant victory for the transparent Susannah Rabin, who succeeded in keeping her thoughts, in all their ugliness, hidden.

The letter was from Bat-Ami, a relation of ours in America. Bat-Ami's first husband was my father's cousin – Uncle Noah – who left Bat-Ami and ran away. He simply disappeared one day, vanished into thin air and left Bat-Ami with a small child and without a penny to her name. It turned out that although he had represented himself as a millionaire and behaved like one too – thereby enflaming Bat-Ami's love after years of enduring the restrictions of Ben Gurion's austerity regime – Uncle Noah, before removing himself from the picture, cleaned out Bat-Ami's meagre savings too, an act which had been forced on him by circumstances but which he profoundly regretted, as he pointed out in his farewell letter. Everyone said that it was terrible and criminal and he wouldn't get away with it and he would land up in prison in the end, not before returning everything he had stolen from Bat-Ami, with compound interest, not to mention compensation for mental anguish and reimbursement for bringing up their child. But nobody knew where to find him, and the truth is that they didn't look too hard either. In short, Uncle Noah was a completely negative character in our family mythology. When anyone took the trouble to mention him it was only to run him down, and the more the years passed the more details miraculously accumulated, and the more the original story was expanded to accommodate them. Some people said, for example, that he was a shady adventurer, a cheat and a compulsive gambler. Others that he was an international crook. They said that he had a wife in every city he'd ever visited. They said that he was involved in transporting uranium on Israeli ships to South

8

Africa. Sometimes they even said that he might be a double agent, working for Israel and Iran at the same time. But whatever the current version of Uncle Noah's life and times, everyone agreed that Bat-Ami was lucky he'd left her, and it was only to be hoped that the child wouldn't turn out as rotten as his father because from the physical and genetic point of view they were alike as two peas in a pod.

Everyone was sorry for Bat-Ami, but they also pointed out that she should have had more sense to begin with. The result of all this talk was that Bat-Ami began to get some sense into her head retroactively, took a course in gardening and went to live on a kibbutz because of the outstanding conditions for child-rearing there. Everyone hoped that on the kibbutz she would at least be safe from problems and adventures, but Bat-Ami had a natural gift for attracting problems and adventures, and she very quickly became involved with an American volunteer. On the face of it, it might have seemed that Bat-Ami's troubles had come to an end, but it turned out that the boy had been a combat soldier in Vietnam and had come home from the war not quite right in the head. But people slightly deranged by war are nothing new as far as we Israelis are concerned, and the ill-effects of combat on a young man's psyche are certainly no reason to stop a woman no longer as young and beautiful as she once was from marrying him. Accordingly, Bat-Ami received all the support and encouragement she could have wished for in her decision to do just that. The wedding took place on the kibbutz, and snatches of its sights and smells are still preserved in my memory – chains of coloured light bulbs stretched between the trees, the cool air of the summer night full of mosquitoes circling hysterically in the beams of artificial light, the faint smell of hay and fertilizer coming from the fields, patriotic Israeli songs and foreign hits blaring alternately from the huge loudspeakers, tables set on the spacious lawn, haystacks and bunches of flowers and swarms of kibbutz children of all ages and sizes bathed and dressed in their best, remote and inaccessible, wrapped up in their secrets and their own affairs, running about between the legs of the tables and those of the adult guests.

But, in spite of all the festivities, the happiness of Bat-Ami and the American did not last long, at least not on the kibbutz. Two weeks before the general meeting which was to approve the acceptance of the couple as full members in the collective, the new husband was caught smoking a joint with a few young-sters. The collective lost no time in pronouncing sentence on the young couple, and they left the kibbutz and the country for America, together with Bat-Ami's son, and after many wander-ings they finally settled down in New York.

Once, when my father was still alive, we even went to visit them there. This trip had been almost completely effaced from my memory, apart from blurred images of endlessly walking the streets behind my mother and Bat-Ami, my father in his under-shirt watching the television in English, the two women cooking in the little kitchen and conversations deep into the night, with the Hebrew parts devoted mainly to our family mythology in all its ramifications and vicissitudes, to bad-mouthing Uncle Noah and analysing his character, and to my mother's and Bat-Ami's stories, turn and turn about, of the difficulties of their respective lives. Bat-Ami's husband, Herb – a big-bodied man with almost transparent pale blue eyes – frightened me in his bearishness, and every word he addressed to me, however soft and purring, sent me flying to safety behind my mother's solid hips.

The child I remember as an obnoxious little creature who chattered non-stop to his mother and stepfather in piping English and ignored us, the provincials who had invaded his life, with ostentatious disdain. I refused to make friends with him because I was afraid of him, even though he was a good few years younger than I was, and his parents said that he was a real genius in innumerable fields, especially in painting, which was also a field that interested me. Because his arrogance was out of all proportion to his defective physical development, my wariness of him was mixed with a certain contempt, which I quickly focused on his legs, weak, white, rabbity legs, which peeped out of his short pants like macaroni *al dente*.

My mother finished reading Bat-Ami's letter and said: Talk about the devil! We were talking about new people and look what turns up! It's a pity we didn't talk about a million dollars too. And I said: Why, what does she write? My mother said: Come, let's go and sit in a café and have an ice-cream, and then I understood that something important had happened. And, indeed, it turned out that it was something well-nigh revolutionary. This is what my mother told me: this same son of Bat-Ami's, the arrogant little rabbit, had grown up into an academic and a businessman and was about to visit Israel. Bat-Ami wrote that he had already paid several visits to Israel, but since he suffered from an individualistic and subversive temperament (a character flaw he had no doubt inherited from his biological father), as well as the usual rebelliousness of youth, he had been unwilling to visit the family, in other words my mother and me, on any of his previous trips. But now he was returning to his roots and she would be very obliged to us, my mother and me, if we could put him up for a few weeks because, although he was coming on business and he could afford to stay at a luxury hotel, such as the Hilton, or the Radisson Moriah, as he usually did, it would make her so happy to know that the family was reunited because with the passing of the years and the onset of old age you came to realize that this was what remained to a person in life, isn't that so?

After the ice-cream arrived – chocolate and vanilla, for both of us – my mother looked at me and asked me how I felt about it. About what? I didn't understand, and she said: About a strange man coming to live in our house. All right, I guess, I said, and she examined me again and said that it seemed to her that I didn't really understand the implications, but on the other hand maybe the lad would turn out to be nice – after all, he was an academic – and it would do me good, and anyway, what could we do about it now, because Bat-Ami, with all due respect to her famous sensitivity, wasn't really asking, but simply notifying us of his arrival, so what could we do but accept the inevitable and hope for the best since obviously she, my mother, wasn't going to throw him out into the street. All this talk had a calming effect on her, and she relaxed and concentrated on her ice-cream. I looked at her and saw that a big drop had fallen off her spoon and trickled down the low neck of her dress, a summer dress covered with little blue, brown and white flowers. She always wore short sleeves and low necks in summer, to give herself more air, exposing the tanned, wrinkled cleavage between her breasts and a large expanse of old, naked skin. Now a large, creamy drop of ice-cream slid straight into this great divide of human flesh, and my mother opened her bag, took out a tissue and wiped herself as if we weren't in a public place with people looking at us. I felt a blush spreading over my cheeks and I was immediately ashamed of myself for being disgusted and ashamed of my mother, but I couldn't help it.

This, by the way, is one of the reasons why I never eat in company. I feel that this is one of the most self-exposing things a person can do. Sometimes I watch other people eating. I watch their chewing, the gluttony they try or don't try to hide, the greediness. The human bestiality disclosed at such moments makes me shrink with embarrassment.

In the outpatients' clinic they advised my mother always to put food in front of me, even when we were in restaurants or in company and when there was no chance I would touch it, so that perhaps, little by little, at the right moment, I might begin to eat anyway. My mother follows their instructions, but we almost always eat at home, except for ice-cream or cheesecake in a café, and then she orders for me and in the end she eats mine too.

In fact, when I think about it in a wider sense, everything connected to the body causes me embarrassment and disgust. In bad times I couldn't even change my sanitary towels or wipe myself after a bowel movement, I was so revolted. I tried not to think about it at all, and if my mother hadn't washed and changed me I would have turned into a real health hazard. Even now, when I'm in great shape, I hate taking a shower and my mother always has to remind me. I find it difficult to see myself naked all over again every time. My body is limp and thin and I don't like remembering it over and over again. That's my right. That's also the first reason why I always wear long, closed garments.

The second reason is that I can't stand the touch of other people's looks. Sometimes I even sense their thoughts without wanting to, and that hurts me as much as the touch of a red-hot iron.

Because of these peculiarities of mine we always try to make sure that I meet as few strangers as possible. This was also the main reason why I stopped going to the groups run by the outpatients' clinic. My mother argued, correctly, that all those encounters with the people in the occupational therapy and the group dynamics sessions only made me feel more exposed. So now we only go once a month to talk to Rivki, my social worker. And the fact is that for a long time now I've been feeling fine, and during the last few weeks I've even started going to the beach with my mother and Nehama. They play with a heavy ball called a medicine ball in order to strengthen their muscles, and I sit and look at the sea. I try to direct my gaze so that nothing else will be in my field of vision, and then this feeling – that everything gets inside me and touches me – turns into a wonderful, beneficial feeling, and I feel that the sea is me and I'm the sea, and it's the best feeling I can think of right now.

So the second thing that happened lately in connection with my name is even more special than the first one, and it's related to Rivki. Rivki is Rivka Finkwasser, the social worker at the out-patients clinic. Although Rivki is my own age, her superior status endows her with a few more years of hypothetical maturity, an advantage which causes her to behave as if I'm an adolescent girl afflicted by deafness. The thing I like about Rivki is the contrast between the round eyes, the plump nose and mouth, and the serious and self-important expression that contradicts the babyish elements of which her face is composed. We've known each other for a few years now, which makes our relations almost friendly. Rivki, who's dying to get married and who despises this weakness in herself because she's a feminist, admires my mother, the strong woman who manages just fine without any men in her life. Rivki has a particularly soft spot for me too, because of my artistic inclinations, for she too aspires to develop herself in many areas beyond the unglamorous field of social work. The truth is that I feel undeserving of her admiration because my artistic inclinations, which once, in my childhood and youth, were the most important thing in my life, have shrunk in the course of the years to attending courses given by the municipality and to the paintings and little sculptures I do at home, an occupation that has more to do with trying to stay sane than the expression of the real creativity of an artist on fire inside. Even thinking about this subject gives me a dull pain and I prefer avoiding it whenever it comes up. I gave up my dreams of becoming a serious artist somewhere in the miserable years after my father's death, and the truth is I consider myself lucky that they no longer return to disturb my rest.

In any event, the last time we went for the regular meeting at the clinic, Rivki looked solemn and mysterious. I brought her a couple of woodcuts I'd made at home and also two clay dolls, which is the real expertise I've developed over the past year. One doll of Yasser Arafat and the other of the English poet, Percy Bysshe Shelley. I did Arafat because he's the puppet from the *Spitting Image* TV programme I like best, and I made one of Shelley because I saw a picture of him in an anthology of English poetry which Armand brought me for a present and I thought that he was the most beautiful person I'd ever seen. The beauty of his poems and of his person moved me so powerfully that it began to seep into me and fill me with a clear, bubbly transparency, like champagne, and a softness of petals – irises, roses and hothouse orchids. Whenever I read the poems and looked at the picture little waves of excitement spread through me, all the way down to the tips of my toes, moving, breathing, as if a flock of rare, exquisite tropical butterflies had been trapped inside me.

The first few times I sank into this contemplation I began to cry. Even my experienced mother didn't understand at first that we weren't talking here about one of my usual fits of crying at the pain of invasion, but about tears of joy. She immediately started massaging my head, grumbling about my father, who loved poetry more than anything in the world and had infected me with this insane passion, until I succeeded in reassuring her and explaining that they were good tears. Tears of inner radiance.

Rivki took the dolls and put them on her desk in order to inspect them and express her learned opinion, but she couldn't concentrate, and after a moment she said: This is exactly what I wanted to talk to you about, and I asked in surprise: About Shelley? And my mother asked: About Arafat? And Rivki asked anxiously: Which Shelley? The fat one? From rape victim assistance? Did something specific happen? And I said: No, not from any assistance, from England, Percy Bysshe, the poet. And my mother pointed to me and said: Look at her, she's starting to cry from too much beauty again, all because of her father and those poems. And Rivki said: Oh, what a lark, I didn't notice it was Yasser. And I said: I'm not starting anything. And my mother said: It beats me why anyone should want to make a doll of that murderer. And Rivki said: And who's the other hunk? And I said: He isn't murdering anyone any more. And I almost did start crying, until in the end Rivki said: OK, OK, let me tell you my news now! And we all fell silent.

And Rivki's news was this: a communal centre was being set up in Rosh Pinna for people with emotional problems, like me, on condition they had artistic talent. The best teachers and artists in the country were going to give classes there in painting and sculpture in metal and marble, professional workshops at the highest level. As well as pure art it would be possible to learn practical artistic trades there that you could earn a living from, such as pottery, gold and silver smithing, enamel work, and so on, and to make connections with professionals in the relevant areas who would help you find work in the future. The commune would be located in an old Turkish building which had been magnificently renovated and donated by an Australian millionaire, who had also provided funds to bring teachers from abroad, to purchase materials and the rest. The reason for all this generosity was that the Australian's daughter had been schizophrenic and had committed suicide, but not before painting a few pictures and making a few little sculptures. At this stage of the story Rivki giggled and rolled her eyes in exaggerated irony. When my mother asked her why she was laughing, Rivki said that she had seen the catalogue for the exhibition the Australian had organized of his daughter's work, and the fact was that the poor girl had been utterly lacking in talent. Then she looked at me and said seriously: That, of course, has got nothing to do with us – in other words, Rivki, my mother and me – although it's a shame that a person with talent like Susannah hasn't got a millionaire for a father. And my mother, who in spite of our friendly relations with the social worker was allergic to her more foolish remarks, immediately protested: What's her talent got to do with how much money her father had? And if she didn't have any talent, it wouldn't have been a shame that her father wasn't a millionaire? And Rivki, who was quite scared of my mother, saw that she had made a mistake and said: Never mind, Ada, it's not important, but my mother persisted: So what is important? And Rivki said that what was important, more than important, wonderful, was that I, Susannah Rabin, had been chosen from hundreds of candidates to be one of the twenty-four members of the artistic commune. And now – Rivki had turned quite pink with pleasure – she wanted to tell us how the final decision had been taken because there had been some hesitation between me and some autistic youth who made wood carvings. It was a real dilemma. The boy was talented and I was talented. The boy was a little sensitive and I was a little sensitive. The members of the specially appointed committee couldn't make up their minds because of all kinds of considerations which offset each other, and in the end they phoned Mr Idelson, the lawyer who represented the millionaire in Israel, and consulted him, and the minute Mr Idelson heard that the name of one of the candidates, in other words, me, was Susannah Rabin, he said that it had to be her – in other words, me – because the name of the millionaire's daughter, just imagine, was Susannah, a name he gave her because of some painting he liked, and Rabin was one of the politicians he most admired, and so it was decided that I was going to Rosh Pinna.

Rivki fell silent, leant on her elbows and rested her chin on her hands, looking at my mother and me with a look that said: Well, am I your fairy godmother or not?

It was quite clear to me that my mother did not think that Rivki was our fairy godmother. She crossed her legs, took a cigarette out of her bag and waited with a frozen expression for Rivki to light it for her with the lighter in the shape of two children kissing which stood on her desk. Then she took a deep drag on the cigarette, looked at me, at Rivki and then at me again, and said: Susannah, do me a favour, go to the vending machine next to the reception desk and bring me a cider. She took a couple of coins out of her purse and gave them to me, and when I was already opening the door to leave the room she almost yelled: Just not the fizzy kind, it gives me heartburn, and I shrank in embarrassment and looked at Rivki and then into the corridor to see if anyone had heard, but Rivki was sitting with her face tense in suspense to hear my mother's reaction to her proposal, and the corridor was empty, so I shut the door behind me and walked in the direction of the vending machine with a slow step, intended to waste time, because I understood that my mother wanted to talk to Rivki about matters that were no concern of mine.

Next to the vending machine a man I didn't know was standing and smoking a cigarette. The minute I saw him I didn't like him, but I knew that I had to perform the task my mother had set me or else she would be angry, and when she's hungry or thirsty there's no talking to her. I inserted the five-shekel coin in the slot and pressed the button for the cider. Nothing happened. I went on pressing, but the machine didn't react. I thought that perhaps the cider was finished and I inserted another five one-shekel coins, pinning my hopes on mango nectar, but here too nothing happened. I started pressing all the buttons, especially the one that was supposed to give me my money back, but the machine seemed to rebel against me. I could feel its resistance, silent and malevolent, and I stopped pressing all the buttons as if I expected to persuade it by these means that I wasn't just another thirsty person, but that my business with it was important and urgent, and then the man with the cigarette addressed me. What's up, honey, he said, did it swallow your money? I didn't answer but he went on: Look, did you try anything else apart from the cola? I bet you didn't. So go ahead and try . . . You want me to do it? Why don't you answer? You're a snob, is that it? OK, it's no skin off my nose . . . You want me to go and call one of the staff and bawl them out for not fixing the machines, the maniacs? No? OK, it's up to you . . . Believe me, these guys here, they don't give a fuck about anything, they think the people who come here are million-aires, what do they think, they can take your money and all the colas stay inside . . . You don't want me to help you? Sure? It's no skin off my nose . . .

All the time the man was talking I went on trying the buttons even though deep down I already knew it was a lost cause, and then he came closer, leant over towards me and whispered confi-dentially: They're all whores here.

I could smell the bad, rotten smell of his breath, he was stand-ing so close. I froze with dread and disgust and suddenly the words broke out of their own accord: Who? Who's a whore? The man moved even closer until he was almost touching me and said: All of them. And then he enlarged on his answer, as if we were engaged in some kind of business deal which had to be clarified in order to avoid any misunderstandings: Everyone here is a whore-son of a whore, and most of all Sigalit from reception. That one, for all she cares a person can go round the bend from stress and nerves, she doesn't give a damn. Until that bitch makes you an appointment with Rosnow you can die waiting. I'll still fuck her one day, the cunt. And that Rosnow's a whore too, you can't get a pill out of her without a prescription from the psychiatrist, who does she think she is? I'll still show her what's what, that cunt.

He stopped for a minute and measured me with his eyes, and I felt as if he was touching me with his broad, brown hands and I shrank, sensing his look slide over my breasts and belly and then over all my inner organs, the spleen, the liver, the ovaries, kneading my womb, probing my lungs with his filthy fingernail, possessively patting my heart, and then going back outside again, to my mouth covered with a dry film, to my unhealthy skin, to my damp forehead, stopping at my eyes, trapping them in the vice of his sly, vacant eyes, enjoying my female ugliness: Why are you trembling, baby? From the Halydol? Never mind, tell them to give you Artane, that'll get rid of it in two ticks. Just don't worry, trust me, Moish knows what he's talking about.

My obvious terror encouraged Moish to go on, apparently out of a wish to reassure me. You know you're cute? What's your name? Let me guess. Orna? Pnina? Shelly? You don't want to tell me? Too bad. Shelly really suits you, you know that?

His last words shook me to the core. What an uncanny coincidence. The pure name of the poet in the mouth of this degenerate. In the meantime Moish started pressing the buttons on the vending machine, repeating my barren actions as if his touch could bring the machine back to life. His need for dialogue increased: So you hear what I'm saying? This whole clinic is a bunch of maniacs, they're all whores. They don't give a fuck. Come on, move, what's the matter with you, don't you care about the money? So say bye-bye, money, au revoir, money, to hell with the money. Or else just get out of my way for a second, and you'll see how Moish fixes the whole thing up in one minute flat.

I couldn't bear to remain next to him for another second. My back was pressed against the corner between the machine and the wall, and like a gecko without a tail I slithered sideways while he ceremoniously took a few steps backwards and then with a savage, ape-like leap, charged towards the silent machine and kicked it with all his force.

For a moment it was quiet and everything froze – the air, time, the strange man, I myself – then with the thunderous sound of the ram's horn blowing on Yom Kippur, dozens of cans of soft drinks began to roll out of the machine, and at the same time, in perfect co-ordination with the roar of the avalanche, Moish began to scream, his deep voice turning into a hysterical falsetto echoing in the deserted corridors of the clinic: Ai ai ai, you bitch, look what happened to me because of you, my foot's broken, fuck your mother's cunt you cock-sucker, I'm going to call the whole staff to bring the police for you because of what you made me do, you fucking cunt, may your father rot in his grave . . .

I started running as fast as I could, sliding over the tiles, swerving round the bends like the driver of a racing car, the sterile, medicinal air of the clinic pumping automatically in and out of my lungs without any help from me, and an invisible hand in my skull pressing against my eyes and threatening to spray them out as I ran and ran and ran, until I reached the door with the sign saying: "Rivka Finkwasser, Social Worker", and I shot into the room, and only there, standing opposite my mother and Rivki, both of them smoking at their ease, coffee cups on the desk in front of them and the fragrance of their pleasant conversation lingering in the air, did I begin to cry.

When we got on to the bus home I was totally exhausted. For my mother, on the other hand, the entire incident was like emotional fuel, serving only to charge her batteries, and even after the clarifications with the nurses, the security guards, the administrative director of the clinic, and curious onlookers who gathered at the scene of the event next to the vending machine, she still had enough strength left to lecture Rivki, who accompanied us to the bus stop, about some man Rivki was romantically interested in, who in return wanted to turn the living room of her little apartment into a studio for photographing models.

Although I sat with my nose and forehead pressed against the window all the way home, staring at the dusty neighbourhoods on the sides of the road, my mother went on denouncing Rivki's proposal about the artistic commune in Rosh Pinna, giving me more and more reasons why it was so important for me to stay at home with her. I was already well acquainted with most of them from previous occasions when the possibility had come up of my leaving home or going out to work or to study. They included examples of women who had lived with their mothers all their lives (the poet Leah Goldberg, the writer Dvora Baron and her daughter Tzipora, and also Tzila, a relation of Nehama's from Petah Tikva), denunciations of the proposal itself (and if this millionaire had decided to set up a commune for bungee jumpers in the desert, would she have wanted to send me there too?), and philosophical conclusions regarding the human condition in general, and ours and Rivki's in particular (there was no one right way to live, everyone found his own way of getting through life, and there was no point in judging or trying to decide for somebody else. What was so great about the way she lived, anyway, letting one man after the other into her home to exploit her and take advantage of her?) All this was completely superfluous, as far as I was concerned at least. I had no intention of leaving my mother either in the near or the far future. She knew this very well and, this being the case, her monologue was presumably intended to resolve certain inner contradictions invisible to the naked eye, which she never shared with me.

These are the two incidents that happened lately and that were connected to my name, which, as I have already said, is Susannah Rabin. Ever since then, everything sailed along as usual. We went to the beach with Nehama, to the HMO clinic (my mother's problems with her legs and back had grown more severe for some reason, in spite of the mild, warm weather), sat in the grocery store with Armand, watched *Wheel of Fortune* and the election propaganda on television. Apart from the approaching elections the main subject on the agenda was, of course, the cousin due to arrive from abroad – speculations about what he was like and what it would be like to have him living in our house. Nehama was excited by the fact that he was an academic and Armand was jealous because he was both an academic and a businessman, and my practical mother was mainly concerned about how he would live with us in our house.

As for me, much to everybody's surprise I couldn't work up any interest in the subject. I read the anthology of English poetry and also a biography of Kierkegaard in archaic Hebrew that Nehama had found in the storage space under her ceiling. I made another two dolls of the poet Percy Bysshe Shelley and I practised drawing, because I have problems with perspective.

At the end of May, two days before my cousin was due to arrive, I went with my mother to Armand's grocery shop to buy provisions for the guest.

Armand's shop, by the way, isn't exactly a grocery but a proper little supermarket, and it's called that too: "Super Duper". Everybody, in other words my mother and Nehama, says that Armand is a remarkable man who built himself up from scratch. Once he was an employee in the aeronautical industry and he had a wife he worshipped, Margalit. They lived in Holon, without children, because Margalit had problems. She was mortally ill, this Margalit, and Nehama, who knew the story better than anyone although my mother wasn't far behind her, hinted that bedpans full of number one and number two had to be taken out from under her while she was dying, a detail that persuaded me more than anything else of Armand's emotional sensitivity, because I myself am barely capable of going to the lavatory without vomiting. In spite of the bedpans and the children they didn't have, Armand didn't even think of divorcing his Margalit. He took care of her needs and looked after her devotedly until her condition deteriorated and she died. And Armand never got married again. He left Holon and came to live in Ramat Gan. At first he had a grocery store, but it grew and flourished until it turned into Super Duper, and he even had an assistant, Aziz, a fat man who always smiles at me when we come in, as if there's some special connection between us, and I smile back at him because his smile doesn't invade me, but hovers over me gently, and I like it a lot.

Armand smiles at me too. A lot. In general he's fond of me, is Armand, and last year he started to teach me French. I accept these lessons because I try to be polite, but I haven't made any great progress and I know mainly how to pay compliments, because this is Armand's own expertise: *Que belle chemise*, for example.

After my mother finished selecting the things she needed for her preparations, we loaded the packages on to Aziz and started walking home. It was an ordinary day and the sun was already hinting at the summer heat about to colour our lives in the coming months. My mother and Nehama walked in front, Armand, who offered to accompany us, was a little behind them, with me next to him, and Aziz brought up the rear with the packages. On the way the usual incident with the Rottweiler almost took place, but my mother saw him in the distance and made us all cross the road. The Rottweiler belongs to Gidi Bochacho, who lives in the building opposite us and is an ex-military man. This Rottweiler, a black beast with a square, heavy head and a humped belly, bursts into loud barks whenever he sees someone walking down the street. Of all the people in the neighbourhood the dog chose me as the focus of his most passionate hatred, and whenever he sets eyes on me, even from a distance of tens of metres, he goes berserk. If I don't manage to cross the road in time or hide in the entrance to one of the buildings, his barks turn into an unrestrained volley of canine outrage. This insults me so much that sometimes I burst into tears even before he opens his mouth. I suppose the reason for my tears is that somewhere inside me I feel that his hatred is justified. He knows who I am, he smells my misery through the distance separating us, through the smells of the street he recognizes my fear, the soft sinews holding my body relatively erect. I could live with his hatred, unfair as it might be, if only it remained a private affair between the two of us, but the terrible thing is that his barks betray me to the whole world. The truth that he recognizes with his nasty, vicious perceptiveness becomes public property and once more I am exposed, naked to the eyes of the passers-by against the pale backdrop of the sky, illuminated by the spotlight of the pitiless sun.

This time my mother acted with precise timing and we crossed the road before the dog noticed us, or perhaps he was preoccupied with his doggy thoughts and decided to overlook our presence. We continued on our way and then all of a sudden the strangest and most uncanny of sights met our eyes: when we approached the entrance to our building I saw the poet Percy Bysshe Shelley.

The poet was leaning with his back against the wall with the mailboxes and smoking a cigarette. He had long hair, darker than that in the picture in the anthology, and he was wearing sunglasses, but apart from these details it was him – the same arrogant and demanding curl of the lip, the same milk-pale brow, the same girlish chin jutting slightly forward, the same cloud of idleness and melancholy enveloping the whole strange and exotic figure.

It was a sight so absurd, so crazy and so far removed from me, from us, from Ramat Gan and the twentieth century, that I immediately attributed it to my recent withdrawn state, and decided that I was simply hallucinating, but to my astonishment I saw that everybody had stopped to stare at him as if the poet himself was indeed standing there, as large as life. A short silence of mutual recognition hung in the air, and then with a quick flick of his fingers the young man threw his cigarette to a distant spot on the lawn, took a few steps towards us, ignoring Nehama, who had recovered before everyone else and hurried to hold out her hand, and stood facing our little group in a relaxed and friendly pose which did not succeed in disguising the impudence in his personality.

He aimed the lenses of his dark glasses at my mother while a pair of eyebrows arched above them questioningly: Ada? I'm Neo, Bat-Ami's son, and my mother cried, utterly confused by the wrongness of the time: But we thought that you were only . . . and he cut her short with the strangest and most glittering smile I had ever seen and said: Yes, I know. I took an earlier plane and flew in via London. There's a Japanese restaurant I like there.

The Blue Vase

There are some people whose very existence makes you, in other words me, want to disappear. Not to let them look at you. To touch you with their look. This isn't because they're bad people. Or rude, or violent, or arrogant. It isn't because they're against you, in other words, against me. It's just so.

Our guest is one of these people.

There are some people who the more frank they are, the more open, the more mysterious they are. The more honest they are the less you know about them. Maybe you don't even want to know more about them, but something about their truthfulness, their sincerity, their excessiveness, gives rise in you, in other words me, to a sense of lack of information. A sense of secrecy. Uneasiness. You know that they're telling the truth. That they're not lying. Maybe it's too much truth. Maybe the truth too needs to be limited in order to be open. Like the few steps back you have to take in order to see a picture by Manet or Pissarro. I know that their experience is authentic – they can encompass something and its opposite with the same degree of conviction. Every claim and its absolute opposite exists in them in perfect harmony.

Our guest is one of these people.

There are some people who make you feel ashamed. Terribly ashamed. Not ashamed of doing something complicated like taking part in a conversation or performing an embarrassing act – going to pee in the middle of a meeting or eating spaghetti. No. Just being in their presence. And it's not because I feel that they're better than I am. It's just so.

There are also people who make everyone want to fall in love with them, but pure as pure can be, for the right reasons, not because they make an effort to charm. Just because that's what they're like.

There are some people who give rise in you to need. Some kind of need. A cosmic, incomprehensible need. So our guest's like that, too.

And there are also people (whose numbers are infinitesimal) who immediately hit it off with my mother.

Yes. Of course. It should be obvious by now – our guest is one of them.

I don't like our guest. He's turned my life in our house into a suffocating prison with no way out. Not because he did anything unusually domineering. That's just the way he is.

My name's Susannah Rabin and I'm no relation to. I sit in my room and I don't want to come out. I don't want to do anything. Not even inside my room itself. Not even paint or model dolls in clay, which usually calms me. I'm careful to sit on a chair and not to lie down because when I lie down I sink into myself, and then it's always hard. When I lie down, at first I feel relief and then I start to feel that I'll never be able to go outside again. I won't be able to open my eyes. So I sit.

Sometimes I want to die. Not because I'm unhappy. It simply

seems pleasant to me. When acting outside becomes intolerably difficult I lie down and close my eyes and feel my universe inside myself, and it's so calm and quiet there that even the thought of going to the grocer's with my mother or taking a shower brings a pressure to my chest that makes me feel nauseous.

It's the month of June and the air is starting to be dense with heat. The fan opposite me moves the air and then I feel really good, I dissolve, I let go, I merge with everything around me – the bed, the objects, the blue vase (oh, the blue vase) – there are no boundaries between the inside and the outside.

The guest arrived on the day of the elections. But he didn't sit with us and watch television till late at night and wait in suspense for the results. He slept. My mother prepared my father's study for him, which my father never used for work – he worked in his office at the theatre. But he argued that a man needed a study. This was during the period when my mother received her reparations from Germany and we moved into this apartment, which is much larger than the old one, and my father got his study. He would shut himself up in it for hours and sometimes I would peep through the keyhole and see him reading, mostly poetry. Pushkin, Rilke, Akhmatova, Byron, Blake. The room smelled of oranges, cigarettes and the breath of a sleeping person. Even in the summer, when there weren't any oranges. When I went inside my father was always pleased and he would read me something from his book, and even when I couldn't understand the meaning of the poem I could feel the hypnotic rhythm, which riveted me, until I learned to read poetry myself and I became as addicted as him.

My father had two reading positions: lying on his back on the bed with the book in his hands and his legs up, carelessly crossed in the region of the ankles and leaning against the wall, or lying on his stomach with the book on the floor next to the bed. Sometimes he would play Russian songs on his guitar. They were called romances. They were sad and obscure, and when the spirit took him he would perform them for my mother and me and translate the words. Even though he only knew a few chords, he would play and sing with a melancholy fervour, his head cocked to one side, his eyebrows coming slightly closer to each other and creating two vertical lines between them, and a dreamy look in his eyes directed at the neck of the guitar. Sometimes I thought that if you licked those lines they would probably taste bitter, like the peel of a lemon, and once I even did it – I hugged him and licked the space between his eyebrows, to see what it tasted like. It really was bitter, but more like cocoa without sugar together with the taste of a baby. And the most important thing is that there was always a lock of black hair falling with glorious asymmetry to cover the right side of his forehead and his eye. Even when he was already bald and he was still playing the guitar I would imagine that lock of hair, as if it was some integral part of his being, like a character trait.

> *Atvari potsikhanku kalitku*
> *I vidzhi vdzhivini sad slovno tzhen*
> *Niye zabudzh potsimnuyu nakidku*
> *Kruzheva na galotku nadzhen*

My mother, who already knew the translation of the words by heart as well as their phonetic sound and who would sometimes move her lips together with his, always sighed at the end and said something about the over-sentimental Russians and pulled a hard face. She couldn't forgive him for his cheating, and he couldn't control himself. Once I heard him say that it wasn't that he loved women – they simply loved him, but for his part he loved only her, and she said in a hard voice with a tremor at its edge: Oh, Avram, do me a favour, I'm not your mother, I'm your wife, and turned away to do something in the kitchen which involved a lot of noise of pots banging into each other.

> Quietly open the little gate
> And enter the enchanted garden like a shadow
> Don't forget the dark scarf
> And the lace on your hair

I remember all these things vividly, and our games too, the jokes with the forbidden obscenities, the book of Greek mythology he would read to me at every opportunity, until the foreign stories in old-fashioned Hebrew became an indivisible part of my world of images and daydreams: the cunning Odysseus, the handsome Paris, Midas of the golden touch, all the denizens of Olympus, the heroes of Greece and Sparta with their muscular bodies, their uncompromising nature, their eternal quarrels with the capricious gods, who alternately made alliances with them and tormented them. All this I remember and much more, but this isn't the time to plunge into the depths of the past. Let the dead years rest in peace.

My boundless love for my father, the memory of the pain of his abandonment, live in me every day, like underground water lying at the base of every thought and every act. I never cease to be amazed at how the pain and despair that a certain person can cause you don't do the right job and make you hate him. Or forget him. It's a screw-up. An evolutionary screw-up. Possible only with human beings. Nature's distorted and dependent children.

My father in his death left me, abandoned me without any axis of security inside me that could have helped me go on without him. He was my life. And, by logical inference, from the moment he was gone my life would never be the same again, or perhaps it wouldn't be a life at all. I was lucky to be able to carry on and survive. This was, of course, thanks to my mother. Thanks to her devoted care, thanks to her endless sacrifice. Because she dedicated her life to me and mingled it with mine until it's impossible to know where I begin and she ends. Hers is a completely different love from my father's. He never thought that I was weak or in need of help. On the contrary. In his eyes I was strength, endurance and order personified. Sometimes he behaved as if it was he who needed me. And in fact when he was alive I never felt needy or helpless the way I've felt ever since he died.

His room remained my secret temple. A temple I would sometimes go into, lie down on his bed, my face buried in his old bedclothes, trying to draw even a little strength from that vanished past where I left myself light years ago.

Into this room my mother put the guest.

Immediately after drinking a cup of coffee he said that he was exhausted and he had to rest because he had hardly slept for a week, and he closed the door behind him. I still hadn't grasped the fact that this man was going to live in our house. One of the characteristics of my peculiar consciousness is to push the awareness of a fact that already exists a little forwards, as if this short period of cheating will give me time to adjust to something impossible to adjust to.

In the evening Armand and Nehama arrived to watch television and wait for the results of the elections. They were both disappointed to hear that the guest was sleeping. Nehama said: What does he have to sleep all day for? In the end day will turn into night for him. And Armand said: Maybe he'd like to take a break, have coffee with us and then go back to sleep? My mother rejected this suggestion and the guest was quickly forgotten as they both settled down to watch television. My mother brought in a tray of eclairs she had prepared and everyone ate and drank tea and talked about what was happening, trying to bet on the final results, each with their own forecast. So we sat, like the guests at the Mad Hatter's tea party in *Alice in Wonderland*, with the television in the role of the dormouse drowsing on the table and only rarely gaining the attention of the participants. Nehama was beside herself with excitement and made the kind of racist remarks about the opposition that in civilized circles you should keep to yourself. Armand maintained a mysterious expression, as if he already knew what was going to happen, and only my mother was tense, staring impatiently at the self-important people on the screen and waiting for the polling booth results.

I don't care about the elections. I don't care who the Prime Minister will be. I have no social or political awareness. I'm a kind of anarchist but for superficial reasons. The world seems to me like an arena that belongs to big, cruel, power-hungry people over whom I have no influence at all. This is one of the few things my mother never succeeded in passing on to me. She always feels that everything is in her hands. That there's no problem she can't change or solve. Usually the situation doesn't actually change, like, for example, the situation in Israel: the influence of the apolitical, phlegmatic Susannah Rabin is no less negligible than that of the involved and caring Ada Rabin. If I told my mother that all her deep involvement and heated debates in front of the television wouldn't do a thing

34

to advance the peace process or stop inflation, she would have thought I'd gone out of my mind. As far as she's concerned, but for her impassioned reactions to the daily news the ultra-Orthodox De'eri would already have been the Prime Minister of Israel. But the fact is that all we've succeeded in doing for our country, both my committed mother and my apathetic self, is exactly the same thing – dragging ourselves to the polling booth to perform our duty as citizens. Peace in the Middle East doesn't even get a look in.

These subversive thoughts about my mother lead me into very strange states. This morning, for instance, at the polling booth in our local elementary school, there was a moment when I was standing alone behind the screen, and I was suddenly flooded by a sense of my total freedom, in the circumstances, to do something unforgivable. The thought suddenly came into my head that I could commit an act of shocking rebellion which nobody would ever know about. I could betray my mother and stain my conscience with an ugly black stain for ever. What if, instead of voting the right and proper way, I voted for some Arab party, or something even worse but just as bold – for Mahal, the contemptible, infamous Likud Party itself, may God damn it to hell? Like a disreputable family doctor imagining the breasts of his patient as he presses the stethoscope to her chest, I stood behind the screen and excited myself with thoughts shocking in their immorality.

Mahal. Netanyahu. Mahal. Netanyahu. Mahal. Netanyahu. Netanyahu. Netanyahu. I passed my finger over the ballot tickets. I, bearer of the proud name Susannah Rabin, was going to screw the country. The party. Everything held dear in the home I grew up in. I was going to screw my mother the old-age pensioner, previously director of the municipal water department, a wonderful woman and an exemplary citizen – Ada Rabin. My departed father Avram Rabin-Rabinyan, who had so symbolically given up the ghost on the very day that Begin came to power. The sad-eyed Mr Shimon Peres and God himself, who had left me all alone here behind the screen and allowed Satan to tempt me, to pull me by the ears and put out his tongue and grin at me mockingly: Do it, do it, do it, sin, sin, sin. A distant childhood memory of a song the children in the street used to sing at me came back and rang in my ears at full volume: Susannah Susannah Susannah, he's coming to get you, Susannah, he'll grab hold of your tits and fuck you to bits, he's coming to get you Susannah!!

But suddenly I heard the voice of my guardian angel. A beloved, familiar voice, a little too loud, as usual, asked an invisible figure, probably one of the cherubs: Pardon me, where are the toilets here? Down the corridor and turn right? Do you know if they've got any toilet paper there? And I heard the flat, but resolute in their heaviness, heels of my mother setting out in the required direction, and I calmed down immediately and everything was clear and pure again. Satan's attempt at temptation had been foiled. I knew what I had to do.

And so at the last minute I saved my soul. I put the right ballots into the envelope, painfully aware of the insignificance of my puny little inner voice in the brutal lion's roar of that vast human mass called the nation. And immediately after the tickets saying Emet (Labour) and Peres had found their way into the dark bellies of the two ballot boxes, I was enveloped in an airy cloud of joy. I emerged into the corridor smiling, full of the sweet childish satisfaction I always felt when I succeeded in doing my mother's will, delighted to see the gratification in her eyes and to know how good, obedient and worthy of her love I was. And when I saw her coming towards me from the far end of the corridor, tugging her skirt this way and that so that nobody could make any mistake about what she had been doing in the past few minutes, I wasn't even ashamed of her disgusting, shameless gestures. I smiled politely at the lady who had examined our ID cards when we came in, hissing at her in my heart: We'll still see, honey, which of us is going to be fucked to bits, and then I took hold of my mother's elbow: Oof, that's over, let's go and have a cola at the kiosk.

And now, on the fateful night in whose results I have played my part, I prefer to look at the moderator and not to think about what's going to happen to the country. It seems that the moderator too isn't worried about what's going to happen to the country. Apparently he's happy either way. Occasionally he gives his lower lip a little lick, addresses an amusing question to the bespectacled lady writer with the thin lips or the cynical entertainer with the yarmulka like Armand's, who Nehama said has become a born-again Jew. I think about them, how they live, what they do when they go home after the programme's over. Their lives are glamorous and glittering. They don't go to the HMO clinic, they're not afraid to eat in the presence of other people, they kiss and cuddle with other writers and moderators, put on perfume, laugh. One thing sure is that, whatever happens to the country, it won't have anything to do with the arch and knowing bacchanalia taking place here on the screen, before our provincial eyes.

From time to time my mother would get up to make more tea and ask in a worried voice when she returned: Well, what's happened? And Nehama would reply: Stop asking. What are you worried about? We're winning. Gradually it became as clear as daylight that she was wrong and that we, in other words they, weren't winning. The more certain it became, the more amused Armand grew and the more noisy Nehama became and the more she yelled. She drank egg liqueur from a teacup and harangued Armand: What's the matter? What are you so happy about? You people with your nonsense are ruining our country. And why? I'll tell you exactly why – because of your nasty, vindictive natures. What's the point of talking, you can see for yourself what's happening – that fascist is going to be your Prime Minister, and why, I ask you? Because you're still settling scores with us! You know very well what I'm talking about – oh, the DDT, oh the transit camps, oh, what Golda said, oh, what Ben Gurion did! And why? I'll tell you exactly why – because you bear a grudge. That's why! And who did you learn it from, I ask you? Well, from who? You don't know? Then I'll tell you! From the people you hate the most – from the Arabs! How do you learn something from people you hate? I'll tell you exactly how, it's a historical fact, if we're already talking about it. You assimilated among them without thinking twice, you got on with them like a house on fire both before the expulsion from Spain and after it, while the Ashkenazi Jews kept themselves pure of Gentile blood – have you read *Tuvia the Milkman*? No? So read it! And you mixed with them and got all their nonsense from them, and now you hate them and Peres too. Anyone would think he did God knows what to you, even though he did nothing to you, nothing! A sweet man, a dear man. Aren't I right? Go on, tell me, tell me what did Peres do to you? Just one small example. So I'll tell you: he didn't do anything bad to you! But you didn't vote for him, and why?

I'll tell you exactly why: on principle. That's all, on principle. Hate, just hate. Well, aren't I right?

Armand laughed and said that she was a terrible racist and that he hoped she didn't talk like this in front of people who didn't have a sense of humour, or they might make kebabs out of her, or some other dish that they learned from the Arabs. This only enraged Nehama more, and she delivered a long speech about the Moroccan Jews who came to Israel and their demandingness and their backwardness and how they didn't serve in select combat units in the army. Armand said that he wasn't a Moroccan but a Tunisian, and Nehama waved her hand at him and accused him of nit-picking. At this stage my mother switched off the television and said that it was enough and it was time to go to bed. Armand looked into my eyes, said: Bonne nuit, ma belle, and held my hand, giving it a secret little stroke with his warm, dry thumb. I quickly pulled my hand away. Everyone said goodbye to everyone else. We heard Nehama's voice still shouting at Armand on the stairs.

I sat opposite my mother next to the table with the empty teacups and the tray of eclairs. We were silent. I looked at her and she looked at me and averted her eyes. And then her thoughts started seeping into my mind. They were thoughts about my father, about herself, about me.

And so I absorbed her into myself, and my inner self began in some involuntary way to organize and order itself until my expression came to resemble hers exactly. My mouth hardened, tightened, turned down at the corners, my forehead became heavy and tense.

She sighed and said: Ah well, too bad, apparently about the elections, and her pain was so unbearable in my chest that I took an eclair and started eating it. I chewed without averting my eyes, chewing the lumps of dough and the fat yellow cream, fighting against the constriction in my throat, chewing, chewing, until I'd finished it all. She looked at me with her dead look, and when I swallowed the last mouthful she said: Well, was it tasty? And I said: Very tasty. Very, very tasty, mummy.

The next morning, before we set out on our daily excursion to the sea, Nehama, who came early, ran to and fro in the kitchen and expressed her disapproval of the fact that the guest was still sleeping. Very strange, she cried, in my opinion you should check and see what's happened to him. Maybe he's ill, or something. Maybe he's dead! Stopped breathing in his sleep. Don't look at me like that, Ada, such things happen! And my mother said: What things exactly? Come along, Susannah, take the folding chair and let's go before it gets hot.

The sea steals me to it. I never get tired of it. We look at each other. Between us – mother and Nehama and the medicine ball. With depleted old knees, with swollen veins, with brightly coloured bathing cap (Nehama), with old-fashioned sunglasses (my mother), they hold the approaching stagnation of death at bay. I'm not afraid of death. I'm afraid of what comes between it and me, of life.

On our way back we meet Gidi Bochacho and his dog again, and my mother, who was deep in an argument with Nehama about her behaviour to Armand the night before, doesn't manage to get us across the road in time.

That dog's hatred for me hurts me as if it were a person. This time too it started off with short, rhythmic, controlled barks that very quickly turned into the desperate hysteria of violence, as if the very fact of me being myself was a burning insult to its existence. It barked and barked passionately, reading my miserable weakness, and so intolerable and repellent was this weakness in its eyes that it could only wish that I would vanish off the face of the earth and cease to remind it of the enormity of the weakness that could exist in a living creature. And me? I, of course, started to cry. We sat down on a nearby bench, and my mother massaged my head until I calmed down.

Evening descended like a damp, dark rag. The guest was still sleeping. My mother occupied herself in the kitchen and I watched a movie on the science channel about sex between dinosaurs. An English professor with long grey hair explained how it took place, with the help of dolls and animated films, and afterwards he even illustrated it on a female assistant wearing a leotard and a bow tie. The assistant's face maintained a serious, scientific expression and I admired her for it. She looked like someone gravely doing their job, without asking questions about what it said about her and life in general, as undoubtedly I would have done in her place. But I don't demonstrate sex between dinosaurs. I couldn't even have demonstrated sex between human beings, with or without a bow tie. The guest, on the other hand, could certainly demonstrate the sex life of any animal in the universe. This thought unnerved me for some unknown reason and I changed channels.

It's time to wake him up, it really is beginning to look strange. My mother, apparently thanks to the sixth sense that she saves to defend me from unsettling thoughts, was standing in the kitchen doorway and taking off her apron.

I walked down the passage behind her, and when we reached the door of my father's study I took a step backwards and she looked at me, asking for confirmation, and then she resolutely opened the door and immediately switched on the light. "Neo, Neo, it's time for you to get up now. The Labour Alignment lost the elections."

Only in the hours that came later, which we spent in the company of the guest, did I begin to grasp the dimensions of the catastrophe that had descended on me.

The feeling began welling up in me the minute he emerged from the shower, wearing jeans and an old white T-shirt, torn at the shoulder seam. His hair was tied back, but a few shorter locks in the front had escaped the ponytail and he pushed them behind his ears. His face still bore the traces of his long sleep, his eyelids were slightly swollen and his lips looked less modelled, less organized, the arrogant sneer was blurred. What happened between him and my mother was one of those special cases when two people understand one another from the word go. Something is understood between them, something works perfectly and precisely in their reactions, in the interest they feel in each other. Like the grace of God.

As in the beginning of every friendship, this one too began by putting out delicate, subtle feelers. The conversation between them lay in the room like a soft, transparent octopus gracefully moving its legs in the air. On general lines, ostentatiously careful to avoid coming too close too soon, with the slowness permitted themselves by participants on such occasions because they know in advance that the intimacy will surely come. First of all the guest wanted to know what the meaning of our big Bavarian cupboard was. The big Bavarian cupboard is one of the objects acquired by my mother during the period when we were a little rich because of the German money. She bought it from a couple of old German immigrants and I thought it was the most beautiful thing I had ever seen. It was huge and heavy, made of dark purple wood and carved all over with flowers, fruit, sirens and centaurs. The middle panel had a sliding glass door, behind which was displayed all the fine tableware my mother kept for holidays: an expensive Rosenthal dinner service, candlesticks, silverware, and a couple of little figurines – owls sitting on a gilt book and a pair of ugly bulldogs fawning affectionately on each other. But the main thing was the cupboard's side doors. From the middle of each door a human head the size of a grapefruit protruded, a woman's head on the left and a man's head on the right. The man had a riddled beard and soft curls surrounding his face, which had a blank, noble expression. The woman was cruder, her hair was loose and her face was that of a coarse peasant girl, but since she was carved on the door of a cupboard with flowers and centaurs, she too had a regal air. Naturally, as a child I wondered who they were. My mother, with characteristic practicality, said they were just people, but my father, ah, my father would invent something different every time – sometimes he claimed that they were the heads of Hitler's parents and sometimes he said that they were the German poet Rainer Maria Rilke and his lover Katherine, who was half a woman and half a man but the source of all his inspiration.

The guest asked about the cupboard, and my mother, who never liked talking about the cupboard because she really didn't have the faintest idea who had made it and what the carvings meant, started digging up scraps of information given her by the original owners from her memory – perhaps they were the heads of the carpenter's relations, perhaps of some local official. As she spoke she served the guest supper: roast chicken, mashed potatoes, chopped liver, aubergines and a green salad. The guest said he hadn't eaten a thing since London, in other words two whole days, and he ate everything and asked for a second helping of chicken and potatoes. He kept repeating my mother's name when he spoke to her: Ada, this is perfect. I'd be glad of another slice of bread, Ada. Ada, I'm dying of thirst. Jesus, what a charming salt cellar, Ada. She, for her part, wanted to know what Japanese food was like, and he explained that it was raw fish cut up in all kinds of exquisite shapes. She was astonished and demanded to know the details: what kind of fish and what did it look like, and if it tasted good. Certainly Japanese food tasted good (My God, Ada, delicate and healthy, and marvellously aesthetic, Ada). And the flights, were they easy (Ghastly, Ada, a nightmare, Ada, luckily I flew business class from New York to London, Ada, but I hate flying so much that it didn't make any difference). Although Ada herself had only flown a few times in her life, and always with as much excitement as if it was the first time, the words of the guest caused her to discover a cosmopolitan sophistication in herself, and she nodded in profound sympathy. Of course, she understood – the discomfort, the confinement. Since my mother isn't a faker by nature, she quickly turned to the next subject on the agenda: And how were Bat-Ami and Herb? This time it was the guest's turn to answer briefly and to the point. (Getting along as usual, Ada. Him with all the Arabs and Puerto Ricans and Mother talking the hind leg off a donkey, as usual, you know her, Ada.)

And what was the impolite and uncivil Susannah Rabin doing while this summit meeting took off like a house on fire? The answer is simple: I sat in the corner next to the fridge on my little stool, half listening, half staring into space.

Of course I would have preferred to disappear. To go to my

44

room. To read the lousy old anthology or Kierkegaard in archaic Hebrew, to look out of the window at the street. Whatever. But I knew that if I left it would attract attention and superfluous questions, and I decided that it would be simpler to stay where I was and behave as if I didn't exist. At one frightening moment the guest tried to include me in the conversation, to ask me how I was coping with the summer heat, but my mother rescued me by launching into explanations about the breeze at seven in the evening (What a pleasure), about electric fans (You need one in every room), about the difference in prices of various air-conditioners (You wouldn't believe it), about the drawbacks of air-conditioners (They dry up the air, Susannah catches a cold right away, they make a noise), how they used to solve the problem in the old days (sitting on the porch at night with a watermelon and raspberry cordial, that was when Avram was still alive). Since the breadth of the guest's horizons expanded her own, my mother also went into the academic aspect of the subject of heat, and supplied him with a piece of information which we had first heard from Nehama (and which the avid for knowledge Nehama had gleaned from reading the supplement *Modern Times*), regarding the manner in which the hole in the ozone layer was affecting global warming in general and Israel in particular. Did he happen to have heard the silly theory that this hole had been caused by – pardon the expression – the farting of sheep in New Zealand? (How shocking, Ada. I never heard that before but I'm sure it's right. Sheep are vicious animals, in spite of their image, Ada.)

The guest reacted to everything she said with as much interest as if she was providing him with riveting and important information. Without saying much he succeeded in creating the impression of a lively, uninhibited conversation. Perhaps because of his narrow-eyed attention. Perhaps because of his relaxed concentration on everything that was said, while his face reacted with subtle and animated changes of expression to every new piece of information.

When the stage of coffee arrived, we moved into the living room. In other words, my mother and the guest made the move with festivity and laughter (Allow me, I'll hold the cookies, Ada. Can you manage the tray, Neo? Is this German porcelain, Ada? Careful of the doorpost, Neo, and so on.) Susannah Rabin the spoilsport trailed behind them with a small still voice, her stool in her hands.

What could I do? I sat on the stool next to the philodendron, hoping to slip out the moment I could. And then, slowly but surely, I began to feel a mounting disquiet, whose nature and causes I soon became aware of. At one of the stations on the route of my aimless staring into space I happened to glance at the guest's wet hair and suddenly I understood: he had taken a shower in our bathroom, my mother's and mine. And immediately the latent disquiet burst into consciousness with all its force. Hot, sticky sweat began to seep though the pores of my palms. Our bathroom is small and crowded with stains of damp next to the ceiling, the bathtub which my mother paints with special paint every year after first washing it with salicylic acid and rubbing it with coarse sandpaper, my box of sanitary napkins, my shampoo, the plastic shower cap I put on my head on the days when I don't wash my hair, and – worst of all – my panties. The same pair that I take off before my shower and my mother puts in the laundry basket after she finishes cleaning up after me and wiping the floor. I remembered the hairs that sometimes stuck to the soap or the sides of the bath, I remembered my mother's vast bras that sometimes hung on the towel rail, the mangy hairbrush, the tubes of antibiotic ointment and the cream for treating piles, and for fungal infections, and the paraffin suppositories for constipation, and the liquid for removing warts, and the pumice stone for softening the hard skin on her feet. Exposed and wide open our bathroom had been displayed to the guest, betraying to him everything intimate, everything private, and making us, me, so vulnerable, unprotected in my ugliness, in my nakedness, in the smell of my mouth, in my pain and in my disgusting carnal humanity. What did he think there with his scornful lips and his mocking eyes as he stood under the stream of water, which sometimes weakens because we're on the third floor? Was he revolted? Did he pass from detail to detail with a curious, horrified look, processing the information he received until it crystallized into a general revulsion? How dared he? How did anyone dare to come inside my house, to observe everything private, and in the space of ten minutes to find out the most hidden, most secret things?

I stared at him with a look full of hatred. He was lounging on the sofa in a half-recumbent position, occasionally wriggling his naked toes in a playful way, puffing cigarette smoke out of the curl of his lip. Why was he so comfortable? How can people be so comfortable altogether? Where do they get those poses from, which are not only really comfortable but also look great? Poses that don't tell you anything about their owners that they don't want you to know in advance.

For example, my poses when I feel comfortable are ugly. I would never expose them to anybody. The way I sit with my legs both tucked under me and crossed at the same time, my back,

47

which always tends to stoop and which I have to remind myself to straighten in company. My arms, which hang like rags at the sides of my body or are crossed under my chest, or for the most part move restlessly between these two possibilities, while he – the guest – disposes his body like a diamond jewel on a velvet cushion, displays it to all and sundry, scratches behind his ear, changes his position in what appears to be an endless repertoire. The private and public are united in him, harmonious, I have no doubt that this is exactly how he sits and lies and moves when he's alone.

I hate him.

I heard my mother telling him about the elections while he listened and asked pointed little questions. Pursing his mouth in revulsion (the demonic nature of the Prime Minister elect), wagging his chin in agreement (the arrogance of the left), biting his lower lip in theatrical shock at the part of the story in which the disappointment was disclosed (the loss of our side, the enemy's victory). My mother said something about the egg liqueur left over from last night, and then with a "Wow, I forgot", the guest raised himself with lazy grace from the sofa and vanished into my father's room. My mother, remembering my existence, asked me with a look: Well, what do you say? Haven't we got a wonderful relative, cheerful and pleasant? And I, trying to maintain a calm expression and not to blink too much, stretched my lips a little in the caricature of a smile. This worried her, and her: What's the matter with you? was already hanging in the air, but then the guest appeared and cut short the mute conversation between us. He was holding bottles and parcels in his hands and he put them down on the little coffee table while my mother urgently and efficiently moved the ashtray and the glasses aside, as if making preparations for emergency surgery on a dying man.

Stricken with dread at the thought that I would have to react to the presents, I watched him extort little squeals of admiration from my mother with the Martell cognac, the shining tin from which emerged a bottle of perfume in the shape of a transparent pink female torso with pointed breasts (Mother: "The kind of things they come up with today. What did you say it was called, Gaultier?") And then, to my horror, a little bundle of silk was spread out into a great floating cloud, searching for the gravity of the earth, until it steadied into a blue-grey dress with narrow straps and all eyes turned to me and his voice said, "I didn't know if it would fit, but I passed Donna Karan the day before my flight and I couldn't resist it, the lines are just so clean and perfect, don't you think so?" And my mother; "Oh, how gorgeous, but I'm afraid it isn't quite right for Susannah, she's a bit too shy for things like that." And he immediately dropped the dress on to the sofa as if it was a used table napkin after dinner, while my mother tore the cellophane from a gold packet of unfamiliar cigarettes and gave the guest, who was already opening the glass door of the Bavarian cupboard, directions as to where to find the cognac glasses as if he was one of us, a member of the household. As if he belonged there.

They drank cognac and smoked. I too held the full glass which my mother forced me to take, dipping my lips into the dense bitterness and waiting for the evening to pass. I consoled myself with the enjoyable thought that after everyone had gone to bed I would be able to pee at last, something I had been longing to do for the past half-hour. An act which would be both a physical and a symbolic relief, a compensation for an evening of torture.

The prospect was so encouraging that even the chit-chat between my mother and the guest sounded less infuriating.

Now it was my mother's turn to ask questions, and she did so enthusiastically. From their conversation I learned that he was not overfond of his mother and that the years had not been kind to her blonde beauty, which was a byword in our family. She had dried up and withered and today she looked like crumpled snack wrapping. This metaphor elicited from my mother, who was already on her second glass, a giggle and a rebuke. I learned that his stepfather, Herb, wasn't in the best of health. My mother repaid him with the story of how Bat-Ami met Herb: when he was on the kibbutz he was the most mature of the American volunteers and also the most hard-working, and at a certain point he was put in charge of the dairy herd, but since it was a well-known fact that he wasn't too focused after Vietnam, they sent Bat-Ami for a few hours a day to supervise him and see to it that he didn't milk the same cow twice. A kind of personal secretary of the milking parlour. At that moment it seemed to me that a tiny shadow crossed the guest's face, and that for the first time since the beginning of this heart-warming family celebration he refused to co-operate, but he did it so gracefully and unobtrusively that my mother didn't even notice how he sidetracked her from the subject of the shell-shocked Herb to the wound my father suffered in the Six Day War, when a sniper's bullet sliced neatly through his right buttock without harming anything else. All this naturally led to a conversation about Uncle Noah, the guest's biological father, and here my mother let herself go, giving free rein to plots, sub-plots and interpretations.

I learned that the guest was an art dealer and that he had come to Israel in order to acquire works of art brought to the country by the Russian immigrants. This wasn't exactly his field, his expertise was American art from the middle of the present century, but since there was a prospect of making a tidy profit and he was experiencing financial difficulties at the moment, he had agreed to do it.

They always say that people like to talk about themselves. I think this is far from the truth. People like telling very specific stories about themselves. A story is a collection of facts which has already been processed, treated, stylized, censored, and refined into its finished form, having a beginning, a middle, an end and a moral lesson. All the undesirable details have been expurgated or blurred, everything the teller wants to stress has been stressed, and so in fact a story is not a living, developing thing happening here and now, but a highly selective recycling of the past. A story is a dead thing. There are complex and sophisticated stories which may include, for instance, facts that are unflattering to the teller, but these facts are always inserted in such a way that, if they expose a certain weakness, the teller immediately receives merit points for his profound awareness of his own weaknesses, an awareness made evident by the very fact that he mentioned them in the first place.

Some storytellers are even more sophisticated. They know how to produce something which is actually a story, but is disguised as ordinary talking. They pause in the right places, lower and raise their voices, stop for a minute to search for the right word. They are actors, and the more talented they are at acting the more the story sounds like true, spontaneous speech.

So yes, people like to tell stories about themselves, but to talk about themselves? I think that people really, really hate to talk about themselves.

The guest was an excellent actor. After the bottle of cognac was half-empty, his narrative talents increased, fed by the adrenalin constantly released in a circle of feedback including both the narrator and his audience. My mother, her cheeks flushed, took off her shoes and tucked her feet underneath her on the armchair. Her ankles were slender and shapely, and her calves too were smooth and round and even youthful, but under her slightly raised dress, in spite of the darkness prevailing there, it was possible to guess at the fat and flabby thighs I knew so well. I was ashamed of this darkness peeping out from under her dress. A treacherous darkness, which with one careless movement could turn into an illuminated lump of pathetic old flesh knotted with veins.

Now she wanted to know why the guest had given up painting. Why, everyone had known ever since he was so high (she indicated the distance from the floor) that he was an exceptionally gifted child – but his main gift lay in drawing. He drew so beautifully. And all his successes later on, and his studies in New York and London. In reply the guest gave his peak performance of the evening. A long monologue, during the course of which he changed the tempo of his delivery and his mood – sometimes fast and enthusiastic, sometimes reflective and as if asking for our opinion (yes, he took the trouble to glance at me too, at the more sensitive parts of the story), and then suddenly confessional and after that a change of voice again to an arrogant and deliberately childish tone. I assume that if I spent a little more of my life in conversation with people and not in silent observation from the side, I would have been convinced that what was taking place here was talking. Real talking, one person to another (guest–mother, of course), like strangers in a train suddenly granted the marvellous miracle of the collapse of all barriers.

Of course he wanted to be an artist. A painter. For years he had directed all his energies to this end, all his willpower. But after he had finished his Master's degree in London and been invited to show his work in a number of prestigious galleries, and even sold pictures for unreasonably high sums for a beginner, he realized that he had nothing new to contribute. That everything had already happened (you know that, Ada). It was like looking at something from the back window of a travelling car. He found himself in a world where the dialogue was conducted in quotes about quotes, in an evasive intellectual sophistication by means of which he was supposed to define himself as an artist (do you understand, Ada?) Oh, Ada understood everything, it was all so similar to the problems she had to cope with in the HMO clinic and the bank. So yes, in a world of post-modernist super-sophistication, where everything had already been done, all that was left for you was to react, as a rule cynically, to what had preceded you. So that from his point of view, to go on creating, to be an artist, meant sinking into an endless swamp of egocentric cleverness (which of course I could have done, Ada). But the mere thought of it wearied him. He was sick of reacting, reacting, reacting. The need to act on his own initiative took him further afield, to places which may have been ostensibly less glamorous but where he felt that he was creating his life anew all the time, on a small, everyday scale, but from within himself and not in some endless chain reaction to what had already been done (because we create ourselves in a thousand little choices every day, Ada). And altogether, these questions are far more complicated. What does it mean to be an artist? What does it demand? To be an artist is to steal the fire from the gods. To be Prometheus. It

53

demands a kind of passion, dedication, a sense of inner direction. The tension between closing and opening. The ability to be detached from the world and at the same time to conduct a dialogue with it that stems from observation and critical thought (life, Ada, humanity, Ada, art, Ada). Yes yes yes, Ada nodded. If she didn't understand these things, then who, in the name of God, did understand them? Yes yes yes.

I listened with half an ear. The guest's voice sang in my ears, sweet and elegant, occasionally flickering with impressive word combinations. A sense of inner direction? The tension between closed and open? What a question! I knew exactly what he was talking about – I felt a cramp seizing hold of my back – my back hurt me as if I was carrying a ton weight on it. I was dying to pee. Now I really had to pee.

The desire had already started to turn into a need when they were still talking about family matters, and since we didn't have a lot of family I hoped that, thanks to this, the conversation would quickly exhaust itself or they would get tired and go to bed. But then I began to understand that they would never get tired, never, never, never.

And, in fact, why should they get tired? The guest was replete and fresh after thirty-three hours of sleep, and my mother was raring to go after countless years of female loneliness and the hunger for new faces. Where was the new postal clerk with the gap between her front teeth, indifferent and barricaded behind the counter, now – compared to the curious guest lying here on the sofa as if he was part of this house, as if he was the third head on the Bavarian cupboard, blood of her blood and flesh of her flesh?

Hatred sharpens the wits. Hatred makes me think of things

54

that I usually don't even notice exist. Hatred makes me not only discern motives but also judge them.

I needed to pee. It was a no-way-out situation. To get up and cross the room to the toilet, to sit bare-bottomed on the lavatory and listen to the sound of the trickle of pee magnified in the silence of the night, penetrating the ears of the people sitting in the living room – this thought made my ears burn and I touched them for a minute to check that they weren't on fire and to cool them a little with my clammy palms.

I tried to control myself and from time to time I shifted on my stool, invisibly contracting my bum and the inside of my thighs, swaying slightly on my seat, trying to distract myself and then freezing, as if enforced paralysis would compel my bladder too to shut down, to stop the insistent pressure of the urine from bursting out and inundating the delta of my thighs with a warm flood.

Occasionally the tension became so unbearable that loss of control seemed the only possibility. I thought that if I peed in my pants, maybe they wouldn't notice the puddle under the stool, and when they finally concluded their joyful encounter I would find some excuse to go on sitting where I was, and after they'd retired to their respective rooms I would get rid of the shameful evidence with a wet rag.

But of course this was an unacceptable solution. The kind of solution you make up just for the sake of thinking about something else which is even worse than the situation at any given moment. A distraction.

And then I came to a decision. As soon as the last wave of pressure passed, I stood up and announced in a faint voice that I was going to bed. My mother and the guest were surprised and a little embarrassed, as if they'd forgotten my presence and said things not meant for my ears. The main brunt of the embarrassment was, of course, borne by my mother, but the guest too sat up: Oho, it really is late, how long have we been sitting here, Ada, how time flies, eh? I had already started walking carefully across the room when my mother suddenly stopped me in a drunken voice that was even louder than usual, and even though she was talking to the guest I froze like a pillar of salt.

"Oy, you know that my Susannah paints too? Not that I understand too much about it, but they say that she's not lacking in talent."

In almost the same breath she turned to me with a look that brooked no opposition and said, "Susannah, show Neo your paintings. The drawings, especially the profile of Nehama, and perhaps one or two dolls, to give him a general impression. Well, go on, what are you waiting for? There's no reason to be shy, he's family."

Her proposal rooted me to the spot. If the situation had been different, I would have been able to look at her and penetrate her drunkenness with my distress. Maybe then she would have seen and understood and protected me from her own generosity. But no. I knew that any effort now would ruin everything, and that right here, in the circle of light cast by the chandelier, I would stand exposed in all my disgrace while a stream of urine splashed down and bathed my legs, the floor, bursting out in every direction, flooding the living room, the furniture, the guest, my mother, all the residents of the building, the Super Duper, all the side streets, the dogs' park, the HMO clinic, the whole of Ramat Gan, without leaving a single survivor.

I took the steps separating me from my bedroom, restraining myself with the last vestiges of my strength from rushing inside.

On the contrary, the closer the longed-for moment came, the more I slowed down, so that I slipped into the room almost nonchalantly, shutting the door behind me and gently letting go of the handle.

Only then did I charge into the middle of the room and look around me like a caged animal, even though I already knew what I was looking for – the blue vase that always stood empty on the bookshelf over the desk. I placed it at my feet, lifted my skirt, dropped my panties, freed them from their entanglement with my shoes, situated myself precisely over the vase, and then squatted down and pressed my tortured vagina to its lips, as if it was a huge cupping glass about to purge my body of all the evil and distress that were poisoning my life.

And then it came.

I peed and peed and peed, flooded by a feeling of growing relief, as moved as if I was experiencing something for the first time in my life. It was like a fit of weeping liberating a long-endured pain into the outside world. Life happened in a pulsing moment, authentic and independent, not as a reaction to anything, just as in the lecture the guest had delivered about the way things ought to happen.

Limp and exhausted I emerged into the living room, holding my portfolio in my hands, and gave it to the guest. I was so tired that I didn't care about anything any more. And he – the cigarette in the corner of his mouth, blinking, protecting his eyes from the smoke – paged through the drawings, and then he raised his face to me and I noticed the violet colour of the blood under his skin.

"Listen, this looks very nice, but I'll take a better look another time, I don't want to be superficial. I'm worn out."

*

Susannah Rabin. That's how I sign my work. A habit from the days when I was an outpatient at the hospital, so that the counsellor wouldn't get mixed up between the drawings.

I'm no relation to. I was never related to anybody. Only to my mother, and she's related to me. My mother – a wonderful woman whom I love very much. In fact it's hard for me to believe that I could or would want to live without her. We're close friends and I have no real secrets that I hide from her, perhaps only little things, when I don't want to worry her or cause her pain.

But now I'm also related to the guest. He'll live in our house. He'll see my panties in the bathroom. The soap I soap myself with in my most secret places. He might see me eating or sitting in an ugly pose, he might hear me flushing the toilet. Little by little he'll invade everywhere, every square centimetre of the house. Of our lives. The only place where I felt safe will dissolve and vanish and I'll remain without a skin, my nerves exposed, until he invades me too and then I won't exist any more at all. And I won't even be related to myself.

Ever since the guest arrived I've been withdrawing more and more. Trying not to leave my room. Listening to his comings and goings. I know that it worries my mother, but I can't help it. After she got drunk with him that first evening she returned to her usual worried, reserved self. She felt guilty.

Once I read something about Oscar Wilde. He was a great spendthrift, and one day he complained that it was getting harder and harder for him to suit his way of life to the two big blue porcelain Ming vases he'd bought.

My way of life is perfectly suited to the blue vase in my room, a vase Nehama once bought for my mother as a birthday present. For a week now I've been peeing into it at night. I'm afraid that the guest isn't sleeping and that he'll hear me in the silence of the night. The jet of urine splashing into the vase. My mother found out quite quickly, but she never said anything to me. Every day when she comes in to tidy the room she empties the vase. We don't talk about it – what's there to talk about? I see her sorrow and anxiety, I feel her pain inside me as if it were my own. But what can she do? Throw the guest out into the street?

Nehama and Armand don't like the guest either. Each of them for their own reasons. There are avowed and also deep, hidden reasons. Nehama's avowed reasons are she can't stand the guest because in her eyes he's a rash, unreliable fellow, involved in shady affairs, most of which he keeps to himself, and he takes advantage of my mother's kind-heartedness and naïveté (!!!). The deep, hidden reason is the guest is taking her place in my mother's heart – the place of the naughty child who is allowed to say provocative and irresponsible things while the loving adults shake their heads in smiling horror. Now now, you naughty little thing!

Armand's avowed reasons are identical to those of Nehama. His deep, hidden reasons? Well, the imperialistic guest has taken his place too – now we have a man in the house. Even though he doesn't do anything manly to deprive Armand of his rights or, more correctly, his obligations – he doesn't drill holes in the wall, he doesn't help my mother carry heavy baskets. But the potential, ladies and gentlemen, the potential!

Unfortunately, the fact that I share this trouble with Nehama and Armand does nothing to help matters. Apparently because of the reasons that led each of us to his or her negative conclusions. Our opposition lacks teeth. We are all too dependent on my mother to go out and demonstrate in the street. And there won't be any guerrilla warfare here either.

It's every man for himself, with all his worries. A state of affairs that can lead to the downfall of states.

I live a quiet life. Very quiet. This kind of life is supposed to bring tranquillity, but I don't feel tranquil. On the contrary. I feel enormous, frustrating tension, with no outlet. I think of Zen Buddhists. Monks. They lead quiet lives of inner contemplation. They're tranquil. I try to contemplate my inner self, but most of the time my inner self is tired out and empty. Everything is blocked. Locked up tight.

Glenfiddich Wedgwood 21

The realization that something has changed comes slowly. Even to people who like changes. Who look forward to them. I hate changes, and maybe that's why I have a lot more difficulty in noticing their silent beginnings. My mind plays strange games, hiding reality from me. Maybe in this way it protects me from shocks. But on the whole I would prefer to see the truth as quickly as possible, however hard it is. That's what I'd like. Yes, change steals in like an ugly, one-eyed cat. It hides under the closet, behind the kitchen towels, sits quietly in dark corners, until the time comes when you begin to see the signs of its existence.

And so it happened that from an almost non-existent entity in the eyes of the guest I turned into a small focus of interest, the kind that is addressed, whose health is enquired after, whose opinion is asked, with whom insights are shared. All very discreet, very low key, but nevertheless there.

For example, the guest asked me to show him my drawings again. The same drawings I had been forced to expose to his indifferent eyes on the first lively evening he spent in our home. When he did so, he addressed me by name, as he had up to now only with my mother: Well, when are you going to let me have a look at your drawings, Susannah? I hugged the wall of the narrow passage leading to the bathroom and the lavatory: Ah, ah, I don't know, this evening, and his understanding smile and the breath of his "OK" scalded my face. Luckily he forgot this proposal, but its existence remained hanging in the air, threatening to renew itself at any minute, depending on the mood and memory of the guest.

And again, opposite the television, the Discovery channel, he chats to me too: Look how small the cheetah's head is, Susannah. A ridiculous animal, but on the other hand, isn't the little tiger sweet, don't you think so, Susannah? Wouldn't you just love to pet it? Admit you would, Susannah!

He's so sociable and friendly to me that already I know he hates films about birds and the weather. Turtles, on the other hand, amuse him: Look at that, Susannah, they're climbing up their own eggs, all the baby turtles are going to turn into pancakes. My mother brings us sandwiches, in other words, him – she eats only at the table, and I, as mentioned before, eat only when nobody's looking. He eats whenever and wherever he feels like it (Damn, I think I've dripped mustard on the sofa, Ada. This roast beef is simply di-vine, Ada. Is there any cola left?)

He began to get up early, and lately he's been sitting and drinking his morning coffee with us before we go to the beach. My mother brings him the newspapers, and he argues with Nehama and for some reason tries to include me in the discussions. Nehama listens to him open-mouthed: You don't have to be so depressed about the election results, Mrs Lieber, a bit of fatalism wouldn't hurt you, the worst thing that can happen is that the state will be destroyed. That is to say, at the moment the odds are that the state will be destroyed, and then we'll go back to being a nation of nomads at last, like we always were. You must agree with me and with history that the Jews distinguished themselves a lot more when they were in the Diaspora. The facts speak for themselves. Note the role played by Jews in the culture and science of the twentieth century – Freud, Marx, Einstein. And what happened when we arrived here? It's too ghastly to contemplate. A nasty little imperialist nation. Who needs it? What do you say, Susannah? Are you attracted to Peres erotically, Mrs Lieber? I think he looks great in a suit, what do you think, Susannah?

Nehama in return wonders about the nature of his business in Israel, but he succeeds in captivating her too: I don't understand why you're so suspicious, Mrs Lieber. There's nothing the least bit criminal about what I'm doing here. If you think the Russian Mafia's got nothing better to do than sell me stolen works of art, you underrate them. Apart from which I have to tell you that the Russian Mafia doesn't exist at all, it's nothing but a cover-up for an FBI plot to take over the Middle East. It's a well-known fact, if you're interested, that your elegant friend Mr Peres is the head of the conspirators in Israel, together with the head of the Secret Service, of course. Why are you laughing? ask Susannah, she's sensitive to hidden truths. Right, Susannah?

And so it goes until we leave to go to the beach and he turns to his own affairs.

And me? I don't react. I couldn't even if I wanted to. I relate to all these appeals as a trifling part of the huge totality of uneasiness caused by the mere fact of his presence in the house. I don't go into details. This is apparently why I took no notice of the fact that until this past week he failed to make even these small efforts to involve me in his existence, not even in the most

63

tenuous way. No wonder then that the conversation that came at the end of this week of little changes took me completely by surprise, and only in its wake did I begin to understand that the whole thing was a plot, of which all his little overtures were part.

In the meantime summer arrived in all its heavy oiliness, leaving no room for doubt. We began setting out earlier on our trips to the sea, because by ten o'clock in the morning the sun was already unbearable and the beach was full of apish teenagers celebrating their youth. I even learnt to recognize the latest fashion – the boys in big, baggy short pants reaching to their knees, affording a glimpse of incipient pubic hair when they lay on the sand exposing skinny calves as scrawny as chickens. The girls with their heavy thighs glistening with suntan oil, in swim-suits with a strange new cut, high and clumsy, that made their bodies look out of proportion.

How ugly and disgusting the human body is. All this brings me back to my eternal preoccupation with my own body. A grass-hopper's body, skinny-legged and stoop-backed. A body whose existence and whose connection to me I try to ignore even in the shower, as if it's an object that has to be taken care of from time to time, a food processor, a lavatory, or a washing machine. I wash it quickly and efficiently, stifling every thought about it.

When we return from the beach the guest is usually sitting in the kitchen, where he has improvised an office for himself – tele-phone, papers, envelopes, files. Later he goes out on his affairs, and my mother feeds me. And then I can get back to myself, my life and my own affairs again, with only the visible and invisi-ble presence of the guest making everything more limited and constrained.

Things became clear when one evening my mother knocked

cautiously on my door. I was lying in my clothes on my bed, listening to the groaning of the fan, trying to draw its barely perceptible effects towards me, letting the heat squat on me like a heavy, hairy animal, say a bear. I am enveloped in clothes and body fat. Everything is suffocating. And then with reassuring, banal words my mother persuades me to come out into the living room. He's there, of course, in his usual pose on the sofa, paging through the newspaper.

The small details are sometimes the solution to impossible situations. Concentration on the small details. It dismantles the situation, empties it of meaning and thus also of its emotional content. And sometimes the opposite – it fills a meaningless situation with little meanings. I'll look at the head of the Bavarian man, at his neat little beard, at the wooden curls crowning his hard, curved billy goat's forehead. I'll look at my mother's hands, at the faint brown liver spots, at the wrinkled, faded skin of the joints. I could look at her mouth or the skin exposed by her neckline, but that would be disgusting and not what I need now. No, I need to concentrate on something neutral. The main thing is not to look at him because then his presence would immediately become invasive, as if he were touching me, tickling my face with his long hair, breathing on me, obliterating me.

Neo, she says to me, has had a wonderful idea – to go to the theatre. To see a play. He works so hard, he needs a break. And why shouldn't I, Susannah, go with him, it could be really nice, because I like going to a show too, but the opportunity doesn't come along so often, and now that Neo's here it's a chance not to be missed.

Naturally I experience the full range of feelings of panic and paralysis at my disposal. It makes no difference: she's already decided, and so has he. My life is in their hands. What does she want of me? She loves me, I answer myself, but what is love? What is her lousy love? I loved my father's love. I was addicted to it. I hate her love. I know this sometimes, not always. I try to be fair. I know that love is important. This is a fact I don't dare question even to myself, but sometimes, when I'm in danger, when I'm terror-stricken, I'm forced to look at love, at her love with my eyes open, and I think that it's the most terrible, meaningless, selfish, deceitful and false-hope-producing thing that God ever created. And my love? I don't want to think about my love now because I know I haven't got any inside me. Only dependency and fear and a great desolation that fills my whole being, and the knowledge that I have no way of surviving alone. But what is all this? I insist on explaining myself to myself. So that at least I won't be a stranger to myself. I don't give up. I try to be precise.

I don't know how to resist. I'm not interested because in any case the game's fixed in advance, and I don't have the energy demanded by resistance at my disposal. Or the words, reasons, pieces of logic that could connect me to the outside world. And so it comes about that two days later, in a flamenco dancer's hairdo, in a blue blouse and a black skirt, with sticky drops of my mother's Estée Lauder behind my ears and a bit on the inside of my elbows too (in the place where they take blood for tests), I follow our guest out into the street, and in a cloud of mosquitoes circling round in the pool of light from the street lamp I wait with him for the taxi to convey us ceremoniously to the theatre. He himself looks a lot less relaxed and amused than he was when he said goodbye to my mother in the stairwell, with little jokes, smiles and waves on his way downstairs. He doesn't really know what to do with me either.

66

There's a strong smell in the taxi – the taxi driver's sweat. I know that we can both smell it, and my embarrassment makes me shrink into my corner on the back seat next to the window, as if it's coming from the pores of my own body. He himself sits in the middle of the seat, in command of the territory as usual. I feel the careful air standing between me and his dark profile, between my huddled body and his elongated thigh, indifferent to my existence. Now that we are alone, without the protecting, softening presence of my mother, even he can't deceive himself and pretend that everything, as he likes to say, is hunky-dory. We travel in silence, occasionally interrupted by the coarse, distorted male voices coming over the driver's radio transmitter. The nervous operator sends the drivers irritably here and there. His voice is dull and exhausted, like that of an Egyptian officer instructing his soldiers to begin pulling out of their posts on the Canal.

I don't know the name of the play chosen by the guest and my mother. I forgot to ask. I try to remember what she said while she was fixing my hair. Something funny. A comedy. "How much tragedy can you stand?" she said. "The whole country's in a depression." She always feels a sense of identity with the country. Or with the world. Or with all kinds of other people. Needless to say, I feel no such sense of identity. Sometimes when I complain of some pain or distress she says, "Yes, everybody's going through the same thing now," trying to deprive me of the privacy of my own experience. Everyone's tired lately. Everyone has a virus. Everyone thinks there's going to be a war. Everyone, by the way, is Nehama, Armand, the telephone operator at the HMO clinic and Nehama's son Amir, who lives with his family in Haifa. That's more or less everyone.

We get off on the corner of Dizengoff and King George, and I drown immediately in humid air stinking of soot, exhaust fumes, and fast-food joints. I begin to sweat. It's awful. I tend to sweat, especially my face. I'm afraid the guest will notice and be repelled by me all evening. But the guest walks two steps ahead of me without even turning his head to check if I'm still there. I push through the crowds while he navigates between them with elusive elegance, leaving the vision of his back behind him. I fix my eyes on the rubber band of his ponytail so I won't get lost, be crushed, trampled under the smells, the feet, the breasts, the sweaty armpits of the passers-by.

The theatre is a converted cinema, I remember my mother's explanations. The old Maxim cinema that had been turned into a theatre. Now they put on commercial plays. Entertaining. Comic. The word "comic" was repeated so many times that now it was buzzing round inside my head like a fly. Comic. Comic. Comic.

So what would happen? I would laugh – ha ha ha. My eyes would fill with tears and my right hand would hold my stomach to prevent it from bursting? And the guest? Would he throw his head back like he did on the sofa at home, like a film star tossing her head? Would his slightly curling lip expose its wet, plummy interior? Would we both laugh, occasionally exchanging glances and laughing louder in our shared amusement? Oh ho ho, ah ha ha! What a lark. What fun.

I doubt it.

"Do you have any preference about where to sit? Susannah, Susannah!"

I stare at him. No, I have no preference. What I'd prefer is for God's watchful eye to whisk me away from here with one divine blink and deposit me back home, in my room. I want to hold the doll of the poet Percy Bysshe Shelley and feel the clay slowly absorbing the warmth of my hand.

I go on staring at him until he shrugs his shoulders, pays, and takes the tickets from the ticket seller. He keeps them both. Another disruption of the natural, familiar order – when I go to see a show with my mother and Nehama they always let me hold the tickets. I'm the one that holds them out to the usher, as if I'm in charge of the expedition. This has been the custom since I was small. A custom instituted by my father. But now he's the leader. I follow his back, squeeze into the auditorium. How does he manage to avoid contact with people even in the crush of a crowd, while everybody touches me, with their shoulders, their groins, their stinking breath, their packaged fat? Touching me is allowed. Touching him is forbidden.

Well, how did you enjoy yourselves, Susannah? Who? Me and the guest's back? Oh, we had a wonderful time, I learned to know every movement of his shoulders. We, you could say, are on almost intimate terms, me and his shoulders. They don't see how frightened and sweaty I am, and I behave obediently. They move here and there and I follow where they lead. In perfect harmony. A bond too deep to express in words.

Our seats are right in the middle – the middle of the hall and the middle of the row. In front of me, behind me, and on either side is a sea of human heads. The ones behind me have faces, mouths that move incessantly, eyes. The ones in front have only various coverings of hair, among which the profile of a person turning to his neighbour is occasionally revealed. A field of strange and hairy fruits: yellow, black, thorny, puffy, smooth and curly. The hall and the world are a colour TV programme about people's lives, and I watch it without being able to understand what they're talking about, what they're happy about, what they want to live for. Their existence is alien to me. All existence is alien to me, sometimes even my own. So I watch, I watch the colourful film being screened in front of me. Like a confused but curious alien, I try to interpret what my eyes see according to what I have read in books, according to what little knowledge I have managed to acquire, and over and again I fail. The thick glass bubble surrounding me prevents me from processing the information in an experiential way. As in our expeditions to Danino the greengrocer, I rummage in a huge bag of rustling garlic skins, my fingers groping for a chance clove of garlic that I can hold in my hand, to feel its cool, solid touch, to bite into it with my teeth and feel its strong, cruel, stimulating taste.

The lights go off and the play begins. On the stage are one woman and two men. It takes me a while to realize that they are acting the same scene over and over in different styles – once in Russian accents, once in Swedish accents, once in operatic tones. A scene from some Shakespeare play or other. I can barely concentrate on what's happening. The ferment in my brain reaches new peaks, more and more poisonous drops of fear, sequences of thoughts sticking to each other like endless chains of mutant molecules from a chemistry book written by a madman. I close my eyes. Try to breathe deeply. To hang on to a single word that will calm me, that will return me to some quiet circle of light. Home, home, home, I mutter to myself in my head, trying to banish the demons running amok inside me. What's this. What is this? An anxiety attack, Rivki, who has a name for everything, would say. I have to stop it, this has to stop. And then I raise my right hand to my mouth and dig my teeth into the flesh between the index finger and the thumb. Tighten my jaws and begin to bite. The more it hurts, the harder I bite.

And suddenly I understand who I am. I understand perfectly. I'm a creature.

A creature sitting in its hole and spying on people. Sharp eyed. Looking for signs of evil. For cowardice. Looking for ugliness. And even if it doesn't look – that's what it sees. Of course, beauty would satisfy it too – even though it's a lot more rare. Looking for ugliness or beauty. Love or hate. Things that mean something. Strong, powerful things.

And why do I need this? It's simple – otherwise I'd fall asleep. Sink into a deep pit of muffled cotton-wool oblivion. So I sit in my deep pit and pronounce sentence: this one to a long, sweet life. That one to death in agony and the contempt of the masses. Off with his head! Comfort him with apples! That's what you get when Susannah Rabin feels like doing you a favour.

My kingdom is hidden deep. Nobody suspects its existence. Nobody suspects my existence. It doesn't matter or it does. It makes no difference to me. I sit deep inside my cave. Only my eyes stick out. Like the eyes of a toad. Hating. Loving. Admiring. That's good. That's bad. That's beautiful. That's disgusting. Small details. Deconstructing into small details. Holiness is in the small details. God is in the small details. And so is hell. I hunt details with power. With strong colours. Otherwise I don't see anything. I'm blind to pastel colours. To the quiet nobility of grey.

I'm disabled. I don't feel anything. I begin to sink and sink. Into the void. I'm afraid of the void.

The poet Percy Bysshe Shelley is beautiful. There is beautiful art. Beautiful people. For example the lousy guest sitting here on my right. My mother's neckline is ugly, the wrinkles round

Nehama's mouth. The human body. The human soul. An inexhaustible source of ugliness.

There's ugly art too. I enjoy it no less. The main thing is the stimulus, that won't let me die. Ugliness, beauty, it makes no difference – the main thing is the intensity. The volume. A lifeline to cling to, to keep my head above the water. The stimuli are little lifelines, elusive rafts bobbing on the waves.

I dig my teeth in deeper. It seems to me that I can begin to feel the salty taste of blood, its warm moistness on my lips. I bite harder.

This way and that, this way and that. Ugliness or beauty. The stimuli won't let me die. I have few stimuli in the life I lead. Is that a problem for a person like me? A person who leads such a quiet, uneventful life? Not really. Salvation is in the details! The small details.

Nobody knows that this is what I do. Luckily for me. Otherwise they might kill me. Strangle me. Tar and feather me. My luck is that I'm not important. Almost non-existent. I appear marginal, I give off no danger signals. An ordinary person. Withdrawn. Drab. That's my luck. Maybe if they looked too hard at me, or touched me, they'd find out – I have no real skin and I'm transparent. There are no real barriers. I have to worry about them all the time. Create them. Guard my frontiers like a dog. Like that Rottweiler in our street. It's very easy to invade me. To find out. I have to watch out. Woof woof woof.

Dullness precedes brightness. Obscurity precedes clarity.

Woof woof woof.

I bark. Inside I bark. My mouth, my lips are wet. It's blood. My blood. The skin's torn. Harder, harder, try to make the teeth of my upper jaw meet the teeth of my lower jaw. The pain is so intense that I can't feel it. Excessive pain equals no pain at all. Woof woof woof woof woof.

Soon it will all be over and all that will be left in my mouth is a bit of skin and flesh. A little bite of raw hamburger. Will I swallow it? Spit it out? Eat up Susannah and you'll be big and strong. Woof woof woof woof. I really didn't notice when I began to cry. Only when the guest's "Susannah" acquired an exclamation mark I opened my eyes and remembered where I was. His face looked at me from the darkness dimly lit by the stage lights, enough for me to see his expression, which was more confused than concerned.

"Jesus, what the hell are you doing? Take your hand out of your mouth. What's the matter? Tell me what the matter is! Do you want to leave? Aren't you feeling well? Answer me!"

I did as he told me, and only then, when I laid my wounded hand on my knee, did the pain strike me in its full force. The taste of the blood, strange and familiar at once, warm and sweetish, filled my mouth and dribbled down my chin. As long as I had gripped my hand between my teeth I had sucked it in instinctively, careful not to let it drip on my blouse but at the same time not to swallow it, and now that I had let go and my jaw hung open, as if I had suddenly been afflicted by cerebral palsy, it trickled out in a slow, dense stream and I wiped it off my chin with the sleeve of my good hand.

My crying grew louder. I couldn't feel it, but I heard the stifled sobs becoming more frequent, my chest rising and falling and the breath going in and out of my lungs in rapid staccato bursts, and I knew that it was me, weeping in a voice that grew louder with every passing second, like a professional wailer at a funeral.

Heads from the rows in front of us began to turn. Hairy shadows in the darkness angrily hissing "Shhhhh", "Quiet", and

"What's going on there?" compelled the guest to take action, and after waiting a few seconds longer he seized me by the elbow and began dragging me out behind him, pushing past the indignant audience, who gave us disapproving looks with their eyes gleaming righteously in the darkness, and immediately returned to what was happening on the stage. And once more it seemed as if the guest in his elusive thinness was gliding through the air, evading the knees digging sharply into me. I squeezed past these hard knees, stooping so as not to hide the stage, feeling their hatred and indignation seeping into me, shame burning my cheeks.

Outside the guest seats me on a bench in Ben-Zion Boulevard. The air is a little cooler. I hide my bitten hand. The pain has become milder and more uniform. I feel so sorry for myself, such great pity for this creature who is myself, that I cry harder than ever. I know this feeling and usually, when I'm with my mother (and of course I'm usually with my mother), she knows how to calm me down. With quiet, monotonous words, and by putting her hand on my forehead so that it covers my eyes as well and isolates me from the threatening world in my field of vision, until I let my head drop into her hand like a heavy, hairy coconut.

The guest, of course, is ignorant of these methods and he has no means of helping me. He gives up and sits and smokes, waiting for me to calm down by myself. I can't stand other people's indifference to pain, especially my own pain. His smoke-puffing silence winds me up even more.

After finishing his cigarette he throws the butt away with the quick, accurate movement that is already familiar to me, sending the glowing orange ember flying into the darkness. Then he gets slowly to his feet, stands in front of me, grips me by the top of my arms next to my shoulders and pulls me up until I'm standing opposite him, my stomach almost touching his breathing stomach, his eyes level with mine. I think: Now he's going to hug me and comfort me. Maybe he'll even press me to his body in an embrace that will absorb me into him until there's nothing left.

The guest looks into my eyes, from which the tears are still flowing. His look is concentrated, free of any hint of amusement. He tightens his grip on my shoulders. Now he's speaking to me. The quietness of his voice does not deceive me as to the utter seriousness of his intentions, and thus immediately after he says, "And now shut up or I'll kill you on the spot," I stop crying. Curtain.

The guest paid no attention to the wound on my hand until we arrived at our next destination, to which he led me by a different method from the one he had employed hitherto. This time I tottered on ahead and he strode behind me, urging me on with light slaps on my back whenever I dared to slow down. And thus, like a straying sheep and a resolute handsome shepherd, we made our way along Ben-Zion Boulevard, past the Habimah Theatre and the Mann Auditorium, and turned into a dark street whose name I did not know, until we reached a bar with a pink neon sign. After a moment during which I tried to attach my feet to the pavement, an unequivocal push from behind shot me inside, into a dim hellish space, freezing cold from the air-conditioner.

In spite of the darkness I immediately noticed that most of the customers were older than us, people who had long ago passed their forties, but before I had a chance to examine the place in detail, the guest pushed me again, towards a corner table, where he seated me on a chair with my back to the other tables and facing an illuminated door, apparently leading to the toilets, and next to it another door, leading to the kitchen, by which two young waitresses stood giggling, one of them short-haired and very thin, in a very brief skirt, and the other with an ample bosom and a cheerful monkey face crowned with long curly hair. The guest put his hands on the table and gave me his usual amused look. This led me to conclude that he was no longer angry with me about the incident in the theatre, and I started really trying to calm down. I held my wounded hand on my knee, trying to relax it and to dissolve the pain with the help of an exercise in concentration I had invented long ago: you concentrate absolutely on the pain until it turns into the only thing filling your consciousness and little by little it starts losing its meaning, just like a word when you repeat it over and over again. The guest waved his hand at the giggling waitresses, and the one with the monkey face and the curls came up to us, not before glancing at her friend and stifling one last giggle.

"Glenfiddich Wedgwood 21. Twice."

The guest ignored her breasts, which hung over the table between us like a pair of strange, giant grapefruit.

"With ice?" She obviously had no intention of departing at once and leaving the guest to someone like me, who it was hard to imagine could be the intimate partner of someone so handsome. The guest glanced at her with the hint of a smile: "For me – without," and then raised his brows enquiringly at me: "Susannah?" The pair of grapefruit swayed slightly in my direction too. Choking on all this unwanted attention, I shook my head.

"Both without then," he said, dismissing her with a jerk of his chin in the direction of the bar.

We remained silent, but I knew that a conversation was coming, and all I could hope for was that I wouldn't have to answer or participate to a major degree, and that the guest would do the work for us both. I knew that I was in the wrong, although I had no idea exactly how, and what was even worse: how I could change anything, because I was me after all, and my possibilities of change were the most limited that I could imagine. The guest took two cigarettes out of his crumpled gold packet, stuck them both in his mouth and lit them with the smooth dexterity of a conjurer, offered me one of them with a flourish as if to say: Olé!, while taking a drag from the one remaining in his mouth, and then leant back in his chair as if to say: And now it's time to do business. I took the offered cigarette in my good hand. As soon as I put it in my mouth the guest made a swift forward movement, leaned on the table and said: "Listen to me, Susannah Rabin. I have a few things to say to you. You probably won't like some of them, but that's part of the banal reality that we all have to cope with every day. Kapish?"

I nodded meekly at the cloud of smoke blowing towards me in a frontal assault on my face.

"The situation, my dear, is as follows. I've been observing you for two weeks now, and what can I tell you – what I see looks bad, not to say shocking. And you know why? Because you behave like a laboratory animal after a cruel experiment on both brain hemispheres. I understand, of course, that at home you're regarded as a nutcase, and nevertheless I find that you're exaggerating. And if we're already talking about a nutcase, I'll tell you exactly what kind you are – the kind that one fine day takes a machine gun and begins shooting up the neighbourhood without any advance warning. But that's not relevant to the

77

business at hand. Not directly, that is. Now, as I understand the situation, part of the problem lies in the fact that I'm staying in your house. I could leave, of course, but I can't even begin to explain to you how inconvenient that would be for my plans and present possibilities. Once I've completed my business in Israel I'll return to the financial balance to which I am accustomed, but at the moment, to put it plainly, I haven't got a penny to cover my arse, and moving to a hotel just isn't realistic as far as I'm concerned. What I suggest is that you get out of the corner of craziness you've painted yourself into, and that we make a common effort to establish friendly relations that will benefit us both. Not to mention your mother, who's torn between her maternal loyalties and duties of hospitality, and all because of the sit . . ."

He fell silent and his expression froze, as if someone had pressed an invisible "Pause" button while the waitress set the heavy, square whisky glasses before us, trying to catch his eye and smiling a smile full of friendliness and goodwill. She recognized the moment with which she must have become very familiar in the course of her duties – a sudden and unwanted intrusion into the flow of a customer's speech – and retired to the kitchen with her breasts heaving and a dignified expression on her face.

"Cheers."

The guest took a quick, thirsty gulp without waiting for me to raise my glass and plunged immediately into the conclusion of his speech, afraid of losing the momentum, which had already been lost in any case.

"Believe me, I understand the inconvenience of having your home invaded by a stranger. I don't know if I could stand it for more than a couple of days myself, and I truly admire your heroism up to now. But nevertheless I believe that you can make a little bit more of an effort, and then we'll all be happy. Perhaps you'll come to see that I'm not as impossible as you think. Well, come on, drink up."

Some things are bound to come out no matter how hard we try to hide them. Even before I had a chance to take a sip from the glass, the guest grabbed hold of my wrist with a loud "Jesus, what's this?!" and the bleeding bite was revealed to his eyes, lying on the table between us. He examined my hand in silence, nodding slightly to himself, and then he gave me the most penetrating and accusing of all the looks I had seen up to now in his repertoire.

A few unreal moments followed, during which I was led to the kitchen and there, with the help of a Thai dishwasher with a shy look and pockmarked cheeks, and another balding, ginger man, whom the guest called Noam and who was apparently the manager of the place, a first-aid kit was produced and the crescent-shaped wound, decorated with teeth marks, was washed with disinfectant, smeared with antibiotic ointment and bandaged by the guest, who displayed surprising medical skill. The procedure was accompanied by quiet and threatening murmurs on the part of the guest directed at me (What a lunatic, fucking crazy, I'll be damned, Jesus Christ, etc.) and noncommittal explanations directed at ginger Noam – something about tripping and falling on to a sharp object.

After this, under the eyes of the waitresses, we returned to our table and the guest immediately ordered another drink, this time a double.

"Do you have any idea what we're drinking, Miss Jaws?"

I took a careful sip. It was whisky, as far as I could tell, of a particularly dry and thorny kind.

"You like it? I should hope you do. It's Glenfiddich Wedgwood 21. The last time I drank it was in extremely unpleasant circumstances in the company of a certain slimy Armenian, and I hoped that this time would provide me with a remedial experience. But why should you give me a little pleasure? You have no family feeling. You remember that we're family, I hope?"

He succeeded in squeezing the hint of a smile out of me. He clinked glasses with me.

"So, in the light of what happened, I understand that you didn't enjoy the play. To tell the truth, neither did I, although, it seems, without any comparison to you." He snickered.

"In general, if you want to know, I hate the theatre. The actresses are all fat and they talk too loudly and all the plays are boring. What do you say?"

To my relief he didn't really expect an answer. His mood seemed to be improving, and I hoped that he would continue to amuse himself in this way until it was time to go home. He went on sounding off about the theatre until he suddenly gave me a look that in other circumstances might have really frightened me, but by now I already knew: however nasty he might be, there would always be something that would soften his words, a tone of voice or a look, or a slight raising of his eyebrow, that would undercut the force of his words and turn them into a childish teasing at most. He had a talent for saying the most terrible things without sounding hurtful.

He reached out his hand and quickly turned my chin a little to the left, holding it there with his fingers.

"That's it. Fucking A . . . I'll be damned!"

"What's wrong?" For a moment I was afraid that he had found some other damage on my face, something I hadn't noticed before.

"Do you know who you are? Do you have any idea?"

I didn't know what to say and I just squeezed my glass of whisky harder with my bandaged hand.

"I'll tell you who you are. I'll tell you exactly. You're Weeping Susannah. Listen to me. Before I came to Israel this time I went to visit someone. A client of mine. That Armenian I mentioned before. He wanted to brag to me, so he showed me a work of art he had in his bedroom. A beautiful coloured mosaic, from about the sixth or seventh century. The beginning of the Byzantine period. The mosaic shows Susannah, who may or may not have been canonized as a saint, standing completely naked in a pool of water and weeping and weeping. Why? – because on the banks of the pool two Byzantine elders are standing and harassing her. They want her to go to bed with them, and if not – they'll accuse her of being a loose woman and a whore and she'll be stoned to death. Understand? There was no feminist movement then and people tended to believe all kinds of respectable old men and sex maniacs and not young women. So that's the mosaic, and what I want to tell you is that you and Susannah resemble one another like two peas in a pod. You get it? I saw it the first day I arrived – that flat, broad face, the golden tint of the skin under the pallor, the meek eyes."

"And what happened in the end?" I asked. I had no idea if we were talking about a compliment here or an insult. Either way, any reference to my appearance caused me acute embarrassment.

"The end of what?"

"The end of the story. With the elders."

"Oh, that. Naturally, everything worked out. Just in the nick of time, when they're already leading Susannah to the stoning place and all the Jews are going: Ho ho ho, here comes the whore,

81

the child Daniel appears, sent by none other than the God of the Jews, Jehovah, in person. And this prophetic child goes to the centre of the stage and announces that Susannah is one hundred per cent and the sons of bitches here are the elders. So they executed the elders instead of Susannah, because the audience were already hot to put a stone in somebody's head, Susannah went back to her husband, and the child Daniel grew up to be the prophet Daniel. That's more or less what I know."

"Is it from the Bible?"

"It's from the Apocrypha. The books written between the Old and New Testaments. The point is for you to understand that you're a winner both from the aesthetic and the historical point of view, and to stop whining like a floor rag over every little thing. Finish your whisky now, drinking with you is a real pain in the neck."

I did what he asked. The place had grown crowded, more and more people were arriving all the time. The waitresses were no longer giggling at the kitchen door but rushing here and there with worried faces. I couldn't remember the last time I'd been in a place so crowded with people at night. Maybe never. I wanted to look them over, to listen to what they were saying. A gentle warmth spread through me, the warmth of the Glenfiddich I was drinking, and I listened to the loud music, which the guest had stopped calling "old people's music". He'd grown tired of talking in the meantime and sat smoking and staring out of the window at the dark street, polishing off his third drink. I felt that life was touching me as it hadn't touched me for a long while, in the smells of smoke, perfume, alcohol, in the murmur of people's voices, the slamming of the kitchen doors, in the foreign music with its dark, unclear connection to forbidden things. Life touched me in disgusting things that became attractive, pulsating on the inside of my thighs, in my embarrassment which didn't disappear but became obscure and hidden, resting beside me like an obedient dog instead of barking itself from inside me.

I looked at the musing guest. Suddenly he didn't look so perfect to me. And he'd always seemed flawlessly carved – albeit from organic matter, but corresponding to the pale, hard perfection of marble. The leanness of his cheeks echoed the darkness in the morbid hollows round his jaws and eyes. His chin was pointed, his hair lay on his shoulders, free of the rubber band, which had been lost somewhere on the way. There wasn't a hint of his usual arrogant glamour. He looked like a child or an old man, photographed in strong, pitiless contrast, like one of those expressive photographs documenting children and old men in underdeveloped countries or prisoners liberated from concentration camps. A wave of painful compassion flooded me, giving rise to a wish to say something to him. Something tender, like the kind of thing I say to my mother when she looks particularly miserable or ugly. Something that would dispel his melancholy and my guilt for catching him out in his wretchedness. For my unintentional invasion of his inner self.

As usual with people who exist in relation to the gaze of the other, the guest was extremely sensitive in this regard. As soon as my eyes lingered on his face for a few extra seconds he woke up, flashed a smile at me, and waved to the waitress, making a sign with his thumb and forefinger as if he was writing, which turned out to be a request for a bill. We went out into the night.

We walked in silence for about ten minutes. The guest didn't say where we were going and I lost the momentary courage I had gained from seeing his vulnerability, and no longer felt an impulse to reach out to him in any way other than the one I was used to – reaction. I therefore walked beside him without asking any questions. Now that I knew he was far from being as dangerous as I had imagined, there was even something pleasant about it. When we reached the clump of tall ficus trees on the traffic island in King George Street the guest suddenly stopped, looked up and uttered a sound while touching his lips with his fingers. A strange sound, like a bird or an animal. Before I understood what was happening, dozens of black creatures with outstretched wings detached themselves from the trees and began gliding over our heads, swooping down and rising up again, flying round in wide circles.

Bats, I realized instantly and clutched my head, rooted to the spot while my memory woke in a panic from its safe slumbers and flooded me with all kinds of horror stories, facts and satanic images connected to the hideous, hellish creatures surrounding us on all sides. Careful not to make a superfluous movement that would bring one of the bats swooping down on me to dig its claws into my hair, I tried to catch the guest's eye. He stood in the middle of the traffic island under the tangled branches with his arms outspread, laughing demonically: "Hey, crybaby, look who your date is – I'm a devil, Ashmadai, Beelzebub, I control the forces of darkness! How about going somewhere to have another little drink?"

How easily he touched people. I'd seen him touch my mother – on the hand, the elbow, light, ordinary little touches, in the course of conversation, to stress a point, to persuade. How easily he had taken my hand, dragged me to the theatre. Me, who never touched people. And now he came up and embraced me without trying to remove my hands from my head and led me quickly, almost at a run, as if he was rescuing me from a place where shells were falling, until the cursed traffic island with the trees and the bats was far behind us and he let go of me.

The next place we went to looked a lot less fancy than the previous one, horribly crowded and reeking of beer, frying oil and cigarettes. The guest seated me on a high chair next to the bar and remained standing next to me. Violent music, frightening in its foreignness, and the roar of voices prevented any possibility of conversation. I sat shrinking, looking at the guest emptying his drink down his throat with the same thirsty desperation I had seen before in the first bar. From time to time he urged me to drink my whisky and soda, shout-whispering into my ear, warming it with his moist, alcohol-sweet breath, "Are you OK? I'm having such a great time, I haven't hit the booze for a million years." And I nodded, as convincingly as I could, afraid he would begin to worry about me and I would have to reply, to react, to disturb the fragile calm that had descended on me, sheltering me like an invisible plexiglas bell from everything happening around me.

I thought about my mother. I always think about my mother when something happens to me that she has no part in. Anything at all. And the thought is always disturbing – if the experience is enjoyable, I feel guilty because she is still shrouded in her quiet, eternal suffering, a suffering I began to be fully aware of after my father died because after he died I too became a sufferer. It wasn't the frightened, bewildered guess of a child. She always shared everything with me. Her family – me, him – was the most important thing in her life. Perhaps because we were the fulfilment of a dream, a new family after her own family – her mother, father, big brother Theo and of course her little brother Aharon with the short leg – had perished in the Holocaust when she was a little girl in Ben-Shemen. And afterwards, oh how I identified with her, as if I had been present at every moment of her ugly youth. She had always worked hard, always gone out of her way, always done all she could to be useful, that was her strength. An ugly duckling who instead of turning into a swan had turned into a perfectly ordinary duck. A duck whose value is measured in terms of how helpful and useful it is. I'm convinced my father fell in love with this tireless helpfulness of hers, even though he always liked complimenting her on her slender-ankled legs – her best feature. With my father she felt a success – as a woman, as a person. And even when he cheated on her, disappointed her, made her worry about him as if he too were her child, she knew that without her his existence would become brittle, empty and lonely. Thanks to this knowledge, every movement she made was full of meaning. When he died the two of us were left alone in the world. And without the separating, softening and demanding presence of my father we became one. This fact makes me feel safe and lucky, except at moments like these, when I feel that I'm taking a bite of some part of life that is inaccessible to her.

The feeling was unbearable, and I took big, determined gulps of my drink, as if it was a medicine, and I didn't even try to resist when the guest quickly ordered another one and put it in front of me with a smiling firmness which left no room for objection.

Time seemed to dissolve in the crowded room and also inside myself. Only the sulphurous taste of the soda water in the whisky with its dead bubbles made it clear to me that it was much later than I thought. The guest polished off his umpteenth drink and at the same time motioned me with a faint movement of his head to slide out of my seat into his embrace, which bore me rather heavily outside. He kept on embracing me too as we began to walk down the night street, looking out for a taxi to take us home. There was something strange in the way he held me, until I realized that he was leaning on me with all his strength, almost hanging on my shoulders, dragging his feet along the pavement. Suddenly he detached himself, took a few hurried, stumbling steps in the direction of a dark alley crossing the street, and before he managed to hide himself he began to throw up, clutching his stomach with one hand and leaning on the peeling wall of a building with the other. He sensed me approaching and signalled me to keep my distance, his slender back convulsing again and again, until he spat the vestiges of the vomit out of his mouth and leaned against the wall, breathing heavily and trying to force a reassuring smile in my direction. Even in the dimly lit street I could see how pale he was, his forehead and upper lip covered with beads of sweat. He spoke in a flat voice, its indifference detached from the apology it expressed.

"I drank too much, I'm sorry. I heard today that my step-father Herb passed away. Last night. He was sick. Cancer. It was expected, but still. You know."

He wiped his mouth on his bare arm.

"Don't tell your mother, there's no need for her to know. Nobody needs transatlantic condolence calls at the moment. I'll tell her myself when the time comes. OK?"

I nodded obediently and at the same time I was astonished to discover that the possibility of sharing a secret with him was even more alluring than the usual, imperative need to tell my mother every new piece of information that reached my ears.

My betrayal of my mother, together with his frankness, filled the space between us with warmth. I felt that I had to ask something. I wanted to ask if he had loved his stepfather, but the guest looked to me like a person who couldn't use the term "love" without feeling that it detracted from his dignity, and I therefore chose a modified version.

"Were you attached to him?"

For some reason it seemed to me that the word "attached" removed the intrusive and off-putting dimension from my question, but the guest didn't even dream of being put off. His eyes glittered at me from the darkness like those of a cat in a pile of garbage.

"Attached? I don't know. Ever since this morning I've been trying to remember his face and I can't. There was some business after I graduated from art school in New York. I burnt all my work. The good stuff too. Don't ask me why because I don't know the answer. I just burnt them one night in my parents' back yard. Then I lay down on the bed in my old room and stared at the poster of Che Guevara hanging over the bed. An old, faded poster that Herb had hung there himself a million years ago. In the morning, after they – he and my mother – discovered that I'd burnt the pictures, he came into my room to talk to me, to try to understand what had happened, and I didn't want to look at him and I didn't give a fuck about what he had to say. So I concentrated on Che's eyes until I nearly started crying, and then I told Herb to fuck off. And all day now I've been trying to remember his face then. His expression. If he was shaved, if his hair was in a mess or combed neatly over his bald spot. And all I can remember is Che's fucking eyes."

The guest let out a strange, mean laugh.

"I can even remember the way the bed creaked when he sat down on it with his bum, but his face – I don't remember. I try and try and all I can come up with is Che's fucking eyes again. So in reply to your question whether I was attached to Herb – shit, I haven't got a clue. Otherwise I'd remember, don't you think? Especially since that isn't the point at all."

My tongue was dry and sticky.

"So what is the point?"

"Nothing. I thought I'd be able to help him a little with the money I made here in Israel. He had lousy medical insurance that didn't cover a lot of treatments. Now, of course, the whole balance has changed."

"So what now? Will you go back to New York?"

"That's just what I don't know. In the worst case I'll make the money and it will be mine. Herb, needless to say, won't be able to use it now, right?"

I moved my lips, unable to find the words to reply, when all of a sudden the guest detached himself from the wall, lurched with surprising speed to the side of the road and hailed a cab, which slowed down with a screech of its brakes. He slid inside without looking at me and I squeezed in clumsily behind him. I hoped that he might go on talking to me during the journey, but until we drew up outside the house in Ramat Gan the guest remained sunk in his corner on the back seat, his head thrown back, abandoning his face to the cool air rushing in from the open window, without saying a single word.

The Poet And The Madonna

The month is the month of June, and the abyss is the usual abyss. In my head I try to describe the exact process of my thoughts to an invisible listener. As if inside my head there exists a kind of supreme being whose concern knows no bounds and, what is more important, who possesses omnipotent powers. The moment I succeed in describing what's happening to me with absolute accuracy, this being will be able to diagnose my disease, the secret of my dark existence, and then as if with the wave of a magic wand it will prescribe the medicine that will cure me once and for all. I have this childish illusion that the whole thing is a question of getting the description of the symptoms right. The moment I succeed – they'll disappear and a great white quiet will descend on me for ever.

I try and try, but the reports come out vague and generalized, the facts fall short of the truth. I'm unable to tell myself even to myself. The main thing is not to stop trying. Susannah Rabin – a weak little Sisyphus – rolls her stone to the top of the mountain over and over again. The main thing is to labour with joy. To sing as I work. And happiness is sure to come.

A whole week passed after the outing with the guest before we had a chance to talk again. He seemed preoccupied and unfriendly, as if in the throes of a prolonged hangover. In the mornings his face was crumpled and swollen, and his mood was bad. After my mother and I had finished getting ready to go to the beach and were waiting for Nehama to arrive, he would sit down, surround himself with piles of papers, and conduct telephone conversations in Hebrew and English to mysterious destinations. Even my mother, who was always so conscious of the laws of her territory, found herself serving this busy, sombre office atmosphere – making extra coffee for the guest before we left, emptying his ashtray, picking up a stapler that had fallen on the floor, and all without saying a word, in order not to disturb him at his work.

As a result of this new and severe order our – my mother's and my – mornings began even earlier than before. And perhaps the reason was also the sun, which now grew white and violent in the middle of the morning. Since my mother and Nehama are afraid of the sun and try to adapt their daily routine to it, as if it were some domineering patriarch who had replaced their dead husbands, we set out for the beach an hour earlier.

The sun really is bad now, full of deception. As far as I'm concerned, too much light equals too little – you stop seeing the details. The small details. The essence of my inner existence. The white light flattens the curves, rounds the corners, wipes out the nuances of what's happening outside me and also inside me.

The pleasantest moment of all is the moment when I enter the apartment on our return from the sea. The moment when the screen of light dissolves and greenish circles appear before my eyes, and little by little I begin to see the details again: the sofa, the heads of the man and the woman on the Bavarian cupboard, the philodendron plant. Dark and vague at the moment of entry, the objects gradually resume their usual and familiar contours, and I absorb them into myself and calm down. Everything is in its place. My life is in its usual cool, safe place.

The guest spends the evenings in his room, listening to music on the little tape he brought with him. A high female voice sings against the background of a cacophony of unfamiliar instruments. I hear the guest's music whenever I pass his closed door. Sometimes, when the heat stops me from falling asleep, I listen to this high voice singing in English, merging into the dense silence of the night, the chirping of the crickets, the noise of an occasional car in the distance, the vague fog of thoughts in my drowsy head.

After a week of this, when I was sure that the friendship between us had come to an end as suddenly as it had begun, he called me. It was an ordinary evening, my mother was sitting in the living room with Armand, who had just started reading Dostoevsky's *The Possessed* and was eager to demonstrate the profound emotional as well as intellectual effect the book was having on him. My mother, for her part, refused to understand what there was to get so excited about: what did he, Armand, have to do with Czarist Russia and the moral dilemmas of the Christian religion? Since this was already their second discussion on the subject, I allowed myself to be bored and stare blankly until I got fed up and walked out of the room, and then, as soon as I entered the passage, the guest's door opened, his rumpled head poked out, and with a loud "Psst, psst, psst", he beckoned me to come closer.

How narrow is the line between the sacred and the profane.

In order to desecrate the sacred there is no need for a slaughtered pig on the temple steps. A speck of shit from an impudent bird on the pure white prayer shawl of a worshipper on his way to say his morning prayers is enough to do the job. My father's room was revealed to me, violated and profaned. I was astounded to see the extent to which a familiar place can be transformed by the invasion of a stranger. A few little changes and the place ceased to be what it had been before – a temple, my father's private sanctuary, the proof of his beloved existence in my past – and turned into the guest's room.

In actual fact only a few details had been changed or added. The table lamp was now standing on a chair next to the bed, casting a golden light that was almost embarrassing in the intimacy it created. The bed, covered not with the neat old burgundy bedspread, but with a mess of rumpled sheets, the travelling bag with its belly gaping like a whale with its guts spilling out, the cube-like little stereo system standing on the floor – everything screamed invasion, violation.

On my father's desk, from which my mother had religiously continued to remove every speck of dust even after it was no longer used, I caught a glimpse of papers, coins, tapes, empty coffee cups, cigarettes and journals jumbled up like a pile of junk in a teenager's bedroom.

But the strongest and most alien presence of all was the smell. The room was now enveloped in hidden, phantom scents which had been brought from distant places and produced the dramatic, unbearably overpowering result: the smell of a strange man.

"Sit down. What are you staring at? You're not in a museum." The guest dropped on to his unmade bed, patted the mattress at his side, and at the same time threw a crumpled T-shirt into

93

the opposite corner of the room. I approached and, after a momentary hesitation, lowered my backside on to the edge of the bed, as far as possible from the inconsiderate guest. He seemed to see this as a sign of intimacy and immediately drew up his legs and hugged his knees with his bare arms, his back leaning on the wall, and a lit cigarette already dangling from his mouth, ready for the talk about to take place.

"So, what's going on, Susannah? Have you forgotten me already? We have to continue what we started, you know. What did you think? That you'd get rid of me with one meeting, however thrilling? The theatre, hand biting, getting drunk together, that was all very nice, but what about what comes next? Oh Susannah Susannah, we have obligations to fulfil. Don't you agree?"

"What obligations?" I couldn't understand.

"Social obligations, social and sociable." The guest giggled at his idiotic play on words. "Your mother, my Aunt Ada, made me promise that as a man of the world I would be the one to take responsibility for our friendship, and I confess that I've been neglecting my duties owing to pressure of work and for various other unworthy reasons. But now the time has come to set things right."

"My mother asked you to make friends with me?" I whispered the rhetorical question. He nodded smugly a couple of times, blowing smoke rings into the air and stabbing them with the dagger of his burning cigarette.

I felt a crimson blush burning my cheeks. I looked away, in the direction of the door, so that the guest would not notice my distress, which almost made me tremble. How shameful that she had asked him to make friends with me! How dared she?

How could she betray me like that, behind my back? And I thought that we both saw the guest in the same way, as a harmless, temporary intruder, whose sojourn among us we could only negotiate successfully by means of mutual support. This was without a doubt my punishment for not telling her about his stepfather's death. Now my act of treachery was coming back to me like a boomerang, to punish me and educate me for the future. I felt myself cringing and shrinking like mother and Nehama's inflatable rubber mattress after they pull out the plug. I stood up, ready to absorb all the embarrassment resulting from this rash behaviour, and turned to the door.

And then the guest did something he was to do a number of times during the course of our acquaintance: he read my thoughts and responded to them immediately, as if he were conducting an ongoing and completely natural dialogue with my unconscious.

"Why are you insulted? What did you think? Don't you know her by now? She's worried about you. Ever since I arrived you've been creeping round the house like a shadow, so she wanted to help sort things out between us. And it's a good thing she did, because I'm so absentminded I might not have realized on my own that there was anything wrong. And how can you expect her not to interfere in your life when the two of you spend your lives stuck up each other's arses? Fat chance. And didn't you ask yourself how come she never kicked up a fuss about the bite mark on your hand? I fixed it up, I spoke to her and calmed her down."

I stood in the middle of the room, my arms hanging long and lifeless at my sides. The moment when it might have been possible to leave the room without embarrassment was gone. No inner voice gave me a clue about what to do next. All I could do was wait for a sign from outside to enable me to decide whether to go or stay, or even take any kind of action.

"And now come here." The guest slid off the bed and began rummaging in the space between the desk and the window until he came up with a large object wrapped in brown paper. "I want you to see something that might amuse you."

I approached him hesitantly, wondering what he was up to. He struggled with the wrapping paper, trying to remove it methodically, but after a few seconds he lost patience and tore it, revealing the object inside – a big Russian Orthodox icon, about eighty centimetres long and fifty centimetres wide, of the Virgin Mary holding the baby Jesus on her lap.

"Well," he flashed me a radiant smile, "what do you say? Isn't it amazing?"

"It's very nice," I replied with restraint.

He looked disappointed.

"Nice! That's not what I'm asking you. Take a good look. You see?"

I shook my head. I couldn't see anything extraordinary enough to justify such enthusiasm.

"You haven't got a clue, have you?" And before I had a chance to feel insulted he quickly took a toilet bag that was lying on the desk, fished out something that turned out to be a little mirror, pushed it right into my face so that I couldn't see a thing, and demanded, "Now do you see?"

When I shook my head again he pushed me towards the old cupboard where my mother kept my father's clothes (only the best ones), flung open the door, and stood me in front of the long mirror inside it.

Examining my reflection in the mirror was the last thing

I needed to raise my spirits. The guest stood behind me and held my head between his hands with a surprisingly gentle grip, tilting it slightly towards my shoulder, and awkwardly moving all my hair to one side. After that he fiddled with my chin, shifting it first to the right and then to the left until he appeared satisfied, and then he returned to the desk, took the icon and came back and stood next to me holding it in his hands so that it was reflected in the mirror opposite me.

"Fuck it, it's the opposite direction, but never mind, you can see what I mean. Or do you still not get it?"

Now I saw. The resemblance between the face of the Madonna in the icon and my own face was striking and unequivocal. Unlike the few Byzantine paintings I was familiar with, her face was painted in a naturalistic way. The shadows, the delicate lines of the eye sockets, the soft transitions from the nose to the cheek and the cheek to the chin were alive and breathing.

"I thought I looked like Susannah from the mosaic of Susannah and the Elders," I said.

"That's what I thought at first, until I realized that you looked like most of the Madonnas in late Russian icons. Isn't that something?"

I was silent.

"Well, aren't you pleased?" the guest asked impatiently, as if I had sent him out into the world to look for paintings of women whose faces resembled mine. He returned to the desk and tried to rewrap the painting in the torn brown paper.

"I don't know. To tell the truth, I'm used to reminding people of all kinds of things. It always embarrasses me, because I know that I've got a peculiar kind of face."

"Is that a fact? So what else do people say you remind them

97

of?" The guest looked put out at having to share me with other perceptive people.

"When I go with my mother and Nehama to see plays at the Library Theatre, which is attached to an acting school called 'Beit Zvi', the director of the school always says to me: Susannah Rabin, if Almodovar ever saw you he would snatch you up immediately for his movies. I never know if it's a compliment or not."

"An actress in an Almodovar movie! You know what, he may be right. But what I'm showing you here is your exact portrait. That's something else again, don't you think?"

"I don't know. I don't really like it when people talk about the way I look."

"I understand. You think there's some sort of criticism implied here? It's exactly the opposite, it means you have a face that's, well, that's full of inspiration."

For the first time I noticed that when he got excited he spoke with a slight American accent, which softened his Hebrew with a kind of drawl, slurring the vowels and the consonants, and gave him the vulnerability of a tourist. I was sorry that I couldn't make him happy by producing a more enthusiastic response.

"Who painted it? Someone well known?" I tried to show an interest.

"Jesus, where have you been all your life? Icons aren't painted by famous painters as a rule. But this one as it happens, since you ask, was actually painted by someone important. It's an authentic Oshakov. The second half of the seventeenth century. See the realism of the facial features? That's his school. The greenish-brown shade of the robe, the gleam in the eyes, the shadows underneath them – see how sad she is, all that breathing softness.

But the general outlines are strictly classical. Exactly like the original icon from the twelfth century. That's why this icon too is regarded as Byzantine art, even though it was painted much later. Look at the posture, the placing of the hands. Everything. This is the Madonna of Vladimir. Do you have any idea of what it's worth? Of how rare it is? It's the kind of article you usually find only in museums, not in private collections. But you, what do you care, living in your shell like an immature pearl? Doesn't it thrill you at all, the resemblance between you?"

"A little. Perhaps. Yes." Again I felt guilty at my indifference. "It's just that I don't understand much about icons, that's all."

"What the hell has it got to do with icons, what I'm trying to show you here? And what do I understand about icons? I specialize in the backsides of David Salle and his like. So what? Does that mean that a person has to lose his sense of wonder, if he isn't a professional in the field?"

The severe look directed at me by the guest made me feel like a petit bourgeois philistine. Luckily for me he abandoned his artistic indignation as soon as he realized that I had no intention of answering him.

"But you know what? I understand you. I understand you completely, because the truth is that nothing really interests me either. I just wind myself up in the hope that in the end I'll be infected by my own enthusiasm."

He sank into melancholy. I felt that anything I said would only irritate him and increase his gloom. We were completely different people. That was clear. Now the difference loomed large in the room, embarrassing as a fart that everybody present was trying to ignore. This was the time to leave but for some reason I stayed and blurted out uncontrollably, "So why do you deal in icons if you don't know about them? Doesn't it make you vulnerable to forgeries?"

"Of course it does, Madam Almodovar. Of course I'm vulnerable. I bought this painting from a friend. It's genuine, but tomorrow I'm going to meet a woman, an acquaintance of mine, who I hope will put me in touch with a restorer of icons who'll be able to help me with my acquisitions from now on."

"But what made you decide to get into it in the first place?"

"I've already told you, it was an opportunity to make a big, quick pile, and I needed the money to pay for treatments that weren't included in my stepfather's medical insurance. And by chance I met this Armenian collector at . . . a social function. He's a kind of colonial type. Texas oil. He's got a huge belly and he wears suits made to order by Armani and Joseph. Half the time you can't understand a word he says because of the Cuban cigar stuck between his teeth even when he sleeps, a real creep. But I can't suddenly say to him: I don't need the money any more, so you can take your icons and shove them up your arse. You can't do that. It's not professional."

"So you're actually doing him a favour?" I wanted to get the facts straight.

"Of course I'm doing him a favour. The Armenians are a long-suffering people, you know. I wanted to help him enlarge his icon collection."

"I thought you said he was a rich creep."

"You're really determined not to understand anything. So what if he's rich, does that make him any less human? Less Armenian? If you pinch a rich Armenian will he not be pinched? If you kick him in his fat arse, will he not be kicked? I wanted to do him a favour, end of story. So for God's sake stop nagging me,

I'm nervous enough already that this fucking paper's torn."

The guest abandoned his efforts to return the painting's wrapping to its former state and sat down on the desk. The lamplight behind him made a golden halo round his head. His hair framed his face softly and gave it a dreamy, unfocused look. He was the most beautiful man I had ever seen. All of a sudden a silly, irrelevant thought crossed my mind and although I tried to suppress it, it kept bobbing up again, until I couldn't control myself and I burst into nervous laughter, already blushing and ashamed in anticipation of the demand for an explanation which arrived forthwith in a tone that brooked no beating about the bush.

"Tell me at once why you're laughing. I warn you that if you lie I'll know immediately, because I'm an art dealer and a poker player and I know when I'm being lied to. Come on, speak up!"

"I don't know if you'll understand."

"Try me, sweetheart. Come on, let's have it, I want to know exactly what was capable of making you behave in such an uncharacteristic way."

"Promise you won't be cross."

The guest rolled his eyes.

"OK," I took a deep breath. "Once I was with my mother at Nehama's grandson's barmitzvah, little Talush. It was at the Ramada Hotel in Tel Aviv. In the small reception hall. In the big hall they were holding a contest between Israeli lookalikes of all kinds of famous celebrities. Under the patronage of some hair-product firm, I think. They had the Israeli Cher, the Israeli Michael Jackson, the Israeli Tom Cruise. Even the Israeli Princess Diana."

I tried to overcome the nervous giggling that was choking me and preventing me from continuing my story.

"Get on with it, stop that hysteria!"

"So I think that we could have entered the competition too. Me and you. I'm the Israeli Virgin Mary, and you're the Israeli Percy Bysshe Shelley."

Even before I had brought the last sentence to its conclusion I knew that I had made a terrible mistake. How could I have imagined that there was anything humorous about this stupid idea, or – what was even worse – that it was worth being taken out of my private consciousness and exposed to the air? But this time the guest proved his good humour and laughed heartily, throwing his head back and restoring the atmosphere in the room.

"The Israeli Percy Bysshe Shelley! You slay me. And I thought you were a kind-hearted girl."

He looked at me with a broad smile and suddenly jumped off the desk, lit another cigarette, and then turned to face me again with a dejected expression, as if he had not been joking cheerfully with me thirty seconds earlier.

I had already come to know his rapid mood changes. The nervous energy he had been giving off just a minute before had been drained out of him, and also out of the air of the room. I looked round, seeking a refuge from the silence that had fallen. Something to lean on, to provide me with a solid backing, to protect me from this enforced intimacy.

And then I understood. Or at least I thought I did. Of course he was sad. How could he not be – he was in mourning. Only a week ago he had told me about his stepfather's death, and here I was making frivolous jokes. If my mother had been a witness to my tactlessness, she would have said: Susannah, you should be sensitive to people. This happened on the occasions when I ignored Armand or argued with Nehama when she talked nonsense. I always put it down to the fact that both Armand and Nehama were easily offended. They had to be, if they could be insulted by someone like me. In my opinion, the whole thing was a farce. And now I had succeeded in offending the guest too. Perhaps I really was an insensitive oaf without being aware of it. How polite of him to go along with me while his heart was bleeding. What a pig I was. How could I have been such a callous pig?

I knew that I had to do something. Something warm, positive. But I didn't know how. I had no previous experience of people like him. People like him were outside my orbit. People like him were the host, the lady writer and the born-again comic from the TV talk show. The kind that lick their lower lips like movie stars. The kind that put on perfume and roll round sweatily between silk sheets with other TV hosts, writers and born-again comics and then drink the dregs from the bottle of expensive wine next to the bed and smoke imported cigarettes, while their eyes gaze at the ceiling, glittering in the darkness. People who live in outer space. Outside the stifling atmosphere of my planet – the Susannah Rabin planet.

If only I could approach the guest. Even touch him lightly on the shoulder, or just sit down next to him. In spite of my awareness of my appalling insensitivity and in spite of the pity I felt for the guest, I was unable to overcome my embarrassment. I remained standing where I was and simply said, "Are you thinking about your stepfather?"

At the sound of my voice the guest started slightly and looked at me in astonishment.

"What?" he asked, as if he didn't have the faintest idea what I was talking about. Gradually the relevant memory rose into his consciousness. "Ah, yes, my stepfather. I forgot for a minute that

I told you about him. Sorry. I was drunk, otherwise I would have spared you the confession. But yes, I was thinking about my stepfather. Strange that you guessed."

In bad American movies, which to tell the truth I liked a lot, especially when the subject was human drama, like the TV series Beverly Hills, there was a regular routine for such moments. At this point in the conversation one of the characters was supposed to say, looking seriously into the eyes of the other: "Do you want to talk about it?"

I knew that this was an inferior option, but rummage in my repertoire of responses as I might, I couldn't come up with an alternative to this idiotic sentence, and since the seconds were flying by I gathered up my courage and in a rapid translation into stammering Hebrew and fluent Susannah-Rabinese, I blurted out, "You . . . that is I . . . he . . ." until the verbal salad in my head miraculously organized itself into "What kind of a person was he?"

A cruel question. I knew very well from family legends that Bat-Ami's American husband was not right in the head. And now I had confronted the guest with the need to give me an account of his stepfather's condition.

I lowered my eyes and smiled shyly, unable to retreat. The guest was silent for a long time, and then he cleared his throat and spoke in a quiet, serious voice.

"He was a moral man. He had a genuine capacity to be hurt for others, he was moral in the deepest sense of the word."

"What do you mean?" I asked immediately, giddy with the success of my question. I felt almost bold, like someone entitled to question and enquire into anything she felt like.

"What do you mean, 'What do you mean?'" he asked.

"I don't understand," I stood my ground. This time my need to understand what he meant overcame my fear of sounding stupid. But the guest was stubborn too.

"What's there to understand here, precisely?"

"What's moral in the deepest sense of the word?"

"That's a good question." He thought for a moment. "OK, I'll give you a rather Christian answer, but it's the truth. Moral in the deepest sense of the word is the recognition of other people's dependence on you. Kapish? And parallel to this is the acceptance of the unavoidability of the attempt to escape this dependency in order to become independent, which in itself is an illusion, an impossible situation. In other words, a knowledge which contains a contradiction in terms. I think that to be a moral man in the deepest sense of the word is to be open, not to block things off out of fear. But we usually live according to conventional morality. The morality which is created by fear. The fear of being out of line which makes us do what we do. Fear, in other words, is a state of moral blockage and openness is the absence of fear, which is the deep moral state. Morality is a concept in relation to which the question Why? is irrelevant. Like love. Understand?"

I nodded, even though I knew that if he asked me to repeat what he had just said I would fail. And nevertheless there was something in his words which touched and moved me. It was beautiful.

"So what was he like, Herb?" I tried to clarify things from the less theoretical aspect.

"Herb? He was a simple man. A man who believed that everything personal is political. He was a very busy lawyer, but he spent most of his time on cases where people couldn't pay him.

Immigrants, second-class citizens. Thanks to him I speak Arabic, Spanish – some of his clients paid him by giving me language lessons. There were periods when he was involved with radical left-wing groups, but his militant side wasn't very highly developed. He had passion, but it was a gentle passion, if such a thing exists. What else? He was crazy about my mother, even though she didn't deserve it."

"And you? Are you a moral person?"

The guest adopted an ironic, amused expression, as he did whenever the conversation focused directly on him. But at this moment I knew that his irony related more to my question than to any hint of self-criticism on his part.

He thought for a long moment, at the end of which he laughed a little laugh, flashing his white teeth.

"I'm a coward. But I try. Once I tried more. I wanted to be like Herb. I didn't really understand what this meant, but I knew the feeling that I aspired to. I wanted to join a left-wing terrorist group. After I finished school in New York and before I started going to the Royal College of Art in London I went to an IRA training camp in Libya."

"So what, are you an anarchist?"

"Me? I'm a dilettante. Anarchist my arse," he said and immediately regretted this self-denigration. "But yes, actually I am. But as you see I don't do anything for the sake of the world revolution, so I prefer not to adopt grandiose titles."

In spite of the amused content of his words, the guest spoke slowly and unsmilingly. "With me everything begins and ends with the ego. I'm a narcissist." He shrugged and spread his hands out in a gesture of: What can I do?

"So did you join a terrorist group?"

"Of course I didn't. That's exactly what I'm trying to tell you. I went to London to do my Master's. But I have to tell you that I have experienced that openness I was talking about. I think that it exists naturally in everybody. Because it's basically intuitive. Inborn. And sometimes it simply lights you up from inside with a clear feeling of renunciation."

"Renunciation of what?"

"Of fear. The fear of death."

"And you've experienced that feeling?"

"Yes. I think I have."

"When?"

"It was during a parachute exercise. At the terrorist camp. The first time I got stuck in the door and I just couldn't jump, even though in the practice jumps from the tower I didn't have any problems and I've never suffered from acrophobia or anything like it in my life. But all of a sudden I was flooded with terror, frozen by it, it was stronger than all my ambition and shame. I hung on to the sides of the door with all my strength, with my frozen fingers, and I couldn't let go. And then I heard the voice. I heard it very clearly, and even though it was so quiet its presence wiped out the noise of the engine and the wind and the commotion, and all it said was, Go. That's all. In this firm, quiet voice: 'Go.' And I jumped. It was almost erotic in the pleasure it gave me. A kind of ecstasy."

"Was it the voice of your instructor?" I didn't understand.

"You don't suffer from an excess of imagination, do you? It was a celestial voice. Understand? That's what it was. The voice of the absolute. What? You've never had that feeling inside yourself?"

I couldn't think of anything in my experience that came close to what he described. What was even worse – I began to feel that barriers were being breached which I had no intention of breaching and that in exchange I might be called upon to contribute information about myself. This thought increased my anxiety. I think that never since my father died had I spent so much time in a face-to-face conversation with a man. A personal conversation. The circle around me had been cracked, and I felt the thought and the presence of the guest seeping into me in a disturbing, almost painful way. A way that made me want to run away and hide until things got back to normal and I was protected again by the poor but only defence at my disposal, my own.

"I have to go now."

I walked to the door and quickly took hold of the handle, encouraged by its metallic coolness, announcing the end of the encounter and distancing me from the option that he might try to go on engaging me in intrusive, disturbing conversations. I waited for him to try to stop me from leaving, but he simply said, "Good night," and only when I was about to shut the door behind me did he call out and stop me, this time in a completely different voice, crisp and amused, his usual voice.

"Wait a minute, I have an idea."

I waited.

"Why don't you come with me tomorrow to see Katyusha? She's the friend I told you about. The one who's going to help me find a restorer. How about it? Don't forget we have obligations towards your mother, and towards ourselves, if we're already on the subject. And Katyusha is really as nice and funny as they come. If you come with me she'll spare me the usual scenes and be businesslike and your mother will be happy about your developing social life. In short, it looks like a perfect solution all round. Especially in view of the existence of Arthur, a little monster who won't let me talk to her in peace. Maybe you'll be able to keep him occupied, you know – nutcase to nutcase, soulmates. Well, what do you say? I'll call right away to tell her we're coming."

And although I thought that this time I really should be offended, and I wanted to ask him who this monstrous Arthur was, and then to tell him that I wasn't in the habit of going to the houses of people I didn't know, I heard myself say, "Yes, OK. I'd like to. Yes."

Katyusha

Just for the sake of seeing the joy on my mother's face when we presented ourselves, the guest and I, freshly bathed and nicely dressed, to say goodbye to her before setting out for his friend's apartment, it was worth joining the expedition.

I've only now begun to understand how worried she's been about me ever since the guest set up camp in our home. And really, what did I think? Hadn't she emptied my urine from the blue vase with her own hands without ever referring to it? And what about the bite mark on my hand, which I had already stopped bandaging to let the wound dry in the air? It too hadn't been mentioned, even casually. I didn't know whether to be angry with the guest at the liberty he had taken in conspiring with my mother behind my back. Something inside me told me that for some unclear reason and in a way impossible to describe he was my ally, and if he already had a confidante in the house, it was me. Which put him in my hands. In my control. If I felt that he was patronizing me behind my back I would immediately expose his dark secrets – the death of his stepfather, how he had made me drunk, how he had threatened in complete seriousness to kill me if I didn't stop crying, how he trampled on my feelings, and various other matters which would give my mother good reason to throw him out of the house without a guilty conscience.

The taxi journey was spent by the guest in preparing me for the meeting with Katyusha. Since it was midday and the roads were jammed, he had plenty of time to enlarge on the subject in detail and in depth, with the result that by the time we reached Tel Aviv I was fully briefed.

To tell the truth, the things I learned from the guest about Katyusha, her chequered career and the vicissitudes of her life, said more about the guest himself than about her, but this too was fine with me. For instance, the thing that charmed him most about Katyusha was her total lack of humour. But in contrast to other people of this kind, he explained, in Katyusha's case there wasn't a hint of stupidity or boredom involved. On the contrary, there was something about the utter seriousness with which she related to every subject under the sun, from fateful decisions to what to order in a restaurant, which was charming and funny in itself.

The enthusiasm with which he spoke banished any suspicion I might have had that the guest was being cynical. I came to the conclusion that the intolerable lightness of his manner of being may have been truly intolerable from his point of view, and in the light of this possibility his enthusiasm about Katyusha's seriousness sounded sincere, and even logical.

Apart from Katyusha's lack of humour, according to the guest's testimony, she had many other qualities that attracted people to her, made them seek her company and become dependent on her of their own free will, as if this dependency was more satisfying than any dubious independence. But, of course, her main talent was as a go-between.

In reply to my question regarding the exact nature of her business deals and for whom precisely she acted as a go-between, the guest said that he couldn't answer me exactly because any attempt to extract information from her beyond that which she supplied of her own free will was always interpreted by her as tactlessness and indiscretion, and threatened the relationship between them, which was burdened with plenty of other problems as it was, which this was neither the time nor the place to go into.

And then, of course, there was little Arthur. Here the guest sighed and shook his head, and for a moment he looked like Nehama when she was watching programmes about sex-change operations or atomic tests on the Discovery channel. Arthur was Katyusha's son. During the initial years of Katyusha's struggle to establish herself in Tel Aviv Arthur had spent most of his time with his grandmother in Haifa. Once his mother had become an independent businesswoman the boy had returned to the maternal bosom, where it soon became apparent that the vicissitudes of his life had turned him into a very disturbed child. The doctors had diagnosed him as hyperactive and suffering from the rare condition, Tourette's syndrome, but it seemed that his problems were far more complex. As he said this, the guest gave me a meaningful look.

Apart from the fact that the mite in question took tranquillizers in doses capable of killing a horse, never mind a child of six, little Arthur slept no more than two hours a day, swore without stopping, and what was weirdest of all – he affected the habit of talking in rhyme. Every now and then Katyusha would ask the guest to send her expensive natural remedies, and this time too he had brought with him a few lethal powders he had purchased from a fashionable Native American in New York – the guest tapped the elegant plastic bag he had pushed into my hands as we left the house. My job – here the guest gave me a meaningful look again – was to help him get through the visit to Katyusha, who asked unnecessary questions, and the psychotic Arthur in the best and most civilized way possible, acting as a kind of human shock-absorber.

Katyusha lived in an affluent new building in a little street next to Rothschild Boulevard. An elderly doorman in a uniform opened the wide glass door of the lobby for us, and we walked across shining marble tiles to the elevator.

"She's absolutely gorgeous too. Not like a model, a true beauty," said the guest as we waited for the elevator. His timing was terrible. The elevator arrived, and while he continued with a more detailed description of his friend's Slavic beauty I was obliged to examine myself in the large mirrors surrounding me on three sides, which afforded me no escape from the sight of my flat, yellowish face, my sunken eyes, my austere mouth.

Katyusha opened the door looking agitated. Her hair was wild and her cheeks were flushed. She planted two smacking kisses on the guest's face, sent a muttered greeting in my direction, and without waiting for a formal introduction rushed inside, shouting something about burnt rissoles.

"Don't be alarmed," the guest reassured me. "She's just tense because she doesn't know how to cook. It's important to her to make a good impression on you, as a representative of the family."

I stepped inside behind the guest and let him lead me to the kitchen, where Katyusha was busy with pots and pans. We watched her from the side, waiting patiently for her to finish what she was doing. She had a potato nose and broad, tanned cheeks. Her slanting eyes bore witness to the three-hundred-year-old Mongolian conquest of the country from which she came. In utter contrast to her aristocratic genes, her hair was piled up on top of her head in an untidy bun secured with a huge, pink, shiny plastic comb. She was wearing high-heeled sandals, and her prominent backside was encased in tight short pants. She was plump but long-legged, with sexy little waves of cellulite at the top of her thighs. She paused in her labours to wipe the beads of sweat from her upper lip with her arm and spoke to us in a tone which held no hint of apology: "I'm sorry. Go away and sit with Arthur in living room. I'll be finished here soon. Everything got burnt."

Katyusha's voice was low and she spoke in an affected drawl that obliterated any trace of the usual grotesque warble character-istic of Russian speakers with heavy accents like hers.

The guest signalled me to stay where I was.

"Wait, turn round for a second. Let me introduce you to my cousin Susannah."

Katyusha gave me a quick, appraising look and brandished the spatula she was holding to sign the impossibility of shaking hands.

"Hi. I'm Katya. Pleased to meet. May I call you Suzy?"

Although every affectionate distortion of my name makes me shudder, this time I nodded graciously, and thanks to this, perhaps, she addressed the following monologue, confiding the difficulties of motherhood, to me.

"Every time I go crazy with these rissoles, just crazy, but he refuses to eat anything else, only rissoles, like at his Granny's, that's all. And I can't say no. I'm tough woman, but with him I can't say no. So I say – he's suffered enough. But what can I do, if I understand nothing about it? Well, OK, so I don't know how to cook, but I know other things – education, love and warmth, chess, dancing, presents, all kinds of things that are also important. Right, Neochik? Well, why are you standing there? Take Suzy into living room, sit with him, he loves company. And I have to finish here without disturbances."

We made our way through the thick smoke to the living room. The guest whispered quickly, "Now you have to help me. I'm relying on you."

We entered a spacious room with a pale parquet floor and a big French window affording a view of Tel Aviv in all its ugliness. In contrast to the view, the interior spoke of elegance and style: a white sofa with a slanting back; instead of a table a rhombus of thick, matte glass resting on a complicated structure resembling an atom made of gleaming stainless steel, low chairs with curving backs made of thick, stiff plastic in green, orange and blue. A tall lamp which looked like a bunch of purple flowers growing on Mars completed Katyusha's temple of contemporary design.

The child was sitting in a swollen red leather chair opposite the television and watching the children's channel. He was wearing nothing but underpants and a pair of huge new Nikes, of the kind worn by tough, street-wise rappers. His belly spread over his underpants in a lordly fashion and everything about him exuded a dignified, proprietary air. He ignored our entry.

"How's tricks, Arthur!" the guest essayed a note of friendly nonchalance.

"Neo fucks from behind, in every arsehole he can find," the

child said indifferently without moving his eyes from the screen.

"I love you too, Arthur. I'm glad you remember my name. For a kid with problems like yours that's an achievement not to be sneezed at."

The child responded to this nasty dig by pressing briskly on the remote control until he stopped at the Turkish channel.

The guest went on trying.

"Learning Turkish, Arthurchik? Planning a vacation in Antalya?"

The child sniffed and returned the face of the children's channel presenter, smiling with imbecilic bliss, to the screen. The three of us looked at her in silence for a few minutes. I couldn't see myself fitting into the campaign to appease Arthur from any conceivable angle. In the meantime the guest called on his reserve troops.

"You want to meet my cousin Susannah?" he said, pushing me forward until I almost tripped and fell over the child's chair.

"Susannah has the cunt of an iguana, she drinks spunk like manna."

The kid was definitely no mean rhymer, but I began to feel the familiar tremor of my lips, signalling that from this point on control over my tears was in the hands of chance.

Now I saw with my own eyes that the guest was indeed lacking in the capacity to be hurt for others, either in the deep or the shallow sense of the word. The only thing that worried him was apparently his failure in the presence of witnesses. He winked at me and addressed the child in a soft, obsequious voice which if I'd been Arthur would have made me suspect his motives from the first word he spoke.

"So you're living with mummy all the time now, are you? That must be fun. I think your mother's very nice. I just hope you're not driving her too crazy with your poetic talents."

The guest laughed nervously, waited a moment, and then added in a tone that didn't carry too much conviction, "Being with mummy's the most fun, right?"

The child replied with a speed that might have made even Donovan Bailey envious.

"Your mother fucks without a slip, she sucks Arabs from the Gaza Strip."

"OK, I see you're not in a very friendly mood, Arthur, I didn't mean to disturb you, I was only trying to be polite. Never mind me, but haven't you got any shame in front of Susannah . . ."

The child switched channels again to ITV. A group of rappers in dark glasses leapt across the screen with cat-like or ape-like movements, waving their hands at the camera. The guest gave me a glance that said: I'll soon put a stop to this bullshit, and set the scene for the final fiasco.

"And while we're already conducting this charming little tête-à-tête, my very young friend Arthur," he emphasized the words "very young", "I would like to point out that my mother hasn't sucked anyone since the early Seventies or thereabouts. Whereas you, on the other hand . . ."

At this moment Arthur pressed on the volume to the point when the threat to our eardrums became very real, intimating that the conversation was definitely over. The guest looked at me with undisguised hostility – I had failed to perform the task for which he had brought me. I in turn looked through the window, trying to breathe deeply.

Only the dramatic entrance of Katyusha, bearing a large platter heaped with pitch-black rissoles and decorated with thick, watery-looking pickled cucumbers, averted the storm about to crash down on the living room.

She set the platter down on the coffee table, crossed over to the child and rumpled his hair, fell to her knees and crushed him to her bosom, covering his sullen face and little paunch with kisses and pinching his fat thighs, and then pulled the table up to his chair, ran to the sofa, grabbed a couple of cushions, pushed one under his backside and the other behind his back, and finally rose to her feet, smiled at us with maternal pride, and switched off the television.

"Well, here I am."

She sat down on the sofa and beckoned the guest to sit beside her. I took a quick look around and positioned myself on the stylish leather armchair next to the big window.

"You're comfortable there, Suzy," said Katyusha without a question mark after the sentence, while she waited for the guest to light the long menthol cigarette she extracted from its packet. "You can play with Arthurchik in the meantime, because Neo here, I understand, wants to talk to me about business." She looked at the guest unsmilingly and blew smoke into his face.

The guest came straight to the point, glancing at me as if the request came from both of us.

"Katyusha, I'm looking for a restorer. Desperately. Maybe you know somebody."

Katyusha responded with a naturalness that startled us both at the ease with which the problem was about to be solved.

"Who? A restorator? Sure I know."

The guest shot me a quick look as if to say: Didn't I tell you she was something?

In the meantime Katyusha reflected for a moment and added,

"Plenty. I know plenty restorators."

"Plenty?" The guest looked at her with an expression of exaggerated surprise. "And you can introduce me to one of them? The one you consider the most reliable, the best in the field?"

"Sure I can."

"Katyusha! You're an angel. I was ready for a big hassle, a whole run around, and here you come and solve everything in a flash."

The coolness and composure with which Katyusha was about to fulfil his request made him almost sentimental, while she licked her finger and rubbed her spit on an invisible insect bite on her neck, tucked her legs underneath her and blew another jet of smoke into his face.

"You know, I've been sitting and racking my brains about it from morning to night. Ask Susannah. That's why I didn't call you as soon as I arrived."

Katyusha raised her eyebrows and pursed her lips in an expression of disbelief, but the guest pretended not to notice.

"Of course I know a couple of restorers myself, the one from the museum and some other guy called Lipkind, but the project I'm engaged on is rather delicate, and I certainly wouldn't want to involve the wrong people in it. You . . . I really don't know how to thank you, you're so, so . . . simply astonishing. You're my Katerina the Great."

Katyusha accepted this brazen flattery without a smile. She no doubt saw herself as a woman worthy of the utmost respect, and she was no doubt right.

"So when do you think you could introduce me to one of them?"

"Whenever you like. Today. Tomorrow. I only have to give a ring."

She gave him a look full of hidden meanings, which were apparently clear to the guest, for he took the cigarette from her hand and took a long, smiling drag on it.

"Who do you think I should meet first? Which of them do you think is the best?"

"They're all very good. Every one specialist in something else."

There was something fishy going on here. That was clear. I couldn't say what. There was a memory, a flicker of a memory that I tried to catch hold of, but it kept flaring up and dying down again, eluding my attempts to pin it down. Something connected to my father, of that I was sure. But what? His stories. His childhood in Odessa. An enchanted city on the banks of the Black Sea. He spent a lot of time hanging around the fishermen in the harbour. He had visited Jabotinsky's house when he was still a young reporter. No, that wasn't it. Him and Uncle Noah. Yes. But what. Him hanging round the fishermen in the harbour. Yes. But Uncle Noah even then – the good life. Sauntering down Deribasovskaya Street and sitting in cafés in custom-made white trousers. Working as a messenger boy for Boris Sichkin, the famous cabaret artist with Mafia connections. Abrashka and Nioma Rabinyan. Uncle Noah. The good life. The fishermen. Watermelons cracked in half against the seat of the boat and guzzled with your whole face inside them – your cheeks, your nose. Tepid beer, black bread whose crust was rubbed with a clove of garlic. Salty little shrimps in newspaper cones. No, that wasn't it.

I went on thinking feverishly. In the meantime Katyusha stood up.

"So, Neochik, are you happy, my soul? Now I want your advice on few legal matters. But first I'm going to get us something to drink. In the meantime, play with Arthur. It's very important to me for you and him to get along. Wine, vodka? Suzy, what do you want? Something cold perhaps?"

"It makes no difference. Whatever you have."

She sailed out of the room with slow stateliness, like a pirate ship loaded with booty receding towards the horizon.

The guest quickly caught my eye. Looking smug and pleased with himself he mouthed "How are you doing?" in my direction, keeping his voice down so as not to be heard by Arthur, who was eating steadily, scattering big crumbs on the carpet. While his mother was busy talking to the guest he had succeeded in getting rid of his fork, and he was now making use of both his hands, taking alternate bites of rissole and pickled cucumber. Suddenly I remembered.

"Restaurant." That was the word. My father said that while he was spending his days with the fishermen in the harbour, Nioma – in other words, Uncle Noah – was already eating in "restaurants". But what was the connection? Maybe something in Katyusha's accent that reminded me of his warm, throaty voice. The slowness of her voice? No. Restaurants . . . restaurateurs . . . and before I even knew what I was saying, a situation I was already getting used to in my conversations with the guest, I found myself whispering in his direction: "Ask her what a 'restorator' is."

"What?"

He had heard me very well. I kept silent.

"What do you want me to ask her?" he insisted.

I moved my lips. Arthurchik, who realized that some secret activity was going on behind his back, fixed me with a stare, vulgarly sucking the cucumber in his hand.

"Ask – restorator. Ask her what it is."

"What? I don't understand."

I wanted to die. I made up my mind that if he asked me again I wouldn't answer him. He could manage on his own. At that moment, as if to confirm my decision, Arthur took the pickled cucumber out of his mouth and burst into song.

"Resto-resto-restorator, in the arse he fucks a tractor. Resto-resto-restorator, in the arse he fucks a tractor."

The guest shook his head and picked up a fashion journal lying on the sofa, as if to say: You're all crazy. Katyusha came in with a tray holding bottles and glasses, and as if he had decided to put an end to the matter and rebuke me for my silly suspicions, the guest turned to her and asked her sweetly:

"Katyusha, tell me, my soul, what exactly, in your opinion, is a restorator?"

Katyusha didn't even take the trouble to be insulted or surprised, and her broad face maintained its blank Mongol inscrutability.

"Well, what do you mean what is it? A restorator is a restorator. Someone who has a restorant. The Golden Apple. Aharoni. By the Sea. What kind of question is that?"

The guest froze for a moment and leaned back, examining Katyusha as if he was seeing her for the first time. She put the tray down on the table and began busying herself about it, pouring whisky and juice into glasses, dishing out ice cubes, adding soda. Only after she had raised her eyes to him a number of times and registered that he was still staring at her, she said in her slow, alto drawl, "Well, what is it, Neochik? What's the matter?"

The guest was quiet for a moment. Then he lit a cigarette and told her about the icons he was supposed to acquire and his shocking ignorance of the subject, and how he needed the guidance of a restorer specializing in Byzantine art to help him make the right purchases. Katyusha did not appear in the least embarrassed by her mistake. On the contrary, the more the guest explained, the more sceptical her expression became, until she stopped him with a look of utter disbelief on her face.

"Just a minute. Why icons of all things? You buy and sell Americans. You understand as much about icons, excuse me, as a pig about oranges. Why the hell should some Armenian trust you to buy icons for him if he's such a serious collector?"

The guest looked a lot more disturbed than Katyusha's simple questions, which even I could have answered, seemed to warrant. But Katyusha was apparently in possession of information that demanded an elaboration of the guest's story, which indeed he attempted to supply, in a rather apologetic tone.

"He liked me. The Armenian liked me. He said that I was a combination of a decadent and a revolutionary. And I learned a little about icons before I came. You can ask Susannah how I explained the one I bought from Shalva the Georgian to her."

Katyusha stared at the guest in silence. She showed no intention of obtaining verification of his claims from me. His distress grew evident.

"He knew that I worked in Israel. He said that after Perestroika Russian museums and private collections were looted of their treasures, and some of them landed up here. It seemed logical to him to make me his man in Israel."

Katyusha maintained her silence, and her look grew more focused and frozen.

"He said he thought it would be a shame for such treasures to fall into the wrong hands. That he had the best and biggest private collection of Byzantine art in the world. You understand. He's an anti-Semite. He hates us because of all the attention we got because of our Holocaust, while nobody cares about theirs, and because we have diplomatic relations with Turkey, and because of the occupation . . ."

Katyusha threw her head back and rubbed her forehead, as if she was having a severe migraine attack. The guest immediately fell silent. The ensuing silence was so dramatic that even the child set his plate aside and stared at us curiously.

"OK, OK," the guest broke the oppressive silence. His resolute expression appeared to indicate that he had reached a decision and intended to stand by it, whatever the cost.

"I owe him money, OK? I lost a few thousand dollars to him in a friendly game at the home of some friends." The guest sighed heavily, as if he had been relieved of a long-standing burden.

"How many?" Katyusha asked laconically.

"How many what?"

"How many thousands of dollars did you lose to him in that friendly game?"

The guest was silent, as if making up his mind whether to lie or to continue along the Via Dolorosa of the truth upon which he had hesitantly embarked.

"It doesn't matter . . . seventy! OK?" Citing the sum he had lost appeared to strike the guest as more terrible than pronouncing the ineffable name of God for a religious Jew.

But he immediately recovered sufficiently to add quickly: "But I've already returned forty. I borrowed it from my mother."

"Your mother gave you forty thousand dollars to pay back gambling debt?" For the first time something resembling a smile crossed Katyusha's face. "That's very nice of her. Very nice.

Altogether, it's very nice to see such good relations between mother and son. So nice that it's hard to believe, especially after all the problems you gave her. A wonderful woman. Give her my regards the next time you talk." At that moment I failed to understand how the guest could claim that Katyusha lacked a sense of humour. Her whole being proclaimed stifled laughter that was about to burst out at any second. She went on smiling at the sullen guest until he lowered his eyes, and then she asked in a completely different tone, dry and businesslike, "And what about remaining thirty?"

"I'm paying them off in work. Buying icons for him. I'll get ten per cent on every deal." The guest was glad to get back to business.

"In other words you have to buy icons at price of three hundred thousand dollars for him," Katyusha made the simple calculation. "That's lot of icons."

"Not if you buy rare, ancient items."

"Even if you buy oldest, rarest items, it's still lot of icons. Believe me. I know."

The guest's eyes flashed at her with a fire that was almost dangerous.

"So I'm fucked. OK? So I started playing again. What do you want me to do now? Kill myself? I'm sorry I didn't tell the whole truth at the beginning, but you understand why. I'm not proud of myself. OK? Now I need you to help me. So do you know a restorer or not?"

For a moment I was sure that I could hear a note of malicious satisfaction in her voice as she answered slowly, stressing every word, "This kind of restorator, of icons, I don't know."

The guest nodded and glanced away, gnawing his thumb.

He seemed sunk in despair. Arthur came and stood next to us, industriously picking his nose, curious about the drama unfolding before his eyes.

Whether it was thanks to her Russian heart, which was wrung at the sight of the guest's disappointment, or whether it was due to the cold calculation of a pimp about to lose his credibility in the eyes of a client, Katyusha put on a sympathetic expression, sat down next to the guest, and put her arms around him. As far as she was concerned, it appeared, he had already received his punishment. Now it was time for conciliation.

"Come, Neochik, there's no need to despair. So I don't know a restorator. But I know plenty of other people. Plenty. This is my work – to know people, to introduce them to each other. If you need a restorator, we'll find a restorator. I know people who sell things too. Who buy things. You know how I am – sociable. I'll ask around, I'll look into it. There are so many Russians, here, in Haifa, in Kfar Saba. If I don't know – somebody else knows. We'll find answer in the end. It will be all right."

"Of course it will, Katyusha. I know. It's just that there was too much going down too quickly, so I'm a little nervous. Don't worry." The guest smiled in order to demonstrate his renewed faith. "What did you want to consult me about?"

Katyusha shot a glance at Arthur and dropped her voice. "There are couple of documents, you know, my Hebrew's not so good for all those little letters and complicated words. I want you to see letter from lawyer in Haifa. Problems with Mustafa's will again, I don't know what to do any more. They've succeeded in holding back payments again." She sent another look in the child's direction and whispered, "Mustafa's turning over in his grave, believe me. This is primitive country. Moroccans and

Arabs. A jungle." Then she added, in her normal voice: "Suzy, maybe you can talk to Arthur in the meantime. He gets little lonely sometimes." And she stood up and left the room, beckoning the guest to follow her.

I looked out of the window. The ugly roofs of Tel Aviv under the pale early summer sky began to turn a tender orange in the sunset. An endless expanse of TV antennae and solar heaters spread out before me, as if the city was a part of the Sargasso Sea, in whose lethal algae thousands of ships had become entangled and drowned. I tried to think of something concrete, focusing, but my head was empty, as if all sense of meaning was being sucked out of the city and of me. Only reality remained, naked, precise, loaded with details and lacking in meaning.

I heard a rustle behind me. I turned round in alarm. The child was standing next to me, rocking and murmuring something in a quiet, rhythmic recitative, the endless repetition of some meaningless mantra. His right hand, plump and soiled by his meal, was clenched in a little fist, which he was trying to press into the palm of my hand. I heard the muffled voices of Katyusha and the guest in the other room. Who did he think he was, this guest? Inviting me to accompany him to some dubious female friend. Confessing to lies he had told to me and my mother too. Losing tens of thousands of dollars at cards. And she was no angel either – Mustafa, lawyers. Knows people! No sense of humour! Why, she had almost burst out laughing in his face! The bitch. And now he was leaving me alone with this half-demented little creature on top of it. Why hadn't he come back from her lousy bedroom yet? What was I supposed to do in the meantime?

The child despaired of his efforts to get me to hold his hand

and went on rocking and muttering like an old Jew at the Wailing Wall.

I measured him with a cold, unsympathetic look and turned back to the window. Now he raised his voice and I was able to hear his words, the usual rhyming obscenities.

"Vadim shits apple pie, Vadim fucks in the sky, Vadim shits apple pie."

I went on looking through the window, but the emptiness which had previously filled my head was now full of the intrusive presence of the child standing behind me.

"Vadim shits apple pie, Vadim fucks in the sky."

At least he had abandoned personal insults, offensive rhymes about Susannah the iguana. If he dared to repeat them I would certainly burst into tears and not be able to stop. Susannah the iguana, he's coming to get you, Susannah. The helplessness of my situation, sitting and waiting for the guest, who was helping Katyusha with shady legal business in the next room and who knows what they were getting up to there in the meantime, sent a tremor through my shoulders. How humiliating. Perhaps I should get up and go, take a taxi home and leave him to manage on his own. But since I had gone out with the guest it had not occurred to me to ask my mother for money. And now, what now?

I turned to face Arthur again, determined to silence him with a look. The child stood in front of me and looked at me. He was very like his mother – broad cheeks, a miniature potato instead of a nose, all the ruined cities of Russia in his eyes, trampled under the hooves of Genghis Khan's horsemen. Now I could perceive the small details too: crumbs of unidentified matter and tiny down feathers from his pillow in his hair, asymmetrical groups of freckles next to his nose, a slight squint that gave him an expression of emotional aloofness. I suppose some people would have called Arthur a "beautiful child".

"Vadim shits apple pie," he repeated.

"Listen, kid, I don't know what you want. I don't know what to do with children, understand?"

I nearly wept.

"Leave me alone. You can't help us find a restorer. So go away and mind your own business."

I turned back demonstratively to the window. To the terrible enchantment of the Sargasso Sea that was already fading. I hoped that now he would leave me be, but I was wrong. He grabbed hold of the hem of my skirt and tugged at it with his fists, beating his head against my thighs while despairing screams bearing the same repulsive message escaped his lips.

"Vadim shits apple pie! Vadim! Shits apple pie!"

I tried to detach him from my skirt, but it was impossible. He hung on to me like a giant crab, rocking his body and shaking his head as he screamed. Katyusha and the guest rushed into the room and succeeded with a combined effort in forcing the child to release his grip.

"Was he trying to hit you?" asked the guest with a measure of concern.

"Never! Probably he was trying to talk to Suzy. He's good boy. Friendly, like me."

Katyusha picked the child up and carried him quickly out of the room, clinging to her neck and screaming his vulgar rhyme.

The guest waited until Arthur finally fell silent in some other room under the loving ministrations of his mother.

"Look, I'm sorry it turned out this way. But it really helped that you came. The kid hates me, he's jealous. With you everything passed off relatively quietly, including the cross-examination. I only hope she'll be able to find me a restorer, otherwise I'll be in trouble."

I didn't say anything and waited for us to leave.

Katyusha came back into the room looking flushed, wordlessly poured chilled vodka into three unmatching glasses and invited us to sit down.

"I have news," she said.

"What news? What did you do to Arthur? Smother him with a pillow?" The guest's voice was full of venom.

"I should have known. He shouldn't listen to adult conversations. It makes him nervous. Now he's playing in his room. He's never bored. But I understood what he was saying."

"What he was saying when, Katyusha? All he says are obscenities strung together with rhymes."

"What nonsense. He says what he thinks. He simply has a style of his own. Like an artist. You should understand such things instead of sitting there with sulky face."

"You're right," the guest agreed indifferently.

"What he said to Suzy is that we know restorator. You understand – we know one. But not a restorator from a restorant like his stupid mother thought. He's a remarkable child. You think he's crazy, but never mind. Everybody thinks so. People don't like him and it has bad effect on him. But I know truth. We have restorator. You understand, he heard the words 'icons', 'art', 'restorator', and he put them all together. Apparently Suzy had good influence on him."

"What are you telling me, Katyusha? I don't understand what you're telling me." The guest looked at me for confirmation, but I held my tongue.

"So listen, please. Vadim. Vadim is father of little girl in his class. For special education. Father of Shellinka. They come from Leningrad. Shellinka lives with Tamara, with her mother, but sometimes Vadim comes to take her too. To play with her. This Vadim is drunk, alcoholic. Disgusting person. I always pity Tamara that she has to give him Shellinka twice a week. But children like him. So this Vadim is painter. Shitty painter. In Russia he calls himself painter, but he makes money from work in museum. I think he even worked in Hermitage. Tamara told me that he is expert on icons. She always said it when he turned up drunk, to show that he was worth something once. Now do you understand that Arthurchik is child genius?"

The guest had no option but to agree.

"Well, so you want me to check out this Vadim, this iconist for you? Maybe he can help. And if not him then somebody else, just don't sit there with long face like that. Right, Suzy? Now go, and I'll ring tomorrow to tell you what's happening."

"Fine. I'm staying with Susannah and her mother, so don't get confused and look for me at the Hilton."

Katyusha sighed with Chekhovian melancholy.

"You have to stop playing cards, Neochik. Otherwise there won't be any money for good life you love."

She accompanied us to the door, and only then did the guest remember the plastic bag with the homeopathic remedies for Arthur which he had left in the hall.

"Here, I got these from the Native American doctor. Although it seems to me now that the last thing Arthur needs is medicines."

When it came to the welfare of her son, however, Katyusha was immune to flattery.

"He needs, he needs. If there's something that can put him

to sleep for more than two hours it will be very good. All night he climbs on top of me, in the end he'll be sex maniac with complex of Oedipus."

"Oedipus Schmoedipus, as long as he loves his mother," the guest repeated an old, unfunny joke that even I knew, and now for the first time since we arrived I saw Katyusha laugh out loud. It was a whole-hearted, throaty laugh, but with the speed of lightning it died down into a smile which was soon replaced by her usual phlegmatic expression.

She planted a moist kiss on the guest's mouth, shook his hand with aristocratic limpness, and slammed the door behind us.

"One word to your mother about the cards and the debts," said the guest as we strolled down the darkening boulevard, "and I'll kill you on the spot."

The Mystery Of Men

I quickly understood why the guest admired Katyusha so much and why it was so important to him to keep on the right side of her. It was simple: there was no problem that Katyusha couldn't solve. There was no promise that she didn't keep. Two days after our visit to her apartment the guest met Vadim the restorer, and when he came home he told us that the man was an expert on an international level, a genius in his field. No longer would the guest, an ignoramus in everything pertaining to the Byzantine period, have to humiliate himself before the stuff made for tourists that Shalva the shady art dealer tried to palm off on him as rare treasures. Not only that, he continued, picking my mother up and despite her protests swinging her round in the air as if she were a slender slip of a girl, not only that, but Katyusha had already started making enquiries and activating her wide-ranging connections, and tomorrow morning, yes, yes, tomorrow morning he was going to see a number of icons in the home of a rich immigrant family in Ganei-Yehuda.

In the days that followed Katyusha supplied the guest with more addresses and put him in touch with more people. He was beside himself. His gaiety and charm rose to new heights.

We spent family evenings at home, watching television, playing Trivial Pursuit or Monopoly or just talking, that is to say he and my mother conducted passionate discussions about lofty subjects (Don't forget, Ada, that fascism too is the result of the romantic revolution), and with no less enjoyment about utter nonsense (In my opinion, the correct diet should be composed of vegetable proteins, Ada), while I listened from my stool, occasionally reacting in brief sentences. Sometimes he would make my mother laugh for whole evenings on end, squeezing shy smiles even out of me. My mother began cooking her more complicated dishes every day, the ones she usually reserved for special occasions: gefilte fish, soup with kreplach, Haman's ears made with yeast dough and crammed with poppy seed. She fixed a torn zip in his trousers, trimmed his long hair while he sat on a chair in the middle of the room like a barmitzvah boy. He would read interesting bits of the newspaper or parts of poems aloud to her, explain the workings of the stock exchange, interpret the characters on the pack of Tarot cards someone had once given her as a gift and which no one had been able to explain to us before. The card representing you, Ada, he said as a blush of pleasure spread over her cheeks, is the Empress (the big, abundant earth mother, Ada). The card representing himself changed from the Fool to the Magician, depending on the period of his life, Nehama – Justice; Armand – the Chariot; while I was represented by the strangest card of all (what else!) – the Hanged Man. A card whose meaning I failed to get to the bottom of – perhaps a sacrificial victim, perhaps a state of incubation, a state of transition from one spiritual stage to the next. Even the guest himself got tangled up in tortuous explanations until in the end he said that the whole Tarot thing was intuitive and explanations only limited the meaning of the card.

There were some evenings when we just sat and watched television. The guest said that at home in New York he abstained completely because he could get hooked in a matter of seconds. I understood what he meant – he could sit and stare at the screen the whole evening long, interrupting the sequence with hurried trips to the kitchen to make himself a sandwich with jam and the oily peanut butter my mother had begun to buy especially for him. When he had to go to the toilet he would announce the fact in the tone of a Shi'ite suicide bomber before his final mission, handing on the torch to his living comrades: I'm going to pee, Ada, but do me a favour, for God's sake, pay close attention to what happens with the prison director, otherwise we won't know what happened about the girl and the old black man.

I enjoyed the knowledge that in spite of the friendship between him and my mother I was his true confidante. My choice to play a minimal part in the family celebrations did not stem only from reserve or shyness on my part. I had no wish to come too close to the guest – attaching yourself to people means being ready to lose them, and who if not Susannah Rabin had narrowed her life down to a state that allowed for a minimum of pain. When I was younger and I met people I felt a closeness or attraction to, like the anorexic Na'ama from the sculpture workshop or the born-again religious guy who was in love with me when I was in hospital for observation eight years ago – after every meeting with them I would imagine that they had gone away, disappeared off the face of the earth, and that I would never see them again. In spite of the terrible grief and sorrow I felt when Na'ama went to study in Italy and after the religious guy slit his throat in the storeroom, the imagined scenarios of their disappearance that I had cultivated strengthened me and gave me a sense of control.

The guest's physical invasion of our faded feminine temple no longer tortured me as it had in the beginning. Although I still took care not to forget my bra in the bathroom, and after using the lavatory I sprayed to suffocation with the rose-scented air-freshener, my initial panic had almost completely disappeared. Once I even absentmindedly emerged from my room bare-legged in an old shirt of my father's, like I used to before he arrived, but as soon as I felt his look burning on my calf I resumed my official dress – a long-sleeved blouse and an ankle-length dark blue skirt.

The guest went out frequently on business and sometimes he stayed away for days on end, leaving my mother and me waiting separately for his return, for his entrance bursting with energy, for his amusing stories, for his presence exuding warmth and optimism to fill the house with a festive atmosphere. Even though our daily routine continued as usual, with all the trivial details of which it was composed, the days were full of a fresh, special meaning. Even the daily excursion to the beach took on a holiday air, free of the dutiful, medicinal purpose by which it had been characterized up to now.

On one of these new mornings Nehama burst into the kitchen, waving the newspaper she had taken out of our mailbox. *Ha'aretz* – my mother's daily paper. The external sign of the stability of our lives in spite of the revolutions raging around us in the out-side world.

My mother was a *Ha'aretz* junkie, hooked on it from the first day I remember. I, on the other hand, hate newspapers. They describe a world alien and remote from me. A world in whose joys and problems I have no part. A world of living people. Only sometimes my mother finds an interesting article for me in the supplement, about an unusual natural phenomenon, a new medical breakthrough, an exhibition I'll never go to see.

Nehama likes newspapers too, albeit in a completely different way from my mother. My mother wants to know what's happening as an observer on the sidelines, who although she feels involvement and is severe in her judgements, has no desire to take an active part in events. Just like my mother, Nehama also feels intensely involved. But unlike my mother, whose involvement stops at the borders of our country, Nehama feels involved in everything, without any connection to her political, civilian or personal closeness to the subject in question, beginning with the treatment of the victims of the volcanic eruption in the Pacific isles and ending with the Cuban government's use of Che Guevara's picture on tourist souvenirs. The trouble is that her opinions are not united in any comprehensive world-view. Scraps of different ideologies attach themselves to her from all directions, like the old-fashioned patchwork quilts made from hundreds of scraps of variously coloured materials. I must admit that this ideological collage of Nehama's is sometimes surprising in its creativity, but for the most part it is full of logical contradictions in every thesis that she tries to put forward. Nehama can be belligerent and tough, almost fascist, in certain subjects and unreservedly liberal in others. When my mother and I point this out to her, she says that she tackles every question on its merits, since she is an authentic person who thinks for herself and doesn't hide behind any ideology, and in any case the era of ideologies has passed from the world and the important thing is the private individual. I'm a post-modern person, she says of herself. And so it happens that her value system, which on the whole aspires to be tolerant, evinces large patches of a fascistic ideology of dubious logic and irrational emotionalism.

But as a rule the subjects that engage Nehama belong more to her and our ongoing daily lives. This time she stormed into the kitchen with her cheeks flushed and yelled: "Nu, so what do you say about this? It's mystic, I'm telling you, simply mystic!"

She threw the newspaper, which she had already succeeded in making a mess of, on to the table, and tapped a peeling, orange-painted fingernail on a small item on one of the back pages. My mother waved a kitchen towel at her, trying to quiet her and stop her from waking the guest, but Nehama was too agitated to pay any attention. "It's not to be believed, simply not to be believed, the things people permit themselves!"

"People", by the way, play a central role in Nehama's discourse, where they are frequently guilty of sins both small and large. I put out my hand to take the newspaper but she quickly snatched it away, leaving me holding a scrap of paper.

"Just a minute," she cried, "first I have to give you the background." Mother placed a cup of Nescafé in front of Nehama and sat down next to her.

"So it's like this," Nehama took a breath, trying to calm herself so that she would be able to step on the gas when she came to the important part of the story without having to waste her energy on the dull details.

"So I'm walking down the street, on my way here, when all of a sudden that Gidi Bochacho appears, taking his dog for a walk. OK. So they're walking along, and I say to myself: Maybe I'll walk a few steps behind them, and see if he shovels the dog's business into a bag or tries to ignore it, because it's early and there's nobody else in the street. This Gidi, by the way, do you know why he left the regular army, Ada? Did you ever ask yourself that question? Just think about it, it's a great job, a good salary, benefits, a pension, all laid on. So why, do you think, does somebody suddenly get up and leave such a cushy job?"

My mother shrugged her shoulders. "How should I know, Nehama? People have all kinds of reasons for doing the things they do. What do I know?"

This was exactly the answer Nehama was waiting for, for her round, swollen cheeks, covered with a tangled net of fine veins – cheeks that always reminded me of little Jonathan apples left out in the sun too long so that they wrinkled and withered – flushed with excitement.

"So I'll tell you exactly why he left the army," her little eyes flashed with a faded blue gleam. "Because he's a homosexual, that's why!"

My mother gave me a worried look. "What a way to talk, Nehama! You're really homophobic, you know that? And anyway, how's that connected to him being in the army or not being in the army? All he did there was work as an electrical engineer or something like that, if I'm not mistaken."

"How's it connected?" Nehama exulted. "How's it connected? I'll tell you how it's connected. But before that tell me honestly: would you want someone like that to defend you in a war, Ada?"

She quickly fended off my mother's protest.

"I know that everyone's terribly liberal about these things nowadays, I know that what I'm saying is unpopular, but I'm asking you seriously, Ada. How do you really imagine him running and jumping over the hills with the Uzi and the mortar and the canteen and the binoculars and everything else they run and jump with, if all he's got in his head is underpants and aftershave? And what if he suddenly falls in love with an enemy soldier? Have you thought about that? With some Egyptian with a moustache? Maybe that's exactly what attracts him, the attraction of opposites? He's blond – the Egyptian's dark; he's refined – the Egyptian's rough; he's intelligent – the Egyptian's a baboon. How do you know? Believe me, people have turned into enemy agents for less. Traitors. I once saw one of their magazines, with pictures, and guess what! That's just what they like – moustaches and Nazi caps. So how can you be sure with someone like that? And you, what are you laughing at, Susannah, and with a cigarette sticking out of your mouth first thing in the morning like some oaf?" Nehama sniffed angrily and took a sip of coffee.

"I want to understand, is this all you wanted to tell us when you came in, or are you digressing again?"

This was another characteristic that made Nehama an impossible person to talk to. She digressed. After starting on a certain story she would suddenly get caught up in some marginal subplot or distant character – a cousin several times removed and so on – and from then on she would unfold the biography of this character in all its aspects and vicissitudes, and she did this over and over again with every new character who appeared in the course of the narrative, until the original storyline escaped her completely and it was only with the help of endless promptings from her audience that she was able to bring it to a conclusion, worn, pale and exhausted, with the thundering climax and dramatic point she had intended petering out instead into a couple of tepid sentences lacking in any moral lesson.

"I'm not digressing, these are all important details." Nehama seemed hurt, but not to the extent of preventing her from continuing her story. "Anyway, so I'm walking along behind this

Gidi, and suddenly they stop, and his animal squats down on the pavement and does what it does. OK. I wait behind the rhododendron, risking, by the way, a certain danger of poisoning, just so you know, Ada, and why? I'll tell you why! You pay attention too, Susannah, it's a point of general knowledge you should know. The rhododendron is a poisonous plant, and once, in the Middle Ages I think, a whole legion of soldiers were poisoned by making plugs for their water bottles from its leaves, just imagine! My Amireleh told me about it when he was doing his preparatory courses for the university, you remember, Ada, it was when we still thought that he was going to study history and literature at Tel Aviv University, but when he decided on the Haifa Technion, even though it was just because of that Russian girl, who's so sensitive and intellectual but who knows very well how to grab a man by the ba . . . never mind, you know by what, I said to myself . . ."

"Nehama!"

This time my mother was about to be seriously annoyed – a danger which the experienced Nehama recognized immediately, and accordingly returned, without pausing to take a breath, to the original story.

"OK, so where was I? Yes, so I'm standing behind the rhododendron and watching the animal doing what it was doing, and then he, this Gidi, patted it on the back as if it had jumped through a hoop of fire at least, and turned to go. You understand, as if nothing had happened! Leaving the whole pile there on the pavement, and I don't want to go into detail but we're talking about a horse here, not a dog, believe me, I'm not exaggerating, it was this size."

Nehama spread out her hands as if she was holding an imaginary watermelon.

"All right, all right." This was a perfect example of my mother's double standards. She couldn't stand it when other people spoke about bodily excretions, even though she herself did so freely and juicily whenever the opportunity offered.

"OK. So I come out from behind the bushes and call him: Excuse me, sir. He turns round, all innocence. Good morning, Mrs Lieber, sweet as pie. I say to him: Excuse me, but you're supposed to shovel your dog's . . . business into a bag, it's a municipal law. Yes, I know, he says to me, but the dog nagged me to such an extent that I didn't have time to take a bag on my way out. I'll just take him to the park and then on the way back I'll find something to clean it up with. So I say to him: I'm sorry, sir, but you're breaking a municipal bylaw here. And he stands his ground: You're right, but I don't have a bag at the moment, I'll get one at Menahem's kiosk on the way back and collect it all. OK, I realized that he was lying in his teeth and I gave him a piece of my mind and told him that I was going that very minute to phone the municipality, even though it was only seven o'clock in the morning and there wasn't anybody there, which I didn't say to him, of course, and then, listen to the cheek, Ada, he says to me: Why don't you mind your own business, and turns his back on me and walks off with his Godzilla as if nothing's happened. And I stood there for a minute, believe me, I felt so insulted that I had tears in my eyes. And then, on my way upstairs to you, I opened the paper, and what did I see? Two Kurzweilers ate a child in Kiryat Ono. So don't let anyone try to tell me that I'm angry and worried about nothing. Here, see for yourself." She pushed the paper over to my mother and folded her hands in her lap, as if to say: I've had my say, now you be the judge.

"What Kurzweil are you talking about, Nehama? He died years

ago." My mother rummaged through her pockets looking for her reading glasses.

"Kurzweiler. That dog, like his. There's a picture. Two peas in a pod."

"Rottweiler, Rottweiler, Nehama, bless you. What made you drag Professor Kurzweil into it?" My mother laughed enjoyably as she read the item. "Oh my goodness, you're right, they savaged a child, how ghastly. Look, Susannah, here's a picture of him in the hospital, with bandages all over his face."

"OK, let it be Rottweiler," said Nehama, encouraged. "That's not the point. The point is that it's a dangerous dog. A murderer, a wild beast. And that Gidi walks round with it here, among people, as if it was a poodle, and look at the way it frightens Susannah all the time. And what if one day it snaps its leash and jumps on her? Have you ever asked yourself that? And altogether, think, what's a dog, when it comes right down to it? Go on, Susannah, tell me that."

I shrugged my shoulders.

"So let me tell you what it is: a dog is a pet. Would anyone want to pet that Kurzweiler apart from the homo? No! And another thing: a dog is a tame animal. Does that dog look tame to you? Wouldn't you say that there was a problem here?"

"Nu, Nehama, get a move on, finish your coffee already, we're ready to go." My mother put a plastic bag containing washed grapes and apricots and the tattered newspaper into the big beach bag. But Nehama insisted on waiting a little longer. The reason was the legend on her bottle of suntan lotion, which insisted that the lotion should be rubbed in half an hour before exposure to the sun. Anxious and upset at this discovery and at the consequences of a lifetime of negligence in this respect, due to her failure up to now to examine the small print on the bottle, Nehama, who in everything directly or indirectly related to her health was quick to abandon her usual rebelliousness and scepticism, began vigorously rubbing the lotion into her freckled arms, her dyed hair swaying in time to her rubbing like a field of sunburnt grass in a dry wind, upbraiding me for my impatience as she did so.

"Stop staring at me like that and put some on too, Susannah. You're as white as a rabbit, you'd better be careful you don't get a melanoma on your nose. That's all we need."

"Good morning, girls."

The guest appeared in the dimness of the living room like a transparent ghost. He was wearing jeans and an undershirt, attire which for some reason made him look immodest, almost pornographic.

"What made you get up so early?" cried Nehama. As far as she was concerned everything the guest did confirmed and reinforced her suspicions that he was a shady character with criminal tendencies.

"A bad conscience, Mrs Lieber, what else?" he yawned. "And also sinister schemes in the framework of my connections with the Mafia." He went up to my mother and pulled the newspaper out of the beach bag, planting a smacking kiss on her cheek in token of his thanks. "Mwaaa."

"You really are up early today, Neo," said my mother, basking in this expression of family intimacy.

"I have to make an early start. I'm driving up to Haifa with Vadim the restorer. Katyusha lent me her car. There's a couple of kids there with a very serious collection. The only trouble is, the air-conditioning in the car's broken down. I haven't got the strength for it, believe me."

The last words were spoken absentmindedly, his nose buried in the newspaper on his way to the kitchen.

Nehama stopped rubbing, still shaking her head as a sign of her disapproval of the inconsiderate behaviour of the guest, who had confiscated the newspaper and showed no signs of intending to return it. But my mother refused to delay another minute and led us firmly to the door.

I love the early mornings. In spite of my natural inclination to lose myself in long, warm sleeps, I would never miss these early morning hours. I marvel at the subtle scent of emptiness in the air. An emptiness not yet filled by the smell of the black exhaust smoke, the familiarity of cooking smells, the sticky smell of the cakes in the pasty shops, the reek of burnt oil at the felafel stands, the miasma of rot hanging over the rubbish bins, the cheap deodorants of the typists hurrying to work, the sourness of the lawyers' aftershave, the stink of the warm breath of humanity – a faceless rabble of Homo sapiens dragged from the imaginary security of their beds into the light of another day of survival. This external emptiness that echoes the emptiness inside me. The emptiness is my distant lover. Don Juan sending his love to his Anita.

This time a disturbing presence made me raise my head and look about me. I soon discovered the source of the alien energy – the guest was standing on the balcony, leaning on the balustrade. His presence was so blunt, so uncompromising, that in spite of the distance I could tell how much coffee was left in the glass cup in his hand.

It seems to me that the suffering of not being beautiful is far more intense than the pleasure of being beautiful. In fact, it seems to me that any pain is more intense than any pleasure. If

I hadn't been convinced that the guest was so perceptive and discerning in relation to the human body, I would have been easier in my mind. I could only shudder inwardly as I went on walking, imagining his eyes appraising my body in casual boredom. I had made myself so sexless over the course of the years that I felt as if a shield had been created around me to protect me from the looks of others. I had become addicted to the magic sense that if you stop thinking a certain thing about yourself, others will do the same. The fantasy of a backward child, convinced that everybody else will be happy to play at being an ostrich with her. Sometimes it succeeded. In fact, almost always. Most of the time I wasn't a woman. I was a creature. But now the dirty guest standing on the balcony didn't know the rules of the game and was examining me from behind. I remembered how he had described Katyusha to me in the taxi on our way there as if I was a male friend in need of information regarding a future mistress. I myself had examined her in this light when she appeared in the flesh. It had never occurred to me that the guest might look at me as if I were a woman among women, possessing a bum, breasts, a walk. And here I was walking down the street, exposed to his gaze with no possibility of taking shelter, while he, bored and sleepy, continued to observe me with an unkind eye.

I walked stiffly, my back muscles clenched, my shoulders hunched. If I could, I would have pounced on the guest, stuck my fingers in his eyes, torn out the slippery little balls and smashed them against the wall and gone on even then digging and digging into the sockets, making sure that there was nothing left, not even a single scrap of tissue he could use to see with. My hatred for him choked me. I was an ugly little ant moving under the all-seeing eyes of God, and there was no escape from that gaze, putting you under a cosmic microscope, enlarging you to millions of times your size, not allowing the single, involuntary tremor of a muscle to remain hidden.

A sharp dig from Nehama's hard elbow interrupted my cruel thoughts. At a distance of a couple of dozen metres, on the other side of the road, Gidi Bochacho appeared with his dog. One thing I knew about this dog – he always had his eye on the ball. If I had seen him, it meant that the recognition was mutual. And as our two camps advanced towards each other on either side of the road, narrowing the gap until it was small enough for eye contact to be established, I set the receding gaze of the guest aside and started organizing myself inwardly for the dog's imminent attack. The time remaining until the explosion filled the air with a concentrated white light. The transparency of the light exposed everything hidden, everything usually suppressed by my selective vision. A little old man with blue eyes stood stooped in the entrance to a nearby building, his unfocused gaze wandering lost in the blinding light of the street. The flies of his trousers were open, exposing a long tube attached to a transparent plastic bag half full of murky, orange urine, hanging from his belt like a canteen. A few steps away from him stood a tired Filipino maid, her swollen face full of laborious concentration as she struggled to open the old man's wheelchair. He waited for her, trying to locate her with his gaze – the gaze of a wingless fly spinning giddily in the tornado of an uncontrollable reality. Gidi Bochacho and his dog advanced slowly towards us. We advanced towards them.

Two young women passed us, apparently on their way to the Beit Zvi acting school. The blonde had a round, pampered face and a soft, weak chin. She had a little case in one hand and what looked like a pile of scripts under the other armpit. The other one, short and aggressive with frizzy hair, was holding a beautiful black and white Pierrot's mask. With my eyes fixed on the approaching dog my ears caught a snatch of their conversation. It was the voice of the one with the frizzy hair. "Whenever people say 'the hubris of the tragic hero' it sounds like something connected to fucking, his penis or something like that."

The coarse laughter of the blonde broke out when they were already behind my back.

And besides all this, somewhere in the back room of my consciousness, was the infra-red gaze of the guest.

The last barrier, bus number 21, hid the dog and its owner for a few moments. Behind its dusty windows I caught a glimpse of the wigs of the religious women on their way to Bnei-Brak. The loud, vulgar fart of the exhaust brought the time of separation to a close, and almost in unison with the receding noise of the engine the dog began to bark. The barks were calculated, measured. He always kept to strict rules in the dynamics of his barking, as if he were conducting the Philharmonic. Careful not to exhaust his strength at the beginning. My mother hastened her step – she was impatient and hoped that it would be possible to get the incident over quickly and efficiently – without interrupting the flow of the story she was telling Nehama, a story which by some miracle had been forgotten and remained untold until now, about how as a young girl she had once had the opportunity of hearing a lecture on Agnon from the famous Professor Kurzweil himself. They increased their pace, sure that I was trailing behind them, red in the face, bathed in the first wave of perspiration of the day.

But I hung back. I slowed down gradually until I was in a straight line with the dog. Facing each other on either side of the road. The attacker opposite the victim. I turned my head in the direction of our building. A large ficus tree hid the guest from view, but he was present nevertheless, in the very air I breathed. A collection of atoms that had suddenly attached themselves to the molecules of the air and created a new compound, the compound of the guest, which I had no alternative but to breathe into my lungs.

Gidi Bochacho wound the dog's leash round his hand. Deliberately he wound it round and round, as if the shortening of the leash gave him more control over events. For him too it was a routine. I looked at him with hate. Sonofabitch homo, let's see you running after the Egyptians. We were opponents. We were WWF wrestlers, each with his own atrocious persona. If we could have, I presume we would have hurled our curses into the ring, goading our opponent.

I stopped and turned to face the dog. He immediately sensed the change and started pulling his master towards me. Gidi Bochacho wound another loop of the leash around his hand. This was already harder – the dog was pulling ahead. I saw Bochacho's biceps bunching in effort. In my heart I had no doubt that what he really wanted was to free the animal and let us meet in the middle of the road like a pair of gladiators in a battle whose outcome was known in advance. The one a handsome Roman – the dog; and the other a skinny, leprous Scythian or Egyptian – me. The chronicle of a death known in advance. My death.

But the desperation of the weak, the doomed, can produce strengths not known to the smug, self-satisfied strong. The power of the hatred of the underdog has made history. Made revolutions. I was brimful of hate. I started to advance towards them. Slowly. One step at a time.

The dog barked louder. In a couple of seconds it would rise to the usual crescendo leading up to the climax, a near howl, which it would sustain until its throat tired, and I would be led round the corner by my mother and Nehama, each holding an elbow, into the friendly street where other rules, considerate of people in my situation, prevailed.

I went on advancing.

A passing car honks irritably: This isn't a pedestrian crossing, lady. I know. I take another step. I stare into the dark interior of the dog's jaws. Deep into the hot, wet blackness, in the middle of which the tongue trembles with eagerness and rage. I take another step. My steps are measured, not slow but not fast either. Mathematical. Precise. With every step I become calmer. I stop thinking about Gidi Bochacho's hostile intentions. He has little glasses and from time to time he straightens them on his nose in a way that almost touches my heart, as if he's the terrified, helpless person under attack here. I go on advancing. The distance between us is getting shorter and shorter. In a minute. In a minute it will happen. I'll stand close. Almost touching. And then he'll jump, knock me down with his forelegs and all the force of his muscular chest and rip my face from my skull. The face of the Israeli Vladimir Madonna. And I, in every split second that I remain alive, will fight him, to my last breath, I'll seize hold of his jaws with both my hands and pull and tear his stinking maw apart. My defeat will be far more glorious than his banal victory.

Step after step. Final preparations. I measured the remaining distance. I marked my way forward, guiding myself. Closed my eyes. One more step. As in a glass bubble, remote and detached from present time, I heard the voices of my mother and Nehama. Susannah, where are you going? What are you doing, child? Come here. I fought them, the warm security coming from them like a promise, I pushed them out of my mind. Only his barks. That's all that matters, me and him. I took another step. I felt the hot breath of his closeness. Once, light years ago, when I was a child, I stood like this before an open stove, sniffing the cookies, letting the heat burn my face, until I couldn't stand it any more and turned my face to the coolness of the room. Now too the heat of the hostile presence spread through my body. Through my chest, my hips. Something contracted between my legs, like a little animal. A hard, frightened little snail. I thought of the guest's face. His curling upper lip, his moist, provocative lower lip. One more step. Another one. The last step. Inside me a celestial voice. The voice of the absolute. The voice of the commander.

The voice of the guest.

One, short, focused word, a bullet fired from a Mauser into my sweating temple – go!

I opened my eyes.

I was squatting like a Bedouin in front of the dog. He was still uttering vestigial howls, staring at me with black eyes gleaming with curiosity. I think I was crying. The tears streamed into my mouth and down my cheeks on to my neck, mingled with sweat. We were so close I could smell him. A strong canine smell. Out of focus – Gidi Bochacho's feet in sandals. I looked at the dog's broad, square face. He was black, with a tawny patch beginning on his neck and spreading over his belly. He pricked up one short ear, tilting his head towards his left shoulder. A stupid, overgrown puppy. He panted. I was right in front of him. Nothing made any difference any more. I closed my eyes again. My quiet breath met his hot, steaming breath. A breath full of meat. The feeling of revulsion was almost enjoyable. Relaxing. Sensuous.

Something moist and rough touched my face, slid over it, wetting it with a sticky, steaming substance. I opened my eyes. His purplish-pink tongue licked my cheeks, my eyes, my chin. A headline in Ha'aretz: Woman has sexual relations with Rottweiler sired by Kurzweiler in Ramat Gan. Kept in custody for additional forty-eight hours . . .

The voices of my mother and Nehama became clearer. Located close behind me. I raise my face to Gidi Bochacho. He is flushed and frightened, he straightens his square little glasses on his nose. Mutters superfluous reassurances in the direction of my mother and Nehama. The leash is still wound as tightly as a spring round his hand, unnecessary now. The dog stops licking me and lets out a meaningless puppyish yelp. He pricks up his ear.

And only now, only now I turn my head towards our building, ready for the fateful meeting. But the balcony is empty. The guest has gone.

Curtain.

For a long time after we arrived at the beach my mother and Nehama were afraid to leave my side in case I got involved in some other incident beyond human comprehension. They discussed the adventure with the dog between themselves, without trying to elicit information from me regarding the hidden motive for my behaviour – the academic debate interested them far more. They even gave up their game with the medicine ball and sat at my feet on the multi-coloured piqué blanket, eating lukewarm grapes and apricots from the moist plastic bag, offering me a pitted apricot or seedless grape from time to time, despite their intimate acquaintance with my eating habits – who knows, maybe this time I would depart from my ascetic practices.

As long as they were hanging around I killed my inner time by staring blankly – me opposite the sea, it–me and me–it. The oceanic sensation as experienced by Susannah Rabin. I waited impatiently for my two chaperones to enter the shallow water next to the sand so that I could really think. I knew that as long as they were near they were liable to hear my thoughts. My mother was so highly skilled at this that sometimes I felt like asking her to bend a fork or guess which of my hands was holding a key or a hairpin. Apparently the thoughts of people like me, people transparent to others, are particularly easy to read. Especially since I was so quiet and secretive by nature, that with my mother and even with Nehama and Armand it had become a kind of non-competitive sport – to guess what was going through Susannah's head. "Now she's cross with me for killing a mosquito, she feels sorry for animals. How about the cow your shoes are made of, why don't you feel sorry for it?" (Nehama the justice seeker). Or: "Susannah feels sad in summer, like other people feel sad in winter" (Armand the frustrated poet). Or: "You think people care if they can see my bra? You're mistaken, people have got troubles of their own" (my subtle mother, needless to say). Now even the guest had been infected by this hobby and he had already made a few guesses that were quite close to home. The net result of all this was to make me try as hard as I could not to think of anything meaningful in the company of others. To count sheep. To think of numbers. Of colours.

In the meantime my bodyguards had begun to sweat so profusely that they were obliged to cut their enjoyable discussion short. They stood up and walked towards the sea. Nehama pulled her bathing costume out of the groove between her buttocks with the movement of a little girl. My mother was talking enthusiastically. She had probably remembered a few more gems from Professor Kurzweil's lecture. Now I was free at last to devote myself to the pleasures of thinking.

I would have liked to ask the guest if there was something erotic about the sense of imminent death. What was the meaning of the hot wave of molten lava between my thighs while I was stepping into the narrow range of the possibility that my body was going to be torn to shreds? He seemed like somebody who would know how to answer me without sounding off about the connection between eros and thanatos, like Armand, or embarking on historical stories that sounded like gossip, like Nehama (French aristocrats would choke each other before having sexual intercourse in order to increase their pleasure, imagine that, Ada, the things people do out of boredom!).

Was it fitting, I thought, as I watched my mother bending down like a giant seal and splashing water with both hands into the pointed cups of the bra of her bathing suit, which made even the oldest and flabbiest breasts look like a pair of cannon barrels, was it fitting to talk to the guest about such sensitive subjects? Subjects which involved the human body in so central, so jarring a manner, like Charlotte Corday's letter in the hand of Marat as he wallowed in the bloody bath? I felt a strange relief at the thought that he had apparently not been a witness to the scene with the dog. I wondered if I should tell him about it myself, without waiting for my mother's report, which would no doubt not be late in coming. I made up my mind not to decide until I saw him in the evening, when he returned from his trip.

After the beach we spent a long time in the Super Duper.

I listened to my mother and Nehama telling Armand about the adventure with the dog. Since in his heart of hearts our grocer was convinced of his spiritual superiority to his two lady friends, he tried despite their protests to interrogate me about my reasons for doing what I did. His soft features crowded together even more than usual in the centre of his face. He looked like a serious koala bear trying to perform a slow, complicated circus trick.

"But why, Susannah," he crushed a bag of raisins emotionally between his fingers, "why did you take such a risk? What if it had ended differently, if the dog had attacked you?"

I shrugged my shoulders.

"Actually she's a bitch," said Nehama, who had received this information from Gidi Bochacho at the end of the incident.

"Who's a bitch?" cried my mother.

"The Kurzweiler. Females in nature, unlike human beings, are much worse than males. They're violent. It's because they have to protect their cubs."

"What cubs are you talking about, Nehama? Where did you see any cubs? Sometimes you simply don't know what you're talking about." It was one of those occasions when the display of Nehama's superficial erudition drove my mother up the wall. This preoccupation with marginal aspects of a situation in which I had nearly been mauled to death, and of my own free will, seemed to her pointless and, especially, indicative of her friend's egoism. Paradoxically enough, this expression of egoism gave rise to precisely those feelings which were its subject, the fury of a female defending her young.

"The child simply wanted to put an end to the never-ending war with the dog. That is to say, the bitch. What's there to understand here?"

"That's obvious. What I ask myself is whether the bitch is actually a lesbian." Nehama showed no signs of a desire to

155

change the subject. "He's a homo, in the first place. And in the second place, why was she so nice in the end?"

"Who's a homo?" asked Armand.

"What time do they stop taking urine samples at the HMO clinic?" Nehama asked, suddenly remembering.

"Gidi Bochacho, the owner of the dog," said my mother.

"But I thought he was in the regular army," said Armand.

"I think they go on till twelve, no, Ada?" said Nehama.

"Go on what till twelve?" asked Armand.

"Taking urine samples," my mother and Nehama answered at once.

"From Gidi Bochacho?" asked Armand.

"Why should Gidi Bochacho have his urine tested?" said Nehama. "Do you think they can cure him of being a homo?"

"Nehama!" yelled my mother.

"Actually I read an article in *Woman*, when I was waiting for my shiatsu, and it said there that it was possible to help them by analysis to stop being afraid of women and even to have a family," said Armand.

"Stuff and nonsense. Once a homo – always a homo. And that shiatsu is as much use as leeches to a dead man." Nehama closed one subject and opened another in the same breath.

"It helped me when I was suffering from piles, don't you remember, Nehama?" said my mother.

"It helped Margalit a lot with her back," said Armand.

"My Amireleh does Chi Chi. It solves all his problems with allergies, although in my opinion that whole business with the allergies started when he married that Russian, the intellectual *de la shmatte*. So he could have not married her and done without the Chi Chi."

"What are you talking about?" said my mother.

"She means Tai Chi," said Armand, "Chinese gymnastics." And he smiled at me.

"Actually she made a good impression on me, the Russian," said my mother.

"You see, Ada, now you don't know what you're talking about. It's all a smokescreen. Listen to what she's dreamed up now . . ."

I went outside. I felt tired. So tired. The tiredest I'd ever felt in my life. I smoked two cigarettes, and when my mother finally emerged and wanted me to go with her to the bank, I said I had to sleep and I went home. I entered the cool apartment with the closed blinds and without even washing the sand off my feet I fell on to my bed and slept until my mother called me to supper.

The steamy evening penetrated the house like some new, demanding guest, requiring attention beyond all the rules of politeness. I slumped in front of the television, damp and sticky, and played with the remote control, too limp to decide on a channel.

Our real guest had not yet returned, but I chose not to mention it before my mother did so herself. He was usually home by this time. I wondered when my mother would remark on this departure from his normal schedule, but she too maintained an obstinate silence on the subject. I knew that she was waiting as anxiously as I was – she couldn't stand any deviation from the daily household routine – but this time she chose to ignore it and behaved as if everything was as usual.

The absence of the guest only underlined the fact of his existence. We waited in silence, sweating, occupying ourselves, me with the remote and she with the morning paper, which was exclusively hers at last, refraining from starting a conversation in case he suddenly showed up and interrupted us in the middle. We had something to drink and put on the clothes we went out in, although before the arrival of the guest we were in the habit of wearing casual clothes around the house: my mother a loose nightgown, and me one of my father's old shirts. Sometimes, on hot evenings like this one, we wore nothing but our panties and bras – because who did we have to be shy of.

My mother broke first. Of course it was much easier for her than for me. She always had her usual weapon – worry. A weapon that enabled her to frustrate any attempt to hide anything from her all-seeing eyes. A weapon as powerful and just as the sword of a crusader.

"I wonder where Neo is this evening," she threw out from behind the newspaper.

"He's in Haifa."

"I know, but it's already late."

I kept quiet. I had no intention of betraying myself.

"The truth is that I'm starting to get a little worried."

I stood up and went into the kitchen. I poured myself a glass of milk, enjoying the cool air blowing from the fridge. I stood there for a few minutes, looking into its bright, cool interior as if it were a postcard of a Swiss landscape with snowy mountain peaks. The fridge was indeed a kind of little Switzerland, spotlessly clean and tidy and air-conditioned. If my mother died, I thought suddenly, I would take everything out and sit inside it all evening, smoking and enjoying the contemplation of the heat outside, just as people enjoy sitting cosily at home when it's cold and raining outside, with a considerable part of their enjoyment stemming from their own good fortune compared to the miserable wet creatures trudging from puddle to puddle in the streets below.

But why should she die? I was immediately overcome by dread. What could have made me think such a thought? Luckily for me, before I could begin to crucify myself for this wicked slip of my unconscious, my mother rescued me, calling out at full volume from the living room: "Close the fridge now, Susannah. Stop standing there praying in front of it. How many times do I have to tell you it ruins the motor?"

I went out to drink the milk on the balcony. The street was deserted, but the windows of all the buildings were lit, emitting wave upon wave of domesticity – TV sets blaring, children scream- ing, snatches of muffled conversation, the clatter of dishes. The air was heavy with the smell of cooking. I counted to a hundred, waiting to see the slender silhouette of the guest coming round the corner. He didn't come. I remembered that he had driven down in Katyusha's car. I wondered if she was his girlfriend. If so, why had he chosen to stay with us and not with her, and why had he done his best to avoid an intimate situation with her when he took me there with him? On the other hand, I under- stood very little about such matters. People conducted all kinds of complicated relationships between them whose meaning was incomprehensible to me. Relationships which had thousands of reasons and sub-texts, some of them even connected with love. Exactly like my own relationships, few as they were. Did the guest love anybody, in fact? As sweet and charming as he was, the notion of love didn't seem to come into it as far as he was concerned.

And me? Did I love anybody? I loved my mother, of course. My father, when he was alive. Maybe in some strange fashion even Nehama and Armand. But this was a quiet, day-to-day love, insep- arable from life itself, like breathing air or digesting food. It had nothing to do with choice. I seeped into these loves. They were completely lacking in the element of the encounter, of that mysterious moment when a stranger is suddenly transformed, as the result of some choice as deep as underground water, external to any system of logic, into someone close. Someone mine. The headlamps of a car interrupted my train of thought. For a moment it seemed to be slowing down outside our building, but it went on. I returned to the living room.

We watched a disaster programme on the Discovery channel in silence. Volcanic eruptions, tornadoes, train collisions. Skilled rescue teams saved people who were drowning, on fire, buried under rubble. My mother made tea. A sour smell of sweat wafted from her when she handed me my cup. I imagined that I smelled no better, but the thought of taking a shower made me shudder. On the screen a racing boat slashed like a giant shark through a row of people standing idly on the bank and watching, and suddenly I thought: Perhaps the guest had left. Left for ever. This was a clear thought. More a certainty surfacing than a momentary idea. He had gone. Disappeared. Naturally he hadn't let us know. This was the only way people like him appeared and disappeared – unexpectedly. Without any connection to previous events. Like a dam suddenly bursting on an ordinary afternoon as the result of a complex set of physical laws operating on it from within, without showing a sign, until it reached the point that caused collapse. An aura of chance surrounded the existence of the guest. He was chance itself. In the past when chance impinged on my life I refused to accept it as such. I had to locate it in the logical centre of my mind. I was convinced that I had played a part in its occurrence. Things happened because I was good or bad. Reward and punishment. Strange how a magical belief in control over one's life exists even in someone like me.

But in fact the guest had appeared without any connection to my deeds or misdeeds. I was neither a saint nor a sinner. He simply came. And now he had simply gone.

I looked at my mother. She was eating a cookie. There were crumbs sticking to her upper lip and her chin. I was filled by an immense, spreading void and inside it the knowledge – like a pea rolling round in a huge mouth, beating against its sides, flung hither and thither, making a shrill, insistent sound – he wasn't coming back.

I went to the guest's room. I wanted to see with my own eyes what I already knew in my heart, and only then to tell my mother. A touch on the light switch revealed my dead father's little shrine, which in the course of the past few weeks had been successfully transformed into the private territory of the guest. The room looked as if it had been abandoned a moment before. The bed unmade, the untidy desk covered with cassettes, ashtrays, papers and coins, the travelling bag standing in the middle of the room with its insides spilling out. Items of clothing scattered every-where, the ragged jeans and used towel hanging on the closet door. The little cubes of the stereo system peeping out from under the bed. And although everything proclaimed his presence out loud, I clung to my belief like a drowning man to a straw. He didn't take anything with him? That was logical. Even expected. He wasn't the kind of person who transported his belongings from place to place. He had no reason to leave? How should I know? Maybe the authorities had discovered his unlawful activities, maybe Nehama was right and he was dealing in stolen or smuggled goods. Perhaps some fateful connection had sprung up between him and the brother and sister whose collection he had gone to see, and perhaps what seemed sudden to me was actually the last link in a chain of moves planned in advance. I went up to the bed. The white undershirt he had been wearing in the morning lay there inside out and crumpled, like a little animal sleeping on its master's bed. I picked it up and without knowing what I was doing I buried my face in it. It was saturated in his smell – a smell I already knew well but which I had never smelled from so close up. An intense emotion engulfed me, almost making me sick. Laundry powder, sweet sweat, smoke, the faint hint of some male toilet lotion and some other unidentified, animal smell. I had to sit down, to calm myself and come back to my senses. I went on pressing the undershirt to my face for a long moment. He's gone, gone, gone, the voice inside me exulted, with a note of panic stirring underneath it. Now I didn't have anything to fear. The danger, whose nature I didn't really understand, had passed. The house was mine again. Nothing would stand between my mother and me. Now I would no longer have to keep other people's secrets from her, worry that they were talking about me behind my back. How strong I was, I didn't need anybody but her. My new friend had gone away and I didn't care, I didn't care at all. Not even a stab of polite regret touched my robust heart. If I liked – I would walk around naked all day. I'd eat in front of the television. I'd pee with the door open, carrying on a conversation with my mother. I'd get back my lost privacy.

I stood up. I switched off the light and closed the door quietly, as if he was there, sleeping or reading, and I didn't want to disturb him.

"He's gone," I announced in the tone of an informant.

"What do you mean 'gone'?" My mother put her cup of tea down on the little table. "Gone where? He's in Haifa."

I shook my head.

My mother looked at me with a frown, as if I had said something silly in company. "I had a look in his room and everything's normal, all his things are there. What on earth put that idea in your head?"

"I had a look too. A minute ago. I'm telling you, he's gone."

"But his things . . ."

"You can donate them to Russian immigrants. Understand? He's left. Gone for good."

I must have sounded so unequivocal that she didn't ask any more questions and we both went together to inspect his room. We stood in the doorway, as careful not to touch anything as if it were a crime scene, and after examining together everything I had already seen for myself, we returned to the living room.

"But he didn't say . . . " She began to speak and was silenced by my look. I felt sorry for her. She looked completely lost. What had happened was so chaotic, so incompatible with the order of her life and thought, that she sat down on the edge of the sofa and stared blankly in front of her with the dull expression of the feeble-minded. From time to time she muttered distractedly, and then sank back into her baffled silence. "Very strange . . . maybe we should phone Armand, he's got that brother in the police . . . but why are you so sure, did he say something? . . . His things . . ." I stood opposite her shaking my head in an uncompromising "no" and afterwards we both sat in silence for a few minutes.

"So what do we do now?" she finally asked in a different tone, more confident and organized.

"Nothing. Get on with our lives." I smiled.

"Are you happy? I thought you'd become friends recently."

"So what? I don't give a damn. Look at the kind of person he turned out to be – leaving like that without even saying goodbye."

"I don't know what to think about such strange behaviour."
My mother rubbed her forehead.

"Don't think. He came and went. People behave in all kinds of
peculiar ways. I do too. And so do you."

This argument somewhat softened the expression of doubt and
resistance on her face, at least for the time being. The "people"
I had referred to, who played so central a role in Nehama's
discourse, were capable of anything. The most villainous acts
imaginable. What was the unmannerly departure of the guest
in comparison to the Holocaust, for example? Or my father's
unfaithfulness? There was no doubt that the world was a place
where, in spite of all the laws of etiquette and morality with which
civilization protects itself, people behaved in the strangest ways.

We looked at each other with profound understanding. I felt
strong. I went over and hugged my mother. We didn't know
exactly what to do next. We stood there for a while hugging
each other, like an archetype of the union between mother and
daughter. Two women left together after being abandoned by
the man of the moment in their lives. An unfissionable nucleus
making its way in time. One more pale reminder of the void
awaiting us at the end of the road.

There was something unnatural in continuing the evening as
if nothing had happened, but at the same time I felt that any
further discussion of the subject would only lead us round and
round in circles of unclear statements and vague speculations.
My mother suggested that we go out for a nocturnal stroll. No
doubt she would have liked to drop in on Nehama or Armand in
order to discuss what had happened in detail, but apparently she
understood that first of all we had to digest the event as a family
duet consisting of the two of us alone.

It was a hot night, but the silence and darkness succeeded in creating the illusion of refreshment and relief, almost of coolness. We walked at a leisurely pace, my hand hooked in my mother's elbow, making occasional meaningless remarks. The disappearance of the guest was constantly present as a powerful taboo.

My mother broke it at last, summing up a private train of thought.

"Listen, Susannahleh, I don't think he's left."

I pulled my hand out of her elbow.

She continued, ignoring this expression of my disapproval.

"You may be right, but at the moment I can't believe it. His things are here. He didn't say a single word. It's not some stranger we're talking about, it's Neo. He's family. And for some reason I had the impression that he was very honest with me. He told me a lot about himself, about his life. Why should he suddenly do such a strange thing?"

Her naïveté outraged me.

"So you should know that there are some things he didn't tell you. For example, you don't know that his stepfather, that his stepfather . . ."

An inexplicable instinct shut my mouth at the last minute. Some inner voice must have told me that if ever, for instance in our next incarnation, the guest should return and discover that I had told my mother his secret, even though it seemed relatively insignificant to me, any chance of friendship between us would be eternally lost.

"What about him, what about his stepfather?" My mother pushed me into a corner, her curiosity aroused, avid for information as a newshound scenting blood.

"He . . . he's . . . an anarchist!"

"Who, Herb? You call that news? Some anarchist! Runs some seedy legal firm that represents illegal immigrants and thinks he's bringing the revolution! Bat-Ami told me that sometimes they nearly starved because of all his dealings with those blacks and Hispanics. He didn't bring home a dollar. You call that an anarchist!"

"Mother, an anarchist isn't supposed to bring home dollars," I laughed, glad that she had swallowed the bait.

"OK, so he's an anarchist."

We walked on in silence.

My mother said, "I'd go to bed, but I'm not tired yet. How about you?"

I said, "No. I'm not either."

We had exhausted the walk, but neither of us could think of a good enough reason to go home and confront the mystery of the abandonment again. It seemed to me that even my optimistic mother was no longer completely convinced that I was wrong. It was clear that we should wait for morning, which by its very nature sheds new light on things and makes it possible to adopt a practical approach to even the most complex psychological matters. We went on walking in the dark until we both despaired of coming up with a solution, and we allowed the sticky air and our sweating bodies to dictate the reason for going back to the apartment.

"You know what I feel like," my mother found the saving formula. "You won't believe it. A bath. Almost cold. Just to sit in and relax. You know, since he arrived I haven't had a single bath."

I noted that she avoided calling the guest by his name, dispossessing him by this act of her love. So, she was beginning to come round to my point of view. I wanted to remind her that she never took a bath in summer, but her need to go back and experience home as a return to normality, and not as an empty, gaping void was so clear to me that as far as I was concerned no explanations were necessary.

I said, "An excellent idea. I'll scrub your back with the loofah. It's good for your circulation. What fun – just you and me!"

We went upstairs arm in arm, insisting on this physical expression of our solidarity in spite of the narrowness of the stairs.

The lights that were on in the apartment illustrated our inner turmoil – we had never gone out without switching off the lights before. I went to fill the bath. I used shampoo instead of bath foam, which we regarded as a superfluous commodity, one more way of extorting money from the consumer. I fetched a chair from the kitchen and sat down, watching the thin stream of shampoo trying with its meagre forces to foam the water filling the tub. Every now and then I dipped my hand in the water and swept it to and fro, helping the bubbles coalesce into something resembling a thin layer of foam. Then I watched my mother undress. I tried not to be disgusted, afraid of my disgust and its capacity to destroy even the pact that had been established between us this evening. I helped her to get in, offering her my shoulder. She leaned on it with all her weight, afraid of slipping, while I held my breath and tried to avoid inhaling the smell of her heavy, flabby body, as if it was the smell of death itself. I looked at her lying back in the bath, her breasts almost completely hidden under the water, which in spite of my efforts had failed to foam, and where between the little islands of bubbles I could see the submerged contours of her body. She asked me to soap her back, and I did so at length, resolutely scrubbing her skin with the help

167

of a ragged old loofah while she guided me to the right and left, and afterwards she soaped herself, raising her arms, taking her time inside the armpits and under the breasts, and only when she had finished and laid the soap on the rim of the tub and closed her eyes, did I permit the torrent of horror that had accumulated in the course of the past two hours to well up from the depths where it had been hiding and to engulf me, washing away all the joy of the exaggerated, newfound intimacy and sucking me in, as if I myself was a slippery little piece of soap liable to disappear down the plughole as soon as the plug was removed, whirling round in the last, gurgling rush of the water.

He was gone. Now it was only me and her. Until the day we died.

In my desperation I turned to her, hoping that she still had a little optimism about his return left.

"Now that I think about it, perhaps it's a bit of a pity after all that he's gone. Do you think he might come back?"

My mother received the breaking of the taboo with quiet joy, as if she had been expecting it.

"Yes, I think that he'll turn up or phone soon." She was silent for a moment, concentrating on her thoughts. "But even if you're right and he really has left, in the last analysis I won't be surprised."

This was new.

"Explain," I demanded. I dipped my hand in the water in an attempt to revive the bubbles of foam, which were dying fast.

"You know, child, people are always talking about the foolishness of men. But I don't agree. I think that men are mysterious. Just like women. A different mystery, of course, but a mystery nevertheless. Sometimes I understand it better, and sometimes

I don't understand it at all. And perhaps not all men have it. The men in this family had a lot of it, this male mystery. Your father, Uncle Noah, and now it turns out that Neo has as well. He looks just like Noah, of course, two peas in a pod, only thinner and handsomer. And then he has a feminine gentleness, which I suppose he gets from Bat-Ami. In any case they all have a lot of imagination, a lot of willpower, but without any inner knowledge of how to get things done. Powerful destructive impulses. And also a very deep, very rooted, kind of impotence. Not only in practical matters, but in them too, of course. The character of artists without the art. It's a kind of lostness. So you can try to explain it this way or that, and part of the explanation might even be right, but I'm telling you that it's not a question of 'why', it's something more basic. Something that 'why' doesn't come into, like love."

These words, identical to those of the guest, almost made me jump out of my skin. My heart was seared with longing, as if someone had pressed a red-hot iron against it.

"So what do you think? Will he come back?"

"Of course he will, you funny girl. Ever since your father died you've had this fear of people vanishing. I know you by now. Of course he'll come back. I'm glad the two of you became so friendly that you care."

How grateful I was to my mother for her wisdom. The flood of terror receded and sank back into the abyss inside me. I wanted to hug her, to hide under her soft breasts, in the folds of her stomach. She looked at me tenderly, effortlessly reading my thoughts.

"Why don't you get in? It wouldn't hurt you to have a good wash. There's not much room, but we'll manage. And I'll shampoo your hair while we're about it."

I got undressed awkwardly under her gaze, refusing to surrender to the pressure of my inner discomfort, and then stepped carefully into the bath and sat down with my back to her, resting my head on her broad chest, feeling her sturdy clavicle at the top of my head, her belly and breasts pressing against my back. The water brimmed over and splashed on to the floor, but she said, "Never mind, I'll wipe it up afterwards." The last barrier of resistance fell and I sank into the engulfing sweetness of her protection, as if I had entered a vast womb that obliterated the last traces of confusion and pain. The emptiness inside me was transformed into a hard, clear crystal, immune to harm.

She soaped me as thoroughly as if I was a little girl and afterwards she shampooed my hair, careful not to splash water into my eyes, and I laughed and shrieked, "Ai, mummy, stop it," and she gave me wet slaps on the back to make me stop wriggling, and then the phone rang.

I listened to the murmur of my mother's voice from the living room and I heard her laughing and raising her voice in a note of surprise and talking again and laughing again, while I sat and stared at the contours of my body in the cold water, completely innocent of bubbles, and afterwards she came back and I already knew what she was going to say and she talked and talked, scolding me for my suspiciousness, laughing at her own gullibility, at the way she had nearly let herself be persuaded that the guest had left without a word, even though everything testified to the fact that he had simply been held up, and see, it was all so simple: he had been obliged to stay overnight with the brother and sister in Haifa because they didn't have all the items of their collection available today, and he was such a scatterbrain it didn't even occur to him that we would be worried, and I –

Susannah – should learn to think a little more positively and not to jump immediately to catastrophic conclusions, and so on and so on, and finally she remembered that I was still sitting in the cold water and she pulled me out and wrapped me in my father's faded old bathrobe and dried my hair with a towel and went on and on talking in an incessant, uninhibited stream, and after she had finished and I was sitting on the bed in my room, looking at the tips of my fingers crinkled by staying in the water so long, I heard her voice telling the whole story on the phone to Nehama, and then to Armand, and I went on sitting there until I heard her closing her bedroom door, and then I waited a little longer, until I thought she'd fallen asleep, and I got up and walked quietly, with an exaggerated show of caution, on tiptoe, like a mouse stealing into the cat's house in a cartoon, and I went into the guest's room, and without switching on the light, relying on my memory, I found his crumpled white undershirt on the bed and I took it and returned to my room and switched off the light and took off the damp, heavy bathrobe and lay on my side curled up like a foetus, and then I pushed that undershirt, the little, breathing animal, between my thighs, pressing it against my vagina as hard as I could with both hands, and I sank my cheek into the cool pillow and said in a quiet voice, pronouncing each syllable precisely and slowly, as befitting a word being pronounced for the first time: Ne-o. And then I did it again, pressing the "Ne" softly against my palate and then pursing and rounding my lips for the "o-o-o".

Not The Lover Of

Katyusha was fuming. She sat in the pose of a model during a serious television interview, taking an occasional sip of the cognac left over from the guest's first night, and spoke with Russian pathos, stressing words that possessed a deeper significance than might be suspected by the innocent listener. The guest had screwed up big time. She too, just like us, had waited for him last night. Very worried. Not for him! (Katyusha's face expressed theatrical disdain.) He, for her part, could jump off a cliff, but because of the child Arthur, who was supposed to come back with him. The main reason, of course, that she had lent him the Golf Turbo Convertible was that he had promised to bring back Arthur, who was staying with his grandmother in Haifa. And when he had failed to return at the agreed time she had gone simply crazy. He had not considered her feelings, just as he had not considered our feelings, and called to say he would be delayed. The grandmother, on the other hand, had called and demanded that Katyusha keep her promise and remove the child at once because she had taken as much obscenity as she could stand, she didn't have the strength she once had. But this Neo, what did he care? He thought that time was a fiction. A human invention. Luckily she had finally succeeded this morning in getting hold of our phone number from Shalva the Georgian – one of the dealers he worked with.

Mother, Nehama and Armand sat round the table and listened with growing fascination, pushing the bowls of crackers and olives, the ashtray and the water jug in her direction. Shalva the Georgian, Katyusha, time as a fiction, Arthur and his obscenities – all these seemed to them like a slow and suspenseful emptying of the guest's Pandora's box, item by item. Nehama and Armand, of course, had long ago reached the conclusion that the guest was a shady character, but now even my mother, who loved and trusted him, was obliged to recognize the fact that there was more to him that met the eye. Sensible that question time had not yet arrived, they all waited patiently for Katyusha to conclude her opening monologue, after which a free discussion with audience participation would take place and the box would open wide, with secrets and lies flying out of it in abundance, spectacular as glittering soap bubbles.

It was midday, and the guest was due to arrive at any moment. Katyusha's sudden appearance had caused quite a commotion in the company, and no wonder – she had burst into our modest apartment in a silver tank-top, which exposed a navel as deep and convoluted as a whirlpool, and sandals with platform heels that made her even taller than Armand. Her striking appearance had aroused automatic respect, even before she explained who she was and what had brought her to Ramat Gan.

Although the subject on the agenda was the guest's irresponsible behaviour, the main thrust of Katyusha's speech quickly shifted to the question of young Arthur and his problems and the way in which these problems were bound up with her own problems as an immigrant obliged to cope with solo motherhood in a harsh Levantine reality. Despite the unspoken collective agreement not to intervene at this stage of the proceedings, the sly Nehama took advantage of a pause in the speaker's narrative to enable her to take a sip of water, and made an attempt to redirect the story on to its proper course, for who was more aware than she was of the dangers of digression?

"If you knew from his grandmother that the child was all right, why were you so worried? Neo is an adult, after all." She slipped in the booby-trapped question sweetly.

Katyusha swallowed the bait. "Sure, an adult. But you know what he's like. You're his family. Here today and gone tomorrow. With him you can never tell."

As she said "family" she glanced around, including us all in the sympathetic understanding implied by the word. Armand's chair creaked uncomfortably. The possibility of being regarded as the guest's relation, even by accident, made him shudder. Nehama on the other hand nodded eagerly, ready to sacrifice her loyalty to the truth for the sake of the exposure of a higher truth.

"So tell me, Katya, what exactly is this work he's doing here, with the pictures? Is it kosher?"

"What do you mean?" asked Katyusha in perplexity. "Why kosher? He's not religious."

"She means is it legal?" intervened Armand, who in spite of his ostentatious nobility had no objections to a detail or two capable of incriminating his male rival.

The word legal switched on Katyusha's red lights. She examined our faces again with a stern expression, hesitated for a moment, and said: "What a question! Of course legal. He buys and sells pictures. What do you mean? Of course legal."

Nehama's impatience brought the interrogation to a conclusion sooner than expected. Afraid that the meagre resources of Katyusha's Hebrew were about to frustrate her designs, she attacked head on, stressing the key word, "stolen".

"But I understand that we're talking about stolen pictures. Pictures stolen from Russia. Thieves. Mafia."

Katyusha flushed angrily with the injured innocence of a resentful immigrant.

"What Mafia? Why straight away Mafia? All you Israelis think all Russians are Mafia and whores. How much is it possible to speak of this? Why Mafia? Neo buys from people who came from Russia. They brought some things with them. So what? Is it against the law? He is art dealer. Very fine profession. Both art and very nice living. Why Mafia? These people in Haifa, brother and sister, this I find for him. The whole family classical musicians, father, mother. And collection comes from grandmother, very famous opera singer. Also in Europe. So what has this to do with Mafia? Only such primitive people as here in Israel can think so, people from Morocco!"

"What's that supposed to mean?" cried Armand, up in arms, and immediately blaming Nehama for letting the communal genie out of the bottle. "You see, Nehama, that kind of talk always leads to the same result. It sounds like some corny melodrama with all those clichés – the Russians are gangsters and whores and classical musicians, and the Moroccans are . . . Moroccans! Instead of a serious discussion between civilized people, stereotypes upon stereotypes. Banana republic is right."

"I just say things straight out. Things that other people think.

And I have to pay a heavy price for my honesty." Nehama shot my mother a furious look.

"But the parents there are really classical musicians. Mother and father. It's not stereotype!" protested Katyusha.

"I didn't mean this specific instance. I was speaking globally. Of course there are gangsters and whores and classical musicians . . ." Armand made haste to appease her.

"And classical Moroccans," Nehama got in, chuckling at her joke.

It was now my mother's turn to take control of the situation, and she did so immediately, calming ruffled feathers, pouring cognac and water into glasses, and moving the bowl of crackers from one to another. The subject of different communities and customs bored her to tears. Her interest was focused on the guest, but since she had to preserve her moral superiority in the eyes of the company, she preferred to leave the dirty work to Nehama. But it was too late. The moment of openness had passed. It transpired that Katyusha, just like Nehama, wasn't born yesterday. Now that her trust had been shaken, she sat nibbling a cracker and showing no intention of reopening discussion about the guest of her own free will.

"So tell me, Katya," my mother turned to her with ostentatious European politeness, "how long have you known our Neo?"

"Many years. Maybe seven. Maybe little less. I don't remember exactly."

"Seven years!" My mother hadn't expected this. "That's a long time."

"Yes, a long time," replied Katyusha, hinting by this laconic reply that the years in question had encompassed a relationship more massive than any of us could imagine.

"So you must be very close?" my mother put out feelers, eager for elaboration.

"Close. Yes," Katyusha maintained her enigmatic tone.

"And . . . and . . . isn't it difficult – with him out of the country most of the time and you here?" My mother hinted delicately that the intimate nature of the relationship was clear to her. Her tone held the hope that in the same allusive manner a few more vital details would immediately be revealed.

"Sometimes difficult. I'm used to it. Men come. They go. This is their nature."

My mother and Nehama responded with vigorous nods. Who knew better than these two widows the way of the world summed up so pithily by Katyusha.

"You see, that's exactly what I'm talking about. Generalizations. There are some men who never go anywhere," protested Armand. His protest was justified, for who if not Armand could testify to a glorious record in the field of male fidelity?

"In end they all go," Katyusha dismissed him contemptuously, being unfamiliar with the history of his life with Margalit. "All. Only I can wait. Heart of a Russian woman." She rounded her eyes and pursed her mouth in rebuke at Armand.

The injustice of this implied accusation overcame even the eagerness of my mother and Nehama to pursue their enquiries with regard to the guest, and they immediately rushed in to set the record straight. With a skill perfected over the course of the years they plunged into the tale of Armand's marriage and bereavement. As always, the two women were the main story-tellers, with Armand's role confined to setting the details straight or drawing a veil of modesty over the glory of his deeds. His official ownership of the story had long ago lost its importance, and his love for Margalit had been transformed into the collective mythology of all three of them. After faltering briefly, they hit a harmonious rhythm, falling silent with ostentatious politeness when one or the other took up the reins, correcting trifling details and offering personal insights and interpretations. They performed their task with the professionalism of a band of travelling storytellers who knew how to catch the attention of a random audience, to build suspense, to make people laugh and wipe away a tear. Their excitement at the chance of performing in front of a brand new audience filled the room with the charged atmosphere of a theatrical premiere.

And me? I sat there in silence. What else?

Almost by chance, like a little parasite getting a ride on the back of a dog and drinking its blood while it was about it, I had learned the truth about the relations between Katyusha and the guest. So, she was his lover. How could I have thought otherwise? And why? Because he seemed so unenthusiastic and nonchalant about her? Because he had spoken about her so lightly when we were on our way to visit her in the taxi? But he treated every subject under the sun lightly. And I myself had recognized, on his very first evening in our home, his tendency to detach himself and his life from his deeper emotions. How blind I could be when I didn't want to see something! In spite of all I knew about the dimensions of self-deception, its endless machinations, I was surprised to discover how loudly the truth had proclaimed itself in the face of my stubborn refusal to recognize it. How clear this truth was – until the moment when it began to threaten my wishes and fantasies, while I was in thrall to my infantile, magic desire to bend reality to my command at the touch of my lying wand.

What an idiot. "The word 'love' doesn't connect with him," I quoted myself to myself contemptuously. And what did I know about love, whom it connected with and how? What did I know about its sounds, its tastes, its colours? Their infinite shades? And how should I know? From books? From poetry? From Greek mythology? From sitting in the bath with my sixty-five-year-old mother? From my French lessons with Armand? From shoving an undershirt between my legs? What did this have to do with other people's love? What did I have to do with the outside world, with its infinite panorama?

Of course he was Katyusha's lover. The impression he had tried to create – that she was interested in him and he was trying to get out of it – was only one more way, one of the many at his disposal, of showing that life didn't really touch him. Of preserving his elegant image: a noble gas undiluted by any other element. He helped her with legal problems, brought her son medicine from New York. She lent him her car, called him pet names. Everything breathed of family, closeness, intimacy. And why not? Katyusha was so beautiful. If I could be so stirred by his beauty, why shouldn't he feel the same way about beautiful women? Yes yes! About Katyusha, full of pathos, long-legged, scheming Katyusha. Katyusha who was connected to life with every fibre of her experienced body, steeped in a femininity nobody could miss. Of course he was her lover. It was the way of the world which I, Susannah Rabin, for some reason chose not to see.

I went to my room. I stared out at the ugly street. I tried to see all its familiar components through the eyes of the guest, just as I had done when he first arrived, only then I had restricted myself to domestic items it seemed shameful to expose – the bathroom, the house, my mother's legs. A narrow perspective which did me no credit as a human being courageously looking reality in the face. And what about all the rest? What about Ramat Gan as a whole, with its dreary, faded, bland streets, lacking even the colourfulness of a slum? And what about me? – stooped, distorted, demented. And our weird friends and our whole way of life. It was true that we were all in the last analysis making our way towards death, flung into life like a stone thrown into an abyss by an indifferent hand, but there were some who in their flight took part in the play of the sunbeams on chips of glittering granite, while for others the walls of the abyss were dusty black basalt.

And if he wasn't Katyusha's lover? What difference did it make? Why was I so upset, as if we, she and I, were competing as equals for the same prize, and may the best woman win? Another idiotic assumption. By what right did I shrink in horror from the thought of his belonging to another woman? As if, were it not for her, he and I would be as passionately in love as Tristan and Isolde, in torments on our sweaty beds, driven out of our minds at every delay in the approaching rendezvous.

And another thing. The child. Seven years she said she had known him. The child was six. And he called him a monster! Deceit upon deceit. He lied to everybody, so why should I be the happy exception?

I was a naïve, gullible old child. Old and gullible. What a loathsome combination! I was a saleswoman in a department store, poisoned by an overdose of romantic novels. And so ashamed! Humiliated by the worst humiliation of all – the humiliation of a person by herself. My romantic hopes had been freed from their ambiguity and lay exposed before me in all their pitiful cheapness.

But it wasn't only myself I hated. I wasn't ready to die without a battle. Just as in the confrontation with the dog, I felt a need to rip the faces of the liar and his lover to shreds. To humiliate them as I had been humiliated. And even if this humiliation took place only in my head, I would make it total, huge, ruinous. I would show them, the dirty liars. I would think terrible thoughts about them. Disgusting thoughts. I would trash them in my mind, strip them of their arrogance, expose their bodies in all their blemishes, their moles, their hairs, the old fillings in their teeth, the corns on their feet. Maybe I was as ugly and repulsive as the heroine in the play by Hanoch Levin (which I had seen with my mother and Nehama, and while they roared with laughter I wailed out loud, even when the actors were taking their bows), maybe I was the personification of female misery, but that was also my weapon. I would stick the sharp daggers of my thoughts deep in their flesh. They were disgusting, disgusting. Yes yes, they too. They shat, they pissed. They had hairs growing in their armpits. Round the holes of their arrogant arses, pulling the wool over the eyes of the world in their expensive trousers. They sweated, farted, burped. Look, Katyusha lets off stinky farts as she sleeps between her black satin sheets, look, the guest sits hunched on the lavatory, tearing off a piece of toilet paper to wipe his bum.

And when they're together? That's the most disgusting thing of all. They fuck. Fuck. Fuck. But not beautifully, like in an expensive American movie. They fuck revoltingly, like in an Israeli movie with ugly, unflattering lighting. Licking each other like pigs, closing their eyes so as not to see the little pimples, the blackheads on their noses, the hairs in their nostrils, the wax in their ears. Look, look, in the middle of a kiss smelling of bits of food from their last meal stuck between their teeth, a glimpse of a hairy mole well hidden from the eyes of the world. And here's Katyusha lying on her back, her hairy black vagina wide open, and inside it, like the contents of a butcher's trash can, moist, shapeless raw meat. The fat on her thighs shakes and quivers. Her sagging breasts swing from side to side. Now she moans. In her grotesque Russian accent, no-ow-w, no-ow-w I come, now Katyusha comes! No-ow-w!

And the guest? That's more difficult. But he's disgusting too. Look at him mounting her: he's naked, his legs thin and hairy, his testicles wobble without any relation to the usual elegance of his movements, they're testicles after all. His penis hangs between his legs long and thin, ugly, circumcised, just like the penis of the born-again Jew who courted me when I was in the hospital and asked me to watch him masturbating in the staff toilets while he muttered verses from the Psalms. Yes, the guest is just as revolting as he was. Now he lies on top of her, they rock like flayed laboratory animals, up and down, up and down . . .

Katyusha was a more convenient fantasy figure, an easy prey. But the guest, the cool, fragrant, handsome guest – I succeeded in destroying him too. I tore his spirituality, his intelligence, his stylish alienation to shreds. Now he was only a body. A stinking human body, a body that death touched with one more touch every day, bringing him closer to the great rot at the end. A mortal.

Despite the disgust that filled me in the wake of my mission, I began to calm down. I felt the warmth of relief from tension in my shoulders, my temples, my upper back. I breathed deeply and evenly. So what do I do now? Live, I answered myself with the same word I had said to my mother when she wondered what we were going to do after the imagined desertion of the guest. I took the drawing pad and packet of charcoal out of my desk drawer, stood the blue vase in front of me and began to work.

It was already early evening when the guest arrived. Before this my mother had managed to improvise lunch for everyone present, and after the group effort involved in clearing the table and washing the dishes, our little gang grew tired both with impressing Katyusha and with interrogating her. The novelty of having a stranger present at a routine event had been completely exhausted. In the living room the tranquillity of a private club where everybody knew everybody else reigned again, and we all settled down to await the guest's arrival. Katyusha, who as time wore on refuted over and over the claim of the guest regarding her lack of humour, removed her platform shoes and lay on the sofa conversing in French with Armand, occasionally giving vent to bursts of wild laughter. My mother and Nehama played Trivial Pursuit on the subject of the world of entertainment and television, and I, resolute in my determination to survive in spite of my secret disgrace, took up my position on my little stool and drew portraits of the company. Now it was the turn of Nehama, who unlike the others paid attention to what I was doing and aspired to demonstrate the professionalism of a real model. Her neck was rigid, stretched sideways, as if she was a victim of cerebral palsy. Instead of turning her head to look at the cards, she raised them to her eyes and squinted at them with the expression of Bela Lugosi in a horror film, afraid of making a superfluous movement. This made it difficult to sketch her. The drawing looked stiff, Nehama's face was distorted and out of proportion. Nevertheless, I made myself continue. My aims were therapeutic, not artistic.

The guest arrived, full of the self-importance and confidence of someone who knows how eagerly he is awaited, and carrying Arthur on his back. I didn't even raise my eyes to look at him. I wanted to preserve his image as he had appeared in my disgusting fantasies. Distant, revolting, a stranger. The minute he came in the idle harmony that had prevailed in the room broke up, with everyone moving from their places and talking at once. Katyusha grabbed Arthur, speaking rapid Russian and kissing his face as if he had just been rescued from certain death. My mother broke into a series of questions about meaningless details connected to his trip: Traffic jams on the way out of Haifa? How long did it take to get there? And to come back? Was it hot? After that she moved on to a detailed description of our thoughts and worries in the light of Susannah's ri-di-cu-lous conclusion that he had left for good without saying goodbye. Nehama reported emotionally on her own experiences in connection with my mother's anxiety. Armand, embarrassed at being found sitting intimately next to Katyusha, shook hands with the guest and told him about some acquaintance the two of them had discovered they had in common.

I persevered in my stubborn refusal to raise my eyes, and went on fussing over the finished sketch, rubbing the oily lines with my finger, fixing the wrinkles round the eyes, shadowing the nose, but the guest called my name, and when I revealed my frozen face to him he gave me a casual wink that exposed the relationship between us in all its insignificance. How handsome he was in his weariness, with his rumpled hair, his clothes which looked as tired as he was from the journey. I quickly lowered my eyes and went on staring at the drawing, detached from my surroundings, allowing the commotion in the room to turn slowly into the buzz of a distant beehive, waiting for the right moment to get up and retire to my room without attracting any attention. The guest threw himself on to the sofa like the naked Maya, answering everyone at once – declining food, agreeing to coffee, considering the offer of cookies, asking for an ashtray, reporting on the journey and the health of the Haifa granny, admiring Nehama's new haircut, complaining of horr-i-ble exhaustion; amusing his audience with stories about the trip, mocking quotations about Vadim the restorer, and descriptions of the brother and sister with the collection. My mother prepared a new round of tea and coffee for the umpteenth time, and the evening turned into an improvised little party, in which I, of course, took no part.

I was grateful to be forgotten. I could go on sitting in my corner like a potted plant until the end of the evening. I didn't want anything. How protected I was here in my dim corner, on my stool, present and absent at once. I was soon absorbed in plans for a new series of dolls – a little zoo of imaginary creatures taken from my favourite books. Werewolves, animals from Alice's Wonderland, trolls and pixies, centaurs and minotaurs, phoenixes, sirens and vampires. I wondered if I should work in clay, plaster of Paris or Fimo, whether to paint them or leave the material in its natural state, whether to go for a height of over ten centimetres or to set myself a new challenge in miniature sculpture. I floated enjoyably on this stream of free, creative thought, completely concentrated on my inner world, until I was rudely awoken by the guest's voice thundering over my head like a bolt from the blue. I shifted my eyes from the pad to the floor and saw his bare feet standing next to me.

"Susannah, mon Dieu, what on earth have you been drawing there for over an hour?" he said, and even before I had time to raise my head and meet his eyes he snatched the pad from my hands with the dexterity of a pickpocket and looked at the drawing. He maintained a pause, enjoying the way in which all eyes were turned questioningly to him, and then gave me a look of comic shock.

"Who's this? Nehama? Jesus, what's wrong with her? Elephantiasis?"

He examined the drawing again, shaking his head, and then sighed with a sympathetic smile, said in French: "*Ce n'est pas facile la vie d'artiste.* Right, Armand?" and gave me back the pad. "Never mind, you'll get there."

Never, from the day we met, had I hated him so passionately. Immediately I became the centre of attention. Everyone wanted to see the drawing. Katyusha glanced at it and immediately turned away, afraid she might be called upon to express her opinion. Nehama began protesting loudly at the aesthetic injustice that had been done to her. My mother mentioned more successful works of mine, and Armand put his softest expression on to his koala bear face and blinked sympathetically, as if to say: Don't take any notice. With the instinct of a trapped animal I turned to the kitchen, the closest avenue of escape, muttering unintelligibly and leaving the disgraced drawing behind me, hugging the rest of the drawings close to my chest, afraid that my heart would burst the flimsy wall of my sunken chest and roll itself torn and bleeding into the middle of the room, exposed and open to every eye.

I sat down at the kitchen table and organized the drawings and the charcoal pencils, and then I heard a rustle. Arthur was standing in the corner between the fridge and the green plastic vegetable stand, his back leaning against the wall. Our eyes met.

The child squirmed uneasily and shifted his weight from one foot to the other. I quickly understood his problem. Now it was my turn to show him what an iguana's cunt meant.

"You're dying to pee, aren't you?"

The child was silent.

"Of course you're dying to pee. But you're too shy to walk across the living room to the toilet."

He shifted his weight in increasing discomfort and then froze.

"I understand your problem perfectly. In fact I can even help you, if you promise to behave yourself, not to swear, not to talk in rhyme. What are you, an imbecile? No. So behave properly. And in return I'll ask you a few questions and you'll answer me. OK?"

The child nodded faintly, afraid to make any unnecessary movements, saving the last of his strength.

I went up to him, took him by the shoulder and led him in front of me. We crossed the living room, where the company were busy discussing the personality of the Prime Minister (negative, negative, negative). I took the opportunity to collect the drawing from the stool.

"I'm taking Arthur to my room, I have paper and crayons there. He's bored," I announced.

Katyusha waved gaily.

I shut the door behind us and gave the child a triumphant look. He examined the room with a curiosity that made him forget his distress for a moment. I took the blue vase off the shelf.

"Now I'm going to turn round and you do whatever you have to."

I stood with my back to him, listening to him pant like a little animal as he laboriously undid his trousers, and then to the jet of urine shooting into the vase. Ah, the dear sounds of home. The music of the motherland.

After he had finished, I instructed him to put the vase in the corner and I said, "And now we'll have a little talk." I pointed to the bed, inviting him to sit down. He climbed on to it obediently and sat down, his legs hanging down like two sausages in sandals. I brought my desk chair up and sat opposite him.

"So tell me, Arthur, how are you?" I wanted to hear him produce an unrhymed sentence before I continued, but he only nodded agreeably, as if to say, "I'm fine."

"OK. In the meantime you don't want to answer. I understand."

He nodded again, this time as if he was pleased at my understanding. Apparently, as a result of his problem, he had worked out a system of nods for use in circumstances when he had no desire to torture and abuse his interlocutors.

"Tell me, Arthur, do you love your mother?"

A nod.

"Yes. She's very nice. I think so too."

A joyful nod at this unanimous vote of confidence in his mother.

"But tell me, isn't it sometimes sad for the two of you by yourselves?"

The child looked at me uncomprehendingly.

"I mean without a father. It must be hard for your mother sometimes."

A nod, confirming the fact that Katyusha was not in the habit of sparing her son her existential complaints.

"And where is your father? Did your mother tell you?"

A grave nod.

"Did he leave you?"

A vigorous shake of the head.

"So what happened? Is he dead?"

Three deep, melancholy nods.

This was exactly what I wanted to know.

"Well, Arthur, I have news for you. Very good news."

The Mongolian eyes rounded in curiosity.

"Your father's not dead. He's alive. He lives abroad but he spends a lot of time in Israel too. Your mother didn't tell you in order not to confuse you, because you're still small."

A silent, round-eyed question.

"Yes, your mother lied to you. It happens with grown-ups. She lied, because you actually know him. Your father."

A frown. The slight squint intensified.

"Would you like me to tell you who he is?"

A freeze, followed by a series of rapid nods.

I drew the moment out. I lit a cigarette and inhaled deeply. Then I blew the smoke out on a long breath, bent over the child, stared piercingly into his eyes, and said in a quiet, precise voice, "Neo. Neo is your father."

The child maintained his silence, his eyes fixed motionless on mine.

"Yes, yes. Neo. Aren't you happy?"

His lower jaw began to drop with an almost imperceptible downward movement, his eyes resumed their slantiness, and his mouth rounded and opened like that of a little carp a moment before the blow on the head. The message had been absorbed, but in order to prolong the pleasure as long as possible and squeeze as much as I could out of it, I brought my face right up to his and moved my lips almost soundlessly.

"Neo." And then, with a viciousness I didn't know I possessed but which now burst out of me completely naturally, I turned the

189

screw cruelly: "Not bad for a dad. Hey? How's that for a rhyme? Not bad for a dad."

A long moment of silence hung in the air, was charged with electricity, organized into form and direction, and then the child slid off the bed, stretched out his hands with fingers splayed, and the next second he was hanging on to my skirt with a deadly grip, his weight threatening to make me lose my balance on the chair. I jumped up and kicked the chair aside as the child began to swing himself to and fro, his head rolling, his grip tightening and a despairing falsetto howl escaping at last from his mouth, a howl that encompassed the terrified shriek of the caveman confronting the mammoth, the yell of the Apache a moment before throwing the tomahawk, the groan of Julius Caesar on the Senate steps. All the castration anxiety of the male of our species, from the beginning of history to this moment, burst out of the six-year-old Arthur's throat.

"Bitch!!! Biiiiiiitchch!" And immediately afterwards, in a crude but telling rhyme that perfectly complemented the previous epithet: "Witch!!! Wiiiiitchch!"

In a hundredth of a second the child had organized himself and recovered his wits. Now he launched into his performance with loud rhythmic yells, shaking himself and me with him from side to side.

"Bitch-witch! Bitch-witch! Bitch-wiiiitchch!"

Immediately they all came bursting in at the door, filling my room with their alien bodies, Katyusha and my mother trying to prise Arthur off my skirt while Armand and Nehama looked on in astonishment behind them, together with the guest, who even took the trouble to show a certain degree of concern, all of them talking and moving and asking questions at once. Afterwards

Arthur was borne off to the living room in his mother's arms, still screaming dementedly, while the rest of us brought up the rear like an idle crowd of curious onlookers, and my mother immediately went into action: How can I help? Can I get something, a glass of water perhaps? Maybe I should call a doctor. Katyusha tried to silence her son and direct the guest to find the little bottle of tranquillizer syrup in her bag, and the guest in his haste dropped the elegant handbag, spilling expensive cosmetics, documents, a mobile phone, sunglasses on the floor, and afterwards Katyusha sat on the sofa with her son and pushed a spoonful of dark liquid into his rattling throat, talking to him and stroking him tenderly, and his yells began to peter out until nothing remained of them but an unintelligible mutter, and he laid his head on his mother's lap and everybody sat down and gradually returned to their previous state of relaxation, when all of a sudden Katyusha let out a piercing scream and pushed the child away, and once again the company jumped up in alarm: What, what, what happened? And she held her right knee and looked up at us in astonishment: "He bit me, he bit me on the leg!"

"What do you mean, bit?" asked my mother.

"Bit! He bit me," her astonishment was now addressed exclusively to the guest. Naturally. The happy father.

"The child is violent!" said Nehama.

"Maybe we really should call the doctor," said Armand.

"Do you want me to hold him?" said the guest.

"Perhaps you should take off your trousers so we can see if there's an open wound," said my mother.

"She needs a tetanus shot right away," said Nehama.

"If there was an open wound the trousers would be torn too," said Armand, and for some reason he blushed.

But Katyusha shook her head, dismissing the speculations and refusing the recommendations.

"No, I don't need anything. But I don't understand what happened here. Suzy, what happened, what did you talk about?"

"I gave him crayons and paper to draw on. That's all. We didn't talk about anything."

Katyusha examined the sore place again, rubbing it with her fingers and fluttering her eyelashes at us from time to time in helpless astonishment.

As far as I was concerned the comedy was over.

"If you like you can put him down to sleep in my room," I said.

Katyusha fluttered her eyelashes again, this time in affected shyness.

"I don't know. Such scandal. I think we should go home."

My mother protested vociferously and everyone followed suit in a modified version of the previous commotion. I went into my room and shut the door. I stood leaning against it for a long time. Apparently I really was crazy. God. I didn't have the strength to think about myself, to understand myself.

I took out the anthology of English poetry and opened it at random at a poem I didn't know by T. S. Eliot. I read it again and again but the meaning escaped me, and only four lines reverberated inside me with their captivating clarity.

> I should find
> Some way incomparably light and deft,
> Some way we both should understand,
> Simple and faithless as a smile and shake of the hand.

A wave of yearning for the guest engulfed me. The sensation was so strong that I buried my face in my hands. I listened to what was happening inside me, occasionally becoming conscious of a tremor in my eyelids, a tension round my mouth, the coolness of my hands touching my temples.

Katyusha came in quietly followed by Armand, carrying Arthur in his arms. The syrup she had spooned into him appeared to be taking effect and he looked confused, his wide-open eyes stunned and owlish. They put him down on the bed, whispering instructions to each other. Katyusha smiled at me in gentle apology, woman to woman. I nodded at them and pretended to be reading, sitting at my desk with my back to the child, and when they left the room I buried my face in my hands again, empty of all thought.

When I turned round I saw that Arthur was sleeping. He lay on his stomach, his limbs outspread, except for his right knee drawn up to his stomach, his eyes closed and his profile sunk in the pillow. I went and sat beside him. An inexplicable need made me touch his head covered with silky hair and then his arm, whose contours still showed a babyish pudginess. He stirred slightly and without opening his eyes took hold of my hand. I tried to free it, but his grip was too strong for me to do so without waking him, and I let my narrow bony hand lie nestled in the marshmallow cushion of his palm. After another failed attempt to rescue my hand, I took off my shoes with an effort that required no mean acrobatic skill, removed the pins from my hair, and lay down next to him on the edge of the bed, positioning myself carefully in the narrow space left. He moved again, raised his head, gave me a look that was more blind than sleepy, and dropped back on to the pillow, facing away from me. I sank my face into the tangle of his hair, and there was something so sweet and cosy and totally unthreatening in the smell of this childish, dusty hair that I quickly fell asleep.

My sleep was restless, full of snatches of strange dreams, and almost as part of it I heard somebody come into the room, and afterwards I felt clumsy attempts to pick the child up without waking me and I closed my eyes tightly so that I really wouldn't wake up, and I felt the child's hand parting from mine limply and unwillingly, and afterwards I heard whispering and creaking and footsteps, and I knew that they had switched off the light and I opened my eyes. I lay relaxed in the dark, my eyes open, listening to the dull echo of voices in the living room and the hum of the telegraph poles outside and the chirping of crickets excited by the endlessness of the summer that had descended on them and the movement of my breathing – faint and dry breathing in and full of Jewish suffering breathing out, and everything merged together into a life that was slow, hollow and inevitable.

I was awake hours later too, when the guest came into my room and groped his way to the chest next to my bed, trying to find the switch of the bedside lamp and scattering my hairpins. I let him switch on the light and discover me open-eyed. He was embarrassed.

"You're not sleeping? So why are you lying here like a corpse? It's scary. I've come to visit you. Get up."

I sat up, drawing the thin summer blanket round me, taking care to cover my feet. Mechanically I raised my hand to tidy my loose hair, but I changed my mind immediately, in case he imagined that I was beautifying myself for his sake. The guest sat down on the bed. His posture annoyed me.

"What do you want? I'm sleeping."

"OK. You're angry. Look, you're right. I want to apologize, it was idiotic, that business with your drawing in front of everyone.

I would have come before, but there was all that fuss over Arthur and afterwards everybody stayed and stayed, and when they left I had a chat with your mother. But here I am."

The fact that he assumed he had hurt me embarrassed me even more. Now he was sure presumably that in all the time that had passed since then I had been busy thinking about him.

"It doesn't bother me a bit. I know the drawing's awful."

"It isn't awful. It's just, how can I explain it to you, stiff, without any flow. There's something unnatural about it."

Now I was indignant.

"You didn't see the way she was sitting. All distorted. Because she knew I was drawing her."

But the guest was apparently incapable of taking a break from his insults. It was a need, just like Arthur's rhymes and obscenities. Now I knew that it was genetic too. The guest's syndrome.

"That's not the point, you know. It's possible to do a good drawing of someone sitting in a distorted position too. Where is it? Bring it here, I'll show you what I mean."

Before I had a chance to protest he got up and began going through the papers on my desk.

"Leave it alone, I tell you I don't care," I almost shouted. His closeness to my drawings, his touching them, was more shocking to me than if he had touched my breasts. But the guest had already set his backside down next to me, holding the accursed drawing.

"You see, you get stuck on the little details and you lose the whole. That's what creates the distortion, the heaviness. And the lifelessness – you see, again, you're preoccupied with the technical, the mechanical, at the expense of the inner understanding of what you see. An image, a flash. A unique human moment."

195

I had no desire to listen to a lecture on the quality of my drawing in the middle of the night. Not even from him.

"I've done better sketches than that in my life you know. Before I met you."

"Stop being insulted all the time. It's enough already."

"And anyway, you're not exactly an artist yourself."

"Don't start with me, you'll regret it." He laughed but his eyes were flat. I was prompted to continue.

"Let's see you draw Nehama."

"You'll be sorry, I'm telling you."

"Why?"

The guest was silent for a moment, smiling into my blank gaze.

"Because ever since I was ten years old it was one of the things I did as well as possible. Because it impressed people so much. So the competition would be unfair."

"Who's competing with you?"

"Everyone. Everyone's competing with everyone else. In this specific instance you're competing with me, and even though we're relations and even friends I'll be obliged to hit you hard. Where do you have clean paper?"

He stood up and turned my desk upside down again until he found a completely new drawing pad, and I wanted to tell him to use the one I'd already started but I stopped myself, so he wouldn't think I was stingy. He sat down on the chair and crossed his legs, and I examined his long feet again and the toes of the foot raised from the floor immediately began to move, curling up and opening out like the feelers of some strange sea creature, and he said, "Nehama, right?" He closed his eyes, frowning slightly in concentration, and then opened them again and immediately began to draw in broad, easy strokes, stopping from time to time but only for a second, and then continuing to sweep the charcoal over the paper with extravagant generosity, narrowing his movements occasionally in order to work on the details with casual hatching, and opening out again in all directions. In the end he threw the charcoal on to the desk, stretched, stood up and flung the paper on to the bed, celebrating his victory with a downward glance in my direction.

I picked up the page. Nehama's face glared at an invisible interlocutor, her eyes glittering belligerently, the wrinkles around them sharpening, her eyebrows rising in a rapid movement, her mouth half open, a fraction of a second before she shot out her next sentence.

I raised my eyes to the guest. I didn't say anything.

"I told you, didn't I? You shouldn't have started with me." He fell back on to the bed, draping himself in a half-supine position, like a Roman aristocrat in *I, Claudius*, making me shrink and hug my knees to my chest.

"Are you depressed? Do you want me to teach you too?"

I shrugged my shoulders.

"Wonderful. Tomorrow I'm in Tel Aviv, so I'll pick up some decent charcoal. And that paper you use, what are you, a schoolgirl? You should know that I'm a terrific teacher. I have a talent for recognizing people's hang-ups. Another brilliant career that will have to wait for my next incarnation. Chuck me a cigarette, but light it first."

I took the pack from the chest and removed a cigarette. Light it first? That meant that I would have to put it in my mouth and then he would put it in his mouth. He was asking me to perform an act that was almost erotic. I held the cigarette between stiff lips, trying to leave it as far as possible outside the wet part of my mouth, and raised the lighter. I could sense the tremor hiding inside my fingers, about to break out. The half-lit cigarette fell on to the blanket round my knees, scattering embers in all directions. I caught it quickly and held it out to the guest, extinguished and slightly charred.

"You're something else, you know that?"

He took the lighter from my hand and lit the disgraced cigarette.

"So now tell me, what happened with the dog?"

"Nothing, it was nothing." I shrugged my shoulders.

"That's not what your mother told me."

I kept quiet.

"Did you want to tease it?"

I looked at him coldly. Sometimes he really didn't understand anything.

"I wanted to kill it. For us to kill each other."

He smoked with languid enjoyment, blowing out the smoke once in a concentrated jet and once in precise rings that dissolved into soft clouds.

"Simply for us to kill each other," I repeated when I realized that he wasn't going to react.

"I understand." He nodded gravely, and went on blowing out smoke.

We were both silent.

"It's funny," he said, motioning me to bring up the ashtray, and grinding out the stub. "I missed you all. I really did. In Haifa. It was strange."

I didn't know what to say. I felt a blush of unexpected pleasure warming my ears. He sat up. "Listen, don't you feel like eating something? I'm dying of hunger."

The danger that he might leave and the conversation would end checked my automatic denial. I slipped out of the blanket, rolling my hair into a round bun on my nape at the same time, and bent down to fumble for the scattered hairpins on the floor, trying to hide my feet under my skirt. With problems like mine I should have been Houdini. Another career that would have to wait for my next reincarnation.

In the kitchen the guest displayed a skill I didn't know he possessed. In my eyes his existence was detached from unglamorous menial tasks such as preparing food. Now he revealed this other, unknown possibility to me. He began to prepare a meal with his usual elegance, moving between rapid ease and strict precision. First he opened the fridge and stood in front of it reflectively, his face the face of a poet contemplating his reflection in a river, and then, with a decision concluding a long and hidden train of thought, he began whipping things out and setting them down on the marble counter – cheese, vegetables, eggs, butter, olives, a bunch of yellowing parsley. Then he turned his attention to the kitchen cabinets and lingered before the shelves, restlessly waving his fingers up and down in front of the bottles of vinegar, oil and spices and then snatching them off the shelf, making mischievous faces at me the while as if we were a couple of imps up to no good. After he had collected the ingredients it was time for consultation.

"Omelette and salad?"

"Not for me. I'm really not hungry."

"You're joking! Are you sure?"

"Absolutely."

That was a lie. I hadn't eaten a thing since breakfast. Because of the company I had been unable to eat the lunch my mother had prepared or console myself with lighter refreshments either – coffee, cookies and fruit. It didn't bother me. But now? I could feel the hunger, stimulated by all the cigarettes I had smoked during the day, nagging at my stomach. I tested the taste of nicotine in my mouth with my tongue, bitter and disgusting, longing to be obliterated by something edible, repelling any thoughts of the menthol aggression of toothpaste. The sight of the food on the marble counter, the fresh simplicity of the cheese, the bread and the vegetables, filled me with a greedy desire to gobble up everything I saw before me.

"No? As you wish. Tell me if you change your mind, I'll make enough for both of us anyway, just in case you do."

The guest began his preparations. It was an enchanting sight. Mesmerizing. He didn't have an ounce of the usual clumsiness of men when they cook. My father, for example, was completely pathetic – with his dreadful doorsteps of bread and his roast chicken sticking up its half-amputated legs, covered with vestigial feathers and smeared with oil and paprika. I remembered supper at Armand's, who considered himself an excellent cook. The way his knife lurched over the cucumber, removing thick strips of peel. The heavy wetness with which they fell into the sink.

The guest too was busy peeling a cucumber. Even his fingers looked as if they were conscious of their beauty as they moved under my gaze. The peel of the cucumber he held in his hand coiled round and round, in a slender, endless strip, and only when the cucumber was completely naked, cool and sensuous in its pale green colour, did the guest make a final cut, and the umbilical cord detached itself and dropped down, with all the pathos of a classical ballet dancer curtseying at the end of her solo.

The rest of the vegetables, which he had already washed,

lay heaped up attractively on the counter, as if ready to be photographed for a commercial. I watched the guest cut them up into fragrant, colourful cubes with the frightening knife my mother used for carving meat. Then he peered into the almost empty mustard jar, poured vinegar and olive oil into it, added salt and pepper, crushed a plump clove of garlic, and then closed the lid of the jar and shook it in the air with all the seriousness of an alchemist in the last stage of his life's work, at the end of which the yellowish mixture would turn to gold. When he had finished he poured the liquid over the salad.

After that he set the pan on the flame and put a huge lump of butter into it, filling the kitchen with a sweet smell that made me turn my head aside to swallow the saliva flooding my mouth. While the butter was slowly committing suicide he broke three eggs into a bowl, stirred them with a fork, added a little milk and salt, and then, without stopping his energetic stirring, poured the mixture into the pan. Again I had to swallow my saliva, while he cut the country bread my mother bought in a special shop and then stood in front of the stove, with his back to me, gently shaking the pan. I looked at his thin back, stooping slightly as he worked, at his hair flowing like a stream of dark chocolate on to his shoulders, and I almost choked with hunger, my salivating mouth imagining the taste of the bread and the omelette, the combination of the salad and the cheese. One thing was clear – I was on the point of experiencing slow, cruel, Chinese torture.

"You're sure you won't join me?" asked the guest after he had laid the table. The question was being asked for the fifth time in the last twenty minutes. I shook my head, stretching my lips into a rigid grimace meant to be a smile. No thank you. With the handle of my fork I sketched an invisible scribble on the empty plate in front of me, as if I was bored.

"Where did you learn to cook?"

The guest looked pleased by my question.

"Baby, I'm a fantastic cook. Yet another career that will have to wait for my next incarnation. This is nothing. I know how to make amazing dishes, stuffed pigeons, pasta, seafood, my soups are works of art. I'll really have to cook something special for you and your mother one of these days." He put a forkful of food into his mouth.

I stared at my empty plate, stealing an occasional glance in his direction. Even in his hunger there was something detached and blasé in the way he ate. His thoughts were on other things. If only I was him. I made up my mind that tomorrow morning, while he was still asleep, I would ask my mother to make me a meal exactly like this. An omelette with three eggs instead of the usual two. Fried in lots of butter rather than sunflower oil. I would tell her to put mustard in the salad dressing and slice the bread as thin as thin could be, and then I would make up for my present hunger and eat everything up, down to the last crumb. Maybe even two meals like this, for breakfast and for lunch and the day after tomorrow too, until I was so full that every trace of this terrible craving, choking me with floods of dense saliva, would disappear.

"Stop that, it's driving me crazy," said the guest. He meant the squeaking noise of my fork on the plate. I hadn't even noticed what I was doing. I put the fork down obediently. He took a bite of bread and butter, and studied me with sudden interest.

"So what exactly happened in your room with Arthur?"

"I already said. Nothing. I gave him paper and crayons. And

then it happened. When we were at their place he went berserk for no reason too."

"There's always a reason with him. He yells when he can't find any other way to explain himself. Then it was in connection with the restorer. He understood the problem and he wanted to help. It wasn't for nothing."

"I'm telling you I have no idea." I began scratching my plate with my fork again.

"Stop it. What's the matter with you?" He raised his voice.

"Nothing."

I put the fork down and stared at my plate. The guest went on eating. I knew that he was looking at me.

"So you're not going to tell me."

"There's nothing to tell."

"As you like."

And as had already happened to me with the guest before, the next minute some inner being, who led a full, independent life inside me, took control of events and I began to speak before I even knew what I was doing.

"I told him the truth. He's entitled to know it. That's all."

"Which truth?"

The guest was so curious that he stopped chewing.

"You know exactly which."

"I haven't got the foggiest notion what you're talking about."

He put his knife and fork down on his plate and pushed it aside.

"I told him who his father is," I said.

"What makes you think he doesn't know who his father is?"

"Fact."

"So why don't you tell me too?" he smiled sweetly.

"You."

I think it was Greta Garbo in Ninochka, a film I once saw on the classic movie channel on television, who opened her arch-browed eyes wide in exactly the same astonishment and then was silent for exactly the same number of seconds before bursting into long, photogenic, perfect-toothed laughter, until she gradually calmed down and wiped the tears from the corners of her eyes, just as the guest did now.

"Very interesting. And how did you come to this conclusion, may I ask?" he said even before the last vestiges of infuriating laughter disappeared from his lying face.

His pretended innocence roused me to a rage which, for a change, was pure and unadulterated by any other feeling.

"Quite simply. Katyusha said that she's known you for seven years. Arthur's six. You're her boyfriend. She said so this afternoon. While we were waiting for you. In front of everybody."

The guest leaned back in his chair, sighed heavily and folded his hands on his flat stomach, as if to say: I've had too much to eat.

"She said that I was her boyfriend, in so many words?"

"Not exactly, but she implied it. You know, in the way she looked and everything. And my mother and Nehama asked her all kinds of questions about you too, about your work and everything. You know how suspicious Nehama is. And then she said it, hinted it, I don't know. It was obvious."

The guest stretched himself, enjoyably and at length. He looked so amused and pleased with himself that I wanted to cry. Then he lit a cigarette and puffed on it complacently.

"My dear Susannah. Allow me to enlighten you. It's all nonsense. I don't know what Katyusha said and what you understood, or your mother, or Nehama, but happily for everyone concerned, I'm not Arthur's father. I knew his father. A great guy. He was an Arab, a doctor from Haifa. Mustafa Elharizi. A very wealthy family. Buildings, land. He married Katyusha after meeting her on a trip to St Petersburg."

"And where is he now, this doctor?"

"He's dead. A year and a half after Arthur was born. He went for a swim and drowned in the sea. A senseless death. Katyusha was wrecked, but she didn't want to stay there with the family and the whole mess. She's still fighting them over his will. So she took Arthur and moved to Tel Aviv. The grandmother in Haifa he was staying with, that's Mustafa's mother."

"I thought the grandmother was Katyusha's mother."

"Katyusha hasn't got any family here. She's a Russian Christian, they're all religious fanatics over there, Russian nationalists. Black shirts."

"And you?"

"What about me?"

"You're not her boyfriend?"

The guest gave me a look that was almost pitying.

"How could you think that a beggar like me could be Katyusha's boyfriend? Katyusha likes the *dolce vita*. She wants stability and security. What's all that got to do with me? Katyusha is someone who takes her life very seriously. She's just a good friend. That's all."

He ground his cigarette into the remains of his omelette, bringing the discussion of his relationship with Katyusha and paternity of her son to a close, and began to clear the table. I jumped up to help him, putting things back in the fridge, wiping the marble counter while he washed the dishes. Then he asked if I wanted coffee. I nodded. He made the coffee, told me to bring the cigarettes and ashtray, and led the way to the dark balcony.

We sat down on the plastic chairs. The guest put his feet up on the balustrade. We sat in silence. The sky was indigo, hinting that dawn was not far off, and despite this dark translucence, the clusters of stars looked dull and depleted, hiding high above the clouds of city smog.

"Jesus I'm tired."

He said this in flat, neutral voice. Although there was no note of complaint in his tone, I felt a panicky fear that I was keeping him, sticking to him like a leech.

"So go to bed. It's way past midnight."

"No, it's another kind of tiredness. Crushing. Sleep won't help," the guest, recognizing my panic, hurried to reassure me. "I'm tired when I get up, tired when I work, tired when I eat, read, think. Even when I sleep I'm tired."

"But there has to be some way to rest."

"For people who've made idleness a way of life it's hard to rest. What usually counts as rest is just another day of normal functioning for the lazy person."

"I'm sure even lazy people could find a way to rest."

"Like what?"

"I don't know. Something calming. Maybe standing on your head, like Ben Gurion. In my opinion you should take advantage of the fact that you're not in New York with all that hurry and scurry."

I felt immediately ashamed of the silly rhyme and even sillier description of New York. The guest on the other hand seemed amused.

"I'll take your suggestion into consideration. The one about Ben Gurion, I mean."

It seemed to me that he was looking at me affectionately.

"When I was small I couldn't rest when I was tired either.

Sometimes I was so tired that I didn't sleep for days on end. I would lie and make a kind of humming noise, 'mmmmmmm', as if something was hurting me, but it was just tiredness."

"I know that feeling very well. But now I'm tired of life. Pathetic but true."

I wanted to tell him that his life, although I knew very little about it, seemed to me so thrilling, so colourful, that it was hard to imagine anyone being tired of it. But for some reason I chose to remain silent.

"I feel done in. Something isn't moving. I do the same things but everything's stuck. I drive and drive, but I don't move an inch. It's terribly frustrating. But it's OK. It will lead to something. Periods like this always end in change. The beginning of another life."

"So what are you going to do?"

"I haven't got a clue. I wish I knew. I suppose that first of all I'd like to rest. To stand on my head. And you? Haven't you ever wanted another life?"

I couldn't tell if he was really interested or if he just wanted to stop talking about himself.

"What do you mean?" I affected innocence.

"You know exactly what I'm talking about. Don't pretend. Look at yourself – stuck here in Ramat Gan with this collection of crazy old people."

The insult and the darkness made me surprisingly uninhibited.

"Why crazy? What do you know? You only see them from the outside. Take Nehama, you think she's just some old busybody and a racist to boot, but that's only words. She snipes at Armand all the time, but when he opened his Super Duper and he had all kinds of money problems and almost went bankrupt, she broke into her life savings to give him a loan, and when he told her that he didn't know when he would be able to pay her back she said: It will be all right, you're such a competent fellow that you're bound to succeed in whatever you do, so I'm not worried. She went through the Holocaust. You might say: So what? All the old people went through the Holocaust. But they all have their own private story. Sometimes terrible. All the Jews in her village near Cracow were killed by a firing squad. They all fell into a pit, naked, her father, her sisters, everyone. And she remained alive and lay there under the corpses for days until she somehow succeeded in crawling out between the decomposing bodies, like a worm. And afterwards she didn't talk at all, until she was sixteen. She simply kept quiet. So she's paranoid. And Armand. He's a simple man, uneducated, but he loves music, poetry, really loves them. And he's completely unpretentious. He's a true friend to us, we've been through all kinds of things together and we could always count on him. And my mother, I don't know how you can possibly call my mother crazy. She's so . . . so strong, she's wonderful . . . so maybe you think all this is banal . . ."

I wasn't used to delivering such lengthy monologues, but the need to explain to the guest that he was mistaken drove me forward. Every now and then I paused to gulp air. I expected him to apologize, to say that he hadn't meant anything nasty. But he said nothing. And for some reason in spite of his silence and his refusal to react to my speech I felt that he was on my side. I wanted to go on talking to him. To rouse him to react.

"And anyway, I'm crazy too."

He sighed dismissively.

"Please, honey, do me a favour. And even if it's true – so what? I think that in the last analysis most of the people I know fit that description. They're all unhappy, they're all mad. And I'm not talking here about some subtle neurosis, I mean crazy big-time. You know, paranoids, corpse-fuckers, people who think they're getting messages through the television, psychopaths without a conscience, melancholic artists, narcissists, perverts, kleptomaniacs, hypochondriacs. Take your pick. They all use all kinds of chemicals, tranquillizers, narcotics, anti-depressants, all kinds of homeopathic garbage. Some of them know they're nuts, others think it's enough if their friends know they're nuts. But they're alive and kicking – in London, New York, Tel Aviv. Earning and spending money, competing with others, cultivating and sometimes realizing ambitions, fighting for principles, loving, envying, hating. In short, living. They go out, they encounter the world, however mean and nasty and personally disappointing it may be."

I said, "There are all kinds of madness." And then I added, "And all kinds of lives too." The lack of understanding between us gave me a feeling of loneliness that was almost physical. Any attempt people (yes, yes, the same sinning people Nehama was always talking about) made to interpret my private experience, which they knew nothing about, from their own point of view, always made me violently angry.

The guest read me, in profile. He took his feet down from the balustrade and turned his chair to face me, put his arms on his thighs, and leaned towards me.

"Don't be angry. I want you to know that I understand you. Your reluctance to go outside. I know that reluctance. In some way, staying with you here in your house is a manifestation of my own reluctance to go out into my normal life. And when I have to confront the world anyway I do it on my own terms."

"How do you mean?"

"I protect myself with a certain type of mask. It enables me to go out even when I'm weak and vulnerable. The problem with you is that you lack this option."

"But I don't know how to be anything else. I only know how to be me. What you describe is like being false."

"I'm talking about the complete opposite. I'm talking about the possibility of choosing full or partial presence. I'm sure you behave differently with your mother than with me."

"I behave the same with everybody."

"Is that so? You don't eat when you're with your mother too? What are you, a yogi? Living on faith?"

I moved my lips helplessly, trying to get some air into my lungs.

"But if that's what you choose – then that's it. You understand that I'm not talking about a false self but about what you choose to show at any given time. Look, you contain all kinds of personas within you, all kinds of Susannahs, and you can choose which of them to let out. Whichever one serves you best. It helps to develop the vital characteristics, to breathe life into repressed, unexpressed aspects of the personality. I'm talking to you about the full extension of the personality. Take the incident with the dog – you weren't falsifying anything, simply revealing characteristics you don't usually show. But that was a little out of control, as if it happened by itself. I'm right, aren't I?"

I nodded.

"So I'm sure you can learn to behave like that as a clear act of will, the result of a conscious decision. Not to rely on your inner destiny."

"And fear? What can I do about fear? It paralyses me."

"I understand. Of course there's also fear that acts as an incentive, the fear that prompts people to act. Perhaps they're actually two different feelings with the same name. But I believe that in the last analysis all fear is superfluous, both the fear that makes you act and the fear that paralyses you."

"But how can you get rid of it?"

The guest laughed.

"That's a big question. I don't know. Maybe just let go of it. I don't have a manual. It's something intuitive. A state of openness."

"And are there people who live like that?"

The guest laughed again, throwing his head back in enjoyment.

"Certainly not. I'm talking about Utopia. It isn't something that can be permanent. But you can get a glimmering of it as opposed to the other option, the closed state, the one that has to defend itself all the time by attributing meaning, reasons, defined forms. I mean opening yourself to the great dread. Being prepared to experience pain which has no meaning. This kind of openness also exposes you to the marvellous."

"I always look for meaning."

"Of course. We all do that most of the time. Otherwise life would be unbearable. But there's something economic in the attempt to give things meaning."

"What do you mean, economic?"

"How can I explain it to you? Calculating, like a book-keeper. To take something that happens, let's say something terrible, dreadful, and say: I'll give it meaning, value – good, bad – and then it will be worth my while to experience it. It turns experience into something profitable."

"But what else can we do? It's unbearable, meaninglessness, especially when bad things happen for no reason and you simply don't understand and ask why, why, why."

"That's exactly what I'm talking about, the ability to bear pain without turning it into suffering. To recognize that pain has no meaning. Mostly it's arbitrary. The whole business of meaning is a fiction. An invention."

"So what's to be done?"

"I don't know. To aspire to reach a place that is empty of meaning. To refuse the temptation to give things a safe, closed, protected shape. To confront them in their unstructured state. Without a hierarchy."

"And do you succeed?"

"Of course not. That's one of the reasons why I gave up being an artist. I'm a very problematic person. Much more than I appear to be. Or perhaps exactly as I appear. But I go on trying."

We were both silent.

"Why does pain exist in the first place?"

"Maybe because deep down inside we know that there's no reason for living. Or dying."

He stood up.

In the creeping greyness of the morning his face looked tired and almost ugly, the way I saw it on the night he took me out to show me a good time, in the bar.

"Come on. Time to go to bed. Listen, I didn't intend to lecture you. Sometimes I get that way. Forget it. I don't know anything, and that's the truth. I know less about life than any of the people you know."

"Even Nehama?"

The guest looked at me sternly.

"Especially Nehama."

And a long moment passed before he let me know that he was only joking, his face breaking into a glorious smile to meet my shy, crooked one.

Blood Drop By Drop

Mother says that the country is in a depression. A national gloom that expresses itself in each of us individually. In her opinion even the Likud voters, in some repressed way, are sad that the Labour Alignment lost the elections. Even the disappearing tribes in Papua New Guinea are saddened by this melancholy reversal.

I myself feel no identification with the national depression because, in spite of the fact that my name is Susannah Rabin, as I have already pointed out – I am no relation to. I do nothing to promote peace in the world or peace in the Middle East either. I'm an escapist. A very small person. As far as I'm concerned the national depression is my mother's depression, and when my mother's depressed – Susannah Rabin thrives.

Mother and Nehama, on the other hand, promote peace in the Middle East tirelessly. But for them we would all be swimming in the sea with a knife in our backs or studying Torah from five in the morning and reproducing through a hole in the sheet. I'm convinced that it's only thanks to my mother, Nehama, and a few other responsible citizens like them, people who read newspapers and have opinions, that the world hasn't finally been destroyed. Parasites like me are lucky that there's somebody to do the hard work for them.

My mother and Nehama discuss the defeat of the Labour Party in the elections for hours on end. They criticize the election propaganda on the television, examine the timing of the suicide bombs, analyse the personality of Shimon Peres, whom they both love but never stop scolding between themselves, as if he's a child who's failed a test. Sometimes it seems to me that this triangle – my mother, Nehama and the elections – is a kind of *perpetuum mobile*, a machine that will never stop, and even when the warming and expanding universe comes to an end, in the eternal empty spaces remaining their voices will be heard denouncing the American appearance of Bibi Netanyahu and the irresponsible members of the extreme left who refused to cast their vote on Judgement Day.

Armand listens to them and laughs to himself. Politics interests him far less than his poetry books and his splendid collection of classical music. Armand is an escapist like me. And perhaps he simply doesn't have the strength to argue with my mother and especially with Nehama, since they are so deaf to his opinions. As far as he's concerned, he says, until there's a Sephardi bourgeoisie and a Sephardi Prime Minister there's nothing to choose between the political parties. Mother and Nehama yell at him and accuse him of not wanting to get into a debate on political and social issues with them, but sometimes, when they let him, he describes with gentle poetry his memories of life in the immigrant transit camp, and then Nehama reacts with theatrical yawns and my mother nods a couple of times and soon changes the subject and goes back to muttering that she simply can't understand it, after everything that happened.

"Everything that happened" is of course a reference to the assassination of the Prime Minister.

I remember that period vividly, not necessarily because of the sense of general bereavement that descended on us all, but because it was in those days that I finally formulated to myself the "Principle of Communicating Vessels of Mother and Susannah", which I shall explain forthwith.

I noticed long ago that close and special relationships like the one between myself and my mother create an independent world of phenomena. In this world there is one cardinal principle around which everything revolves. This principle is complex and full of nuances, but basically it is simplicity itself: when my mother is strong and confident I am weak and trembling. This is usually the situation between us. But there is also another, rarer state, and perhaps this rarity is the reason it took me so many years to formulate the physical law: as soon as my mother weakens, the mousy, dependent Susannah turns into a little tiger, full of power and energy.

It is important to note that this situation is not the result of some deliberate act of will, as when the corporal steps forward to take command because the leader lies wounded and bleeding on the battlefield. What we have here is not the result of a conscious choice stemming from some existential imperative. No. It just happens. Without any intention, and shamefully, instead of sorrow and concern, the weakening of my mother gives rise in me to a hidden, inexplicable joy. Since these shifts are very infrequent and my mother hardly ever abandons her position as the strong woman at the head of the camp, I was never obliged to confront this embarrassing feeling in significant doses – until the assassination of our Prime Minister.

What happened was that she reacted to his murder by total collapse, as if in his death he clearly defined the possibility of her own death. After she heard the official announcement on the television she let out a shriek that made my blood run cold and then began to cry. Nehama had already rushed round to our house, stunned and confused, and Armand soon arrived, also in a state of shock, and together we tried to calm my mother down, but she couldn't stop crying in spite of all our efforts, and she kept it up for a whole week, tireless and unconsoled. I, on the other hand, felt a rising tide of strength such as I had never experienced in my life before. I tidied the house, did my best to calm her down, and coaxed her patiently to eat. Not only that, but I even allowed myself to be angry and scold her, for example, for not reacting with such grief to the death of my father, and she, submissive as a child, replied: "But we're almost family. He's Rabin and so are we." At that moment I was sure that she had started to go off the rails. And for the first time I wondered what would become of me when she died. After all, she was older than me. It was inevitable that she would die before me. How would I survive? What would I eat? Who would I love? I couldn't talk to her about it, she was in no state for conversation. For days on end she sat with Nehama and Armand and looked at old pictures, read everything written in the newspapers and watched everything shown on television. And she didn't stop crying. When she was still lighting memorial candles three weeks after the murder I yelled at her: "Stop it, this has gone far enough!" She obeyed, and from that moment everything returned to its former state and the principle of communicating vessels of Susannah and her mother received its final definition.

So now the country is in a depression and my mother with it.

I, of course, am feeling fine. And so, luckily, is the guest. Mother is shocked at our indifference. And since the guest has been with us for quite a while now, she allows herself to criticize him.

"I don't understand this apathy, Neo. Don't you care what happens?"

"I care a lot, Ada," answers the guest from the sofa where he's lounging, his head hidden by the newspaper, "but what can I do? You all got what you wanted. Every country gets exactly the government that it deserves."

Nehama too has something to say on the subject.

"You call that caring? You didn't even take the trouble to vote!"

"Who do you want me to vote for, Mrs Lieber, those fascists from the so-called left-wing Meretz?"

The guest drops a grape into his mouth. The plate next to him with its huge bunch of grapes gives him the air of a decadent hedonist.

"I agree with Nehama," my mother continues. "You don't like Meretz, don't vote for Meretz. Vote for the Communists, for the Arabs, but vote. I don't understand how with a father like Herb you turned out so indifferent to what's happening around you."

"As Herb's son I don't recognize the institution of the state. Certainly not this synthetic, imperialistic entity that calls itself the State of Israel."

"Why don't you become a Muslim terrorist and join the Hamas if that's how you feel?" Nehama pounced.

"How perceptive of you, Mrs Lieber. I already have. Now I'm on a special mission from Sheikh Yasin to blow up the Super Duper. *A'lan ana bi-muhimme khassa min qibel el Sheikh Yasin bi-tafjir el Super Duper*," says the guest, showing off his fluent Arabic.

"Go on, laugh. Some leftist you are. I'm a leftist too. Really, some people – they get out of the army on psychiatric grounds, live abroad, don't go to vote – but they've got a mouth on them you wouldn't believe."

"It's from pacifism, Nehama, not indifference. You know – young people who care about the environment, about the animals," my mother jumps in to defend the guest, even though in her heart of hearts she tends to think that Nehama's not entirely wrong.

"Sure they care about the animals. They'll drive their families to an early grave, but if somebody says boo to some Kurzweiler – they take them to court. Voting is beneath them! They were so busy smelling flowers and kissing the Arabs that we lost the elections to the fascists and the religious!"

"And why should you have won the elections? Go on, tell me why." The guest begins to warm up. "And what have you got against the religious? At least they operate on the basis of some logical sectional interest. And you? You took over this country, you speak this language, and you don't even understand that there's absolutely no justification for it apart from the one that exists in the Jewish messianic faith! What is all this nonsense about secular Zionism anyway? It's a logical contradiction!"

The guest has not yet learned that Nehama and logical contradictions are like David and Jonathan.

"It's a fact, mister smarty-pants, I'm an Israeli and a Zionist and I feel just fine!" Nehama wags her raised forefinger in the air.

"Sure, because you repress the deep reasons that give you any right to settle here and speak this language without feeling like a criminal. Otherwise what right would you have for all this endless injustice to the Arabs?"

"I did something to the Arabs? I came to settle in my mother-land. What did they have here? Nothing! Two goats and a camel. And when they saw us they suddenly woke up and realized that it was possible to make this a place fit for civilized people to live in." With the righteous expression of an innocent person falsely accused, Nehama invites me and my mother to join the union of noble swamp-drying pioneers.

"Do you really think it's possible to isolate Jewish history from the Jewish religion, my dear Mrs Lieber? Or the Jewish people from the Jewish religion? It's absurd! The Jewish religion is Jewish history itself! All this secular Zionism is shallow and based on repression and self-deceit. You're secular? Cosmopolitans? Go and settle in Uganda, speak Esperanto, and then we'll talk. At least the Likudniks and the religious are rational and consistent."

Nehama listens to this heated speech with an expression of demonstrative disgust.

"Ay ay ay, what interesting opinions! But the National Religious Party would demand that you go and vote too, you know."

"I'm not voting until the Palestinian state is declared," the guest concludes and returns to his newspaper. He's tired of the argument, he's done his number for the day. Encouraged by this sign of retreat, Nehama returns to the attack.

"I thought you didn't recognize the institution of the state, Mr Bakunin *de la shmatte*."

And so on and so forth.

I say nothing. I voted.

My mother says, "You're a strange generation." As usual, she robs me of my private experience, even when it comes to something as personal as indifference. I'm part of a generation. An indifferent generation. Not only I am absorbed in my private affairs and occupied with trifles, but the entire generation. But this time I don't mind. Because the guest too is part of the generation. Both of us are part of a syndrome. We have an identity. At least in my mother's eyes.

Nehama can't bear the sight of the swollen-bellied children in Africa. Armand's heart breaks at the sombre eyes of the humiliated, jobless men in the development towns. My mother's blood boils at the thought of battering, murdering husbands, while I, Susannah Rabin, contemplate the outside world from inside my protected pit. A world which secretly worships the God of power. A world full of human creatures climbing over one another, trying to crush and trample whoever they can, to conquer their place under the sun. What I feel about it isn't important. Feeling not accompanied by action is worthless. An abortion. A dead foetus. A creature who will never be born.

Better to shut up. Or talk to the guest.

The day after our nocturnal conversation the guest kept his promise and came home in the evening with expensive boxes of synthetic charcoal and a pad of fine drawing paper. First we sketched the blue vase. For me it starred in our drawings as the symbol of the pact we had signed after weeks of negotiations. Susannah Rabin and Neo Arafat. The guest, of course, was unaware of the symbolism of the blue vase and the reasons for its choice. In the following days we sketched each other. In profile, three-quarter profile and *en face*. Upper torso, full length, seated, lying on the sofa, with our chins resting on our hands. We made lightning sketches and slow, thorough ones. The guest was a virtuoso, no doubt about it, I didn't even try to compete with him. Sometimes he drew with the dense detail and precision of a Dürer, sometimes with the showy sensuality of a Leonardo, and sometimes with the ragged-ended economy of a Cocteau.

When he was out I would draw the objects he had left for this purpose – a nut, a bit of crumpled velvet dangling from a bowl, a fan, a statuette of Aphrodite Armand had brought back from a trip to Cyprus, a pile of books next to an alarm clock.

Afterwards we drew my mother, in every possible pose. Serious and smiling, in the kitchen at the stove, and sitting deep in thought with the newspaper. We met Gidi Bochacho and his dog in the park and we drew them too. We drew Katyusha. We drew the man who came to offer us a deal on cable television. We drew Uzi the plumber when he was fixing the water pressure in the shower. We sprayed the good drawings with fixative so they wouldn't smear and put them in a special cardboard portfolio. The guest stuck a big label on to the portfolio and wrote on it in gold ink: "Neo and Susannah, July '96". The bad ones we threw away. After two weeks the guest looked at my latest efforts with undisguised satisfaction and said that I was beginning to make progress. That my hand was growing lighter. That the lines were beginning to breathe.

"In honour of your progress I have a gift for you," he announced with a flourish. I was sure that he would give me a special box of paints or something like that. I had already noticed that with the guest an expression of affection was always connected to the purchase of expensive objects. But he got up from the sofa and gathered his hair into a rubber band, without showing any sign of leaving the room to fetch my prize. Then he went over to the wall and moved the philodendron and the magazine holder aside and taking a quick step backwards he turned around and stood on his head, his hair falling on to his face, which was red with effort, his flat stomach arching forwards, his feet trying to grip the wall in a desperate struggle to keep his balance. After a few seconds, which he seemed to think sufficient to demonstrate his new skill, he dropped to the floor with a mighty thud, his limbs falling every which way in total disarray, as if they had become detached from their owner and turned into a collection of disparate objects. My mother, alarmed by the noise, burst into the living room with the carving knife in her hand, looking like Anthony Perkins dressed up as his mother in *Psycho*, but before she had a chance to cry out in surprise, the scattered limbs collected themselves and turned back into the guest, safe and sound, his cheeks flushed and his eyes glittering, sitting wild-haired on the floor and rubbing a bruised knee, looking at us in proud triumph.

"Well, what do you say, Susannah? An almost perfect headstand, after exhausting practice in secret. As you see, I haven't yet reached the stage enabling rest and clarity of thought, but I'll get there."

He raised himself from the floor, still rubbing the sore spots, went up to my mother and planted a kiss on her cheek. "Who are you planning to kill, Ada?" he pointed to the knife.

Mother touched his hair, tidying it with her fingers, stroking his head.

"Just be careful, children, I heard the noise and I thought something terrible had happened – my heart almost stopped beating."

My own heart contracted. Suddenly I felt guilty at my cheerfulness. In recent weeks I had been so absorbed in the guest that I had almost forgotten her existence. Eager for achievement in the improvised drawing course, I had stopped joining her on her daily excursions into the outside world. Look, I thought, she goes out every day to take care of all the problems of our lives with the officials in the post office, the income tax, the national insurance, dragging her old body under the glaring sun, just so that I, the Princess Susannah, can sit on my backside opposite the fan and draw potted plants and walnuts.

She went on absentmindedly stroking the hair of the guest, who pulled faces of exaggerated pain and rubbed the sore places on his body. Her face was full of tenderness, the knife in her hand a striking contrast to her maternal expression. The scene was so strange and picturesque that I suddenly felt that I didn't know her. That she had secrets she didn't tell me. Not concrete details, what she did, where she went, but thoughts. Thoughts that were hers and hers only. And in fact, why not? Didn't I myself have thoughts that were mine and mine alone? Thoughts I wouldn't dream of revealing to her, not even under torture. Thoughts about the guest, for instance – or even worse – bad thoughts about her, when I was physically revolted by her, or when I felt sorry for her.

The possibility of my mother having a secret life appalled me. It reminded me of the terror I felt that night when I was ten years old and in passing my parents' room I heard quiet sounds that tempted me to peek inside. I saw them moving in unison, with the blanket covering them revealing body parts that created a kind of mythical, many-limbed, two-headed monster. I remembered how I ran for my life, choking in disgust, full of shame at having witnessed this unparental act, as if at the exposure of a dirty secret, and more than that – something quite inconceivable.

Parents are people without secrets. Parents are people without a sex life. Parents are people with limited wishes and modest hopes, which are mainly focused on us. On their offspring.

From the minute we emerge into the light of day the world of their desires narrows into one single desire, in all its subtle variations – the desire for us to be happy. Anything that upsets this scheme of things, in which we believe with all our hearts, horrifies us. And now, just as after that chance peek at my parents' sex life, I sensed a dangerous whiff of chaos and an imminent breakdown in this natural order, as it was confronted by one of the innumerable faces of reality. But what was the source of disharmony in the family scene I saw before me? Was it the knife in my mother's hand? Or the steady stroking of the guest's head? Or the combination of both? On the first night he spent in our house she drank cognac with him, laughed and chatted playfully like some Parisian society lady, forgetting her unadorned Israeliness, her manly haircut, the Birkenstock sandals on her feet, her modest tent dress. Their friendship, so delightful and direct, had been plain to see from the moment he arrived. The fact that parents live not only for their children I had learned to my cost on that night so many years ago. So what was to stop them from going on living their secret lives day after day, ignoring our interests and needs in the pursuit of their own selfish desires?

But on the other hand, this was my mother. The person who loved me above all. No one had ever loved or would ever love me like she did. The greatest, most devoted, most self-sacrificing love in the world. So why was she stroking his hair? Had she forgotten that she had stopped being a woman long ago? She had passed the torch on to me the minute we bought my first bra, with two little Donald Ducks in the area of the nipples. Yes, yes. Her femininity had ended on the day I called to her from the lavatory and with downcast eyes showed her the first bloodstain on my tricot panties, and she had responded with tribal joy, diluted by endless instructions regarding the laundry, sanitary towels, moods and stomach cramps. Although to be strictly honest I have to admit that the end product was a woman in theory only. The creature called Susannah Rabin wasn't even a hermaphrodite but a congenital eunuch, just like one of the dolls she played with as a child. Girl dolls with long hair and dresses, whose panties I pulled down again and again in some unclear hope, only to discover the slitless pink plastic between their legs.

So what. Creature or not, the femininity in this house belonged to me. Murky as it might be. And so did the life. Murky as it might be, of course. She had no right to a life of her own. That was the code. Signed and agreed between both parties. In return I was hers for eternity. A very serious return. A respectable return. She was entitled to stroke the guest's hair only because he did me good. Because he made friends with me and had a positive influence on my social skills and self-confidence. Because I had stopped peeing in the blue vase. Because thanks to him I had almost bitten a dog. Because having a family was a good thing. But she had no right, absolutely no right at all, to stroke him because he was a man. Because he was a handsome man.

Stop it, jealous Susannah, it's only Mother.

Is that so? If you're paranoid it doesn't mean you don't have enemies, in the words of Nehama.

"Mother, why don't you make tea?" I said, astounded at how natural and ordinary my voice sounded.

"Of course, gladly. Right away. Why don't I make supper at the same time?"

The last question she addressed exclusively to the guest. Me, she knew, she would feed later on, when he went to his room to read.

225

"Brilliant idea, Ada. I'm starving. I forgot to eat since the croissant this morning," said the guest ingratiatingly. He was never just hungry, or tired. He was always starving, or finished, or destroyed, but his tone was never one of hysterical exaggeration, as might have been expected, but rather of sorrowful restraint, as if the sensations felt by ordinary mortals assumed in him such immense proportions that any attempt to communicate them to others was doomed to frustration.

"Have you seen Susannah's latest drawings, Ada?" the guest asked as my mother set the bowl of salad on the kitchen table and sat down opposite him. The guest and I were already seated in front of our plates, our hands washed, like nicely brought-up children, watching my mother as she placed more and more of her plain dishes on the table. Yes, she put a plate in front of me too, for the sake of keeping up appearances. Even though he had already discovered the reason for my abstinence, we went on behaving as if I was simply not hungry, but happy to keep the others company.

"I certainly have." Mother put a thick piece of French toast on the guest's plate. "It's extraordinary, such outstanding results in such a short time." I felt ashamed of the old-fashioned way she expressed herself, but the guest didn't even notice in his pride at the results of his teaching.

"You haven't seen anything yet. She just has to keep on working. Oh, Susannah, you're such a star. Determination and perseverance are thirty per cent of the matter."

"And what about the other seventy per cent?" my mother enquired.

The guest opened a container of sour cream and licked the lid.

"Come on, Ada. Talent, of course. And of course all kinds of other trifles like originality, cultural breadth of vision, expressive power. Nonsense like that."

"And in your expert opinion, is she talented?"

She, without a doubt, was talented. For what precisely, I couldn't say, but the manner in which she succeeded with one short sentence both in flattering him and in embarrassing me to death certainly indicated considerable capacities. I gripped my cup of tea in both hands, seeking refuge in the amber liquid with my eyes.

"Expert my arse. But seriously? It's too early to tell. I really don't understand these things. Processes. Beginnings, buddings, flickerings. I only know when something is absolutely good. Which is nothing to brag about."

"You're so modest." My mother pushed the salad bowl towards him. "But that reminds me, Susannah, Rivki phoned. We have to go and see her. She said that she's prepared a list of all the municipal courses and activities for you, so you can choose what interests you."

"All right," I mumbled. "Next week."

"I don't understand what you need those dreary courses for." The high spirits of the guest, heady with our common success, made him cross lines he had already learned not to cross with us. "Go and apply to somewhere normal, like the college in Ramat Hasharon, for example."

He took hold of the salad bowl and piled a generous portion on to his plate.

For the first time I wondered what my mother had told him about me in their private conversations. Presumably quite a lot. Till this moment I hadn't stopped to think about it. Where did he know everything he knew about me from? In the meetings between us I had certainly not filled him in on my life history. Had she told him how I vomited in the middle of the class, splashing in all directions, when I was required to talk about my latest work in front of the entire staff and student body of the School of Visual Art, as a condition of my continued attendance there? Had she described to him in detail all the treatments I had undergone, in both private and government frameworks, with the aim of extricating me from the pit in which I had entrenched myself, making me fit to function among strangers, to express myself, to study, to ask for the time, for a light? Had she accumulated hours of intimacy with him with the help of little betrayals of me, the dubious apple of her eye? Was their friendship, at least partially, at my expense? Of course it was. I didn't have the shadow of a doubt.

I raised my eyes to the guest. He was still holding the salad bowl in the air, licking the fingers of his other hand, which he had dipped by mistake in the dressing.

"Salad, Susannah?" His face turned in my direction, relaxed and more beautiful than ever, his mouth uttering the sentence as casually as if in the middle of a lively conversation with his date in a restaurant. Without taking my eyes off him, I sensed on the tip of my left ear and all the exposed area of my cheek my mother's immediate alertness, the mobilization of her energy to protect me, to act with speed and efficiency, to spread a sheltering wing. The red light in front of her eyes signalled "Fire, fire, fire." Too late, traitor.

"Yes, thank you," I said. I took the bowl from his hands. I was surprised to see that my hands weren't trembling. Slowly I drew the bowl towards me and put two heaped spoons of salad on my plate. Then, with the same slowness, I returned the bowl to the guest so that he could put it down on the table. I picked up the knife and fork next to my plate, organized a little heap of salad on my fork with the help of the knife, raised it to my lips and put it in my mouth. I chewed with my mouth closed, without haste, like the Duchess of Windsor, and when I had finished chewing and making the swallowing motion that slid the food from my mouth to my throat, I took a sip of tea and said, "So what exactly did Rivki say? I hope that this year they'll open the advanced ceramics class at last. I'm fed up with their promises."

More lemon on the oysters, Sir Charles?

How tender are the feelings of the pervert lying in wait in the park for the little girls returning from their ballet lesson. Now he sees them in the distance, chattering to each other, in their satchels their little ballet shoes (black for beginners, pink satin toe-shoes for advanced), and leotards, damp with sweet pre-puberty sweat. Now they come closer, their budding breasts bouncing underneath their T-shirts – undeveloped milk glands in the eyes of the ordinary adult, but full of life and meaning in the eyes of our hero. And now, one step before they are in a straight line with him he emerges quickly from the dusty clump of rhododendrons and hop – the black raincoat opens and the organ of his lust jumps out at the little ballerinas. Now comes the thing he has been anticipating – the space of time that will pass from the moment of recognition to the moment when they begin to run, raising dust on the path with their slender legs, looking back to make sure that the bad man isn't chasing them. Yes, those few seconds when they stand there paralysed, until their unpractised minds sound the alarm and send them flying from the scene, these are what the exhibitionist waits for. The shock appearing on the face of his victim is the source of his pleasure.

At those moments, just like that pervert, I rejoiced in the stunned confusion spreading over my mother's face. Unlike those light-footed schoolgirls, she couldn't get up and run, and so my enjoyment lasted longer and longer, increasing from moment to moment. What more does the poor pervert need, when he finally dares to perform the only act of love he is capable of? The wide, startled eyes, the little bodies frozen like decorative fountain statues – and he is flooded with the greatest joy and triumph that he knows.

We'll see who'll stroke whose hair here.

To my disappointment, once my mother understood that my behaviour wasn't an act of caprice no sooner conceived than regretted, her expression of shock gave way to an excitement that she tried without any marked success to control. The meal continued. I ate a piece of French toast, two triangles of pro-cessed cheese, and then another piece of French toast, this time with sugar and cream. We all tried to behave as usual, but the only one who fully succeeded was the guest, who chattered away, and recounted the story of the brother and sister whose collection of icons, inherited from their grandmother, he wanted to buy. I co-operated as best I could between my careful chews, asking questions, exclaiming at their tragic biography – their parents had been killed in a road accident some five years before; nodding understandingly at the dilemma with which they were faced: the wish to keep the rare collection as opposed to the desperate need for money, which would enable them to move to Tel Aviv and study at the university.

Only my mother failed to come close to a realistic portrayal of normality. Oh, ballerina. Oh, swan. If only I could have, I would have made clucking noises with my tongue: Tsk, tsk,

tsk, just like she and Nehama did when it turned out that the hero of the movie was cheating on his wife, or when the CNN cameras caught an Israeli soldier hitting a Palestinian child. She sat straight up in her chair, picking indifferently at her food, her mind distracted by thoughts and feelings about what was happening before her very eyes. Her eyes and nostrils reddened, her throat convulsed as she swallowed in the attempt to overcome her emotion. She took care to replenish our plates until nearly all the food on the table was finished – the guest insisted on drawing the event out to the bitter end, as if leaving my eating in public in the realm of the symbolic would detract from the significance of the achievement.

Only when we moved into the living room and my mother brought in the tray of coffee and cookies and sat down opposite us in the deep armchair, did her ability to speak openly and directly return. The guest lounged on the sofa with an exhausted expression, in a pose that declared: I'm full, or, as he said: I'm bursting. I took up my position next to him, nibbling cookies, trying to trap the elusiveness of the event by turning it into a non-stop routine.

My mother examined us, letting her gaze slide from one to the other, from the masticating Susannah to the bursting Neo, with an expression that bespoke boundless excitement and emotion.

"I don't know what to say to you, children. Neo. I'm so excited I can hardly speak. You know, to be perfectly honest, when I got the letter from your mother, I was very worried. A strange man in the house, who knows? Family, yes, but we never really met. And here I see what's happening, and I'm simply speechless. Such a wonderful friendship between you, between us, it makes

231

me so very happy. You know, I'd already got used to the idea that Susannah and I were alone in the world, and managing, thank God. We have friends, Nehama, Armand, they're like family. But then you came along, and suddenly I understood what a real family means. Even though you're only cousins, I see how you've become a real brother to Susannah. To find a lost brother at her age! Apparently it's true what people say: blood is thicker than water. There's no getting away from it. And for me you're like a son, I hope you know that. I may be a sentimental old woman but I . . ."

She cleared her throat, took a big, crumpled man's handkerchief out of her apron pocket, blew her nose and immediately afterwards wiped the tears from her eyes before they could roll down her cheeks.

I stole a look at the guest, trying to discover what he thought of this wet speech, but his face was blank and grave, waiting for her to continue.

"In any case, what I wanted to say to you, Neo, is thank you . . . for the friendship . . . thank you . . ."

Now she was really crying, sniffing noisily and moving the handkerchief back and forth between her nose and her eyes.

The guest slid off the sofa, sat on the arm of her chair, and put his arm around her shoulders.

"What's got into you, Ada? What are you thanking me for? I feel exactly like you do. Stop it, do me a favour."

I looked at the comedy taking place before my eyes and felt alienated from both of them.

Brother? I heard a malicious laugh echoing inside me. If I'd felt he was my brother maybe I would have joined the touching family scene, sitting on the other arm of the chair and shedding a sentimental tear. I don't want a brother. I'm happy as I am. Thanks, but no thanks.

So what do you want? I heard the malicious voice stop laughing, and try to set me on the blessed path of clear thinking. What do you want then? What would you like the guest to be? Your husband? Your lover? Well? You dimwitted ugly provincial retard?

The laugh returned, rolling between the sides of my skull, echoing, rising on a crescendo to intolerable heights. I raised my hands and pressed them tightly to my ears, until I heard nothing but the quiet humming of my brain. I listened to the billions of tireless cells never resting for a second, releasing countless neurotransmitters into the synapses, endlessly transmitting information, logical, instinctual, automatic, voluntary and involuntary responses. A totality of voices, whispers and murmurs uniting into one broad, low and marvellous sound – the eternal roar of the ocean waves inside the shell pressed to your ear.

And out of this low roar I heard the sentence spoken by the heroine in a play by Lorca – I simply couldn't remember her name or the name of the play.

"I'd like to drink his blood. Slowly. Drop by drop. That's what I'd like."

Navels

The heat rules the streets. Slowly and skilfully it increases its presence, invading corners hitherto protected by a deceptive shield of shade. We bought a special fan to hang on the ceiling and the guest installed it, drilling with an enthusiasm that made up for his lack of skill, covering the house in a fine film of white powder that transformed the living room, with all its furniture and objects, into a room in the palace of the Snow Queen, until my mother with the help of cloths and cleaning agents made the magic disappear.

I feel admiration mingled with guilt at my mother's refusal to adapt her lifestyle to the weather. She confronts the heat like David facing Goliath, placing her faith in the limitless power of the human will and the ability of the body to keep itself cool under any conditions. Every day she celebrates the momentary victory of the perishable flesh over the constant, pitiless glare of the sovereign sun. Even when the evening news reports the tragic death of hundreds of thousands of chickens on the farms, the dehydration of workers in the fields and ordinary citizens who forgot to drink, she goes out every morning on her chores.

I go out only when I have to. I hide.

We've stopped going to the sea. The official reason is the heat, but the real reason is that Nehama is ill. Since the beginning of spring she has been complaining of weakness and exhaustion, but we were all convinced that it was just her usual moaning, until she announced that she didn't have the strength to schlep to Tel Aviv in the bus, and my mother quickly agreed with her and gave up our regular summer routine. And ever since then Nehama has confined her excursions to the operations necessary to her survival – going to the Super Duper and of course to us, until a few days ago the phone rang in a way that we all knew spelled trouble, perhaps because of the ominous way the usual screeching noise vibrated between the walls. My mother answered and listened with a serious expression on her face, and after the first "Oi vay" she only nodded again and again, letting out an occasional understanding "Aha, aha", as she did so. When she hung up she reported gravely that Nehama had fallen downstairs and been taken to hospital. It wasn't yet clear what was the matter with her, but she had already been moved from the emergency room to the internal medicine department, and since the guest had forgotten his key I would have to stay at home and wait for him while she went to see what was happening and to take care of things. When she returned in the evening accompanied by Armand it was clear that the situation did not bode well. She switched off the television and rebuked us for smoking so much in the house that you couldn't breathe, and then filled us in on the details, together with Armand, each taking over from the other like a pair of practised travelling storytellers. While Nehama had escaped from the fall itself relatively unharmed, a few bruises and a cracked rib (even though she had tumbled down half a flight of stairs), that was only part of the picture. The initial tests indicated the onset of a degenerative neurological condition, and while the doctors said it was still too early to make a final diagnosis, it was apparently something serious, perhaps even multiple sclerosis. They had decided to keep her in the hospital for a couple of days and after that to continue examining her on an ambulatory basis.

Although the story was told in a stern, matter-of-fact manner, for the first time in my life I saw real loss in the faces of my mother and Armand. All these medical facts that confirmed Nehama's disease removed her from the category of fusspots and hypochondriacs and transformed the tension of old-age-illness-end into part of an inevitable reality, not only hers but all of ours. The same actuality transformed death itself from a hypothetical fate waiting somewhere or other beyond the horizon into the hollow sound of the murderer's footsteps behind our backs in a dark street at night.

Even the uninvolved guest said, "Wow," and also, "Jesus."

In my mother's eyes Nehama's illness was nothing but a natural outcome of the miserable state of the country as a whole, and since she could do nothing to improve the national condition in any significant way, she threw herself into caring for her friend with all the fervour of a frustrated fighter on the barricades. After Nehama was discharged from the hospital she spent hours with her every day, doing her shopping and her chores, and reporting the latest news to her son Amir and his Russian wife, damn them to hell, who were too busy to come in person and managed the care of their mother/mother-in-law by remote control from Haifa.

This was made possible by the fact that I, the fragile daughter, the delicate forest flower, the shy deer, was being taken care of by the guest.

I can't say exactly what it was that changed the nature of our relationship and made us inseparable. Like bosom friends, or perhaps, as mother would have it, like brother and sister? Was it the heat that dominated everything, imposing its uncompromising laws on every smaller, more modest system? Or perhaps it was the loneliness of the guest, who began to show signs of social distress? Or perhaps my own yearning for him, which in spite of my timidity began to seep out, controlled only by its own intensity, crossing the walls of secrecy with which I had surrounded it, spreading like toxic waste with every breeze, infecting everything in its path and appropriating it to itself. In any case, the guest and I began to spend together all the time when he wasn't working or sleeping.

Our drawing lessons grew less obsessive. As soon as my drawings reached a satisfactory level the initial, surprising rate of my progress slowed down, but even though I was no longer as interested in the occupation itself as I had been, I took care to produce one or two drawings every few days, simply in order to enjoy the physical proximity of the guest as he bent over my shoulder. To see his finger turning black, leaving prints on the paper, touching the weak lines, pointing out my sloppiness or laziness, and feeling his breath, bearing trivial words of explanation, brushing my nape and the tip of my ear.

Sometimes I just watched him as he prepared a sophisticated quiche for supper or fixed something in the house (my mother's energetic activity succeeded in infecting even him with a sense of general mobilization). I liked watching him from an angle I found in the living room that afforded a view of him as he sat in

237

his improvised office in the kitchen, speaking on the phone in Hebrew and English, arranging meetings and clarifying issues, as if I were a little girl eavesdropping on adult conversations, dull and obscure in themselves but thrilling in their mysteriousness. His work was going well, he said. Katyusha, with a finger in every pie, continued to find people interested in selling works of art to him, and he followed them up assiduously with Vadim the restorer (a small, broad-shouldered man who never said a word to me apart from a curt, or perhaps shy greeting), making acquisitions, taking photographs, insuring, obtaining permits and doing laboratory tests.

Sometimes we sat for hours in the silence of old friends who've already talked about everything, watching television or reading different parts of the same newspaper. Sometimes I read books while the guest pored over catalogues from Sotheby's or Christie's or the American magazines that he bought assiduously and left scattered all over the house – *Time*, *Newsweek*, *Details*, *Vanity Fair*. Some of them even lay in the lavatory, embarrassing me with their presence, forcing me to imagine the guest sitting with his trousers round his slender ankles, absorbed in an article about the economic situation in east Asia with his bum covering the opening of the lavatory bowl and – Oh my God, spare us the sight, the sound, the smell, the thought – taking a crap.

I learned to suppress these revolting thoughts in the same way that the religious manage to avoid thinking of God while they are engaged in performing similar functions. Now I, a Peeping Tom against my will, was forced to confront the low, physical life of the guest, just as I had feared he was doing to us at the beginning of his stay. But to my surprise what happened was the opposite of what might have been expected – the confrontation with this part of his life did not disgust me in the least. It was a strange, unnatural feeling. At first I would close my eyes and turn my head to the wall in order not to see the bright magazines lying in the narrow space between the lavatory bowl and the wall and testifying so grotesquely to the guest's mortality. But after a few days I carefully picked one of them up, and a few minutes later I was eagerly reading about the eating habits and political opinions of Susan Sarandon, making one more secret alliance to add to those I had already made with the guest without his knowledge, this time concerning mutual bodily excretions. About which the guest himself would doubtless say: Everyone gets the alliances he deserves.

And of course we talked. Or to be precise, the guest talked and I listened.

I could never understand from his stories whether he was satisfied with his life or not, but what difference did that make? The stories themselves were riveting, full of subtle insights about human nature, sometimes cruel and sometimes hilariously funny. Many of them smacked of a certain boastfulness, which the guest took care to balance with measured doses of self-criticism. He was a master of the art of anecdote and his life was packed with incidents both great and small, all so original that they could never have happened to anyone but him. His successes at the universities of New York and London were flavoured with many infringements of discipline and practical jokes. It was only thanks to his artistic and academic brilliance that someone as anarchic and subversive as he was had succeeded in getting through his studies and acquiring both a Bachelor's and a Master's degree. His friends and acquaintances were fascinating and ridiculous at once, invariably unique, extraordinary, obliged to fit into the narrow dimensions of an anecdote, but worth a full-length novel, each and every one.

In additional to his narrative talents the guest displayed great gifts as an actor, gifts that were recognizable as soon as he made his appearance among us but that now, encouraged by his grateful and insatiable audience and liberated from the bonds of credibility, were given full expression and reached full bloom. The heroes of his stories came alive before my astonished eyes in all their mannerisms of speech and gesture, their uniqueness and absurdity.

I came to know many of his friends well. Andrei Troikorov of London, for example, son of an aristocratic Russian family which emigrated to England during the October Revolution. Andrei was an antique dealer who owned three magnificent shops in New Kings Road, dressed exclusively in suits of velvet, silk and brocade tailor-made to fit his great girth, and had been madly in love with the guest ever since their student days in the Royal College of Art.

I knew Sandra and Nicky, owners of a New York gallery and the guest's best friends. Nicky was so ginger that even her feet and knees were covered with freckles, and Sandra, Dutch Surinamese, a former model, had been brought up in an orphanage and suffered from a mental disorder called obsessive slowness which she treated with hypnosis and medication.

I knew the golden boy Nisim Babjani, an emigrant from Israel, a financial wizard who played the stock market and by the age of twenty-seven had accumulated three hundred million dollars and retired to devote his time to fishing and reading the Encyclopedia Britannica.

I even knew Shalva the Georgian from the pawn shop in

Ben Yehuda Street, who kept trying to sell the guest forged icons. Shalva hated Vadim the restorer, who sabotaged his business deals, and claimed that he was an agent in the employ of the organization that had replaced the KGB, and that the guest should get rid of him as soon as possible, before he fell with him into the clutches of Interpol.

And so on and so forth, a long and fascinating parade of characters who passed before my eyes and with the help of the dramatic and descriptive talents of the guest stirred my imagination and strained my curiosity and admiration to their limits, like a parade of revellers at a Venetian carnival with a motley crew of lovers hiding behind their masks, insubstantial as the bursting bubbles in a brimming glass of champagne.

Sometimes we played chess and I always won, except for the times I lost on purpose because I felt sorry for the guest. He was a very bad loser. The moment I made my final move and timidly announced "Checkmate", he would start to rub his forehead and complain of exhaustion, hinting that this was the reason for his defeat, scanning the board again and again to make sure that there was no mistake, examining me with an unfriendly eye as if to expose the slyness that had enabled me to beat him, and then going to sit in front of the television and grumbling that I had distracted him on purpose, and that spending my life shut up in the house had enabled me to perfect my performance to a degree that owed everything to endless hours of practice, and nothing to the kind of natural talent that characterized his own game.

Sometimes we went to do the shopping at the Super Duper, and while I passed between the shelves the guest would chat to Aziz in fluent Arabic, bringing a smile even to his stern face. Sometimes he joined me on my visits to Nehama, who seemed vulnerable and quiet, sitting in the shiny new wheelchair she had to use until her condition improved.

In the light of the near-idyllic relations between us it was only natural that the guest should take my mother's place and accompany me to my next meeting with Rivki, and on a morning glaring with white sunshine, the guest equipped with his gorgeous sunglasses and me blinking all the way to the bus stop, we set out for Ramat Chen.

Rivki was sitting behind her desk, peering sideways into the mirror of an open powder compact set on top of an improvised tower composed of the telephone directory, the *Yellow Pages* and the files of her patients, waging war on a stubborn pimple that had sprouted on her chin.

The entrance of the guest had a dramatic effect that took even me by surprise. In seconds the compact was on the floor, its mirror shattered, surrounded by hard pink pieces of compacted powder. The stack of patients' files lay scattered freely over the desk, and Rivki scrutinized the open telephone directory lying upside down in front of her with the expression of a surgeon performing open-heart surgery.

"Hello, Rivki," I tried to balance the little commotion created by our entry with a matter-of-fact tone, "this is a relation of ours from America. My mother couldn't come today because she's busy. Our friend Nehama, the one we used to go to the beach with, is sick, so today he's come in her place. Neo – Rivki. Rivki – Neo."

"Glad to meet you. Rivka Finkwasser, social worker." Rivki stood up, trying as she did so to kick the remains of the powder compact under the filing cabinet next to the desk.

"Neo," the guest flashed his standard introductory smile at her.

"I'm glad you've come," Rivki began to recover herself, careful for some reason to look only at me, "I called Ada two weeks ago. I have all the material ready for you, all the courses, all the activities. There are wonderful opportunities this year. Everything sponsored by the municipality is free, with us footing the bill. With regard to other things I'll make sure you get a reduction, but first of all you have to see what's on offer and decide what you want." Rivki riffled through the files and papers on her desk.

"Is there an advanced pottery course?" the guest intervened.

At last Rivki dared to look at him, and from that moment on she didn't take her eyes off him until the end of the meeting.

"I see you're in the picture. I understand that you're a close relation?"

"Cousins," the guest drawled, and immediately narrowed his eyes and lied: "I've heard wonderful things about you from Ada and Susannah."

Rivki began to melt. "It's so great to have family abroad. I have a sister in Romania. She went there to study dentistry and married a Romanian."

The guest looked suitably impressed.

"Much older than she is," Rivki hurried to put the record straight. "But I say: if he's a mensch then it makes no difference if he's young or old. Even though I'm a dedicated feminist, I believe in the importance of partnership. In the Nineties our approach is not one against the other but one complementing the other. It's not like it was in the Seventies, when you had to grow a jungle in your armpit. Femininity isn't a swearword. I say: a woman is a woman and a man is a man. We'll put on perfume, you'll scratch your balls, the main thing is equality of opportunity. Aren't I right? Here, Susannah, why don't you look through the programmes now, so that we can sign you up and get it over."

She pushed a bunch of prospectuses and sheets of paper stapled together towards me.

I flipped through the bundle. All I wanted was to get up and leave. Suddenly the whole meeting seemed completely pointless. Rivki was flirting with the guest. Presumably he would reply in kind. And what did I think was going to happen? Bringing a handsome man to Rivki was like throwing a raw, bleeding fillet steak at a Bengal tiger. I cursed myself for my mistake, but it was already too late.

"Excuse me for asking, but what do you do?" Rivki interrupted the silence that had fallen.

"Business," the guest smiled. "But why apologize? It's a legitimate question."

"It's just that it suddenly seemed to me, please don't laugh, but don't you model for Armani? For their new aftershave? The resemblance is amazing." Rivki pursed her lips in a cupid's bow pout. For the first time I noticed how much they resembled the lips of Cabinet Minister David Levy.

"Me an Armani model," the guest burst out laughing, nudging my chair with his leg. I joined in the laughter.

"What's the matter?" cried Rivki. "Did I say something funny?"

"No, no," the guest made haste to reassure her. "Just a private family joke."

So, I had private jokes with the guest. A tremor of joy ran down my spine. Perhaps he would keep faith with me after all, and not turn the meeting into an exhausting sequence of embarrassments for his poor cousin. The letters on the pages in my hand merged into a meaningless mishmash. Course upon course. But no advanced pottery.

"So what field of business are you in?" persisted Rivki.

"I'm an art dealer. Modern art. Post-modern, to be exact."

"I don't believe it," shrieked Rivki. "It runs in the family, it's genetic! You're all sensitive to art. It's amazing."

"Yes," the guest agreed. "In fact, I came along with Susannah today because I wanted to talk to you about something concrete in relation to that very subject. Not that I'm not delighted to meet you and chat about this and that, but . . ."

But Rivki had a few more things to say before turning her attention to the trivial matter of her work and her client.

"I have to tell you that I myself am mad about art. It's very deep with me. I've always been drawn to art. All my boyfriends were involved with art in one way or another."

Rivki rolled her eyes up in affected reminiscence, counting them off on the fingers of her right hand.

"There was a television presenter, an actor, a musician, and once I even almost had a director, but it didn't work out. I'm too independent, it frightens some men off. They want a little woman who stays at home. In the bedroom and the kitchen." Rivki gave the guest, and for some reason me too, a probing, meaningful look, as if I was a fifth column in the service of an army of power-lusting male chauvinists whose only aim in life was to force Rivki to her knees and fuck her in the arse while analysing the Saturday soccer game.

The guest opened his mouth to respond, but she shut it for him immediately, propelled forward by an irrepressible stream of thought straining to get out.

"Of course it's not enough for a woman to have a man who's somebody. The woman has to realize herself too."

"Without a doubt," said the guest.

"Take me, for example, I did a correspondence course on Plato

245

and it was a really enriching experience. In the past I also studied piano, lithography, folk dancing, yoga, Vipassana meditation, nuclear physics, macramé, a cure for acne by use of a pendulum, scriptwriting and rectal contraction on the Paula system. But I don't feel that I've achieved self-realization yet. There's still a long way to go." Rivki smiled modestly.

In spite of the celerity with which the guest put in: "That's exactly what I wan . . ." she cut him off and continued.

"I have a few ideas about things that I'd like to do. I'd be happy to tell you about them, because you strike me as someone who'd be interested to hear them."

This time the guest didn't even try to respond. Apparently his interpersonal skills led him to the conclusion that he should give Rivki her head and allow her to express herself in full before attempting to engage her in rational conversation. But she interpreted his silence as disapproval and immediately changed course to correct any misunderstandings.

"Not that I don't love my work," she pouted again (David Levy threatening to resign from the government). "Social work is a wonderful profession – helping others, it's so fulfilling. I receive by giving. You know that feeling when your satisfaction comes from the enjoyment of others?"

"I've heard of it," the selfish guest said evasively.

"But you know, sometimes you have to do something for yourself as well. Because otherwise you give and give and give and it can just empty you out. A person has to connect with himself as well."

"Definitely," said the guest.

"Which is why I want to develop my artistic side too. I've never studied art but to tell the truth – I don't believe that art is something you can learn."

"Interesting," said the guest.

"Art has to come from inside."

"I'm sure you're right," said the guest.

"From feeling and intuition."

"Certainly," said the guest.

"So I have this idea, and when I decide to carry it out I'll go straight for a show. I don't believe in doing things for the drawer."

"That's the way," said the guest.

"Navels," said Rivki and suddenly fell silent, her eyes like those of an orphan looking at the sunset. There was silence in the room.

"I'm not sure that I understand," said the guest in the end.

"An exhibition of navels." The expression on Rivki's face was one of evident disappointment, that after having reached an almost telepathic understanding with the guest she was still obliged to put things into words. "To take photographs of navels, of all kinds of different people. You know, thin, fat, old, ugly, and have an exhibition. I don't know what it means but I feel in my guts that it's right."

"I'm stunned," said the guest.

"There you are, I knew you'd understand. You know, in Israel everything's so small, so provincial. People here don't understand things that are a little special. Although I've heard that over there in New York there's a lot of rubbish too."

"No question about it," said the guest.

"But in the meantime I'm stuck here. In the outpatients' clinic," Rivki summed up sadly. "A pawn in the hands of reality. Like something straight out of Kafka."

"Not for long, I'm sure." The guest drew his chair closer to the desk. "Rivka, I'm delighted to discover such a sensitive person in a government position. And I think you'll be able to understand what I'm about to say and to help."

Rivki rested her chin on her hands.

"Look," the guest went on, "all these courses are very nice, but I believe that what Susannah needs is a more serious framework. More comprehensive. I think she's already wasted enough time on all this bullshit."

He took the bundle of typed pages and prospectuses from me and threw them on to the desk.

"Why don't you look into the possibility of long-term study for her? That would constitute real help and real rehabilitation."

The guest's seriousness took Rivki aback, as if she suddenly realized that she had been rambling. Her expression hinted at hidden anger. Anger at the guest for misleading her and making her believe that he was interested in her and her soul, and now all of a sudden he was talking in such a dry, businesslike manner. It was clear that she felt she had been betrayed into exposing herself to an indifferent stranger, cunningly tricked into feeling special and important and fascinating, and now the realization was dawning that the thrilling meeting of minds had taken place only in her own head.

Who could understand her better than me? I felt a stab of pity. But Rivki had no intention of suffering in silence. The guest had betrayed her, and he would be punished.

"With all due respect, I don't think that what you're asking for is possible." She sat back in her chair and lit a cigarette.

"Why is that?" enquired the guest.

"Look." Rivki blew out smoke and looked at the papers in

front of her. "You must be aware, as a member of the family, of Susannah's problems. She has many problems." Rivki stressed the word "problems" as if to hint that it was an understatement. "Very many. The truth is that we made her a very interesting offer recently and she refused. To be precise, Ada refused, and she's Susannah's legal guardian. In any case, we had to drop the idea."

"What exactly was this idea?"

"The College of Art in Rosh Pinna. The only project of its kind in the entire Middle East." Rivki's lips stuck out (Minister Levy had new budget proposals). "Ninety per cent of the financing comes from a billionaire philanthropist. A remodelled old Turkish building, private rooms, work spaces, free materials, the lot. Top artists will teach there. Local and foreign. This billionaire is very well connected, and he's bringing all kinds of international celebrities. Jeff Koons is going to conduct a summer seminar there, and believe me it's not for the money. Only twenty-four candidates were accepted from all over the country, and Susannah was one of them. So there you have a special project for gifted people – is that serious enough for you? But they turned it down, so her place was taken." She pointed at me with her chin.

"Listen," the guest sounded very determined. "I want you to check it out again with the people in charge."

"There's nothing to check," Rivki sounded almost triumphant. Now she would show the guest what it meant to seduce an innocent girl and then throw her to the dogs. The sleeping Amazon hiding in every woman's heart woke at the kiss of the false prince and rose up to kill him. "The list is closed. You have no idea how many people jumped at the chance. Ada said no two months ago, and I passed it on."

The guest leaned forward and put his hand on the desk, next

to Rivki's, whose nail-bitten fingers were tapping on a personal file labelled in handwriting: "Menahem Shriki, Ramat Chen, 378". And once again, for the first time since that evening when he had cast his spell on my mother, I saw him in action. He bit his lower lip as if pondering what to say next. I could see his girlish eyelashes fluttering slightly, shading his eyes, the tension in the long line of his nose, and the lizard-like swiftness with which his tongue flicked out, licked his lip and withdrew into his mouth. His eyes glowed with melting tenderness. No, it was not in vain that Rivki had bared her artistic soul to him. He was at her feet, a tame lion cub, a willing slave, and at the same time a powerful, authoritative patriarch.

"Listen, Rivka. In the course of my work I meet a lot of people, strong, talented people who know how to get what they want. But it isn't often that I meet someone with such a harmonious combination of artistic sensitivity and professional assertiveness. And so I know", he covered Rivki's hand gently and meaningfully with his own, "that you can arrange it. For Susannah."

"But Ada would never agree. Have you checked with her?" Rivki was not about to sell herself cheaply.

"Leave it to me. I'll take care of Ada. And you find out what's happening with this project and how to get Susannah back in." I didn't know if I was imagining it or if he was really squeezing her hand. He looked deep into her eyes. Rivki made one last attempt to stifle the smile that broke on to her face with all the obstinacy of an old woman pushing in to see the doctor at the HMO clinic.

"I can try. But I can't do anything until September, closer to the opening of the school year."

"Take your time," the guest removed his hand from hers.

I stood up. Even though I knew that more subtle messages

would have been swallowed up in the impermeable armour with which my social worker protected herself from an unbearable reality, there was something outrageous in his crude flattery. And what gave him the right to represent me anyway? How did he know what I wanted, what was best for me? What gave him the right to take charge of my destiny? What gave him the right to disagree with my mother's decisions!

I wanted to be angry with him but the thoughts chased each other round my head divorced from emotion, as if they were neutral facts. I was unable to admit that I was glad about what he had done, however crude and intrusive. His motives lay revealed before me in all their purity, and no suspiciousness or pride on my part could besmirch them. And perhaps I was also glad of this subversion of my mother's will – a subversive act in which my very presence made me an accomplice, without my having to say a word.

The guest stood up too.

"I'll be in touch," Rivki waved at us. She looked tired, as if she had been subjected to an inner turmoil invisible to the eye of the outside observer.

We walked to the deserted bus stop. The guest seemed to have forgotten all about the meeting and hummed an English song to himself. He appeared to have no intention of talking to me about what had happened.

"There aren't any taxis here," I said after we had waited at the bus stop for ten minutes. As far as the guest was concerned he had exhausted the proletarian bit on the journey here, and now he stood stretching his neck like a goose, looking from one side of the road to the other in anticipation of rescue, as if all he had to do was look harder in order for his efforts to be rewarded by the appearance of the desired cab. There must have been a hint of spiteful satisfaction in my voice, because the guest desisted from his barren efforts and sat down on the bus-stop bench, patting the plastic next to him in invitation to me to join him there.

"You're angry with me."

"I think you might have asked me what I wanted. Why do you think it's so obvious? It isn't even obvious to me."

He thought for a moment.

"You're right. But look at it this way: I didn't really do anything. No revolutionary change took place. I only reopened the option. It's up to you if you take it up or not."

A dusty bus stopped next to us.

"Let's go to Tel Aviv. We'll go somewhere for coffee," the guest decided suddenly. The landscape surrounding us – the drab apartment blocks, the wretched shopping centre, a grocery, a greengrocer's, a stationer's and an empty car park – depressed him to such an extent that he was ready to compromise on the plebeian mode of transport in order to change the scene. Presumably he also hoped that travelling in the bus would restrict my scope for further complaint. We got on.

I fixed my eyes on the back of the seat in front of me. It was scratched and peeling and in the middle someone had carved a crooked heart with two arrows sticking out of the side like two calcified arteries. The names of the lovers greedy for immortality were Ofer and Zahavit. I tried to imagine them in my mind's eye. It was easy. Ofer, a soldier in the Golani brigade with a shaved head, twinkling eyes and pimples, had a small Swiss Army knife that his brother had given him when he joined the army. Zahavit had a big bum and sickly sweet perfume and she knew all about the signs of the zodiac and astrology. They were on their way home from a night out in Tel Aviv, maybe a movie, maybe a club. From time to time she rested her head on his shoulder. They weren't drunk, but they laughed and talked too loudly. While Ofer carved the heart with their names on the seat in front of them Zahavit kept slapping his arm with her nail-painted hand in pretended, provocative rebuke.

The guest sat next to the window withdrawn into himself. He certainly wasn't amusing himself with fantasies about Zahavit and Ofer. His thoughts were too precious to waste on speculations about the sources of the vandalism on our public transport. A large woman with a basket from which peeped a bunch of coriander as big as a broom stood in the aisle next to me, holding on to the rail and assailing my nostrils with the smell of her body. I remembered a film in which the heroine said that if your boyfriend has the window seat in a plane and you have the aisle seat and he doesn't offer to change places with you it was a sign that he didn't love you, and suddenly I was flooded with profound sorrow at this sign, which although it wasn't in the least bit relevant to the situation between me and the guest, nevertheless rang true, for all its silliness. I began to feel the familiar lump forming at the bottom of my throat, the poisonous burning in my nostrils. I tried to control myself and think of something logical, or not think at all, but it was stronger than I was, and although I managed to hold back until we reached Tel Aviv, the minute the bus turned into Dizengoff Street I began to cry.

There were so many reasons for my tears that I succeeded in identifying only part of them. The other part glimmered fitfully, exposing one heart breaking detail after another, until in the end I was unable to tell what came first and what came last and I cried for everything at once, without any order or chronological

253

sequence or any other classification, and only a dull feeling, of pain, of sorrow, of infinite longing, combined all the reasons together and transformed them into a homogenous mosaic, parts of one whole, and saved my consciousness from being torn into shreds of madness.

I wept because I would never sit on a plane next to the guest, neither in the window nor in the aisle seat.

And I wept because I was white and stooped and encased in all my clothes, and it was years since anyone had told me I was beautiful, not even my mother.

And I wept because my father used to take a shower with me until I was eight years old, a big girl, and we would laugh and sing and my mother would shout at him, "This can't go on, Avram, she's a big girl now, in the end she'll have an Oedipus complex," and my father would lather the shampoo on my hair into a giant cloud and shout back, "Oedipus Schmoedipus, as long as she loves her father."

And I wept because Diti Vardimon's parents had caught us smoking when we were in the sixth grade and wouldn't let her be friends with me any more, and I was sure that we were being separated by force like some Romeo and Juliet and I would wave to her with secret signals in the playground, until one day I couldn't control myself and I waited for her, hiding from her parents behind the dustbins, and when she came home from her piano lesson I jumped out at her and said, "Diti, let's run away, let's go somewhere and talk," and she said she didn't want to, that now she was doing folk dancing and she was in the youth movement, and she felt that with me she had been phony, with the cigarettes and everything, and now she was sincere, and that it wasn't because of her parents that she wasn't friends with me any more, but also because of herself.

And I wept because during my father's illness, when Michael the gangster, who they said became a junkie in the end, would stand a few buildings away from ours and start masturbating when I walked past, I didn't even know who to tell, because my father was weak and not to be worried.

And I wept because of the time they sent me to a kibbutz for the summer and the kibbutzniks would stare at me when I entered the dining hall, because I had sandals made of silver mesh that my mother bought me in Tel Aviv next to the central bus station, which made them laugh.

And I wept because of that time long ago, even before the Intifada, when we went on a trip to Jerusalem and saw soldiers arresting an Arab boy next to the Damascus gate, and he stood there with his hands behind his head until they put him in the car and the people went on walking past and talking and laughing, glancing at him casually as if he was a hawker selling almond water or something even more banal and uninteresting. I tried to catch his eye so that he would see that I was good, that I was on his side, but his eyes full of hate slid over my face and I felt more ashamed than I had ever felt in my life.

And I wept for the time that I was in Tel Aviv with my mother and Nehama and together with a crowd of passers-by we stood and listened to a couple of street singers with guitars, a young man and woman from a foreign country, and a man came out of his shop and wanted to chase them away, and I intervened and tried to defend them and he said to me, "Shut up you bitch," and none of the people standing there said anything.

And I wept for how my father always defended me against my mother and even against my teachers if I talked in class or didn't do my homework and how he always took my side if I quarrelled with my friends, even if I wasn't right, not like my mother, who always wanted to understand both sides.

And I wept because of how we used to go to eat ice-cream in a café on Saturdays, my mother and father and me, when we were still a family and before I got so fucked up.

And I wept because I hadn't succeeded in preserving even a little of the strength I had when he was still alive, the feeling of being protected, the ability to face the world.

I wept for my mother's wrinkled breasts with the drop of ice-cream dripping into the cleavage between them.

And I wept because I was crying like an idiot and I couldn't stop, and the guest saw me in my misery, but the humiliating misery of self-pity and not the noble misery of poverty or mourning.

And I wept from inertia, tired out by my efforts to resist, throwing myself into a whirlpool of emotions and letting myself be swept up in it without a struggle, passive and powerless, my eyes dripping and my body limp.

The guest. Ah, the guest was already experienced, or at least he thought he was. At first he behaved naturally, completely ignoring my weeping, leading me down the stinking, sweltering street between people who in spite of living in the big city looked ugly and ground down by hard work, tired, sweaty people making their way through the hooting cars, the shops, the cafés.

"Should we go in?" he asked and without waiting for an answer he pushed me into the gust of cold air blowing out of the entrance to the air-conditioned Dizengoff Centre. Gripping my elbow, he led me through the winding corridors, slowing down next to shop windows that looked interesting, apparently in the hope of distracting me by a bit of window shopping. We stopped in front of a men's gift shop with antique globes, office accessories, lighters and expensive fountain pens. We stopped outside a shop selling towels and bathrobes where you could have your name embroidered on every item you bought. A shop that sold Persian carpets and Chinese vases. We stopped next to a shop that sold theatrical make-up, a shop for hikers in the mountains of Latin America, a shop that sold bridal gowns and even a sex shop, whose display window was hidden behind a dark curtain with only a small poster portraying dozens of different kinds of colourful condoms, as if they were toys for toddlers, betraying what went on inside.

All this time I kept on crying. The guest took absolutely no notice of my tears and most of the time he remained silent, apart from an occasional comment on the goods on display. His attempts to treat me like a normal human being touched my heart and made me cry even harder. After about half an hour of this he was fed up and he dragged me to an unappetizing little café with a counter holding huge cellophane-wrapped sandwiches. There were two little tables standing right in the passage, exposed to the passers-by. He ordered coffee for himself and mineral water for me and then he turned to me, abandoning his manful attempts to ignore my situation. And even though his words were rather mean, his distress was so sincere that the insult welling up inside me was replaced by pity for the guest at having to cope with a chaotic creature like me.

"Listen, I'm serious: stop crying . . . I hate it when women cry . . . what have you got to cry about? I don't understand it. You cry in idiotic movies, you see a beggar in the street – you cry, one word out of place – you cry. After fucking – you cry, you get a present – you cry, you see starving children on the news – you stuff your mouths with cake and cry. Now I see that you cry after seeing your social worker too . . . I don't know what to do . . . it's horrible . . . do me a favour and stop it, or this time I'll really kill you."

I nodded, sucking the cold water through the straw with slack lips, but even the thought of trying to overcome my distress increased it to such an extent that little sobs began to escape from my mouth and threatened to turn into a deafening wail.

"OK, OK," said the guest. "I've got a great idea. First we'll go and buy you some dark glasses, and after that we'll see what movies are showing downstairs and go in to one of them. How does that sound?"

Naturally the wretched Susannah Rabin wanted to take part in these attractive activities, especially since there was someone compassionate enough to invite her to join him in spite of her inappropriate behaviour. Yes, yes, I nodded, that sounds fine. Yes, indeed. I walked next to the guest, examining him from the side, trying to imagine what he looked like to all the people walking past. All the women. How handsome he was with his dark hair, the perfect cut of his nose, the clear grey of his clever eyes. What kind of a life was led by someone blessed with looks as unequivocal as his?

Beauty can stop the breath of the coldest, most indifferent people. Beauty can make people kill, abase themselves, write poetry, conquer countries. Beauty can drive people mad, arouse love, jealousy, envy. Beauty can bestow infinite pleasure. Beauty can reveal qualities in you that you never suspected, in the wildest of your dreams, that you possessed. Beauty has healing properties and sinister powers. Beauty is honey, poison, light. Beauty is the opposite of chaos. Beauty is the daily proof of the hidden existence of God.

These are facts known since the dawn of history. I wondered if Rivki had learned about them in her correspondence course on Plato.

Male beauty is rarer than female beauty, I went on musing. Men shy away from their own beauty. They hide it and cover it up. They undervalue it. In the hierarchy of male virtues beauty is relegated to the area of the unsound. The marginal.

But male beauty exists. In spite of the cloud of insignificance surrounding it, it shines out like a stubborn ray of sunshine on a stormy day. It demands its proper place, the place awarded it by the ancients, with no bones about it. It demands justice. And sometimes justice is done. Because justice too wants to come out. To be exposed to the grey light of reality. And although I once read in the newspaper that research showed that men possessed a more highly developed, almost genetic, sense of justice, while women were ruled by capricious emotions, it was clear to me that justice in the matter of male beauty would be done by women.

A little of this justice was done in the optician's we went into. Three female sales attendants, one middle-aged and two young, rushed to do his bidding. How much patience and sympathy these three women showed towards the handsome customer, who behaved like a terrible nag – he asked them to pull out more and more drawers of sunglasses, demanded to see the items on display in the window, upsetting the careful arrangement, decided to re-examine a pair that had already been returned to its place, and so on and so forth. I must have tried on thirty pairs of glasses, my face wet with the tears that kept on flowing without a break, until at last the guest set a pair of small, oval glasses with silver frames on my red, swollen nose, took two steps backward, gnawed reflectively on his right thumb, wrinkled his nose, sighed, kept quiet a moment longer, and then said, "I think that's it."

He threw his credit card on the counter and as he signed the bill with a careless hand I managed to catch a glimpse of a sum that seemed to me astronomic for so mundane an item. And then he looked at me again, gave me an exaggerated pinch on my wet cheek, and exclaimed, "You're a movie star."

The ticket booths at the cinema complex were open, but there was nobody in the queue. From the expression on the guest's face, as I read it from next to the stand of postcards where he had parked me, I understood that the film had already started. He waved to me and we hurried in, stumbling on the steps, groping our way through the popcorn-scented darkness. In the end, after I had almost fallen, crushing his toes, we squeezed into one of the first rows, too close to the screen, and sat down.

"I've been dying to see this for two years," whispered the guest, "cry quietly and look. This is a great movie." He turned his elongated profile to me and left me weeping in the dark, holding the smooth black case of my new sunglasses in my hand and feeling the legend on the lid, trying to identify each separate letter as if I were learning to read Braille. Dolce&Gabbana. My tears, which during the course of the purchase had turned into a quiet, steady flow, began to seek a new form of expression. It wasn't difficult. Show me a life, gentlemen, and I'll find a reason to cry.

On the screen two men were riding in a taxi and conducting a meaningless conversation about hamburgers. The black actor was unfamiliar to me, but I was horrified to discover in his partner the former star John Travolta, grown fat and old with long, greasy hair. I remembered the giant poster in Diti Vardimon's room, where he appeared in a magnificent white suit, his legs parted and his hands raised in a frozen dance step. I remembered how Diti and I had gone to see the movie *Saturday Night Fever* about seven times because we were both in love with John Travolta, she openly and I secretly. So secretly that I didn't even tell Diti, giving up the consolation of a shared sorrow, because I knew that I, the strange skinny Susannah Rabin, didn't have a chance of gaining his affections, as opposed to Diti, who was tall and had blazing red hair that came down to her backside and was already wearing a black bra in the seventh grade, and it was clear to both of us that if she ever met him he would fall in love with her at once, and therefore she had the right to fantasize about him and I didn't. We never tired of bad-mouthing the actress who played opposite him in the movie, she was so drab and ordinary in comparison to him, and Diti would spend hours at home practising the steps of his dance, wriggling her hips, churning her arms round, pointing her finger at the ceiling and singing, "Night fever night fever, we know how to do it, night fever night fever, we know how to show it," and every time we went to see the movie we would burst out laughing when he said to the fan he'd made love to in the back seat of the car, "What did you say your name was?" and I would pretend to laugh loudly, but in my heart I knew that if I ever met him and he deigned to notice my existence at all, this would presumably be what he would say to me too. "What did you say your name was?" And he wouldn't even ask me if I was any relation to, because what did he care about Israel and Rabin and the Six Day War?

At this stage of the movie Travolta appeared on the screen in the company of a black-haired girl he was taking out to eat in a restaurant. The girl behaved with spoilt arrogance and demanded that he take her on to the floor to compete in a dance contest.

And then I saw him dance again. The legendary John Travolta, fat, old, in his stockinged feet, in a stylish twist, lazily wagging his heavy bottom. What finally broke me was the gratified face of the guest as he gazed intently at the screen, and my great loneliness in the darkness, illuminated by a close-up of Travolta's new face, led to a stormy burst of weeping accompanied by little barks and loud sniffs, and the guest didn't even wait for the threatening "shhhhhh's" of the people around us in order to begin pushing me through the narrow space between the rows of seats with stumbling little steps, and when we found ourselves in the street, which was already dark but still hot and stinking, he shoved a lit cigarette into my mouth, lit one for himself, and led me to the other side of the street, to find a taxi to take us home, muttering in an almost indifferent tone, having finally despaired of me: "I'm finished with you. I wanted to see it. The last Tarantino. I missed it in New York when it came out because of all the work I was putting in and all the shit, and now you. You're finished, I swear."

The apartment breathed a pleasant, cosy dimness that spelled home. On the kitchen table we found a note from my mother saying that she would be back late and giving us instructions about what to take from the fridge for supper. I drank a glass of water and went into the living room. I sat down on the sofa and hesitated as to whether I should go to my room and finish the humiliating evening in splendid isolation, or remain where I was and go on dying of shame but with the consolation prize of the guest's company. I listened to the clatter of dishes in the kitchen, the fridge opening and closing. The beloved sounds of home. I huddled up in a corner of the sofa, trying to calm down. My crying was quiet and long devoid of meaning or content. All those memories, thoughts, chains of association of sorrow trapped in sorrow trapped in sorrow, had dissolved long ago and I was crying for no reason, hiccuping from time to time, wiping my nose on my sleeve, my eyes swollen and burning.

The light went on, startling me out of my limp, exhausted pose. The guest was standing in the kitchen doorway holding a plate of sandwiches in his hand. He advanced with a rapid step and stood in front of me, slamming the plate on to the coffee table between us. The violence of his movement frightened me. I sniffed, trying to make as little noise as possible, but it was enough to snap the patience of the guest, which in any case had lasted far longer than I had any right to expect.

"Stop crying, you hear me! Sorry for yourself, are you? Life's hard. What are you going to do about it? Life is terrible by definition. We were kicked out of the Garden of Eden a long time ago. Learn to live with the facts. OK, life's terrible, but human beings are drawn to the light. Understand? To the light! You think my life isn't terrible? It's terrible. But I don't ruin movies for people when they're dying to see them."

I was so startled by the suddenness of his entry and so shocked by his outburst that the question escaped me before I could take it back. "Why?"

"Why what?"

"Why is your life terrible?"

"For a million reasons." The guest sighed impatiently and looked round as if inviting an invisible audience to take note of my foolishness. "Because nothing in my life happened the way I planned it. Because all the choices I made were always, but always, for the wrong reasons. Because I've got no one to blame but myself. Because I'm stuck in Ramat Gan without a penny to my name. Because I owe a pile of money. Because I always owe a pile of money. Because I'm enslaved to some Armenian swine and I have to work like a dog for money that I owe in advance. Because my body's a total wreck from cocaine and cigarettes and stress that never lets up for a minute. Because I'm a compulsive gambler. Because I don't keep my word. Because I never did a thing for Herb. Because I hate my work. Should I go on? There's more."

His outburst was so emotional, so uncharacteristic, that I wasn't even insulted when he said that he was stuck in Ramat Gan. The things he said astonished me.

"I thought you loved your work. All those fascinating, unusual people, places, all that glamour."

For the first time since we met I heard the guest raise his voice. His barely perceptible American accent slipped out, giving his strange words an added strangeness.

"I detest my work. Understand? I de-test it! I don't feel any connection to it. Every day of my life I cast pearls before swine. Sell masterpieces to degenerates. Unusual people my eye! Moshe from El Paso. Meyer the jeans king. Nouveaux riches idiots! Baboons. And I drink with them, joke with them, crawl to them."

"Why are they degenerates? They buy works of art."

The guest laughed a nervous, artificial laugh.

"So what if they buy them? They don't understand the first thing about it. You know how they talk? Your ears would fall off if you heard them. But I go on licking their arses because that's how I earn my living."

It was a little chilling to hear these things from the guest, the prophet of freedom and independence, the wild anarchist, the spoilt child who wouldn't even say "Good morning" when he didn't feel like it.

"You don't have to talk to them. Sell them the paintings and leave," I said.

"You don't know what you're talking about. I have to keep my customers sweet. It's part of the deal. You have to make them feel they're rubbing shoulders with culture. Otherwise why should they buy? I go to Meyer, for example. Meyer is the self-made effendi of the jeans industry. I go to sell him two beautiful works by David Salle. He buys. But then he wants to talk. I'm part of his social life. Understand?"

"And what does he say?"

"Nothing humanly tolerable."

"Give me an example."

"You want an example? I'll show you an example."

The guest thought for a moment. Then he leant back, parted his legs and let out a long, repulsive belch. He lowered his voice an octave and his face took on a slack expression on the verge of idiocy.

"Jesus, Neo, I gotta tell you, boy, you put me on to a good thing with that Salle. I spoke to a couple of people, they tell me he's hot shit. If you get a line on anything else by him, tell me first thing. Even Claire said to me, let's put the smaller one, with the fanny, in the bedroom. She's crazy about it and believe me, is that babe hard to please or is she?"

The guest paused for a moment and examined the smile that had spread over my face without my intending it.

"You see the kind of people I have to deal with?"

"More," I pleaded, giggling in anticipation. The guest belched again and then spat, shooting straight into the ashtray. He went on with his monologue, probing his teeth with a hairpin he found lying on the table as he did so. His acting talent conjured up the

265

vulgar figure of Meyer the ex-Israeli jeans tycoon before my eyes as vividly as if I was sitting opposite him by the side of his pool in Long Island while he smeared himself with 15SPF suntan lotion, his 24-carat gold Magen David medallion hiding in the luxuriant growth on his chest like a mouse in a bundle of straw.

"But the truth," the guest scratched his balls, "you know who gets to me the most? Kostabi. Boy, that guy is really something. Made it big time, a financial genius. I'm telling you, that's the kind of guy I really take my hat off to. A stinking Greek, comes here without a cent to cover his arse, and look where he is today." The guest sucked his teeth and gave me a look of stupid admiration.

My laughter, which slowly lost its woodenness and flowed out, occasionally restraining itself in order not to disturb the performance, encouraged the guest, who rose to new heights of enthusiasm, inventing more and more disgusting acts, picking his nose, his ears, scratching his head. The enjoyment of an actor hitting his stride and successfully connecting with his character raised his performance to a peak of artistry.

"But what I don't get is the people. They buy pictures for the name, in other words Kostabi – and it isn't him who paints them? What kind of a mug's game is that? Let me tell you something, but the truth now. This whole business of what they call plastic art doesn't really grab me. You tell me Salle – OK, I go for Salle. Even though the guy's obviously sick. Hasn't he got anything in his head except for his wife's arse? Some bunch of flowers, some view, do I know? No, the guy's a sicko for sure, and I don't like it. No, give me a good movie, something with Robert de Niro, Harvey Keitel, there's a guy with soul, he's the one I like best, even some concert with Pavarotti, there's a voice for you, something else. It beats me why people are so crazy about all these

pictures by someone who can't even paint a girl in a normal way."
The guest paused, looked at his laughing audience, and said,
"And on top of it all, he wants me to marry his daughter. Should
I go on?" I nodded vigorously, snorting into my hand, like a
country girl at the harvest festival.

The guest sat down next to me on the sofa and put his arm
round my shoulder, alternately slapping my heaving back and
patting my thigh.

"Neo, what do you think of Elinor? Look how she's grown.
Isn't she gorgeous? Last weekend we threw a party for her
eighteenth birthday. Catering for a hundred people, sushi, the
real thing. Time flies all right, before you can fart the birds have
flown the nest. It seems like yesterday that all she could think
of was dieting and shopping, crying because they didn't choose
her for a cheerleader, and all of a sudden she wants to be a
businesswoman. You know what she said to me the other day?
Daddy, I want to invest all the money from my birthday on the
stock exchange! Believe me, that girl's something else."

The guest took a sandwich from the plate before us and began
to eat it with giant bites and his mouth open, making piggish
noises, with whole pieces of bread and cheese dropping from his
mouth on to his knees and mine.

"Elinor, come here a minute, I want you to show Neo your
tattoo! At first when she told me: Daddy I want a tattoo, I flipped
my lid – but her, when she sets her mind on something, forget
about it! Crying, screaming, and she says to me: But Daddy, only
a little one, a dainty one, just a little rose on my titty. So in the
end I said, OK, let her have her tattoo if she wants it so much.
So what do you say, why don't you take her out for a date, you're
a nice-looking boy, maybe she'll end up by marrying you."

The guest removed his hand and moved to the other end of the sofa. He looked at me writhing about, my eyes streaming, my hands clutching my stomach, squealing and gasping helplessly for breath, trying in vain to overcome the laughter that was shaking my stomach and breasts, filling me with an unfamiliar and exhilarating feeling of happiness.

"And now you're laughing. Didn't I say you were stupid? If you'd had the sense to watch the movie to the end you would have really had something to laugh about."

Mer-maid, Land-maid

In the interval between acquiring the icons and shipping them to the Armenian, the guest keeps them at Katyusha's because she lives on the eighth floor of a building with an intercom, the door to her apartment is steel-plated, and it is under the surveillance of a special security company. All of which, according to him, makes her feel safer. But sometimes, when he's depressed or fed up and his peace of mind is threatened by the Russian temperament of his friend, he brings them to us.

The guest, so he says, is becoming enthusiastic about Byzantine art. This is because he is finally beginning to understand the works of art he is purchasing, thanks to the expert knowledge passed on to him by Vadim the restorer. The guest tells me excitedly about Slavic iconography, and I too begin to grow enthusiastic about the paintings, sometimes peeling and in poor condition, which at first seemed to me simple and primitive. I have even learned enough to enjoy guessing when and where the works shown me by the guest were produced. Although most of the icons he purchases were painted after the Byzantine period they are still called Byzantine art because of their strict adherence to this tradition of painting. The main differences lie in the colours. Green icons, for example, were characteristic of the Moscow school. Pale, transparent shades of green were mainly used in the second quarter of the sixteenth century, and they grew darker, stormier and more violent during the second half of the century, when the methods of the Moscow school spread to local centres such as Novgorod and Pskov. The Madonna of Yaroslavl, on the other hand, dating from the end of the fifteenth century, is painted in delicate pinks, soft blues and watery orange decorated with gold. The infant Jesus presses his cheek to that of his mother, his hand touches her chin. Next to them stand Sts Zosima and Savvatei, with the Holy Trinity overhead. This is a delicate, lyrical painting. I would be happy to hang it over my bed, I say to the guest, and he laughs and immediately boasts of the bargain price he paid for it in comparison to what it would have gone for in a public auction at Sotheby's.

Both the guest and I have already developed a personal taste in icons. I prefer the paintings of the Madonna from the six-teenth century on, he likes stranger and more ancient things. His favourite is St Nikola, a bald old man painted in an archaic style – his head resembling a giant electric bulb, his look hard and probing, with the garish red background evoking an atmos-phere of menacing power.

But after a few days the paintings are shipped off, and we fall in love with the next ones, and thus there pass before our eyes John the Baptists, St Katherines, Georgis, Lukas, Andreis, Leontis, sad-eyed Madonnas, and of course – the face of Christ the saviour, Christ crucified, as the infant Emmanuel and as Pantokrator – the wrathful and merciful lord of the world.

In Byzantium, says the guest, the ideal was the preservation of what already existed. This was because of the medieval belief that from the moment of Christ's appearance on earth the world kept on getting worse. Therefore the artists took care to paint exactly as their predecessors had done. They tried to penetrate the secrets of their colours, kept strictly to the forms and gestures of their figures. Changes and additions were so minute that apart from the chronological age of the painting, which could be established by laboratory tests, experts like Vadim were required in order to perceive the developments and details that nevertheless distinguished one generation of icon painters from the next.

My ideal too was the preservation of the status quo, with slight modifications. From my point of view, the life of the guest in our house, the summer, the relations between us, and all the trifles revolving round this trinity, were eternal. A permanent model that renewed itself every day, with nuances imperceptible to the naked eye, just like the figure of the Madonna of Vladimir or St George with his sword, with their flat gaze, their stiff posture, their eternal meaning during hundreds and thousands of years of history.

But it is in the nature of things to move. To change. Everything flows, said the Greek philosopher. Sometimes the movement is minor, elusive, hidden from the eye, sometimes it is grandiose and full of drama. This way or that, it will always take place.

Katyusha went on holiday with Arthur to a spa near Prague, and the guest was entrusted with her white Golf for his unrestricted but careful (!) use. After he had driven twice to Haifa and back, and made several forays to Tel Aviv, he began to insist on driving my mother, in spite of her protests, to the Super Duper and the HMO clinic. It was clear that new reasons to use the car had to be found, and it was therefore decided to take a drive out of town. He and I. To an unknown beach. The guest's special beach.

The interior of the Golf had the intoxicating, synthetic smell of a new car. We set out in the afternoon so that it wouldn't be too hot and so that we would be able to see the sunset. My mother had provided us with thick sandwiches and washed fruit in a plastic box, but as soon as we left the crowded urban roads behind us and got on to the expressway, the guest directed me to open the bags on the back seat. I did as he told me, exclaiming admiringly as I did so – the bags contained three bottles of French wine and a bottle opener, a loaf of country bread, fresh baguette rolls and a vast assortment of imported cheeses and cold meats bearing the label of an exclusive delicatessen on their wrappings.

"Today we're treating ourselves, but without hurting your mother's feelings," the guest explained his surprise, smiling complacently as I removed one item after another from the bags and read the names on the labels out loud.

In spite of the blazing sun the guest opened the collapsible roof of the car and exposed us to the hot wind. His loose hair flew like that of an Indian brave galloping to the horizon, while mine, severely pinned back, tried desperately to remain within the confines of the little bun bouncing on the nape of my neck. The guest turned up the volume of the expensive stereo system until it was loud enough to be heard in the cars driving past us and sang along at the top of his voice, "spendin' most their lives, living in a gangsters' paradise". We were both wearing our sunglasses, just like the black gangsters in the song, and the air was full of one of the most intoxicating thrills in the human repertoire – the thrill of driving, and driving fast.

After about half an hour the guest turned off the highway and we drove down a narrow dirt track, raising clouds of dust, bouncing over low hillocks, surrounded by an expanse of grass and thorns burnt dry by the sun. A jeep full of soldiers drove past us and we waved at each other like a bunch of kids on a school hike, until at last, behind a ragged, dusty stand of eucalyptus trees, the sea came into view.

The guest had not exaggerated in his description, it really was a marvellous, broad beach with no breakwater to block the view. We advanced until the sand was so deep that the wheels began to grunt in resistance, spitting jets of sand in all directions and refusing to go any further, at which point the guest switched off the engine.

The sea lay spread out about a hundred metres in front of us, shining with a blue so dazzling that it looked artificial, exaggerated as a picture in a glamorous tourist brochure. Not far from us another car was parked with a little family beside it – a man, a woman and two small children running about with bright, plastic buckets. There were a few more cars dotted along the beach. Next to the waterline were three youths in a jeep. Despite these alien presences the beach looked almost empty, inviting in its rolling expanses, persuading us that it was private, special, chosen. Our beach.

In the meantime the guest had taken off his shoes and broken into a run towards the water, hopping like a grasshopper with his feet, burned by the blazing sand, high in the air, stopping from time to time to beckon me with vigorous waves and then continuing his grotesque, hopping run.

I got out of the car and gulped in the air, abandoning myself to the intoxicating feeling of freedom bestowed by nature on an urban creature like me with my polluted lungs. Immediately I wanted to stay here for ever, to stand bare faced opposite the sparkling expanse of blue, examining it through my sunglasses with the satisfaction of a wealthy landowner surveying his property, breathing in the faint smell of seaweed and observing the guest, who was already standing with his feet in the water, talking to the boys in the four-wheeler and waving to me alternately.

I began trudging towards him, feeling the heat of the sand through the soles of my shoes, embarrassed by my clumsy progress under his watchful eye. The sand was deep and dry and pulled me down as if I were walking through a swamp. I felt a trickle of sweat between my shoulder-blades sticking my dark shirt to my back, and I stopped to recover my balance. The guest looked at me uncomprehendingly and then set out towards me, this time at a more normal gait – apparently his feet had had time to get used to the inquisitorial heat of the sand – shouting unintelligibly, until he reached my side with a couple of final bounds, and before I realized what was happening he picked me up, hoisted me over his shoulder and carried me, collapsing under my weight, groaning exaggeratedly, calling me a "phlegmatic, spaced-out astronaut" and ignoring my embarrassed protests and nervous giggles, until we reached the place where the sand became dark and damp, next to the waterline.

"There, you can stand here," he announced, dropping me to the ground with an expression of relief. "And take your fucking shoes off, for Christ's sake."

The boys with the four-wheeler greeted me and I nodded in reply. Then they parted from the guest like old acquaintances, promised to come back later, and raced off along the beach, their bodies tanned, their hair and shoulders wet from the sea, their movements showing a calm confidence.

"What do you say, isn't it amazing?" demanded the guest and

without waiting for an answer he ran back to the car. He came back laden with things – the big piqué blanket provided by my mother, the bags of food, magazines to read, cigarettes, suntan lotion and a bottle of mineral water. He unloaded it all on the damp sand next to me, spread out the blanket and put things on its corners to stop it from blowing away in the briny breeze.

"Come on, grab hold of the other corner and put something on it. What are you standing there for like a mummy?" he scolded me when I showed no signs of mobilization, displaying the passivity habitual to my excursions to the beach with Nehama and my mother.

I broke into an awkward, guilty run around the blanket, picking up objects at random and handing them to him, until he dismissed my efforts impatiently, finished organizing everything himself, and then stood up straight, surveyed the results of his labours with a self-satisfied air, and commanded me with a regal gesture to park my bum on the blanket. I sat down and hugged my knees to my chest, trying to take up as little space as possible, while the guest, looking even more at ease than usual, took up his position at my side and gazed calmly at the sea, after which he took off his T-shirt with a leisurely movement and exposed his pale torso, unused to the Mediterranean sun, puffing out his chest and raising his arms at his sides.

I lowered my eyes although they were hiding behind the dark glasses, trying not to catch even a sidelong glimpse of this boastful, inconsiderate nudity, but in spite of my efforts I could sense in the vicinity of my left cheek the unzipping of the zip, one foot hopping on the sand while the other extricated itself from the stubborn trouser leg, the sound of the coarse jeans material peeling off the body, which was then lowered gently to my side – the body of the guest, abandoned and relaxed, spread over three-quarters of the blanket.

"Light me a cigarette, gorgeous," he commanded, pulling the latest issue of *Newsweek* out from under me and beginning to leaf through it, wrinkling his nose. I did as he asked, and after he took it from me I began to examine his bare back lying next to me, at first cautiously and then with growing confidence, as if I were examining a piece of evidence from a crime scene under a microscope. I felt like a voyeur ashamed of his squalid deeds but unable to stop, compelled by an impulse stronger than any moral conditioning. Now in the pitiless light I could see everything hidden from my eyes in the considerate dimness of our home. Down to the last pore. The guest's skin was as thin and delicate as that of a woman, with a mauve undertone, and in complete contrast to this delicacy the muscles on his back were prominent, well developed and highly visible due to the leanness of his body. I discovered three pinkish pimples under his right shoulder, and a few beauty spots and freckles scattered about with a chaotic lack of symmetry. A downy growth of dark hair began low on his spine and disappeared under the elastic band of his swimming trunks.

I went on examining this defenceless back, scrutinizing every square centimetre as if it contained the answer to my agonized yearnings. Perhaps my salvation would spring from there – in the horrible, monstrous shape of the flawed human body. Now I would recoil in disgust, now I would be cured of my addiction! If anyone could do it, I could. But the longer my inspection of every flaw and sub-flaw lasted, the more intense my yearning grew, and the more inappropriate its objects. Every new discovery of a scratch, an insect bite, an unruly, misplaced hair, filled me with growing compassion, with a great tenderness and a strange pain, until I was obliged to close my eyes and bury my face in the inhospitable angularity of my raised knees.

Even after he got up and ran to the sea, revealing his nudity in motion, my salvation did not arrive. Although he had lost the protective armour of his clothes and he was too pale and too thin and showed brutish signs of maleness such as hair on his legs and even, alas, on his chest, his human beauty still cried out aloud in the salty sea air.

Suddenly the sun began to set, like an actor making his entrance when the curtain goes up and the play finally begins, after the audience has begun to grow bored and rustle sweet papers and read the programme notes for the third time. The sun swelled and turned orange, steeping the beach and the people on it in an atmosphere of awe. The couple near us called their children and gathered them close. Those scattered further afield could be seen too quietly organizing themselves in obedience to the age-old laws of the cosmos, one of the most basic of which is the awe that overcomes the human ant at the sight of the sunset.

The guest abandoned *Newsweek*, soaked with the salt water dripping from his hair, and sat up. We unpacked our bags and opened the first bottle of wine. Every time, before passing it to me, the guest would rub the mouth of the bottle with the palm of his hand in a symbolic gesture of politeness, to remove his spit. I was too shy to follow his example. We sat side by side and gazed in front of us, silent and solemn. The sun went on setting, refusing to disappear into the water. We opened another bottle of wine. The couple with the children began getting ready to leave. The sea gave up bits of seaweed coloured a shiny, artificial green. The August air stood still even here, innocent of any hint of a breeze, and only the darkening sea gave off a promise of freshness and coolness.

And afterwards all that was left was a film of orangey blue above the horizon, and the beach emptied of all its few visitors, except for us. We didn't stop drinking and smoking cigarettes, clinging to our little urban sickness, as if, were we to stop, we would merge into this sweeping oceanic idyll and become nothing more than a couple of grains of sand lacking any distinction or importance.

The guest stood up and said, "I'm going for a walk on the beach. Maybe I'll find those guys with the four-wheeler." His receding silhouette grew small and dark, and I thought: Why is he so unhappy? Even I, with my pathetic little life, feel that I have a place under this setting sun, while he doesn't seem to feel that he belongs even to the world that he's supposed to be a part of. And I thought: Why is he doing what he's doing with me, talking to me, showering me with all this charm and sweetness and kindness, shaking me and waking me up as if I'm his equal, a gallery owner or a model? Why does he make it seem a matter of life and death to him for me to behave like a normal person, with the strength to do things? What does he need it for, what can he gain from someone as plain and pathetic and peculiar as me?

And I asked myself: And you? What do you want from him? And this time too the answer was the same, clear and unequivocal: I want to drink his blood drop by drop. To wrap my arms and legs around him, to press myself to his chest until his heart beats in time to mine and then to stick my teeth into his neck. To feel the skin resisting and tightening, to deepen my bite until it tears, to taste the sweet wetness on my lips and then to attack with all

I've got, my tongue probing the stripped flesh, my mouth locked round the wound, choking on the force of the jet gushing out of the slashed vein, sipping and swallowing more and more and more until my thirst is slaked.

I finished off what was left of the wine.

I stood up, swaying on my feet. I was very drunk. The wine we had drunk like water in the face of the little spectacle God had put on for us had done its job. My feet were almost in the sea, black and dark, betraying itself by its incessant murmur and the white foam of the low waves of the incoming tide.

I know what I am, I thought. Now I know: I'm a vampire. All I want to do is drink blood, I even wanted to bite Gidi Bochacho's dog to death. A sinister, morbid creature. A creature who doesn't want a real life. Who doesn't want to fuck. Who doesn't want to get married. Who doesn't want to have a career and wear tailored suits. Who doesn't want economic independence. Who doesn't want to eat health food and work out. Who doesn't want to contribute to world peace. Who doesn't say "No" to terrorism. Who doesn't donate to the soldiers' benefit fund, or the fund for disabled children. A kind of bat. The bat-woman of Ramat Gan. An apolitical comedy in one act that lasts too long.

"Jesus," I said aloud and laughed. I took a few steps forward and felt the water seeping into my shoes. It was pleasantly tepid, inviting in its steady movement, full of life. I stooped down and dipped my hand in the water. Then I licked it. It tasted faintly of decomposition, testifying to the billions of minute organisms filling the infinite expanse opposite me. Organic compounds of molecules, single-celled, dual-celled, sea urchins, medusas, fishes, dolphins. A giant womb in which life came into being by parthenogenesis, by sperm sprayed on to eggs laid in coral reefs, in foetuses curled up in the depths of the bellies of great mammals, in miraculous creatures like sea horses which fertilized themselves. A vast multitude of life forms coming into being according to their inexorable laws of procreation, never still for a moment.

I took a few more steps. The water now came to above my ankles, dragging the hem of my skirt down. My shoes were heavy and waterlogged, sinking into the sand, full of broken bits of shells.

And what about the sirens? The licentious mermaids who enchanted even the wily Odysseus with their voices. How did they reproduce? Did they have a cunt, excuse me, private parts, excuse me, pudenda, excuse me, a vagina, excuse me, a female sex organ? Oh God, why wasn't there a word to describe this place without making me blush for a different reason every time I did so – for the rude vulgarity of "cunt", or the old-fashioned absurdity of "private parts", or the priggish primness of "vagina"? But why worry, I never had much of an opportunity to discuss this organ, and to my mother I simply said "pipi". Mother, make an appointment for me with the gynaecologist, I've got an infection in my pipi again. We're a really cute couple, my mother and me, no doubt about it.

I walked further in. Already I had to exert strength against the waves, pushing with my stomach and rowing with my hands. My skirt swelled up like a kind of wet balloon, a tricot growth on the body of the siren Susannah Rabin. I squashed the ballooning skirt with my hands and pushed it down until it yielded, absorbing the water, and sank with heavy submission into the sea. I had neither a vagina nor a pipi, I had a fish's tail covered in silver scales – that's what I have, Doctor, shall I lift it up? Open it? Do

I make you think longingly of Friday night gefilte fish? Sorry, that's what you get when you make the kind of career choice you did, looking at cunts, sorry, vaginas, sorry, female genitalia, every day. Would you like to hear a joke, Doctor? A blind man passes a fishmonger's and says: Hi, girls! So it isn't a chauvinist joke about the smell of what-do-you-call-it, like you always thought, no, it's simply about us sirens.

I heard myself laughing rudely among the waves.

The water was nearly up to my chin and I had to jump up with every wave in order not to swallow it. On one of these jumps, when I dropped softly down again, I didn't feel the bottom. And after a moment I touched it again, groping with my leaden shoe, but this time in order to feel the ground beneath my feet I had to hold my breath and let my face sink into the salt water, which at this depth was far less tepid, with deep cold currents sliding over my body.

After that everything turned into a vortex of water and foam and salt and stinging bitterness in my throat, and my body in its wet, heavy clothes no longer in control, no longer arrogantly facing off the waves, and the voice of the guest, small and distant, first on my left and then on my right, calling in broken syllables "Su-sa-nnah", dying away and coming back again, without an echo, swallowed up in the tempestuous breath of life of the sea. And all the time the nagging thought: The sirens, where are the sirens, where are those dirty whores, those irresponsible bitches, why don't they hurry up and take me and put a stop to all this unpleasantness for ever?

And afterwards I threw up in gushing jets while the guest held me from behind, crushing my stomach, after bringing me out to the dark shore. Oh my sweet Odysseus, who goes on holding me close after my body has stopped convulsing, stroking my forehead, loosening the superfluous pins in my bedraggled hair plastered to my head and rolled up in a wet lump like a floor rag. I could have gone on standing like this for ever but he suddenly cried – "The blanket!" And we both ran to save the blanket with our possessions from the rising tide. The guest insisted on carrying the bundle by himself, looking back from time to time to make sure that I was behind him, keeping me close to him with a rhetorical, "Are you all right?" We spread the blanket out next to the car, on the dry sand which was still hot. The guest got into the car and switched on the headlamps and when he came out he examined me in their deathly light, as if he was examining the puddle made by a pedigree puppy for the tenth time that day. He seated me on the blanket, handed me a lit cigarette (an out-of-place habit of intimacy he had brought to our relationship from relationships with other women), lay down on his back next to me and stared at the starry sky, and only then he said in a tired, dreamy voice, "This time I'm really going to kill you. That's final." And he also said, "Jesus."

And I said, "I haven't swum in the sea since I was sixteen."

Although it seemed that half the night had passed, a glance at the clock in the car showed that it was only eight o'clock. After a short consultation with himself held by the guest in my silent presence, it was decided that we should stay a while longer, in order to forget the traumatic event and get back on track as normal, civilized people enjoying a pleasant evening on the beach. We opened the bags which had not been completely drenched by the sea and began to eat, silently breaking off pieces of baguette with our fingers and passing each other the various kinds of cheese. We must have been very hungry, for even my mother's thick sandwiches received our attention. The sweetness of the summer evening relaxed our limbs and worked its soothing magic together with the food and the third bottle of wine, which to my surprise the guest agreed to share with me despite the bitter lessons of our recent experience. After we had finished eating he switched off the headlamps and left us in the deep violet blue of the night.

We had nothing to talk about. This was a situation with which we were both familiar and with which we felt quite comfortable, sitting and staring into the darkness, each sunk in his own accustomed loneliness.

The guest broke first.

"If you think you've got a chance in hell of my letting you ruin the very expensive upholstery in Katyusha's very expensive car with those wet rags you insist on keeping on your body, you're very much mistaken," he announced.

I knew he meant what he said. In spite of the heat in the air my clothes hadn't even begun to dry, wrapping themselves sourly and clumsily round my body, like seaweed round a drowned sailor's corpse. I remained meekly silent.

"Do us all a favour and take them off. Spread them out to dry on the hood of the car. I'll turn my back, OK? Nobody will see you." He turned his back to me ostentatiously, making fun of my shyness.

The wet clothes seemed to sense the horror about to overtake me and refused to part from my body, sticking and tangling round my head, my shoulders, my ankles. I battled against them in silence, trying not to pant with effort.

My heart, aware of the guest's physical closeness, was beating like a drum roll in a circus during the execution of a dangerous acrobatic trick. Tum-tum-tatum. Bam-bam-babam. The animal tamer with his moustache and velvet trousers puts his head into the lion's jaws. Naked and violently agitated, I lay down on the blanket and tried to calm down, abandoning myself to the touch of the hot night air on my skin. I crossed my hands over my pelvic bones, which stuck out like a shark's fins.

"You know where we should have been, you and me?" The guest paid no attention at all to my nudity and spoke as if continuing a previous, private train of thought.

"Where?"

"In Alexandria. At the turn of the century. I once read this terrific book. We should have been a brother and sister travelling in the Orient. Probably English. Rich. But not too rich. Too rich would be vulgar. We would stay in a luxurious apartment-hotel, with mute Sudanese servants in white kaftans. You would draw and I would write travel notes. At night we would wander round the city, smoking hashish, frequenting dark, sinister clubs intended for decadent Europeans like us. Going to parties thrown by wealthy local nabobs. Having affairs. Drinking tea on the roof in the mornings. What do you say? Do you have a favourite time that would be more suitable to your destructive personality?"

I couldn't think of anything to say. I remembered a rerun of a programme about the history of the universe on the Discovery channel.

"I'd like to live in the prehistoric swamp where human life came into being."

The guest turned round and lay on his back next to me, his eyes fixed on the sky.

"Sounds interesting, if stinky."

His indifference to my physical presence was insulting, to say the least. But why should I be surprised? What did I expect? That he would fall on me passionately like a Latin lover? That he would do sweet perverted things to me like a sophisticated Frenchman? That he would tremble at my very proximity like a virgin school-boy? How repulsive I must be. Even though according to all the spoken and written reports men were unable to resist the sight of a naked woman, however ugly. Lies upon lies.

I turned on my side and leaned on my elbow. I stared at the calm face of the guest as he lay on his back. My nakedness no longer embarrassed me, it was as neutral and empty of content as a cardboard box. The nudity of a big, twisted plastic doll.

"Neo."

"What, honey?" he said in a low, relaxed voice, almost a whisper. He didn't turn to look at me.

"I want to ask you something."

He nodded and closed his eyes.

"Do you think that anybody could ever be attracted to me, anybody normal that is?"

"What kind of a question is that?"

The irritation in his voice boded no good. He turned over and lay in a pose identical to mine, face to face. Now we lay facing each other like a couple of Greek philosophers holding a pleasant twilight conversation. Except that one of the philosophers asked stupid questions and the other one was angry.

"I . . ." I wanted so much to skip the stammering, to say what I had to say straight out, however hard it was. "It's just that I know, that is, I think, that I'm repulsive. Very repulsive. And you've got a lot of experience, and you know about these things, so I thought you could tell me." That was it. The words were out. I heaved a sigh of relief.

"What do you want me to say to you? You want me to flatter you? To console you? To contradict you? Eh?"

I felt myself blushing. It was just as I had feared. Now he was cross with me, and rightly so. How hypocritical my question must have sounded. I had no idea how to convince him of my sincerity.

"I don't want you to console me. I just want you to tell me what you think."

My meekness didn't help. The guest's sails swelled belligerently.

"What do you think, that only attractive people fuck, fall in love, have children? Have you lost your wits completely? You know that's nonsense. It's so obvious that I don't even want to waste my energy on the words."

I nodded silently, ashamed of myself. It was obvious, of course, but it wasn't what I meant. But how in the name of God could I explain what I did mean? I could only hope for some superior, super-subtle understanding. How demanding and deceptive was the need to be understood. More seductive than love, than happiness, than the supple and glorious body of the guest. And the fate of this need was always to be frustrated. To end up with precisely the same longing as it had started out with, in spite of all the acrobatics and heroic efforts at communication on the way. I knew this.

So why was it so hard for me to accept the fact that I would never be understood? Anyone would think that I had been indulged in this respect in the past and it was difficult for me to adapt to the deterioration in my circumstances. Whereas, in fact, even the almost wordless understanding I had with my mother was a fiction. A kind of habit fostered by a rhythm of life in which the changes were so few and the routine so well oiled that it wasn't hard to maintain the illusion of mutual understanding.

I knew that the fate of humanity in general in this respect was no happier than mine. I knew that an abyss of misunderstanding gaped even between the closest of friends. Sometimes, in rare moments of grace, this abyss narrowed to a crack, but it very soon opened up again, leaving each alone on his desolate cliff.

Nevertheless I wanted desperately to be understood by the guest.

The guest began to speak again. This time there was a conciliatory softness in his voice – perhaps he was afraid that I would start howling or run away to look for sirens in the depths of the sea. And perhaps he was simply sorry for me.

"If you want to know what I really think, I'll tell you: in my opinion there's nothing's that's exclusively repulsive or exclusively attractive. In order for something, or for the purposes of the present discussion, someone, to be attractive, there has to be something repulsive about them too. The repulsive implies the existence of something that's dangerous to you, and if you feel that something puts you in danger it means that you're attracted to it, no?"

"But only some people are attractive," I said.

"Who, for example?" the guest snapped as if I had said something that challenged an absolute truth and at the same time insulted him personally.

I wanted to say "you" but I couldn't. Then I wanted to say "Katyusha" and again I couldn't, as if involving other people in the discussion would remove it from the category of the personal, belonging exclusively to him and me.

"Come on, give me an example," he insisted.

"I can't think of one at the moment," I said evasively, "but there are people like that. It's a well-known fact. All kinds of models and TV hosts."

"Who told you that only they were attractive?" The guest's voice expressed profound contempt. His vehemence excited me, as if it contained some incontrovertible proof that he really cared about me and he wasn't just throwing himself into a theoretical debate with his usual verve. "And who told you that they were attractive to begin with? Try to remember the things you were attracted to in the past. That aroused and excited you. Weren't you ever attracted to anything repulsive?"

Now of course I could have spoken to him about what had happened with the dog. About the unseemly excitement I had felt when I was almost torn to pieces. But it was too sick, too deviant. Presumably, in spite of the sharp and dangerous edge to the discussion, what the guest expected from me was some confession about being attracted to an ugly boy or something human of that nature.

"Maybe. Sometimes. But my feeling is that there's something unnatural about it."

"That's exactly what I'm trying to tell you – there's no such thing as 'unnatural'. It's absurd. Things are many-sided, ambiguous, don't you know that really? Nothing that's homogenous, even beauty, can ever be as powerful as that place where all the conflicts come together – repulsive and attractive, beautiful and ugly. There's nothing that isn't beautiful. Only we find this fault with ourselves – ugliness. The flawed has tremendous power. It's the place where we fall in love. Where we lose our senses. It's the most erotic thing there is. Fuck it, who the hell wants perfection any-way? Not only in looks, in everything. Even totality isn't perfect."

He fell silent and waited, but I didn't open my mouth. I agreed with every word. But it wasn't the blessed agreement that kept me from reacting. Oh no. What made me keep quiet was shame. Shame stemming from the recognition that the guest had been right in his initial, angry diagnosis, and that all I was really fishing for was for him to say that I, Susannah Rabin, was OK. Acceptable. Not utterly disgusting. That I had beautiful eyes or hair, that I was tall, or some other rubbish – he could always find something, like my mother and Nehama did when the occasion arose. There's a whole arsenal of compliments for plain women. I knew a lot of them. I would even have made do with "special". Even "interesting" would have satisfied me in the circumstances. I was ready for any crumb he threw me. He had wasted his pearls of wisdom on me in vain. My wishes exposed themselves to me in all their lowness.

"So what do you think?" He was waiting for a response to his ardent monologue.

What could I say?

"It's all very theoretical."

"Theoretical?" The guest shot up next to me, his face examining mine in the darkness. "What are you actually saying to me? What do you want, you crazy girl? Tell me. For us to start fucking? To have an affair? Would that be practical enough for you? Have you gone completely mad? We're blood relations. You're my sister! I'll go away at some point or other. What do you want to happen? Hey? Theoretical she says. Jesus!"

I turned my back to him and curled up in the foetal position. I could sense him standing up and afterwards I heard him shaking the sand off his clothes and putting them on briskly and crossly, concluding as the teeth of the zipper snapped shut with a hiss.

I felt so empty and despairing that I have no idea where I found the insolent words I addressed to him from my curled-up back.

"With your sister you can drink tea on the roof in Alexandria. I'm your second cousin, that's all, and I don't want a thing from you."

It was quiet with that night stillness which is never really still. Somewhere behind me the guest was standing, dressed, shielded and beautiful. Between us lay a space and a time which however beautiful were not intended for us. I remembered how Nehama always said, "I'll be happy in the grave."

Suddenly the thought of home and my mother and Nehama and Armand seemed almost consoling. Definitely preferable to this spectacular setting of the sea and the dark night and the star-studded sky, where I lay curled up like the drunk usher who fell asleep on the stage in *La Traviata* in one of my father's theatre stories.

A warm dry hand touched me and turned me over on to my back: Oh poor astonished Susannah Samsa, and the guest gripped me under the armpits and lifted me up, stood me on my feet and led me a few steps backward, in the direction of the car, until my bare bottom touched the metal, where he lifted me into the air again and seated me on the hood, simultaneously sweeping my damp clothes on to the sand, after which he stroked my cheek lightly with the back of his hand, as if to signal the opening of a new dialogue between us, utterly different from the one before.

I sat opposite him with my knees apart, my feet resting on the bumper, and he put his hand on the inside of my thigh and stroked it gently, as if it was a Persian cat, his invisible look focused on mine, revealed by the light of the moon.

I leaned slightly backwards, trying to remain upright, not to slip, letting him stroke my inner thigh with lascivious slowness, pressing my hands to the warm hood. Would you believe it, my siren sisters? The "special" Susannah Rabin had seduced the handsome guest. I wanted to laugh and naturally I wanted even more to cry. How ambivalent is victory. The joy of achievement immediately diluted by the terror of what is to come. Time, however fictitious, has laws of its own. It is never satisfied with the status quo. It strives to fill itself with event, invites action, and we obey it like slaves. It is beyond our will. It simply happens.

The guest's hand made its way from my knee to my crotch, closing in on me, barring the last, secret escape route. As if someone had opened my chest and touched my heart, my lungs, my blood vessels with naked hands.

I shuddered at the alien touch as at a sudden, startling noise.

The first impulse was to brake, to stop the invasion. To kick him with a bare foot and drop quickly to the sand, cover myself with my damp clothes, and turn back the clock! With a heroic effort I mobilized all the self-discipline at my command. Be still! Be still, Susannah. Sit still, foolish woman, fear junkie, let things happen, let life show you its real face, however terrible it may be. Isn't this the thing you wanted most of all? And as in those idiotic seventh-grade English lessons on television, I said to myself "Look and Listen" and abandoned my body to the touch of the guest, listening as his fingers crossed the permitted boundaries and made for places even I wouldn't have dared to touch myself, groping with surprising delicacy, like the fingers of a blind man over the face of a beautiful woman, assessing their location and gradually beginning to move with confident skill, giving off the bitter smell of the hundreds of women who had preceded me.

I looked at the guest's face, trying to make out the expression in his eyes in the dark, but all I succeeded in sensing was the serious concentration of his breathing, and I wondered what he was feeling and thinking and whether in spite of all his years of erotic experience it didn't disgust him to touch me and all my gaping female wetness. I tried to remember how it looked and felt, but the memories were so distant, somewhere in the first years of high school on the big double bed in Diti Vardimon's parents' bedroom, with her father's little shaving mirror and blurred images of a kind of strange exotic sea creature or the mouth of a carnivorous tropical flower, and afterwards the memory of the touch of Dr Arika the gynaecologist's latex-encased fingers, a touch which didn't really remind me of anything except for the paralysis I imposed on myself in order not to get up and run away.

My thoughts returned to the present, where I found my tense body seated with its legs apart on the hood of a car while the royal hand of the guest made itself at home between my thighs. I felt my face stretching in a stiff, unnatural grimace, until I was obliged to push my forehead against his shoulder, hugging his neck with my hands, as if I was trying to hide what was happening to me from myself. I didn't understand exactly what was happening because it didn't look like anything I'd seen in the movies or read about in books, and only the hot steamroller in my stomach and the muscles stiffening in my legs and back persuaded me that it was something human. I didn't even know if it was pleasant or terrible, there were too many elements involved in this event for me to be able to isolate the pure element at its core, and I only clung more and more tightly to the guest's neck, pushing my forehead harder and harder into his shoulder as if my life depended on it, until I felt a shock wave jolting me out of my skin, and the tension relaxed, fading slowly away like the warmth fading from the body of a person who's just died.

Afterwards I sat hunched and shivering from time to time, and the guest stood next to me and gently patted my back as if I were a child who had behaved heroically while the nurse was taking blood from my vein, until the shivering passed, and then he said with a down-to-earth sweetness that immediately banished the embarrassment that prevented me from raising my head, "Come on, let's go for a walk on the beach." I said, "Then I'll get dressed first," and he said, "Don't bother, your clothes are still wet," and he picked them up and threw them back on to our multi-purpose hood.

We walked almost joined together to the waterline, the guest in his clothes and me naked, embracing. A naked woman and a clothed man. At first we walked silently until the guest, who as usual spoke first, began to tell me about all kinds of difficulties he was having with the Armenian, and how he had sent back three icons because they were in worse shape than they seemed in the slides he had received in the mail, and I asked, "Are you worried then?" And he said, "I'm always worried," and I thought how much I wanted him to be happy, and how I had no way of making his life happier because I was – me.

We went on walking and I asked him if he'd had a lot of women and he said, "For God's sake don't start one of those after sex conversations with me," and I said, "But I don't know what you're supposed to talk about afterwards," and he said, "I'm sorry, I'm sorry," and then he said, "I've had fewer women than you might think, but I was with one woman for a long time, which is what counts," and I asked, "Did you love her?" And he said, "I think so," and then he laughed. "What's certain is that she loved me, a lot." I wanted to know if she was beautiful. The guest thought a minute as if this question had never crossed his mind before, and then came up with an evasive reply: "She's a lot older than me, almost twice my age," and I asked, "What's her name," and he laughed and said, "Why do you want to know?" And then he said, "Miriam. Her name's Miriam." And then again, as if he liked hearing the sound of her name, "Miriam Sullivan."

Afterwards he detached himself and splashed me with his bare foot and I shouted, "Stop it, idiot," and he began to run away and suddenly I remembered how young he was, younger than me, only twenty-eight, a baby. And perhaps because of this when we turned back in the direction of the car I gathered the courage to ask him, "Why are you so nice to me? Where do you get the patience for all my problems? After all, you're quite screwed-up yourself." And he hugged me hard, too hard, as if we had just finished a naval officers' course, and said, "Are you crazy? You're my Byzantine Susannah, you're my magic charm. I love you most in the world."

We returned to our blanket. The minutes ticked by slowly, holding us in the enforced calm of people on the run who had finally reached a hiding place and were basking in the short, artificial freedom granted them, talking and falling silent by turn.

We drove back with the roof down and without music. The guest drove with quiet concentration, turning his elongated profile towards me, occasionally giving me a penetrating look. I stared at the road, trying to get rid of a silly childhood song, another one of the chants the children used to tease me with, which kept on coming back and buzzing in my head, refusing to make way for more suitable thoughts. The coincidental compatibility of the words with what had actually happened made the silly song even more mocking.

> If you love her
> Don't be shy
> Take her to the beach
> And show her what you've got
> Tell her Oh Susannah
> Don't you cry
> I love you a lot
> And that's the reason why
> I want to marry you.

And so on and so forth, with the words "marry you" occasionally being replaced by a version regarded at the time as more insulting, "fuck with you". Today, presumably, things were different. Completely different. Did the guest want to fuck with me? I had no idea. Oh Susannah.

The dark entrance to the building smelled strongly of cat pee. We climbed the stairs and stopped in front of the door. Suddenly I was afraid. It was late. I was wet and wild and sinful, and I was about to meet my mother. I looked at the guest, seeking reassurance. It was his role to confront the authorities, to hand out explanations, to smooth rough corners. But he leant against the banister and showed no intention of taking command. The light in the stairwell went off. He pressed the red switch to put it on again and resumed his former position. I stood in front of the door, filling with more and more anxiety in anticipation of my transparency under my mother's appraising eye. I looked imploringly at the guest again, begging him to rescue me, but he only narrowed his eyes and then, accompanying the order with a commanding jerk of his chin, said, "Go!"

I pressed the bell button.

In a loose dressing gown disclosing the broad white night-gown underneath it my mother looked like Medea in her madness. In the dimness of the passage behind her I caught a glimpse of Armand, making it clear that the graph of her panic had jumped far higher than I could have imagined. According to the protocol observed in our parts, Armand was summoned only in cases that bordered on emergency. Her opening words "Have you taken leave of your senses?" were only an introduction, an overture containing hints of what was still to come. We were led into the living room so that she could acquaint us with the entire course of her thoughts from the afternoon on, and unburden herself of the full weight of her anger.

"I simply didn't know what to think. So late. I woke everybody up. We were just about to phone Armand's brother in the police, otherwise they only start looking for missing persons after twenty-four hours, and his brother's a Chief Inspector. Nehama's hysterical too, we've been on the phone all the time."

She went to phone Nehama, to tell her the news. We were left standing in front of Armand in embarrassed silence. What must he think of us? My clothes were creased and dirty, my hair was loose and wild. I was exposed and ashamed, while the guest stood to one side and chewed his thumb, waiting for the moment when he could retire to his room, far from all this family commotion, which interested him as much as last year's snow.

It was only when she returned from reassuring Nehama that my mother had a chance to examine me, which she proceeded to do, measuring me from top to toe, after which she stepped up to me and felt my wet clothes. Then she looked sternly at the guest, refusing to be seduced by the ingratiating expression he usually assumed after some trivial wrongdoing, such as throwing out the paper before she had read it or forgetting to buy milk. She looked from me to him and back again, like an archaeologist examining a wall covered with hieroglyphics which she had no trouble reading.

"So where have you been all this time?"

"At the seaside." The guest made a mistake and smiled.

"Till now? And why are you wet, Susannah? What happened to your hair? Did you go into the water? Since when do you go into the water? And what about a bathing costume? What's there to do on the beach at night for so many hours? And where's the blanket? I nearly went out of my mind. How could you behave so inconsiderately?"

She didn't expect an answer and went on hurling rhetorical questions at me, abandoning in her anger our usual ethical code, according to which explanations about important things took place in private, between me and her. She talked and talked, refusing to spell out what appeared clear and obvious: that if she stopped she would be forced to see the truth, which was so awful and inconceivable that it was better to concentrate on our irresponsibility and lack of consideration for her in coming home so late, on my ruined clothes. Anything rather than the thought that the worst of all had happened. After finishing with me she rebuked the guest with a hard expression on her face, without a trace of the affectionate indulgence she usually displayed towards him.

"Neo, I must ask you to behave more responsibly from now on. We don't have many rules in this house, but I expect you to respect the few we do have."

"I'm really sorry, Ada. It was just such a warm, lovely night. We had a wonderful time. It's true we forgot about the time. I'm sorry you were so worried."

The last thing on her mind was to hear about how we had enjoyed ourselves. The fact that we had been enjoying ourselves while she was worrying herself sick was even more infuriating than the lateness of our return. But she had already said what she had to say. Anything further would only detract from the eloquence of her rebuke, and she sank into her armchair with the expression of one whose sufferings would never, but never, be fully understood, and sent us on our separate ways with a sullen "Go on, go to bed."

I lay on my bed in my wet clothes without switching on the light.

What did the guest think of me?

What did he want from me? What did I have to give him?

In The Heat Of August

I try to remember when I learned to say "no" to life, that same life which is so desirable a product in the eyes of others. When I decided finally and hermetically to close the iron door of the basement in which I live and from which I survey the outside world through a periscope. I have no answers. I can identify moments, glimmerings of decisions throughout the time I have spent here, on our sinful globe. I recognize turning points. The deepening of knowledge. I have no dates.

Somewhere in the receding dawn of my childhood I understood that the world was a terrible place. This didn't happen because I experienced abuse or trauma that wrecked the foundations of sunny optimism on which I was supposed to build the rest of my life. My biography is drab and ordinary, innocent of those personal experiences full of the drama of evil, that harden the heart. I was never beaten, oppressed, tortured or made to suffer beyond the usual degree which is the lot of all mankind. My parents were as good to me as they knew how, I can't find any real answers in their human failings as educators and child-rearers.

So, when did the embryo of renunciation begin to take shape

inside me? Who set me on the path to where I am now, contemplating life as if it was a picture in an exhibition?

Perhaps it was the first mosquito crushed by my chubby, childish hand and the close examination of the squashed insect on the wall, its torn-off legs stuck to a reddish-brown bloodstain, with the knowledge that it was my blood it had sucked doing nothing to alleviate the horror rising in my throat like vomit?

And perhaps it was the child Eviatar, the son of our friend from the farm, who showed me how he fed his tame hawk with live chicks, and I watched with a frozen heart as the bird of prey in its elegant leather collar bit off their heads, and the balls of yellow fluff went on hopping and jumping about for long seconds in their demented death throes?

And perhaps it was the run-over body of the tabby cat right in front of our house, the sight of its innards spilt on the road in a wet mess? Perhaps its intestines poking through the torn fur? Its gaping head? Its milky, glassy eyes?

And perhaps it happened when I was taken to the emergency room when I succumbed to food poisoning at a summer camp between the second and third grades, and the open curtain next to me exposed a four-year-old toddler sitting bowed over on the high hospital bed and between his delicate shoulder-blades, which looked like a pair of undeveloped wings, was the undeniable crimson print of an iron?

Perhaps it was my father's head bald from the radiation, swaying on his shrivelled neck when we went to visit him a few days before he died?

And perhaps it was simply the result of accumulated information about great and small acts of injustice, oppression and evil, about wars, about hospitals and prisons and entire countries full of human beings suffering unbearably? The inevitable outcome of the human screams that fill the air wherever you turn and that my ears did not know how to muffle?

And so I have to answer unequivocally. I don't know when it all began.

I turned off the apparatus of my will little by little. Heel to toe. I was happy to do so. I wasn't calculating. My intuition led me surely through the winding corridors of the labyrinth. I knew that I was doing the right thing. I couldn't do otherwise, nor did I want to.

There was love. There was love in me. For example, my love for my mother. But in my heart of hearts I despised this love and was disgusted by it – it was just another expression of that loathsome, covetous will, which appraised everything according to the degree to which it could serve me. Supply my needs. Act as a means of survival. Of course, there was also my mother's love for me, but I sometimes suspected that her love too was contaminated by practical considerations which were out of her control – she was human too, wasn't she?

The only purity was in contemplation. In wonder. That was how I once felt about the guest, aeons ago, enchanted by his physical beauty, his charming ways, his polished speech. But that was over. Finished. Instead of wonder I felt only desire. A terrible yearning which I had dared to express and which had submitted to my will. Like a dolphin caught in a tuna fisherman's net I had been thrown terrified, gasping for breath, on to the polluted shore of desire.

Not to want anything from him but his continued existence in the world. Did he want anything from me besides my continued existence?

I had to return to my previous purity in relation to the guest. But how?

My war was a war of surrender. Surrender was the only way I knew. It had power and it had served me faithfully always, so why not now? I would surrender to my desire, I would let it overcome me to the bitter end. And then I would be cured. This was exactly how I had rid myself as a child of the craving I developed for honey cakes. I demanded of my mother that she bake me one every day, and she would say: What's got into you, child? In the end you'll get sick of them. But I stood my ground, filling my mouth with the sticky brown slices, until the day came when I couldn't even stand the smell of the honeypot on the breakfast table.

Of course, this decision was ridiculous, absurd in its very claim to be called a decision. As if I had any other option.

I had no other option.

I no longer cared about anything. Nothing could restrain my craving for the guest. I even gave up the need to disguise it. From now on the surrender and I became one. The surrender was me. I was the surrender.

On the days following our trip to the sea I didn't take my eyes off the guest as long as he was within my range of vision. He was in a bad mood, he looked depressed and uninterested. At first I was afraid that it was connected to what had happened on the beach, but he rid me of this fear the very next evening. I bumped into him in the passage on his way from the bathroom, giving off a warm, damp, scented smell. He put his hand on my shoulder and asked, "Are you all right?" And even after I had nodded eagerly, he went on examining my face, searching for signs of hidden distress, and in the end he said, "If you have any bad thoughts or anything, tell me at once."

I hoped that his depression would soon go away, as had already happened in the past. But this time it was more persistent. On a walk we took one evening he told me that the Armenian had returned two more paintings, and he felt that his labours would never end, as if he had made a pact with the devil himself, like some fucking Faust. In the mornings he continued to get dressed neatly and go to town in pursuit of his affairs, with his hair still wet from the shower, and in the evenings we watched television or played chess. I was careful to let him beat me whenever I could, but this too brought him no joy. Our conversations turned on his reports of the progress, or rather the lack of progress, in his affairs. After exhausting the list of people with whom Katyusha had put him in touch, he was hard-put to find any further sources of icons rare and precious enough to satisfy the demands of the Armenian. I wondered what had happened, what had changed recently to make him so preoccupied and lifeless, and I came to the conclusion that more than any objective increase in the severity of his problems, he was simply tired of disguising his distress, just as I was tired of disguising my own. Now that we both knew each other so well, we could take off our masks and rest.

It was a relief. At least for me. Faithful to my decision, I cast off all restraint and abandoned myself to my addiction to his presence, trying to soak up his existence inside me, to poison myself until there wasn't a single cell of my body that wasn't completely saturated with him. I tried to spend every minute I could in his company. The guest showed himself open to my purpose. One afternoon he even took me to Tel Aviv with him, to Shalva the Georgian's dusty shop in Ben Yehuda Street. We went on going to the Super Duper to do the shopping together, filling the trolley with the items on my mother's list under the eye of Armand, who had recently become reserved and correct and had stopped greeting me in French. But for the most part we just sat in his room, drawing or reading from the anthology of English poetry, while he made me laugh with rude and ridiculous interpretations of words I didn't understand.

And my mother. Ah my mother. The day following our return from the sea, I learnt that sometimes the intelligent detective has only to lean back and listen to the nervous chatter of the murderer in order to reconstruct the event in full. Somewhere in the depths of his sinning soul the criminal will always long to be caught and thus be cleansed, even if partially, of the guilt weighing heavily on his heart. And the nature of love, at least in this sense, resembles that of a criminal act; even a love which is secret, forbidden, whose very existence depends on its remaining hidden, will always long to be revealed – by a careless embrace next to a nosy neighbour, by a couple of tickets forgotten in the back pocket of the lover's jeans, by a cigarette stub of the wrong brand in the family ashtray, and above all, by its own ostentatious nature, which craves witnesses, as if the moment love visits the happy pair of mortals their lives turn into a work of art, a theatrical performance thirsty for an audience, a poem, which, however conscious of the miracle of the act of creation itself, still longs to boast of the results. For otherwise even the greatest masterpieces would rot deep in the desk drawers of their modest creators.

My love too was subject to this cruel law. And who, if not my mother, the person closest and dearest to me, knows how to provide me with an audience? And so, without her having to ask me a single question, I couldn't stop talking about our trip to the sea, adding more and more trivial details, beating about the bush, dwelling on descriptions of the beach, the boys with the four-wheeler, reporting innocent snatches of conversation, making acrobatic efforts to dispel any hint of suspicion and, of course, achieving the completely opposite effect. And the longer I kept up these compulsive ramblings, conscious of the paradoxical effect they were having, the less capable I was of stopping. The pleasure of talking about the guest was addictive. The need to talk about the object of my love, which for lack of any confidantes had remained unsatisfied, burst forth and dulled my wits in the joy of confession.

My mother listened with half an ear, busy about her usual household tasks, giving me the impression that she had swallowed my innocent version of events, as if we were talking about the annual excursion of a group of religious Girl Guides here, but the days to come showed that the information received had been sorted, processed and analysed very thoroughly indeed, the appropriate conclusions had been drawn, and an alternative programme of activities for the wayward Susannah Rabin had been formulated. She put on a show of being preoccupied and out of sorts, insisted on my accompanying her on her chores even when I had no desire to do so, didn't stop complaining about all kinds of aches and pains, and even forced me to go to our dentist Dr Malul with her and watch while he lanced an abscess on her gum. To her credit, it must be said that for the most part she was satisfied with indirect distractions, except for one day when she was apparently particularly nervous, and when she saw me making for the guest's room with a drawing pad and pastels she actually barred my way with her body and said, "Leave Neo alone now. Go and occupy yourself with your own affairs!" And she refused to budge until I gave in and returned to the living room.

Nehama, on the other hand, was getting better all the time. She no longer used a wheelchair, but she still needed supervision so that she wouldn't fall down the stairs again, and my mother spent long hours with her, grumbling that nobody helped her and insisting that I accompany her on their walks in the park. And so, reluctant but surrendering to this reality too (which was, after all, part of the greater, sweeping reality), I would trail behind them stunned by the sweltering August heat, while they strolled up and down the same ten metres, Nehama's shrunken hand hooked in my mother's elbow.

Here I have to point out that all this bothered me a lot less than might be supposed. And no wonder – my usual alertness to my mother's moods had dulled due to my vigilant attention to the guest. I had no room to hear or see anyone else. I was almost completely empty of the nagging sensitivity which had always been my lot and had made me experience the feelings of those around me as if they were my own. I was brimful of the guest.

In the hours of his absence from the house I would steal into his room, look at his scattered belongings, touch his pillow, his still damp towel, the useless American coins lying on the desk, examine the view from his window in the attempt to merge with him and identify with him down to the last detail in his field of vision.

When he was at home I would stare at him while he was watching television, putting something on a shelf out of my mother's reach, reading, talking on the telephone. Sometimes he would catch me at it and, smiling, shake his head, or pass his finger over his throat to show me what I could expect if I didn't stop. He was prepared to bear the burden of my lust for him, and I felt more grateful to him for this than for anything else he had ever done for me.

At night I suffered torments with the sheets wound round my sweating body – a giant grasshopper trapped in a spider's web, raped over and over again by the memory of that night on the beach, as if it were a scene from a film shot tens of times from different angles and now being screened before me without my being able to take my eyes off it. I tried to reconstruct the way he had touched me by myself, but it was crude and barren, empty of the added value of the otherness of his presence. I was more revolted by my body than I had ever been before. I loathed its demandingness, its active existence, busy as a swarming anthill. An existence which would not be ignored. I stood under the shower for hours, stroking my belly, my breasts. A number of times my mother opened the door, as if by chance, and every time our looks crossed like swords, empty of any mutual understanding. I had no inner space to think about what it meant. What she felt or thought. I set her aside as if I was putting my sweaters away on the top shelf of the closet for the duration of the summer. I consoled myself with the thought that it was only temporary.

Miserable and happy, bemused by the unfamiliar weight of feeling, I discovered how being flooded by emotion blurred every concrete wish and purpose, set me afloat on the surface of existence like an abandoned dinghy. The self-absorption imposed by my situation was no less repulsive than the crude demands of my body. The never-ending contemplation of "me me me me me" wore me out, as if I had been forced to look at the photograph album of some boring relation (here we are next to the Leaning Tower of Pisa, here we are at the Louvre, here we are on top of fucking Kilimanjaro).

But above all I was troubled by the unhappiness of the guest, an unhappiness I already knew so well that even when he put on his polished, cosmopolitan self, even when he drew rude caricatures of the poet Shelley, his wife Mary and Lord Byron with bare, hairy bums and engorged sexual organs, even when he made his comments on the evening news, denouncing the complacent left, contradicting my mother's arguments, admiring the autumn collections of Vivienne Westwood and Alexander McQueen, then too his distress cried out in countless signs and signals, breaking my heart, torturing me with my helplessness and lack of initiative, which for the first time in my life struck me as a real disability.

The movement from myself to the guest and from the guest to myself made me dizzy. But what could I do, Susannah Rabin the greenhorn, the siren, the mermaid, the virgin of the sea, the virgin of the land? When you surrender to reality and throw yourself on your back in a self-inflicted knock-out and lie there staring at the sky, be ready to be dazzled by the twinkling light of the stars.

A week, or a year, or an eternity later, the guest went to Haifa to try to persuade the brother and sister to sell him more paintings. They were his last hope, he told me the day before. Otherwise he would be the Armenian's slave till the day he died. Oh Faust.

I woke late from a bad morning sleep that failed to make up for yet another sleepless night. The guest had already left. The house greeted me steeped in a mixture of stillness and heat. August was everywhere. In the sun spitting through the slats of the closed blinds, in the oppressive gloom lurking in the corners, in the familiar household smells transformed by the heat into a suffocating, overpowering miasma. Hiding between the walls of our house August betrayed its presence like a plague betrayed by the dead rats in the stairwell.

My mother wasn't at home either. Reassured by the guest's absence, she had taken pity on my sleep and gone out to do her chores without dragging me along. I wandered from room to room, enjoying the touch of the tiles on my bare feet and the fact that I had the house to myself. I couldn't remember the last time I had been alone at home. Since the arrival of the guest my eternal sanctuary had turned into a glass cage exposed to the eyes of the world. I peeped into his room in order to absorb the daily chaos, to examine the nuances in the dispersal of his belongings: the massing of the Benson & Hedges stubs in the ashtray, the cascade of crumpled sheets sliding from the bed to the floor. I tried to reconstruct with their help the nocturnal choreography of his sleepy body. A still life innocent of a paintbrush. I lingered for a long moment on the threshold and decided to postpone the physical examination till later – the guest was not due back until the evening of the next day. I had plenty of time to indulge my fetishistic addiction.

My mother's room spoke of order and routine, the polar opposite of the guest's picturesque mess. The double bed was made, the floral cover stretched smooth, the pillows symmetrical, the simple, old-fashioned dressing table displayed a single bottle of scent – a monk in isolation on a Tibetan mountain – and a decorative carved wooden box (a souvenir, Nehama, a trip to Romania).

I examined the medicines on her bedside cupboard. I picked up and returned to its place the half-empty glass of water, I glanced at the weekend supplement of the newspaper. After a slight hesitation I decided to go through the drawers. They contained dozens of female articles lacking in femininity – needles and thread, silk stockings which had seen better days (in case they ever came in useful), more medicines, an enamel necklace (a gift, my father) a broken gold watch, buttons of different sizes (in case they ever came in useful), a pair of scissors, an old address book, something Chinese and stinky for backache, an embroidered velvet purse (a gift, Armand, birthday). I remember how I had longed for these objects throughout my childhood, regarding them as a precious forbidden treasure which only rarely, when I was ill or as a prize for good behaviour, I was allowed to raid at my pleasure. Oh Susannah, all grown up and disillusioned now.

My father's bedside cupboard, like a dried-up widow, boasted a huge, shining cut-glass ashtray on a lace doily, which only served to stress the absence of anyone to use it. I wanted to throw myself on to the big bed and roll around on it, another of those forgotten childhood pleasures, but the thought of straightening out the cover afterwards – a complicated task demanding patience and co-ordination – made me desist. Nothing in my mother's room told me anything about her beyond what I had always known. I opened the fitted cupboard, door after door, inspecting the clothes, the bedlinen and towels neatly arranged on the shelves. Hanger after hanger of floral dresses, pastel blouses for festive occasions, winter coats smelling faintly of mothballs, passed before my eyes like one-dimensional silhouettes of my mother. When I reached the drawer where she kept useless gifts in order to pass them on when the occasion arose, I recognized immediately the fancy shopping bag lying on top. The bag containing the presents the guest had brought us when he came. I pulled out the grey dress and the scent bottle in the shape of a female torso. I fingered these alien objects delicately, as if I were touching the guest himself. I sprayed some scent behind my ears, unfolded the dress and held it up against my body in front of the mirror inside the closet door. How out of place it seemed in its narrow-strapped airiness, like a cloud of artificial smoke.

I couldn't help thinking of the crazy bag lady I had once seen in the street in Tel Aviv. She was pushing an ancient, overloaded pram and rummaging in the garbage bins. Her age was unclear, her mouth almost completely toothless. She was wearing layer upon layer of faded, unclassifiable rags, except for the baseball cap on her head. This was brand new, bright orange, with the logo of a foreign oil company, apparently the donation of some compassionate tourist. And although I knew it wasn't nice to stare at the maimed and the mentally ill, I couldn't stop staring at that lousy baseball cap boastfully proclaiming its bourgeois sanity on the head of that beggar woman. I wanted to snatch it and run, to save her lost-lost-lost honour in the eyes of the passers-by, but of course I did no such thing (I'm Susannah Rabin aren't I?). For weeks afterwards I remembered that baseball cap. And now it rose before my eyes again, redolent of family barbecues and healthy children with computers and roller blades in futuristic designs. I quickly pushed the dress and the scent back into the bag and closed the cupboard door.

I went on wandering round the house, eager to assert my rights of sole ownership to the full, even looking into the toilet, inspecting the water dyed a poisonous blue in the lavatory bowl, overturning with my foot a forgotten magazine lying unhygieni-cally next to the cleaning brush, eyeing the friendly farmer's face of the US President. In the living room I stroked the hard heads of the Bavarian man and woman and greeted them with a "Sieg Heil", I switched on the television. I zipped through the channels until I stopped at the Discovery channel. And guess what? Certain kinds of small fish change their sex from male to female when they feel the need to reproduce. Was the opposite possible too? To change from a little female fish into a little male fish? If only I could change into some cheeky, cute-arsed Ronen or Nimrod Rabin, I would strut round the world driving salesgirls in optician's crazy, adopt a world-view full of sex appeal, maybe neo-Marxism, or even better, nihilism. On the other hand, who could promise me that I wouldn't turn into someone like Armand and have to get up every day at five o'clock in the morning to open the store? It's impossible to know anything in this world any more, I said to myself, repeating the sentence Nehama was in the habit of pronouncing when some fact or other (a mistress, plastic surgery, a criminal past) about a neighbour or a public figure came to light and upset her previous opinion of them. I turned off the television and stared into space. No, it was impossible to know anything at all in this mixed-up world any more.

I wandered into the kitchen. I inspected the full fridge, took out a peach of giant dimensions, swollen with hormones, and sat down at the table. I leafed indifferently through the dismantled newspaper (the guest's patient hands, the newspaper, my inner thigh, my racing heart: stop it, disgusting Susannah), glanced at my mother's open mail – accounts, bank statements, a flyer advertising a manicurist-pedicurist beautician. Another letter from the bank, this time addressed to me, the annual report on the state of my savings account, a newsletter about the activities of the community centre in September–October, another advertisement, this time a brightly coloured promo for a new pizza joint – open twenty-four hours a day, a letter from the municipal water department confirming the installation of a separate meter for the apartment.

The essence of my life lay spread out before me on the

table, depicting its drabness with the minimalist precision of a powerful artist.

Life is terrible, said the guest. Every life. His. Mine. But people are drawn to the light. I don't even know where to look in order to find the source of that fucking light. The difference between us is that he has himself. His problems are outside himself. As soon as they're solved, he'll be able to carry on as if nothing has happened. And me? Can I solve myself? I felt angry with the guest for daring to compare my chronic misery with his temporary, almost accidental misery. All he needed, in order to reorganize his life, was money. Nothing but money. To pay back his debt to the Armenian and all his troubles would be over!

In my heart of hearts I knew that I was making light of his character, and that the financial difficulties of the guest, trailing behind him as endlessly as the train of Princess Diana's wedding dress, were only a natural extension of his troublesome self, like a misshapen hand or a six-toed foot, or even something more bizarre, like a tail. But this thought was completely unhelpful, and I pushed it aside and concentrated on the problem at hand.

Money. All his declared problems began and ended with money. Because of money he was stuck here in Ramat Gan, forced to chase after all kinds of shady Russians only to discover that the icons they were selling were poor forgeries or dated from the last twenty years. Because of money he was forced to smoke two packs of cigarettes a day, to be depressed and despairing.

I flipped though the pile of mail on the table and took out the savings account statement. One hundred and twenty-one thousand shekels. Or one hundred and thirteen thousand, if I decided to withdraw the money now.

It was an account which my mother had opened for me

313

years ago. I couldn't even remember when exactly. A modest sum, deposited when she received her reparations from Germany, which had grown over the years. We had never actually considered taking the money out of this account. There had been times in the past when we had thought of it and wondered if we should put the money to use, but that was in the days when there was still hope that I would fit into the mainstream of life like a normal person and need money for things like college fees, or even as a down-payment on a small apartment of my own. But the more these life opportunities dwindled the less we thought about the savings scheme, until in the end it turned into one more piece of official business, automatically renewing itself every two years, leading an independent life of its own parallel to ours, like some distant relative sending an occasional reminder of their existence in the shape of a New Year greeting card, only to be forgotten again until the next holiday comes round.

Unlike the rest of our meagre possessions, this account was in my name. My father had insisted on this formality. For some reason it was important to him to emphasize, however symbolically, that this money was mine alone. At the time it had seemed a charming caprice, one of the many that characterized him. Everything we possessed belonged to us all in common. My mother had the slight advantage of being placed in charge of our financial affairs, thanks to her skills in conducting a dialogue with reality, skills which neither my father nor I possessed to the least degree, but it would never have occurred to any of us to think that any part of our property belonged exclusively to them.

I paged rapidly through the newspaper, looking for the rates of exchange. More or less thirty thousand, I made a quick calculation in my head. Thirty thousand dollars that belonged exclusively to me. Exactly the sum mentioned by the guest when we went to visit Katyusha. This was the sum he owed the Armenian. Presumably part of the debt had already been repaid on account of the work he had done during the past three months. Great. That left us with change. Room to manoeuvre. Air to breathe.

I was so excited that I had to get up and walk around a bit and then sit down again and get up again. My heart beat as if at the sudden slamming of a door, the thrill at the birth of a brilliant idea going hand in hand with anxiety about its expected results.

Thirty thousand dollars. How cheap redemption was. I lit a cigarette and went back to restlessly pacing the length and breadth of the apartment, which in the blink of an eye had been emptied of the dense heaviness filling it only moments before, and was seething with restrained energy dying to burst out, without a quiet corner for rest and thought.

And what would happen to me? After he had paid his debt to the Armenian there would be no reason for the guest to prolong his stay with us, a stay which in any case had lasted far longer than expected. Of course, I knew that the time would come when he would have to leave, but the more the days went by, creating more and more points of contact between us, the harder it became for me to imagine the inevitable future, until I reached the stage when I was completely incapable of preparing myself, even by imagining the worst, for our anticipated parting. Our steadily developing relationship changed the scenario so many times that I could no longer conjure up any realistic picture of the future and I stopped thinking about his departure altogether.

In the light of the new situation, I could no longer avoid confronting the facts.

He would leave. And what about me? What, in the name of God, would become of me?

I went to his room, took off my clothes and got into his bed, straightening the tangled sheets as I stretched out. I closed my eyes and tried to calm down.

I could, of course, give up the whole idea. Who said that I had to rescue him from his financial difficulties? Me, his poor relation? I could forget the idea before I did anything about it.

I ran these thoughts through my mind, inciting myself against him, formulating arguments, elaborating justifications, but even as I did so I knew: my efforts were in vain. It was too late. I wouldn't be able to live with the knowledge that it was in my power to help him and that I had refrained from doing so, it would be a crime against the moral code governing my inner relations with him. The kind of behaviour prompted by calculations of profit and loss that belonged to other, awful people. The people I had been running away from all my life. It had nothing to do with my love for the guest. In spite of all the reasons I could come up with for retreat, there was only one right thing to do. I had to give him the money.

And what about me? I asked for the umpteenth time.

I could go with him. To New York. Why not? We would have a little money left even after he had paid off his debt. I could use this money to find my feet. Hadn't he himself brought up the idea of us living like brother and sister in Alexandria? That was a fantasy, of course, but why not take it seriously for a minute?

No, I had no intention of forcing myself on him. Although our relations went beyond any definition that I knew, I would be quite content with the relations between brother and sister. I wouldn't be in his way. He could live his life exactly as he had always lived it, and I would be there, by his side, far from my mother, true, but I was sure that when I wrote and explained she would understand. In spite of the worry that sometimes blinded her and clouded her mind, she was so sensible, so open. Who understood better than her that there were innumerable ways of living this short life of ours? Didn't she herself always say that all ways of life were equally legitimate as long as they didn't hurt anybody?

And over there? What would I do there? It was so hard for me to fit into the outside world. All my previous efforts had failed. But, on the other hand, I had never had the compelling motivation I had now. On the contrary, on all the previous occasions I had had to put myself through endless mental acrobatics in order to find any justification at all for taking part in the violent, uncompromising activity of the outside world. Now I had all the justifications in the world. Perhaps I could find work in Nicky and Sandra's gallery, office work, even cleaning. I wouldn't turn up my nose at anything. And perhaps they would agree to teach me how to dress and do my hair. Maybe I would even have it cut in a fashionable little haircut.

I could start painting and sculpting seriously. Dedicate myself to something I had never dared really to commit myself to. Maybe there, far from home, far from the sticky, suffocating drabness of my present life, I would find the courage I needed. Maybe I would study part-time under some painter or sculptor. I would do whatever it took to make the guest proud of me. I would be his most loyal, undemanding friend, he would be delighted to have me there. Of course he would, he was so lonely, in the final analysis, in spite of all those people around him. We would go and visit them all, so that I could get to know them personally, Nisim Babjani, Andrei Troikorov, even Meyer the jeans man and his daughter Elinor with the dainty rose tattoo on her tit, and Moshe from El Paso.

And of course Miriam, Miriam Sullivan. She would open the door to us, tall and statuesque, with a wide jaw and full lips like Liv Ullmann, wearing black trousers and a tight polo-necked sweater, strands of silver in her well-groomed hair. I would say to her: Miriam, I've heard so much about you. Perhaps they would get back together and I wouldn't be jealous because it would be completely different from what there was between us. We would all love one another, and perhaps Miriam would even be a bit of a substitute for my mother, whom I would certainly miss badly.

My thoughts drifted into daydreams. Fantasy pursued fantasy, rising in stormy waves, reaching their climax and smashing on the rocks of the impossible. So it went until I fell asleep, and when I woke up I saw my mother standing over me, holding the sheet that had covered me in her hands, her face more sad than surprised as she inspected my nakedness. The same strange sadness was in her voice when she asked, "Susannah, what are you doing here?" I mumbled something about resting in a cool place and she said, "What are you talking about? This is the hottest room in the house, get dressed," and she walked out of the room, leaving the door open behind her. I was grateful to her for not staying to humiliate me with her looks while I got dressed, which would have been typical of her.

When I joined her in the living room, all buttoned up, I was ready for anything she dished out. Injured innocence. This was the policy I had decided on while threading my legs through the opening of my waist-high cotton panties (oh nymph, oh diva). Not a very sophisticated strategy, to be sure, but now that I knew I was about to leave my mother in the lurch, it wasn't the right time for frank and painful confessions. Yes, I knew I tended to hang round the guest too much, especially lately, but let's not forget that it was she herself who had been so keen on the idea of us becoming friends. We enjoyed each other's company because of our common interest in art. And after all, he was the only relation of my own age I had. Thanks to him I had made a lot of progress in my drawing and I was in a good mood, and in general – as I saw it – our relations were only part of the whole wonderful family relationship in which she played as full a part as I did.

Mother, mother, our love for each other is a tangled Gordian knot, about to be cut with the axe of my betrayal. I stepped into the lion's den with the calm confidence of a trained spy, his true identity hidden under a disguise so perfect that not even the most up-to-date methods of interrogation can expose it.

But my mother had no intention of talking about the guest. Or about him and me. And instead of clarifications and didactic lectures she hugged and kissed me as if she hadn't seen me for weeks. And then she said that she felt she had been neglecting me lately because of Nehama and everything, and that she wanted to make it up to me and for us to be together because she really missed me. She had never been so sentimental, and I, already rehearsing our impending separation, responded with all my traitor's heart. We went together to the kitchen and made ourselves an early supper, acting in perfect co-ordination. She soaked pieces of matza in eggs and fried them and I stirred cinnamon into cream cheese, added sugar, and threw in some raisins. My mother told me proudly about her triumphs at the municipal water department and the cancellation of the inflated bill. How proud she was that although she was already retired she could still pull strings in her historic place of employment. I showed a keen interest in every detail, asked questions, laughed at her descriptions of her toughness with the clerk. Afterwards we ate and chatted, just like old times, predicting the apocalyptic future in store for the country because of the new regime. We washed up together – me soaping the dishes and my mother rinsing and drying, and then she asked me if I felt like going to see a film in Tel Aviv, just the two of us, and was there anything special I wanted to see? And I said: Sure, why not, how about the new Quarentina, Neo recommended it. And she looked for it in the paper and said there was no such movie, maybe it hadn't come here yet, and I said: Never mind, you choose, whatever you like, and she said: Maybe that Danish film, *Breaking the Waves*, they say it's excellent, and I said again: Whatever you like, I really don't care, and she said: It starts early, I'll call a taxi because today we're celebrating, and I said: Great, cool, just like the guest.

We drove to the Tel Aviv Cinematheque and saw the movie about a feeble-minded girl in a remote village in Scotland and her boundless love for her paralysed husband. When the lights went on some of the people stayed in their seats as if they were afraid to break the spell and return to the little everyday pain of living. Couples sat dotted round and I heard weeping on my left and right and saw women with their shoulders heaving, grieving like widows identifying their dead on a battlefield, lamenting their lives, their female nature that was stronger than a thousand years of civilization, a nature which had once been glorious but had gradually lost its dignity and turned into the greatest symbol of weakness. Their partners comforted them speech-lessly, hugging them like helpless children, at a loss in the face of this powerful female grief.

My mother too cried terribly, howling uncontrollably, exactly like she had cried after Rabin was murdered. I patted her back until she grew a little calmer and then I led her gently out. As we were standing in the plaza outside the Cinematheque we met Rivki with a curly-haired boy wearing little glasses and a ring in his ear, and Rivki said, "This is Ido, he presents the weather reports on the Bat Yam cable television," and then she noticed my mother's swollen eyes and cried, "Oh, Adaleh, you're crying, don't tell me it's because of the movie! I was just saying to Ido that with all due respect to love, no woman should abase herself like that for a man."

In spite of her tears my mother was so incensed by these words that she turned angrily on Rivki and said, "Really, Rivki, do me a favour! What's it got to do with what a woman should or shouldn't do? Sometimes that's just the way things are, what did you expect, a WIZO propaganda movie?" Rivki was offended: "I don't know, Adaleh, I have a problem with the message, but then I'm a fanatical feminist so you can't take me as an example for everyone." Then she turned to me and put her arm around me and whispered, "Well, what do you think of Ido, isn't he cute? You see, sweetie – it's only artists for me." She went on to say, "I want you to know that I haven't forgotten about Rosh Pinna. But I'll only be able to set things moving in October," and then the curly-headed Ido interrupted her and said, "Come on, Rivki, I'm parked on the pavement," and we parted from them.

When we got home we took out the bottle with the remains of the cognac that the guest had brought when he arrived. We settled down on the balcony with cigarettes, grapes and salty little bagels – to break the taste of the alcohol, and my mother told me for the millionth time about how she had met my father and how handsome and mad he was. This time the story had a different flavour, full of new layers of meaning. After that we reminisced about the two of them, the three of us, about me – how a picture I drew in the fourth grade won first prize in a worldwide children's competition, how I had once painted in gouache all the pages of the Chamber Theatre's income tax returns which I had taken out of my father's briefcase. My mother recalled that Nehama had read about an interesting private collection on show at the museum in Jerusalem and suggested that we drive up to see it after Armand fixed his car, which had given up the ghost again, and I confided my idea of making a series of miniature sculptures of legendary beasts to her, and I also told her, with an enthusiasm springing from an unclear source, about the tragic life of Jackson Pollock, and how he had started his career with figurative paintings which while competent were not particularly original, until he developed the unique individual style that made him the greatest of all American painters.

We sat and talked until late at night, and after I had already gone to bed she came into my room, sat down next to me in the dark and stroked my head. "My gifted little girl," she said, "it's wonderful that you have your art." I wanted to tell her that I didn't have any art and I never had had, that I was just messing around and distracting myself, without daring even to think of painting or sculpting something with true, serious intention, because that was meant for noble beings and not frightened little worms like me, who were so confused they didn't even know what they thought about a table or a cigarette, let alone about life itself, and what kind of an artist could you be without having a point of view? But I didn't want to get involved in an argument with her and have to listen to her arguments about my special qualities.

I was grateful to her for not having mentioned the guest once all evening, however artificial this was, and I held her hand. In the end I pretended to be asleep until I heard her close the door quietly and carefully behind her and I thought, soon none of this will exist, home, childhood memories, her love, all of it will be behind me. And with dry lips I said goodbye to myself, goodbye, goodbye, goodbye.

The next day I was sent to the Super Duper. This was strange, since only the day before my mother had done a big shop for the whole week, but she excused it on the grounds that she had forgotten to buy yeast and matches. I took what I needed from the shelves, intending to pay and hurry off. In my skirt pocket lay the phone card I had stolen from my mother's purse. My subversive plan at this stage was to phone the bank and make enquiries about the savings account and how to go about withdrawing from it. I didn't have the faintest idea of what procedures might be involved in taking out such a large sum of money. Could I just walk into the bank whenever I wanted to, or did I have to let them know in advance so that they could get the money ready? I was afraid that they didn't keep such sums in cash in our little local bank and I wanted to prepare the ground for action.

Armand, however, had no intention of letting me go. After the customer in front of me, a sloppy woman with black roots showing under a topknot of woolly yellow hair, finished paying, he sent Aziz to unload some crates of canned goods in the back, closed the door to prevent any new customers from entering, and asked me to wait until the ones already inside the store left because he wanted to talk to me. I sat down on the counter, an old habit I had preserved from the days when I was a lot younger and I was allowed to because I was regarded as a child, and swung my legs. Armand's cash register caught my eye and I stared at the black plastic compartments containing notes and coins. I played with the idea of banging Armand's head against the wall until he lost consciousness and then taking this money too – every penny was important in my new scheme. Maybe the guest and I would even turn into a new Bonnie and Clyde, roaming the country and robbing greedy capitalists. But the idea of robbing Armand seemed childish and mean and I abandoned it. I had money. I didn't need the miserable earnings of a grocer.

"Susannah, thank you for staying," said Armand after he had got rid of two nagging old women and locked the door.

"Do I have a choice?" I said archly, pointing at the locked door, but Armand wasn't in the mood for jokes. He came and stood next to me, and wiped some invisible crumbs off the counter with his hand. His koala bear's face was sad and serious.

"I'd like to tell you a story."

"*Alors,*" I said when he remained silent, organizing his thoughts.

Armand spoke in a low voice, stopping to think before every sentence. For the first time in my life I found his faint French accent, which he exaggerated on purpose, to be irritating and affected.

"Once the Pope asked Michelangelo to prepare something for a big, important religious procession that was to be held in the city. He wanted it to be something special and impressive, unlike anything that had ever been seen before. Michelangelo thought and thought and came up with an idea. He took a small child, a beautiful boy, the son of a widow he knew, and painted him gold. From top to toe. It was an amazing sight. In the procession the boy was drawn along in a splendid chariot decorated with ribbons and flowers, and the people couldn't stop marvelling and trying to guess if it was a statue or a living person. It was a great day for the boy and he was thrilled with the honour and attention he had received. But that night, when he went home, he began to feel ill. His fever rose and he vomited and had convulsions. The poisonous fumes from the paint had penetrated his pores and poisoned his blood. The doctors tried to save him but it was too late. He died two days later in terrible agony."

I kept quiet, turning the story over in my head. The metaphor was grotesque and humiliating. Its intention malicious. I jumped off the counter on to the floor.

"That's a very nice story, Armand," I said. "It's just a pity you never had the opportunity to ask the gilded boy what he thought. Maybe in his opinion that one day of happiness and fame was worth all the days of his life beforehand, and all the ones that might have come later." I smiled, mobilizing all the composure my anger permitted, and then I added in French, "I have to go now. Please open the door."

"Wait," he barred my way with his body, standing so close to me that I had to press my back against the counter. "Let me finish."

I breathed heavily, lowering my eyes in case my hatred split him in half and killed him on the spot.

"I've known you for a long time. You and Ada. I love and respect you. Please listen to me. We're friends. I worry about you. Your mother worries about you. But sometimes she's helpless before you, afraid of hurting you, of giving you pain, of how you might react. So let me tell you now, you have to take care of yourself. To think of yourself. You're a delicate person. Special. Not everybody sees this. People might hurt you not out of any ill intention but out of coarseness. Of ignorance. And you need to be handled like a flower – gently, considerately. I've always been careful with you . . . and I, I care about you very much, believe me . . . more than you know . . . but I've always been careful and I . . . "

The realization that Armand, even in his secret thoughts, dared to see me as a potential lover filled me with horror, as if I had been touched by scores of filthy hands. Coming on top of his intrusiveness, his halting confession wiped away the vestiges of the politeness that had kept me standing obediently next to the counter with my head bowed. I pushed him with both hands and yelled, "Open the door at once or I'll scream." And all the time he struggled obediently with the lock with trembling hands I stood next to him, furiously stamping on the floor with my left foot like a crazed foal, and then I ran as fast as I could to the payphone on the corner.

August lay on the universe. August was everywhere, even on the remotest stars of the galaxy. August covered Ramat Gan like a cloud of toxic waste. A human invention that nothing had the power to negate. A monster risen up against its creator. What was August but one of the many terrible faces of God?

That night, when the strip of light under my mother's door disappeared, I tiptoed barefoot to the guest's room. Since his return early in the evening we had only exchanged a few words. I had nothing to say until I told him my news. I had decided to reveal my plan to him in stages, not to stun him with one blow. First I would offer him the money, and only after he had grown used to the idea would I inform him that I was going to join him in his life in New York or Alexandria or the suburbs of Katmandu, or wherever else he chose.

He was lying on his bed in his clothes listening to music. It was the same dark music with the high female voice that he had listened to when he first came to stay with us.

"What's cooking, good looking?" he nodded to me without changing his position. I pulled a chair up to the bed and sat down and then I told him quietly and in detail about the money in my possession, where it came from, how much it amounted to in dollars, and my intention of handing it over to him as soon as possible.

The guest turned on to his side and examined me with narrowed eyes. It seemed to me that he was grinning.

"Have I said something to amuse you?" I asked, ready to be hurt.

"Nothing in my life has ever amused me less. Don't offer me money, sweetheart. It's one of the few offers in the world, if not the only one, that I have a hard time refusing."

"I'm offering it so that you'll take it. I'm serious. It's not out of Polish manners or anything like that." I was insulted that he could even suspect his acceptance might threaten me in any way whatsoever.

The guest resumed his former position on his back, and looked at the smoke rising from his cigarette.

"It's awfully sweet of you, really. But I can't take money from you, baby."

I didn't think it was going to be easy. I was prepared for a long round of arguments and persuasion, but something in his tone was surprisingly firm.

"Why not?"

"For all kinds of reasons. It's too complicated to explain."

"Tell me one reason."

He smoked in silence until he had finished his cigarette and then carefully ground it out in the ashtray next to him.

"There's something in me, in my personality, that makes people want to give me things. It's something I know well. Once I regarded it as extremely convenient from the point of view of survival. A kind of positive attribute along the lines of intelligence or beauty. But today, on balance, I see it as something, how can I explain it . . . even degenerate. But all this is terribly boring. Come and sit next to me."

I slipped off the chair and sat on the edge of the bed. He pulled me towards him until I was lying next to him on my back, straight and stiff as a corpse in a coffin. He bent over me and we looked into each other's eyes for a long time, and then he seemed about to say something but immediately changed his mind and stroked my cheek instead with the familiar touch of the back of his hand, and I said: Switch off the light.

We lay and stroked one another and afterwards he said: Let's get undressed, and we got undressed without getting off the bed. We went on lying and stroking each other's bodies for a long time. There was something strange about this sudden familiarity, in my hands touching him, studying him as if in an anatomy lesson, straying all over. Even in the dark, even by touch alone, I could sense how beautiful he was, like an object, and I hurried to seek out with my hands unknown, vulnerable, human places, in order to arrest this fetishistic adoration. I went on searching until I put my hands in his armpits. It was like putting my hand into a box full of blind kittens, and immediately the barrier fell and he was a human being, a man, flesh and blood, and I felt that I loved him so much that there wasn't enough room inside me to contain my wild, swelling emotion. I wrapped myself around him, kissing and licking his face and neck, and he said: You're mad, and then: Are you sure? And I said: Yes, yes, I'm sure, groping between his legs, surprised at myself for knowing how to behave like this, like some whore, and he said: Just a minute, slow down, and I said: I can't slow down, and he said: Sure you can, and he went on stroking my face, but I couldn't relax and I pulled him to me until I felt his body relaxing its resistance, and he immediately lost his dreamy passivity and suddenly he was on top of me and around me and inside me, and again I thought about how I was capable of behaving like some sort of animal, but the thought was detached, as if somebody else was thinking it for me, and I pushed it aside, afraid of wasting this closeness on thinking, trying to contain as much of it as possible in real time, as if it was my life I was fighting for and not some lawless fuck with my cousin.

I wanted to scream but I couldn't, I felt as if I was dying, just like the boy in Armand's story, and he pressed his cheek to mine and I listened to his breathing and tried to breathe in unison with him, as his belly pressed against mine and pulled away and the old bed creaked insultingly. Afterwards he detached himself from me and slid down the bed and sank his face between my thighs. I had to control the impulse to stop him, not to let him pollute his precious face by contact with that place whose names are all too ugly to pronounce. I listened to what was happening inside me quietly and intently, breathing in hot, panting breaths, my fingers sliding over his cool hair, until the shock wave I already knew from the beach came back and forced me to push my hand into my mouth to stop the scream from escaping and waking my mother. I wanted to suck him right into me and keep him there for ever, and then his movements became tense and concentrated, almost detached, and he froze for a long second like an animal listening in the forest, until he laid his face in the hollow of my neck, and I wanted to stroke him but I restrained myself, afraid of spoiling the purity of the situation with cloying sentimentality, when all our intention had been to fuck, just like our forefathers in their caves.

And afterwards we smoked cigarettes and he said that he would like to write me a poem only he didn't know how, but maybe one day he would paint me a picture, even though he didn't know how to do that either, but who could tell, and we laughed, and that promise that implied a common future, however amorphous, filled me with joy. I asked him if he knew any poems by heart and he said: Sure, anything you like, and I teased him: What if it's something you don't know, and he said: There's no such thing, and I said: OK then, "Through nightmare" by Graves, certain of catching him out with this little-known poem, but he said: No problem, and recited the poem in a cool, expressionless voice. His American accent breathed a new, strange life into the text, illuminating the obscure places, brushing aside the banal, the sentimental, until I almost cried, listening to the familiar words as if he himself was saying them to me, as if he were speaking from his heart.

> In your sleepy eyes I read the journey
> Of which disjointedly you tell; which stirs
> My loving admiration, that you should travel
> Through nightmare to a lost and moated land,
> Who are timorous by nature.

When he finished saying the last line he touched me lightly on the tip of my nose. And in an attempt to dispel the emotion thickening the air and charging it with electricity I asked: So you like Graves? And he laughed and said: I don't know him at all, I just came across it in your anthology and I've got a photographic memory. And all this time I lay on my stomach and he stroked my back with light fingers, all the way down the spine to the tail bone, and then he drew me to him, pressed my back to his stomach and chest, and we did it again. This time it was completely different, slow and intent, and in spite of our synchronized movements we were each absorbed in ourselves, tuned in to what was happening inside us, and again I felt his body freeze and relax, but he went on moving inside me and stroking me at the same time, and just as before on the beach his skill conjured up before my eyes an endless and anonymous gallery of other women.

And afterwards we were silent for a very long time and then we smoked again and talked about nothing again until the window started turning blue.

I stood up and got dressed. I sat on the edge of the bed and said confidently: "So you're taking the money."

He said, "I'll think about it, I promise. Now go!"

And he drew my head towards him and kissed me hard on the mouth with his lips closed, like Michael in the movie The Godfather before he went to kill his brother Fredo, but I freed myself from his grip and flew light-footed to my room, because I knew that everything would turn out exactly as I wished and dreamt. Exactly as it had happened up to now.

The Smell

A single sinning woman will ignite a thousand imaginations.

It seems that in the past two days everyone wants to talk to me about life. The day before yesterday Armand with his idiotic metaphor and his confession, and now Nehama, who while she had no confession of long-suppressed lust for poor unfortunate Susannah, was positively overflowing with worldly wisdom illustrated by examples from her personal experience, from which naïve virgins could learn a thing or two about their own lives and the dangers to which they were exposed at any given moment.

How had I fallen victim to a situation in which Nehama was given the opportunity to put on her horror show to a captive audience? My mother had asked me to spend the night at her apartment and I had no option but to agree. During the past month my mother herself had spent a number of nights on the couch in her friend's home. On days when Nehama felt particularly weak and slipped in the bathroom, dropped vases, bumped into the doorposts and so on, putting life, limb and property at risk, the members of her intimate circle were persuaded that her situation required round-the-clock supervision for the next twenty-four hours at least.

And so it came about that early yesterday evening, after first bribing me with a strawberry milkshake, my mother said to me, "Susannah, do me a favour and take over for me at Nehama's tonight – she toppled the bookshelves today and I can't sleep on her couch any more, my lower back's killing me."

I had reasons of my own for wanting to get out of the house for a few hours, and I agreed with a willingness that surprised my mother. Yesterday morning the guest had gone out early, saying that he was going to spend the day with Katyusha, who had returned from the spa claiming that the hydrotherapy had done wonders for Arthur – he now cursed separately and rhymed separately. And so, armed with a toothbrush and a nightgown, I set out for Nehama's place without having exchanged a word with the guest since our night of love. I had no intention of letting him vacillate over my offer. Time was against me and demanded speedy action. Talk wasn't enough, he needed to see the cash with his own eyes. I decided to take the money out of the bank and spread it out in front of him, like a Comanche warrior flinging down a bunch of fresh scalps at the entrance to his fiancée's tent. Staying at Nehama's would give me time to carry out my plan unburdened by my mother's latest attack of family feeling.

Luckily for me, I managed to avoid a nocturnal chat with Nehama. After we had watched all the programmes showing on Channel Two one after the other I announced that I was tired and made up my bed on the couch, which was really terrible, hard and sagging in the middle. But what kept me awake wasn't the couch, or my usual difficulty in falling asleep in a strange house. It was a smell, very faint but demanding and persistent, whose source I was unable to determine. It may have been naphthalene, or the stink of old age, or just a lingering whiff of Nehama's cooking. In any event, it disturbed me and kept me awake, and I occupied myself with daydreams. Only at daybreak did I fall, exhausted, into a deep and dreamless sleep.

In the morning Nehama, disappointed by the lack of sociability I had demonstrated the night before, was raring to go and determined not to let me leave before a heart-to-heart, woman-to-woman talk. And so, although I was in a hurry to get to the bank and withdraw the money, to ransom my happiness and the happiness of the guest, I was obliged to sit and listen to Nehama's unbelievable story, and while she spoke and filled and refilled my cup with pale, weak tea, I became conscious once more of the disturbing smell.

This is the story she unfolded before me.

After the war in 1967, when they were still living in Jerusalem, the late Mr Lieber had gone off to run a natural gas plant in Eastern Europe, and the grass widow had met and fallen in love with a young Arab from East Jerusalem. He was very good-looking, said Nehama, and apropos any feelings of guilt, as she had already mentioned more than once before, Mr Lieber may he rest in peace was partially impotent and in the course of time he had become completely impotent, it was a wonder they had managed to produce Amireleh at all, bless him, a wonderful boy only that Russian had turned him into a floor rag, because who had ever heard of such a thing that . . . Here I intervened with my mother's battle cry: "Nehama!!!" and she immediately abandoned the digression and resumed her story. So, this Arab boy was from a very good family, not the run-of-the-mill stinking kind of Arabs with their olives and goats' milk. A family of jewellers.

And she, Nehama, was very different then, a very striking woman to say the least, she had nothing to be ashamed of, not when it came to her figure and not when it came to her face, blouses with Yemenite embroidery, tailored suits, hairdos à la Sophia Loren. Mr Lieber of blessed memory may have been impotent but he knew how to make a woman feel good. In short (Nehama sighed, the very word "short" inducing the sadness of an artist suffering the constraints of an ignorant patron), in short she and the Arab, one thing led to another, until in the end he said to her: Nahima, that was what he called her as a pet name, Nahima, my dear, my eyes, my dove, my soul, *ana bahibk*. In a word, he loves her and he wants to marry her. How can that be, says Nehama. I'm a Jew, you're an Arab, I have a child – and there's Lieber too, who for all his impotence is a good man. I don't care, says the Arab, *ana bahibk*, I love you and that's it. Everything is from Allah and everything will be all right. Infected by her lover's fatalism, Nehama phones Lieber in his Serbian village and explains the situation. Lieber immediately announces: I'm coming home. Impotent or not, a real man. Good, so Lieber arrives, boom, bang, scandals, scenes, cross-examinations, since when, how long has it been going on, how did it begin, but Nehama stands her ground: she wants a divorce. Lieber starts to cry: My love, my darling girl, my goddess, my beauty – don't ask. But Nehama stands firm. If the Arab *bahibk* she *bahibk* too, all the way, with no half measures. In the end Lieber asks: And who's the other man? Nehama says this and that, a serious fellow, rich, not one of our Ishmaelite cousins with pitta bread instead of brains, trying to appease him. But the minute Lieber hears Ishmaelite he nearly drops dead on the spot.

Nehamaleh, he says, what's come over you? You're betraying your motherland! But Nehama doesn't give way to this piece of demagogy and she replies: I believe in peace and brotherhood between nations. And I also have the kind of sexual relationship with this Arab that I never had with you. So then Lieber goes berserk, and so on and so forth, and suddenly this friend of his, Aryeh, starts coming round, a person Nehama can't stand at the best of times because he always uses their toilet for, how to put it, number two, as if he hasn't got a home of his own. People think they can come to other people's houses and . . . (Nehama!!!) To cut a long story short, this Aryeh was some kind of big bug in the security services, something Nehama doesn't exactly understand because she's not interested in all that dirty business and it certainly doesn't impress her. So all of a sudden this Aryeh starts coming round every couple of days, sniffing round, God knows what he's after. In the meantime Nehama goes on meeting the Arab, and all of a sudden he changes his tune, comes up with all kinds of excuses, this, that and the other, look, there's a problem, and so on. What problem, says Nehama, I thought we said *bahibk* and everything, I've already told Lieber, and Amireleh picks things up too, because even though he was only ten he was very advanced for his age. No, says the Arab, I can't do it. My family objects. Our community wouldn't stand for it. We'd be ostracized for the rest of our lives. In short, he begins to recite all Nehama's own texts, but from way back when he first broached the idea of marriage. She says: Something's happened. No, says the Arab. Nothing's happened, that's what I've decided. But we love each other. Yes, says the Arab, but sometimes life is stronger than we are. It's because of Aryeh, isn't it, asks Nehama. I don't know any Aryeh, says the Arab. OK, Nehama isn't about to humiliate herself for the sake of any man. Crying and grovelling aren't her style. He said "no" so let it be "no". To cut a long story short she went back to Lieber. Naturally he didn't make it easy for her, sulks, silences, pouts, but little by little things settled down – impotent or not. In short, what does this story teach us? A number of things. First, that the Arabs are a treacherous people. And the occupation drove them completely round the bend. But that's another story. The important thing is that men are a treacherous people. If it doesn't suit them down to the ground – weight, height, nationality and shoe size, then all you'll get from them is *bahibk, bahibk,* throw your husband to the dogs, and in the end – you can kiss me you know where.

I finished my tea and stood up.

"An amazing story, Nehama. I'll have to tell it to my mother the first chance I get. She'll be fascinated."

"Wait a minute. Where are you going?"

"I still have a few chores to do for my mother before everything closes."

She accompanied me to the door and she really did look weak, as if she might collapse at any minute, and she said, "Look after yourself, *meideleh,* you're still our sensitive little girl."

"Sure, don't worry," I called on my way downstairs. It seemed that my mother had not spared her friends her concerns. I was at the heart of a general mobilization to get me back on the straight and narrow. I wasn't interested – I didn't have time for trifles. When I stepped outside and stopped, dazzled by the white light next to the rubbish bins, last night's smell rose in my nostrils again mingled with the reek of the garbage rotting in the heat, and this time I knew for certain that I was already acquainted with it, but on no account could I remember from where.

I hurried to the bank.

I had never seen so much money in my life. Nevertheless when

337

the teller Nitza finished counting the bundle of pink two-hundred shekel notes, I nearly exclaimed: Is that all? The bundle seemed too meagre for my expectations of such an astronomic sum, but its weight in the little travelling bag I received from the bank as a gift, light as it was, was the weight of reality itself.

And whether it was a flicker of the inner fever that had me in its grip or a nagging memory, when I sat in the fake leather chair in front of the low counter, nodding and signing forms, the faint smell was there too, alien and out of place in the cold, synthetic, air-conditioned atmosphere.

I went home, trying not to hurry. It required a huge effort of the will to restrain the impulse to break into a wild, breathless gallop. Another street. Another corner. Another building. Three more buildings. Fifty more paving stones. Ten. Five. The entrance to our building. I stopped in the stairwell. The smell was there. Persistent, sly, present.

I climbed the stairs slowly, deliberately. On no account did I want to arrive panting and red in the face. Slowly and surely, one step at a time.

To be prepared, to be organized. To keep chaos at bay for the next hour at least. In one hand I held the little travelling bag with the money and in the other my destiny, mine for the first time, mine at last, like a baby returned to its unfit mother after dozens of orphanages and welfare bureaux.

The house breathed freshness and cleanliness, testifying to one of those spring-cleaning fits that attacked my mother from time to time and flung her into a whirlwind of washing and scrubbing in the middle of the week, with the fanaticism usually reserved for feast days and holidays. The living-room floor was still damp and the chairs upturned, their slender legs pointing at the ceiling. I heard her busy in the kitchen, but before announcing my arrival I looked around, examining the house as if for the last time, trying to absorb all the beloved, painfully familiar details, registering them in my memory so that they would remain as fresh and vivid as possible. The green sofa, my mother's deep armchair, the Bavarian cupboard, the old-fashioned coffee table, the philodendron, my stool, the only stage set where I would ever appear in the main role – the drama of my life. I crammed the travelling bag into the plastic bag with my nightie and toothbrush. Now I was ready for what was to come.

The smell took me almost by surprise. This time it was stronger, overcoming the artificial pine scent of the cleaning agent, mocking me, distracting me from my objective, imposing itself with rude familiarity, like a rapist whispering to his victim: We know each other, honey, we know each other very well. I sniffed my armpits and shirt sleeves – the banal smell of Susannah Rabin – vanilla and dry leaves. I could only suppose that it was something that had stuck to me in Nehama's house, maybe some old-fashioned cleaning agent she used, Lysol or something, and it was only when I called my mother and she came out to me, and the smell hit me with violent force, and my eyes locked on to her wet hands as she dried them with a little kitchen towel, at that very moment I knew what the smell was and where we knew each other from.

The smell of disaster.

That's what it was.

The terrible smell of disaster.

Clinging to the single second before this impossible present, I asked: What's up? And she said: Everything's fine, I'm cleaning, and I said: Can I help with something? And she said: No, no, I'm already done, afterwards you can take down the garbage if you like. I turned to go, careful not to dirty the clean floor with my footsteps, and she said: Where are you running to? And I said: I'm just popping in to see Neo for a minute, I have to ask him something, and she said in a neutral, almost casual voice: Neo's gone.

And although I already knew everything I went on clinging to the ignorance of five minutes before, trying to win another moment of sanity before plunging into the abyss gaping beneath me, and I said: What, Haifa again, those two are driving him crazy, and she said: No, not to Haifa, and I said: I'll give Katyusha a ring, he must be there, and then, finally surrendering to the importance of the occasion, she stopped wiping her hands and looked straight at me. A look that said: I've mobilized all the reserves. I know and I'm ready for everything that's going to happen now.

"He's gone for good. For ever," she said.

"Where to?" I asked. "New York?"

"I don't know," she said. "I don't think New York. But I'm not sure."

"When did it happen?" I asked.

"Yesterday," she said.

"But he didn't say anything to me," I said.

"I know," she said.

"Then he'll come back, I'm sure. Maybe it's something connected to his work," I said.

"He isn't coming back, Susannah." Susannah, she said!

"I'm sure you're wrong," I said. "It's just a misunderstanding, like once before, remember, that time with Haifa?"

"It isn't a misunderstanding. He's gone for good. This morning. He isn't coming back," she said.

"You're lying to me. Why are you lying?" I said.

"I've never lied to you in my life," she said.

"You are lying. You liar. He hasn't gone anywhere," I said.

"Don't you dare talk to me like that," she said. "I know it's difficult, but those are the facts, Susannah," she said. "Neo's gone," she said.

And already running I yelled, "You just don't know, you just don't understand anything," and I tore the door of his room open.

And the room spat in my face, empty of any trace of the guest, naked of his possessions, his clothes, his cigarette stubs, papers, coins, breath. The bed was covered with its old cover. The closet was closed. The desk was wiped clean.

I flung myself on the looted, desolate room with the obsessive desperation of a junkie, opening drawers, closet doors, over-turning the mattress, crawling under the bed in the hope of finding some sign, some remnant, a fingerprint, and when I was through with his room I pushed my mother, who was standing in the doorway like a sentry observing my madness, out of the way and ran to the lavatory – maybe the magazines, and then to her room – maybe he was hiding, playing a joke, and from there to my room – maybe a letter; and then flew to the bathroom – hoping for a toothbrush, a used undershirt hanging on the towel rack, a forgotten bottle of shaving lotion. But everything was dead, tidy and scrubbed, as if his presence in our house for the past three months had been wiped out by some powerful and sophisticated espionage agency.

I returned to the living room, and only after taking a few steps into the room I thought: The floor's still damp, I'll dirty it with my shoes, and I stopped, afraid to move, as if I had been surrounded by a satanic circle.

"Now I suggest you try to calm down," she said and took one of the upturned chairs off the sofa. And since all the places where I could have looked were finished and I was standing in the middle of the room without the faintest idea of what to do next, I sat down. And she, determined to tame my frenzy with her composure, went on taking down the rest of the chairs, moved the armchair, returned the coffee table exactly to its place, and then sat down opposite me.

"I want to tell you everything, exactly as it happened, so that you'll never again be able to call me a liar. There's no reason to crap on everything you have just because you're upset," she said.

"This isn't about you and me," I said.

"I don't have to tell you," she said.

It was her game. I was in her hands. I rolled a bit of dry skin torn from my lips round my tongue. My head was empty, every now and then insignificant details flickered in the emptiness – the slovenly bank teller, Nehama's couch, Lieber and the Arab. Marginal images trying to push aside the single thought that was too terrible to bear – me. I was to blame for everything. Me, the tick hanging on with all its force, the greedy leech. In my greed I had chased him away, in my attempt to make him dependent on me, grateful to me, tied to me.

My mother spoke in a measured voice, in the sober tone of one adult to another.

"For some time now I've had a very uncomfortable feeling. A kind of suspicion. As you know, I'm a warm, simple, straightforward person. I welcomed Neo with open arms. I wasn't interested in all Nehama's and Armand's nonsense. I trust my instincts."

"But what happened yesterday? What?"

"Let me go on." She was determined to show me that the

342

reins were in her hands and I had no choice but to submit.

"Over the past two weeks my feeling of uneasiness grew even stronger, and I decided to phone Bat-Ami, who it turned out had left the old address I had ages ago. I managed somehow to get hold of her new number and I rang her up. She was very surprised to hear about the letter she had never written and the fact that Neo was staying here with us. It turns out that she's in mourning. Herb passed away in June, and Neo didn't say a word about it."

"He did!" I yelled. "He told me. He just didn't want to upset you, that's all." A wild hope rose in me: if this was the whole story all I had to do was explain it to her, and then we would find him and bring him back. A little white lie to preserve her peace of mind, that was all it amounted to. I almost laughed.

"You knew and you didn't tell me?" She raised her voice for a moment, but immediately controlled herself. She still had a long way to go.

"He said that he would tell you himself when the time came. But that's nonsense."

"It turns out that it's far from nonsense," she said in a tone that showed no intention of mitigating the gravity of the situation. "I myself think that the reason he failed to tell me wasn't that he didn't want to upset me, but that he was afraid I would call Bat-Ami to condole with her, and then the truth would come out."

"What truth? What are you talking about? What truth?"

She lit herself a cigarette without offering me one.

"I had a long conversation with Bat-Ami, and a great many things became clear to me. Bad things. Three and a half months ago securities to the value of forty thousand dollars disappeared from her safe. Money she had taken out of the bank and kept at home in order to pay for Herb's treatment at a clinic specializing in alternative methods of treating lymph cancer at the University of Philadelphia. You know yourself – medical insurance in America covers very little, and in the end she was battling for every cent. The safe hadn't been broken into, someone who knew the code had opened it. She has no doubt that it was Neo, because there were similar incidents in the past. Neo is a compulsive gambler, he's undergone a lot of therapies, mostly paid for by Bat-Ami and Herb. And a few months ago he apparently started gambling again, after keeping away from it for two years. She put me straight on the subject of his academic career too: he never even finished his BA, never mind his Master's in London and all the rest of his stories. She cried so much it broke my heart. She said that child was the tragedy of her life. Disappointment after disappointment. She keeps getting phone calls and threats from people he owes money to. An ex-lecturer of his from Columbia University, Miriam something, complained to the police after he pawned her family jewellery and . . ."

"Miriam!" I seized on the familiar name as if it was a clue that would lead me to the guest himself. "Of course, Miriam Sullivan. She was his girlfriend! She'll be able to help us find him."

"Didn't you hear what I said – she pressed charges against him! Stop making such a fool of yourself! You're not a baby! You're not an imbecile! Bat-Ami went to the police too, so the minute he sets foot in the airport he'll be arrested. I can't believe he'll go back to New York if he's got a drop of common sense left."

"But why did it shock you so much? You knew he was a little problematic. It never bothered you before. You were friends. He made us feel good. He made us happy. And why did he leave so suddenly? Why didn't he wait to say goodbye to me? I don't understand."

344

The answer to each of these questions was fateful, but I couldn't wait for her to answer them separately, the pain of not understanding was too disturbing, I had to know everything at once.

"I told him to leave right away. Without waiting for you."

"You did what?!"

Although I spoke in a near whisper, my expression must have been terrible because she looked at me in alarm and stood up to move towards me.

"I told him to leave the house. Immediately. And to leave the country within twenty-four hours."

I too got up and stood behind my chair, gripping the backrest, trying to stop my trembling, gritting my teeth which had started chattering as violently as if I had been thrown into an icy river.

"And he agreed? Just like that? I don't believe you! You're lying to me again! He had to say goodbye at least!"

"I told you not to call me a liar!" she screamed. The composure in which she had begun the dialogue between us evaporated before my eyes, giving way to rage, the terrible rage of those with a guilty conscience.

"But you are a liar," I said coldly, as if stating an incontrovertible fact. "Go ahead," I encouraged her to refute my argument. "Tell me what you said to him." My voice was quiet and dangerous.

"I'll tell you exactly what I said to him. I've got nothing to be ashamed of. I told him that I'd already notified Armand's brother in the police, and that if he didn't leave the country within twenty-four hours I would lodge a complaint about dealing in stolen goods. I wasn't born yesterday – a brother and sister in Haifa? I've already made all the necessary enquiries, my dear!"

"And it's true? You went to the police?" The slowness and

quietness of my voice frightened even me. And in total conformity to our principle of communicating vessels she became more and more agitated.

"What do you think, that I'm joking? This is a sick man we're talking about. A psychopath. You should have heard the way he talked to me. I'm to blame for all your problems, he says, I buried you underneath me."

"And what else did he say? Tell me exactly," I spoke almost pleasantly, doing my best to overcome the violent chattering of my teeth.

"The most absurd things. That because of me you gave up a life of your own. That I'm perpetuating your problems. And so aggressive! The big expert on the human soul! What does he know? What does he understand? He'll tell me what I did and didn't do for you! That good for nothing! And you ask me if I went to the police? What a question. How do I know what he'll decide to do next? Maybe he'll kill somebody?!"

And then everything went white, me, the room and everything in it, the inside of my eyelids, the air itself. I felt as if my very blood had turned white in an instant, and as I leapt on her I reached for her face to gouge out her filthy eyes, but she quickly stepped aside. I fell, and as I rose to my knees, trying to grab hold of the hem of her skirt to pull her down to me, I let out a hoarse animal growl. "I'll kill you. I'll kill you, you hear. I'll kill you, I'll kill you. I'll kill you."

She slipped out of my grasp and stood with her back to the Bavarian cupboard, without a trace of her former composure, shouting at me in a trembling voice, "Susannah, stop it, what's got into you? What did you think, that he would live with you, give you a home? A family? All lies and illusions. That good for nothing, that human garbage! All my efforts to protect you, to guard you from harm, and he . . . he rushes in and tramples it all down with his boots, destroys it like a bulldozer!"

And I, half lying on the floor, twisted as an animal in a trap, out of some instinctive obligation to answer and explain, yelled back at her, "I didn't want him to give me a home and family, I didn't want a home and a family. You understand? I didn't want a home and a family."

But she didn't want to hear, afraid that something in my words, in my pain, would unbalance her, slap her in the face with a remorse too great to bear. She began to speak again, shouting me down, "And what was I supposed to think when they called me from the bank to tell me that you wanted to open your savings account? What did you want? For me to let him rob you in broad daylight, like he robbed his parents? Everybody he ever knew?"

"He didn't ask me for the money," I yelled, "he never asked me for money." I crawled to the sofa, where I had put the plastic bag, took out the travelling bag and tried to unzip it. The zip was stuck, and in the end I simply tore it apart. I took out the bundle of money, loosened the rubber band, and threw the bills up at her. They flew through the air like pink petals, like a stage set for a political cabaret denouncing materialism. And the sight was so theatrical that even she fell silent, and I crawled round the floor, collecting the bills and throwing them up in the air again. "Take it, take the money, take your rotten money, go on, take it, take it . . ." I kept this up until I began to feel that it was completely idiotic and I began to laugh at the whole grotesque scene. I rose to my feet and stood looking at her and laughing. She said, "Have you gone mad? Stop that at once!" I tried to stop, stifling giggles like a scolded schoolgirl. I couldn't understand what there was

347

to laugh about, but I went on until the giggling subsided, and as it died away I perceived the bottomless pit of the abyss.

I started to cry quietly. She made a movement in my direction, but I stepped back and she stayed where she was, next to the cupboard. We stood there like that for a while. I listened to the warm movement of the voiceless tears over my cheeks, trickling into my mouth, falling from my chin into my blouse, on to the floor. A long close-up of a dripping gutter in a black and white art film.

She said, "What did you want, child? What did you think would happen?"

I said, "I loved him. I didn't want anything from him. I loved him."

She said, "That's not love, it's falling in love, it happens and it passes. Love is something else entirely, believe me."

And for some reason the gentleness in her voice outraged me more than all her rage and toughness. I ran up and pushed her against the Bavarian cupboard with all my strength, hearing the sound of breaking glass. I gripped her by the shoulders and pushed her and pulled her towards me and pushed her again, and with every thud of her head against the shelves exposed behind the broken glass I repeated in a low, ragged voice, "What do you know about love, you crazy bitch? What do you know about love?" And every time I paused and looked at her, as if I expected her to answer me, but she was so terrified that she didn't even try to resist and submitted to my blows like a rag doll. I saw a thin trickle of blood begin to drip from her hairline, startling in its bright, fresh red. It only maddened me more, as if I was a hunting dog. I went on banging her head against the cupboard, sweeping the shattering china from the shelves, again and again and again, until I was worn out, and then we both slid to the floor, holding on to one another among the fragments of glass and china, like the survivors of a pogrom.

She sat with her back leaning against the cupboard, and I, emptied of the last of my strength, rested my head on her vast bosom, with the smell of her body encompassing me like morphine fumes. I sobbed quietly while she stroked my head and her voice full of sorrow and pity mesmerized me with its familiar melody: "My child, my poor, beloved child. It will pass. It will all, all pass."

The greatest grace that God can bestow on a human being whose heart has turned from a beating muscle into a pile of splinters is to give him a physical disease. There is nothing more calculated to distract the thoughts and at the same time to alleviate the rebellious pain of the soul. This time, unlike after the death of my father, there was no such distraction.

I remained as healthy as an athlete. Naked in the gas chamber of heartache.

On the day of the big scene with my mother I could already guess what lay in store for me in the area of distraction from above. Instead of collapsing and burying myself between my bedsheets I helped her, with the apathetic diligence of a kibbutz volunteer, to tidy up the living room. Meekly I held the dustpan while she swept up the smithereens. I took the pink banknotes she picked up from the floor and rearranged them in a bundle, fastened it with a rubber band I found in a kitchen drawer, and handed the barren, meaningless money over to her. I lifted the chairs while she ran a wet cloth over the floor tiles covered with my aimless footsteps. I took down the bags full of garbage. We both acted with serious co-ordination, trying to efface with our humdrum activities the memory of the exaggerated, uncharacteristic drama, to rewrite the scene full of Russian pathos and turn it into a short story in the American style, restrained and grey. When the house had returned to a semblance of order we sat silently in the living room. From time to time I tried to cry, but the tears broke off of their own accord, blocked by a new and unfamiliar sense of responsibility that obliged me to contain whatever happened inside myself and alone.

When I phoned Katyusha she sounded preoccupied by her own affairs and impatient. "Suzy," she said, "Neo is the kind of person that even if he goes out to buy cigarettes I don't know when and if he's coming back. His life is now very very complicated. It's better this way."

In the evening Vadim the restorer arrived with a letter for me from the guest. My mother offered him coffee and he declined and looked even shyer and more embarrassed than usual, as if he himself was the villain and deserter.

I soon knew the letter off by heart. I knew every character, every space between the words. In the course of the following weeks I occupied myself with turning the letter over in my head, examining its contents, searching for hidden intentions, until the words lost their meaning and the text turned into a satanic anagram which I had to decipher at all costs – to organize the letters in a new order that would give it its true meaning.

When a man falls out of a plane in the middle of the night only God himself can save him, the poem says. But my private God has revealed himself again and again to be particularly silent, and if I hadn't been the obedient Susannah Rabin I might even have had the nerve to declare, like one of the great philosophers, that he was dead. But this is a luxury I can't afford. My atheism is superficial. Deep in my heart I have to hang on to faith, however anaemic, because without the hope of God's grace there would be no point in anything. I hoped to find grace by deciphering the guest's letter. I lost myself in it. And after I despaired of penetrating its subtle mystery, which was too sublime for my understanding, the letter returned to its original meaning, assailing me with all the weight of its profanity.

Dear Susannah,

The temptation, yes the temptation, is to say to you: we heard the sirens sing, but human voices woke us and we drowned. Because parting is always a kind of nightmare. I wasn't meant to be your lover. This is the truth. And perhaps at this moment this truth seems like a kind of nightmare to you. But you're wrong. Here you'll have to trust me, and even though I believe that all pain is meaningless per se, in this case I tell you: there was a point to our meeting, and there was a purpose, which you may find it difficult to see now but you'll see it in the end. I know.

You may remember that the evening I arrived I said that in order to make art you have to steal the fire from the gods and give it to human beings, like Prometheus. Well, you helped me to feel like a kind of Prometheus. And the punishment, of course, is part of the deal.

In all my life I've never succeeded in creating anything that came even near to my fantasies. And I wanted to so much! As Ada will no doubt tell you, I never even made it through the first three years of art school, and altogether my CV is nothing to write home about. I never justified even one-hundredth of all the expectations I aroused somewhere back there in my childhood, with my high IQ and all my many talents. But with you I felt that maybe, for a few months, I had become what I was meant to be. Not because you in your innocence were impressed by my baroque façade (I know very well that you saw beyond that too), but because of what you made it possible for me to be for you. It's a thrilling feeling, and I want to thank you for it, because I never hoped to experience it.

Now pay attention, because this is the main thing: everything we were together is pointless if you don't go on from there. You have to go. You have to be free. I believe in your star. Don't be afraid. I know that you have the power to create, to invent yourself, to make your own world wherever it may be, to open an escape hatch for the dark forces and also the forces of light that are curled up inside you. It's true that freedom is a kind of prison too, but the fact is that it's a punishment we were sentenced to and we shouldn't try to escape it, because escape conceals the big lie. And the big lie, unlike the little lies, is death, is desolation, and your place is not there.

I wish you all the courage you'll need. Go.

Sanity In Flight

The summer gave way to a warm, bland Israeli autumn.

Heavy and withdrawn I dragged myself dully round the rooms of the house, which had almost completely lost the protective, sheltering quality in which it had always been steeped. I was exposed, flayed. There was nowhere to escape. The pain was inside the house, outside it. Like the air I breathed. Like the light. Like the darkness. It was built in, like an integral part of every cell in my body. Even if I chopped off this superfluous body the pain would go on existing in the labyrinth of my brain. Even if I died, it would still live.

After I had exhausted the letter, I had to look for new contents that would help me to push the pain into the back room of my consciousness. This time God ignored me, refusing to fog my mind with illness, a romantic fevered brow, an anaesthetizing daze. I had no one but myself to save me from the pain worse than death, the flickering insanity – or perhaps it was actually sanity – that threatened to crush me with all its weight.

There were days when I was struck by a wild hope that the guest would return. Days when I waited, jumping when the phone rang, standing for hours on the balcony, my eyes riveted on the angle of the street corner, like the camera lens of an agile paparazzo, ready to snap the slender figure of my private celebrity the moment he appeared.

There were days when I hated the guest, conducting long, insulting conversations with him in my head, hurling accusations at him, analysing his character faults or simply repeating my mother's nasty words: You're nothing, you're a good-for-nothing miserable little liar, and I wish you were dead.

There were days when I worried about him, when I felt this worry pushing aside all other thoughts related to him, and I mumbled prayers to my mute and slandered God: Just let him take care of himself, just let him be all right, just let him be safe and sound and all right.

There were days when I wept in my room without stopping, like a grief-stricken mourner.

There were days when I suffered agonies of infinite longing, reliving moments, snatches of conversations, fears that proved unfounded, quarrels and reconciliations.

There were days when I wandered from room to room as if possessed, trapped in a restlessness of body and soul, unable to sit still for a second.

There were days when I felt a little better, and then I would say: It's all nonsense, I'll get over it, I have myself and my life, but these thoughts would be refuted with insulting speed and immediately I would be thrown back into the great empty void.

There were days when I drew for hours, trying to abandon myself with the addiction I once knew, but these fits were sporadic and short-lived, coming and going of their own accord, unrelated to any decision of mine, and in the end I gave them up entirely.

There were days when I tried to analyse and understand what had happened to me, to us, and why each of us had acted as we had. Who was to blame. What I had done wrong. These were inner conversations with myself, and since all my life I had been used to conducting similar post-mortems with my mother, I failed to produce any interesting or illuminating insights without her.

There were days when I dozed fitfully and woke pierced by the knowledge that the guest would never return. The pain would never go away.

There were days when I went back to cursing and interrogating my mother. This happened several times, until there was no angle or nuance in her story that had not been raked over in previous discussions. As soon as I realized this, I began to treat her with quiet, matter-of-fact politeness.

When I had no will or hope, no anger or tears left in me, and the need to get to the bottom of what had happened had also departed, all that remained were the senses. I concentrated on each one separately, as if I had lost the ability to use them all at once.

With my eyes closed I listened to the sounds of life. The dark, pagan blast of the ram's horn announcing the silence of the Day of Atonement. The voices of the born-again hippies singing religious songs in the *sukka* booth on the roof of the building next door. The sound of water flushing in the toilet in the middle of the night. The busy cement mixer two streets away. The chatter of the birds in the grey dawn. The whoosh of the first rain, unexpected and dramatic as the entrance of a beautiful woman into a crowded room.

I would isolate random observation points, empty of content, and watch them intently – a scrap of dirt stuck to the stainless steel of the kitchen sink. The long bar of fluorescent light shining on a neighbour's porch. A little lump of grey cigarette ash that had fallen out of the ashtray. My mother's faded, shabby slipper under the sofa in the living room. A forgotten price tag on the base of a lamp, a fingerprint on the bathroom mirror.

I felt the pillow on which my wakeful head rested at night. The dry, indifferent wood of the foot of my bed, the smooth lacquered surface of the living-room cabinet, the little rough patch in the distemper on the wall.

I sniffed my menstrual blood, coarse and out of place as a baker coming to collect his money for the birthday cake of a child who has already died, the smoke of a cigarette I'd lit and forgotten to smoke, the palms of my hands, the coolness slowly invading the air and leaving the summer behind, turning it into the past tense, mummifying the organic reality of the experience and putting it behind the glass of the museum of memory.

Only my sense of taste betrayed me. It had almost completely gone, and it was only thanks to some ancient animal instinct that I was able to distinguish between the saltiness of a pickled cucumber and the prickly sweetness of a guava. Perhaps for this reason I ate more and more, refusing to surrender to my new handicap, like a newly paralysed soldier in a melodrama about handicapped veterans furiously insisting on trying to walk, throwing himself again and again off his wheelchair. Until one day I grew tired of these hopeless attempts and I simply stopped eating altogether. Sometimes I gave in to my mother's worried coaxing and tasted a little gruel or bread and butter – foods which seemed to her nourishing and harmless in their blandness. To me it made no difference, everything tasted the same. I did as she asked.

Winter came late, interrupted by superfluous sunny days. My physical weakness forced me to spend most of my time in bed.

I found this convenient. My mother's figure turned into an empty hologram flickering and disappearing sporadically, and in the apathy which had finally descended on me, muffling the pain, blurring the memories, I felt a gloating little worm of spite moving in my brain – the only sign of life which I could recognize and to which I clung with all my might. Whenever my mother appeared in my room with a glass of fresh orange juice or the newspaper's weekend supplement, the little worm sent out a signal of life, a prodding little pulse. How cunning was the fate of Susannah Rabin – now too, when she had succeeded in losing interest in everything, the only life left in her was dependent on the eternal existence of her mother by her side. My God may be a silent audience, but without a doubt he enjoys the show: watching the laws which he laid down prevail in the most adverse conditions, triumphing over every obstacle of changing circumstance.

We would exchange a few humdrum words. Our conversations were brief and always initiated by her – sometimes she would tell me about the chores she had done, about Armand or Nehama. Sometimes, in a last-ditch attempt to retrieve something of the sweet routine we had lost, she would speak of her thoughts or her worries. The fate of the Oslo Accords. The nagging pain in her back. Human nature. In the course of time I stopped responding even with an occasional question or nod to show that I was listening.

I remember – after my father died God blessed me with meningitis, making me hover feverishly between life and death for a number of weeks. The damage done by the disease was so severe that I became a weak and sickly girl. It was during these years that the fateful, marvellous bond between my mother and me came into being. A secret alliance whose meaning only we could understand. An alliance that had a language, laws, humour, a history of its own. A kind of miniature culture possessing all the attributes required for independent existence. Now this culture had been contaminated, become confused, had collapsed. Its foundations had been shaken by the invasion of a foreign force, influential and powerful.

How do you begin to restore the ruins of marble temples after conquering troops have passed through the city, burning and destroying everything in their path, all the glories it took years of labour to build and acquire? Who will bury the dead, succour the wounded? Who will teach the little children their forgotten mother tongue? The customs of their fathers? Who will restore their faith in the whole, the good, the eternal? Who will repair the irreparable harm of the failure? The betrayal? The damaged wholeness?

And for what?

I was indifferent to everything, apart from the spiteful satisfaction occasioned by my mother's sorrow. As we know, her pain is like the fountain of life to Susannah dying of disappointed love. ("Tsk, tsk, tsk," the vindictive Moirais on Olympus click their tongues. How unfilial.)

As for her, she was wrapped up in and preoccupied by her sorrow, which despite her efforts to radiate confidence and stability betrayed itself in every move she made – in her strained smile, in the slight tremor of her hands when she set the bowl of gruel on my bedside table, in the difficulty she experienced in leaving the room and letting me be after I closed my eyes in pretended sleep.

And then, one day, as she sat on my bed, I saw the decision in her eyes. The decision to bring me, my silent and emaciated corpse, back to life. Her life and mine. From that fateful moment she stopped wasting her resources on sorrow and worry. Her timid, hesitant, guilt-ridden conduct became brisk, decisive, full of energy and zeal. From now on she had a goal.

I had always known how great her love for me was, how far she was prepared to go for my sake, but this time she succeeded in surprising even me, and perhaps herself too.

When I stopped getting out of bed new emergency measures were taken. Every other day I was taken to the shower, where she washed me in a clumsy but meticulous ritual – soaping, rinsing, turning me this way and that under the jet of water, patting me on the back while I slowly and mechanically moved the toothbrush in my mouth. Then she would dry me and comb my hair, clean my ears with cotton buds meant for babies, clip my nails when they grew too long, push my resistant head and arms into a clean nightgown or the grey track suit that Nehama once bought me in a sale. Luckily I was able to drag myself to the toilet under my own steam. Thanks to the ultra-Spartan diet I had adopted this was not something I had to do very often.

I submitted willingly to the new regime. It allowed me to give up the last of my attempts at functioning. I could be silent. Not move. She had stopped looking for any signs of reaction on my part. From now on she wanted nothing of me. And what's the wonder – she didn't need anything, her mobilization on behalf of her rescue efforts filled her to overflowing. She had everything. Her gifts of herself to me poured out with the abundance of an inexhaustible horn of plenty.

Every day she would sit next to me for hours, reading me books and newspapers and talking to me, sometimes gently coaxing and sometimes simply telling me about her day, reminiscing, complaining about trifles, laughing at old jokes. The blue vase was put to its proper use at last, and each week its flowers were exchanged for new ones, different every time. She bought a little stereo system and put it on the desk in my room, after clearing away all the little figures, drawing pads and boxes of crayons piled up on it, and from then on she never stopped playing me music, mostly Mozart (recommended by her women's magazine to improve your mood) and Vivaldi (the same reason), but also old Israeli songs (your father liked them), various local pop stars (the young people like them), Charles Aznavour (recommended by Armand) and a group called "Baby Lymphoma" (a heavy rock band led by Talush, Nehama's grandson, and called after King Hussein's disease). There were other discs that had been purchased in order to fill out the collection but were out of bounds at the moment: Schubert (too sad) and Chopin (ditto, and also Polish schmaltz). When I lay awake at night I would hear her heavy steps trying to tread softly as she came in to fix my blanket, to smooth my rumpled hair. Now she ate only in my room, at a folding table she bought especially for this purpose. Sometimes she would lie down next to me and gently stroke my back, massage my shoulders. Armand had attached the television to the wall opposite my bed with a special metal arm, and in the end, crammed with all these electrical appliances and resuscitation kits, my room began to look like a storeroom for stolen goods. Heavy, expensive new art books were placed next to me, waiting patiently for my attention. Jasper Johns, Pollock, Rauschenberg, Cézanne. A beautifully packaged parcel was opened before my eyes and from it emerged elegant little volumes of Byron, Shelley and Keats – contributed by Nehama's Amireleh, who had ordered them on the Internet from the famous Amazon shop.

I could no longer eat solid foods. On my bedside cupboard stood little cans of special body- and muscle-building foods. They were full of a dense white vanilla-flavoured liquid, high in calories and essential nutrients, and I would drink them with a straw three times a day, too exhausted to resist her monotonous coaxing: "Come on, child, a little more. You must get strong. Come on, one more sip, one more and that's it. Good girl."

She saw to it that I had visitors – the return to normal as she saw it included an active social life. Nehama turned up every second day. Although she already felt much better now, she spent most of her visit complaining about the thirty-six steps leading to our apartment. Apparently the reason for her fall had been the onset of multiple sclerosis, but with the help of a considerable measure of optimism, together with a healthy dose of denial, she went on clinging furiously to her truculent lust for life, as if it were some new miracle drug, and refused to surrender to the knowledge of what the future held.

One day Katyusha arrived with Arthur, who was wearing a yellow plastic coat and a woolly hat and looked like one of Snow White's seven dwarves in a performance by Antonin Artaud's "Theatre of Cruelty". Katyusha said, "You got very thin, Suzy, sometimes too thin is not beautiful any more. I have opposite problem – only fatter and fatter all the time. Size forty already. I have to buy new clothes and I like only designer clothes – Versace, Donna Karan. Very expensive." And she also said, "Next year Arthur goes to normal class already, not class for special education." I smiled at them.

Rivki came twice. The first time she said, "Remember Ido? The guy you met at the Cinematheque? We split up. What a schmuk. He tried to make himself out to be some big sexy stud and gave me herpes and then had the cheek to complain that I talked too much. Well I'm sorry, but for me a relationship means intimacy, it means talking. All men can talk about is their work and their cars. It's all ego with them – who's got the biggest prick and the smallest cellphone. They're pathetic. I'm volunteering once a week at the Centre for Victims of Sexual Assault, and I took a half-Persian cat from the Society for Prevention of Cruelty to Animals, but it died after a week, and now I'm thinking of getting a dog."

On her second visit Rivki glanced at the open door to make sure my mother wasn't in the vicinity and then said, "I want you to know that I took care of Rosh Pinna for you, because that's me – if I say I'll do something I do it, and it could work out because one of the people there killed himself, some sculptor, and a place has become available, but of course it's not really feasible at the moment. Never mind, first get better and then we'll see."

Armand read me poetry by Verlaine and Baudelaire in French, and when he grew bolder in the face of my endless silence he began to read me his own translations into archaic Hebrew: "Ancient of days am I, a thousand years of memories . . ."

My mother got hold of all the video tapes of the Israeli *Spitting Image* for me and showed them to me every evening. Sometimes she would get a film from the video shop and show that too, sitting on my bed, making comments, sighing, identifying, just as she used to do when we watched films together in happier days. Sometimes she talked about my father, strewing the bed with old photographs, somehow managing to inspire them with new life despite the fact that I knew them like the palm of my hand. She would describe the circumstances in which each snapshot had been taken, what they did that day, during that period of their lives, what their plans and expectations for the future were, where she bought the dress she was wearing in the photograph, where I was and why I wasn't there.

I knew that one day the wall I had built around myself would collapse beneath the avalanche of her stubborn love. For who knew like I did – change, however hidden and subversive, would always come.

The worm of spiteful satisfaction curled up into an inanimate cocoon, and after many days of feeding on her abundant love and care, obedient to the eternal laws of nature, it shed its skin and burst forth into the light of day as a glorious bright butterfly of longing and gratitude.

First came the dreams, usurping the place of the empty random naps and the sleepless nights. The dreams were clear and full of light. The guest appeared in every one of them. Sometimes I saw his face, smiling and remote, sometimes he was part of a strange, complicated plot, most of which I forgot on waking, and sometimes we were drinking tea on a roof, with a spectacular view of the mosques, palms and distant seashore of a Levantine city spread out before our eyes, still sleepy after getting up late in the morning, and I would say to him: James, have you pawned Grandma's pearls again? And the guest would reply in an aristocratic English drawl: Susan, darling, be reasonable – on Sunday we're organizing a picnic at the pyramids, someone has to pay for the porters.

Then the sense of taste returned, filling a void of dullness with every variety of sweetness, sourness, sharpness and saltiness. At first I only took little titbits from my mother's dinner plate, but very soon I began to receive and eat full helpings of my own, taking dainty bites of bread and butter, pieces of chicken, brown cookies, orange segments, like an enquiring alien in his first culinary encounter with the local civilization.

My mother watched me with bated breath, complying with my laconic requests without saying a word, as if afraid of destroying my timid progress and blowing it away, like a tender leaf from a bough shaken by a spring breeze. She no longer had to bathe me – one day I released her with the words, "No, mother. Today I'll manage on my own." And from then on I continued on my own, punctilious in every detail, sitting weakly on the edge of the tub until the conditioner took its softening effect on my hair, slowly shaving my armpits and my legs, rubbing handcream into my hands, inspecting my face in the mirror after wiping away the film of steam covering it.

The television was returned to its former place in the living room, and I would curl up on the sofa opposite the evening news, dropping random sentences into my silence: That's the end of Oslo. Who's that Knesset member with the beard? Lieberman's really running the country! Check and see when *Seinfeld* begins. And my mother would jump in, elaborating trivial remarks into theories, explaining, reporting on gossip not written in the newspapers but well known to the intelligence agency of the Super Duper (That Sara Netanyahu, Mrs Bibi, she suffers from a compulsive obsessive disorder, like that fat girl with the pimples in drama therapy, remember? Nehama says that it was the security services that killed Rabin, what do you say to that? Of course she also claimed there was a Yemenite conspiracy, the nonsense that woman talks. Hillary Clinton is just like me and your father – a serious woman with a childish husband. In my opinion she's really something. Good luck to her. They say she earns more as a lawyer than he does.)

Later on we began conducting proper conversations, albeit more reserved than they once were, but I began to smile at her jokes, take an interest in the neighbourhood news, Nehama's health, the character and qualifications of the new ear, nose and throat specialist at the HMO clinic. She told me she had met Gidi Bochacho with his dog and he had sent his regards and best wishes for a speedy recovery. Nehama and Armand sent their warm regards too. Lately they had stopped visiting us at my request (convalescing, needing rest), and my mother had taken care of it with practised tact. When she was busy in the kitchen or cleaning the house I would sit next to her on my stool, volunteering myself for light tasks: peeling carrots, pouring sugar from a paper bag into a plastic container, setting the washing machine to the correct programme. In the mornings we sat in the kitchen with our coffee, exchanging pieces of the newspaper, reading aloud items about political scandals, advertisements for sales, new medical discoveries (babies' urine as a treatment for allergies, the effects of whole-wheat bread on mental states, a computerized hearing aid). The guest was never mentioned, and only once, when she was tidying the wardrobe in her bedroom, she suddenly pulled out the parcel with the grey dress and said, "What should I do with this, it just takes up space. Should we pass it on to the new immigrants' aid association?" And I said, "No, leave it, I've got someone to give it to." She looked at me, but when I said no more she handed it over to me with no more ado, as if to say: I'm not interfering in your affairs.

The ice wall melted gradually and pleasantly. Attentive to each other we tiptoed over the fragile bridge of rapprochement stretching between us. Be careful, don't push, don't exaggerate, beware of crude movements, out-of-place words. And in spite of the delicacy of this hidden emotional activity its positive results seemed to indicate stability and success. Our love had returned, even if it had not yet steadied into an established norm, and it expressed itself in an exchange of smiles at some nonsense mouthed by a transvestite or a fortune-teller on a television talk show, in a seemingly accidental touch, in small, everyday expressions of concern: Here, Mother, take this cushion, you'll be more comfortable.

Spring showed its face with suspenseful gradualness, like a stripper in a nightclub filling in the intervals between the removal of various items of clothing with sexy dance steps, which nobody has the patience to watch because they're waiting tensely for her to undo the hooks on her bra. In the beginning I went downstairs leaning on my mother's arm, and we would sit on the low concrete wall opposite the building entrance and raise our faces to the anaemic sun. Later I began to go out for walks on my own, postponing as long as I could the meeting with Nehama and Armand and the routine of the Super Duper. I would take leave of my mother and set off in the opposite direction – to the park with the dogs and back again. One day I met Gidi Bochacho, who looked pensive and withdrawn. I sat on the edge of the bench next to him and lit a cigarette. He smiled at me: "How are you? It's good to see you." The dog came up and sat down in front of me, panting and examining me with its head on one side.

"Here, throw it for her, she wants to play." Gidi handed me a short stick in the shape of a bone. I threw it weakly and it fell right into a clump of ragged hibiscus bushes not far from where we were sitting. The dog raced over to the bushes and started trying to reach the toy.

"What's happened to that great-looking cousin of yours? Has he gone back already?"

This reference to the guest seared me with longing.

I nodded. Then I asked, "What's his name, your dog?"

"It's a she," said Gidi. "Her name's Zara."

In the meantime the dog succeeded in fishing the stick out of the bushes and came back and sat down in front of me, holding it in her teeth.

I touched her square, heavy head.

"She's mad about you," said Gidi. "It often happens like that. First you hate someone and then you fall madly in love with them." He sighed.

I threw the stick again. It flew into the distance, passing the litterbin I had taken as my goal. For some reason this manifestation of physical strength flooded me with idiotic joy.

I said, "OK. I'm off. I'll probably come again tomorrow. I go for a walk every day now."

"Keep well," said Gidi.

That evening I decided not to watch television and lay on the bed in my room, trying to read Keats. I couldn't concentrate and I switched off the light, staring into the darkness, listening to the sounds of the television coming from the living room. Later my mother came in and sat down on the edge of the bed.

"So, child. You're tired today."

And her careful, quiet voice sounded so sweet in my ears that I turned over and laid my head on her lap, and in the security I felt in our renewed relationship I decided to break the taboo barring any mention of the guest. I said, "So do you think that he didn't love me at all?"

She kept quiet for a long moment, stroking my head, and then she said, "You know, with people like Neo you can't talk about loved or didn't love. They don't love anyone. Not even themselves, for all their egoism. Do you understand?"

I nodded into her lap.

For the first time in my life I started to paint with oils. An act that for me bordered on blasphemy. Who was I to use materials that real artists used? I no longer cared that I had nothing to say, no firm view of the world, cultural depth, intellect, sophistication. It no longer made any difference to me what I thought of myself. I wasn't looking for some transcendent redemption but immediate, physical rescue, a place where I could stand, even on tiptoe, to escape being engulfed by the savage loss threatening to drown me for ever. I threw myself into the work as if I was possessed by demons, trying techniques, attacking the canvas as if it was my final battle, a Japanese Kamikaze pilot in a last, proud farewell. I had no idea of what to do or how to do it, I was equally unfamiliar with innovative and traditional methods. Full of a demanding, almost erotic restlessness, I threw myself into the work with abandon, forgetting myself, remembering myself, slapping the paint on to the canvas in the dark forgetfulness, in the sobering memory. I taught myself to work out of despair, out of indifference, out of pain, depression, happiness and boredom. My inner state no longer dictated my daily agenda. Sometimes I spread the canvases on the floor and splashed paint on to them as I knew Pollock had done, bowed over, sweating, in my underpants, not allowing my mother into the room for days on end. I painted on canvas, on plywood, on industrial cardboard. With paintbrushes, with my hands, with my whole body. When the excitement and concentration refused to clad me in their blessed armour I sat for hours erect on a chair, smoking and staring into space, waiting for them to return. Sometimes, frustrated, I felt a disturbing tension in my groin, between my legs, a tension I had known up to now only in one context – the context of the guest. A tension that gripped me whenever I looked at his long-muscled back, his fine-skinned arms exposing their inner anatomy in the tracery of their veins, the delicate pulse beating in the wrist.

Every day I went religiously to the dog park.

On the days when it rained and I couldn't go out I waited impatiently for the next day.

On the days when Gidi and Zara were late I found myself in the throes of an anxiety attack in case they didn't come at all, smoking nervously, unable to take my eyes off the side of the park from which they always approached.

I sometimes chatted to Gidi about this and that, but mainly I enjoyed playing with Zara. This black and terrifying dog had really fallen in love with me. I couldn't remember a single living being who had ever greeted me with such joy, such unrestrained enthusiasm, before. On the days when I arrived in the park after them she would break into a gallop the minute she saw me, jump on me, almost pushing me over with her forepaws, whine like a puppy, run round me in circles trying to lick my face, and I would pat her neck, which was as broad and thick as that of a young calf, kiss her moist muzzle and say, "What's cooking, good looking? You're a piece of work, sweetheart!"

Gidi told me how she had come into his possession when she was already two years old. He had actually saved her life. Before that she had belonged to two spinster aunts of his, his mother's sisters, who had acquired her as a watchdog. They had no idea how to treat a dog. They had punished her, let her go hungry for days on end. When she refused to obey them they would beat her and lock her up. "That's why she's so frightened of people she doesn't know, especially women," said Gidi, "and she behaves aggressively. As soon as she realizes that nobody's going to hurt her she becomes as mild as a lamb."

"So do you think my mother and I reminded her of your crazy aunts?"

Gidi looked embarrassed, but the theory he was about to expound to me was too interesting to keep quiet about for the sake of politeness.

"Well, perhaps your mother and Mrs Lieber. But maybe you too. See how attached she is to you now. I think that all our lives we seek out people who remind us of the initial, primary trauma, because it's only with their help that we can perform the repair, or *tikkun*."

I shrugged my shoulders. "That sounds like pseudo pop-psychology to me."

"Maybe," he said. "But let me remind you that *tikkun* is a Kabbalistic term, not a psychological one."

"OK, then popular pseudo-Kabbala."

We laughed.

Gidi turned out to be an easygoing person, who did not insist on his ideas. This showed him to be of a sceptical disposition, and I liked him for it. He was tall and ungainly, and cultivated an elegant appearance. I liked looking at his feet shod in highly polished, expensive Italian shoes, at the perfect seams of his retro-style leather jacket. On his right hand he wore a signet ring with an aristocratic coat of arms which he had bought in an antique shop in the Portobello Road in London. He wasn't a big talker, but my silence gradually had an effect and he began to talk. Unlike the guest, Gidi Bochacho always talked about himself and didn't tell stories about himself. He was terribly human in his melancholy honesty and his slight tendency to self-pity. These too were characteristics that I liked.

Gidi Bochacho's heart was broken. About two months before he had met a wonderful man who lived and worked in America and who was on holiday in Israel. Now this man had gone back to America, and although he had declared his love for Gidi and invited him to go too, Gidi was miserable and beaten because of the distance separating them from each other and his inability to make up his mind whether to go to America. Indecisiveness was another of Gidi Bochacho's outstanding character traits. On a bad day he could spend ten full minutes trying to make up his mind whether to smoke the third of his daily ration of five cigarettes now in the park, or at home with his coffee.

"At first I couldn't stand him." He described the course of his love affair to me. "I met him at a party in a fancy penthouse in Tel Aviv. He looked to me like one of those rich middle-aged business types, the kind that fuck a different boy every night for the price of a dinner. You know the kind I mean?"

I had no option but to nod. For reasons best known to himself, Gidi Bochacho had seen me from the first as someone familiar with the darker side of life.

"Afterwards it turned out that he was the kindest, cleverest person in the world. A great scientist. The head of a special institute for the alternative treatment of lymphatic cancer."

"At the University of Philadelphia?" I asked.

It took me a long time to convince him that I wasn't a witch or a psychic. He believed in every superstition going, another characteristic that for some reason touched my heart. All men were my brothers.

Gidi was so neurotically indecisive that the best thing anyone could do for him was to decide for him. Smoke now. Take Zara to the vet first and go to your date afterwards. Tell the cleaning woman to come on Tuesday. Forget the movie on Channel Four and watch the one on Home Cinema instead. To his credit it must be said that he never made any objection and was always grateful for the decisiveness I learnt to display towards him, as if it was an expression of sincere concern.

"In my opinion you have to go," I said after he had described to me in detail the full dimensions of the impossibility of his going to America.

Afterwards, item by item, I explained to him how each of the problems standing in his path could be solved with almost insulting ease.

For a moment he was silent, taking in what I had said. It was all too simple, and simplicity, however seductive, gave rise in Gidi to suspicion, and what was worse: to a truly astonishing creativity in finding new obstacles.

"And what will I do with Zara?"

This was definitely a weighty argument.

"Leave her with your parents or one of your friends."

"Don't make me laugh. She's got the reputation of a demented cannibal."

"I understand," I said. "I'll think of something."

That evening I complained to my mother that I had a feeling of emptiness.

"What kind?" she enquired. Anyone who knew Susannah Rabin knew that emptiness had many faces.

"The lonely kind. I thought that perhaps I should have a pet to take care of."

"You had a hamster when you were small. The one who took care of it was me. And anyway, if you don't mind me saying so, a hamster can only increase feelings of loneliness, not alleviate them. Besides which they stink."

"Yes, you're right, perhaps a more intelligent kind of animal would be better," I put out feelers. But my mother, who had a firm way of dealing with dangerous subjects, put an end to the discussion by saying, "You'd do better by coming with me to visit Nehama, or Armand. They're intelligent animals." And she roared with laughter at her mean joke.

I had no option but to act on my own, in the hope of smoothing things over after the event.

A week later everything was ready for execution. Gidi Bochacho had booked a ticket at a travel agency, under my bed lay a large packet of dog biscuits and two deep plastic bowls, and immediately after my mother's broad back had receded in the direction of the Super Duper I collected Zara in the park and took her up to the apartment. My arrangement with Gidi was that I would start taking her home for one night every two days, both to get her used to the idea and out of consideration for the blow about to descend on my mother when she found herself faced with the *fait accompli* of the new reality.

The first thing Zara did on her arrival in our home was to mark the occasion with a puddle the size of Lake Victoria in the rainy season. Immediately after that, in a burst of mischievous glee, she smashed the blue vase. I joined in her glee and cavorted with her round the fragments of blue china flooded with water and yellowing day lilies, clapping my hands and crying, "Bravo!" The god of department store sales himself had apparently destined this vase to be a multi-purpose symbol in the life of Susannah Rabin.

In the hours that followed I gained the impression that Zara had definitely taken a shine to our apartment – she ran from room to room, sniffing the corners, overturning objects, inspecting the beds, and leaving a layer of short stiff hairs on the covers. After eating all the pastrami, schnitzels and cookies I found in the kitchen, our new pet lay down on the sofa, drooling and diligently chewing one of my mother's favourite cushions.

In the evening the three of us, Zara, my mother and I, went out for our first walk together.

"Isn't there anything," said my mother, "anything," she repeated the word with feeling, "that would make you happy apart from that creature?" And she tugged nervously at the leash of the frisky, bounding Zara, who was all set to break into a light gallop along the dark street.

"Nothing that I can think of at the moment," I muttered from below with my nose blocked, trying to refrain from breathing. I was busy attempting, with the help of a crumpled piece of cardboard, to push a massive pile of fresh dog shit into a plastic bag. My revulsion from bodily secretions turned this everyday task routinely performed by all conscientious dog owners into a mission no less complicated than the attempt to escape from a missile attack with chemical-biological weapons. Our first walk with Zara was an exercise in familiarization and adjustment.

At half-past four in the morning the dog woke me up with a low, miserable whining noise, and as soon as I put her on the leash she pulled me forcefully to the door. I managed to snatch my mother's old coat from the rack and let her drag me down the stairs, barefoot and barely awake.

"You miss Gidi, is that it?" I asked wearily. I sat down on the edge of the pavement, huddled in the coat, and undid the leash. "Go on then, go for a run." But the dog sat down next to me, refusing to take advantage of her sudden freedom.

It was cold and the moon seemed like the quintessence of sparseness, saying in its paleness, its incomplete circularity, that life is never what it should be.

I covered my face with my hands. I had no heart left. Only the memory of the guest pulsed inside me. His face was tattooed on the inside of my eyelids. I loved him more than ever. The dog peed, looking at me with round, anxious eyes, as if she felt guilty for her earthiness, for the life filling her to bursting.

"We'll have to find you a more suitable match, sweetheart," I said to her.

I let her sleep in my bed, under my winter eiderdown.

Two days later, after Zara had gone home to Gidi, my mother summoned me for a talk. She insisted that I leave the painting I was working on and she looked solemn and mysterious. The occasions are rare when my mother dresses up, puts on her blue Egyptian satin dress, pins on her silver brooch in the shape of a pair of open roses, and encases her feet in her black pumps with their heels as low and broad as a cow's hoof. Even rarer are the occasions when she dabs her sweet French scent behind her ears and smears her dry lips with her coral-coloured lipstick. Usually when she wishes to honour any occasion with her presence she makes do with one of the above. Just the dress. Or just the lipstick. That's enough for them. We're not taking part in a beauty competition here. This time it was the full monty, dress, brooch, shoes, scent, lipstick, the lot. How handsome and elegant she looked! It was only to be regretted that she didn't choose to make the effort more often.

"Who died?" I asked, flopping into the armchair, irritated in advance. Now I noticed her best handbag too, the one she kept for going to the theatre or going shopping in Tel Aviv. She clasped it to her stomach with both hands, as if it held stolen jewellery.

"I want you to listen to me now, Susannah," her voice was pregnant with fateful importance. "Over the past few days I've been thinking and thinking. And suddenly I realized what has to be done."

"About what?"

"About you. And me. And life."

"What did you think about life? Why are you all dressed up? What have you got there in your bag? Let's hear it." I knew that my everyday impatience was out of tune with the dramatic tension she was trying to create, but I couldn't help it. The mystery was more than I could bear.

"We've been through a difficult period," she put the bag down on the table but went on holding it with both hands. "A big crisis. I'm afraid even to speak of my happiness now, in case I tempt fate, when I see you beginning to recover, to return to yourself."

"OK, OK, let's just see what you've got there already," I prompted, but she only tightened her grip on the bag.

"And I thought that it didn't happen for nothing. Perhaps everything we went through was intended to show us something."

I listened with a sour face, hoping that my expression would make her hurry up and get to the point.

"I realized that what we needed was a change. Something significant. I thought and thought and made up my mind. I decided what we're going to do." She fell silent and looked at me, as if I already knew what it was all about and I was now expected to react.

"Mother! You're worse than Nehama, I swear."

She pushed the handbag over to me and crossed her arms. I opened the bag, and although my expectations were completely vague I felt a stab of disappointment when I saw that it was crammed with papers and colourful brochures. I pulled one out at random and saw a picture of a white beach and a turquoise bay.

"What's this?"

"Go on, take them all out."

I emptied the contents of the bag on the table. A pile of prospectuses confronted me, pamphlets put out by a big travel agency with information about various package tours illustrated by brightly coloured photographs of tourist sites and pastoral scenes of Greek beaches.

"You want us to go on a package tour to Greece?" I looked at her in astonishment.

As I live and die, the next chapter in the comic drama (or perhaps the tragicomedy?) about the adventures of the madcap pair from Ramat Gan. Susannah and her mother strike again. The return of Susannah and her mother. Susannah and her mother in the footsteps of the Argonauts.

My lips twisted and my cheeks swelled a second before I fell apart in rude laughter. I snorted like a pig.

My mother hastily thrust a packet of cigarettes in my direction. Calling me to order.

"Stop it at once! Listen to me. I want us to go on a private tour of our own. We have the money, thank God – your savings scheme." She smiled and immediately grew serious. "And I have more,

377

money I've been saving over the years. I can't take it with me to the grave. We have to live as long as we're alive, don't you agree?"

"To Greece?" I asked, trying to take it in. "Just you and me?"

"Actually I thought we could start out with Nehama and Armand, have a rest on some island, and then they could return to Ramat Gan and we could go on. You and me. You remember how when your father was still alive you had all those fantasies about the mythological heroes, Olympus and the Pantheon and Troy and all that Odyssey-Schmodyssey and God knows what else. Look, Armand's even bought you a book of poetry in honour of the trip." She handed me a slim volume entitled *A Greek Island*. The name of the poet was unfamiliar to me.

"But . . ." The prospect of being on a Greek island with Nehama and Armand was hardly enticing.

"But what? There are no buts. We only live once. We deserve a bit of happiness after the nightmare we've been through."

That *we've* been through? I wanted to ask, but I restrained myself. Was I going to compete with her in the matter of who suffered most too? I was incorrigible.

"Aren't you pleased?" She stood up and came over to me and hugged my shoulders and looked with me at the cover of a pamphlet illustrated by a picture of the headless statue of the goddess of victory.

"I'm not sure what to think."

Why not, in fact? The proletariat have nothing to lose but their chains, as the guest used to say when I hesitated like Gidi Bochacho over a walk to the park or a talk show on television.

My mother was too determined to waste time on doubts whose nature, knowing me as she did, she would have no difficulty in guessing.

"There's nothing to think about. Where would you like to go? Where do you dream of going?"

In spite of myself I thought for a moment.

"Sparta. Could we go to Sparta?"

"Sparta, Athens, anywhere. What's the matter, child? Aren't you happy?"

I got up and put my arms around her, burying my face in her shoulder, rubbing my nose on her perfumed neck.

"Of course I'm happy, mummy. As happy as can be."

For the first time in my life I learned that happiness, like emptiness, has too many faces to count.

Hesitantly at first and then with growing enthusiasm I joined my mother in examining the coloured brochures, until we were like a couple of excited schoolgirls poring over a pile of pornographic magazines discovered in the bedroom of their respectable parents. Giggling, interrupting each other, snatching the material from each other's hands, stopping for a moment and looking at each other in profound mutual understanding and then returning to serious perusal of the text again, and again breaking the tense concentration with laughter, jokes, fantasies about what the future would bring.

My mother took off the clothes she had worn to the travel agency and changed into her shabby robe, and we both moved to the sofa and cuddled up under a plaid rug, using the coffee table as a desktop, laden with papers, ashtrays, pads and pens, as befitted a pair of active go-ahead women like us, full of plans. From time to time we got up, by turns, to make tea, and then returned to planning our campaign.

We pored over the brochures late into the night, selecting destinations, examining prices and timetables, arguing and reaching agreement, noting down questions to be clarified, leafing through my father's old atlas, choosing, regretting previous choices in the light of new and more thrilling possibilities, and so on, until mother made the last round of tea, pushed Armand's book into my hands, and sent me to bed.

I was very tired, but to my surprise instead of dropping straight into bed and falling into a sweet sleep, as soon as I entered the room I felt disturbingly wide awake.

The room was dark. I went over to the window and looked at the street. The pavements were wet with a sudden shower, one of the last of the season. I opened the window and breathed in the air that held within it the signs of an early spring, banishing the echoes of staleness with its wet freshness. My life lay before me here in this undistinguished suburban street, in the light of the street lamps reflected in the puddles, in the banal magic of the night. Sometimes I would be surprised at how people as drab and unimportant as me were able to benefit from all these marvellous things, no less than the rich and famous – the smell of the rain, the pale cool moon, the full, spine-tingling sensation of being alive.

I existed. I was alive.

This was me, me, me. In the strong smell of the oil paints in my room, in the bed as narrow as a young girl's, in the lungs breathing in oxygen and nicotine, in the memory of the touch of the skin of the guest, in the dark pit inside me that would never be full, in my dry, bony fingers, in my mother, sleeping her old, heavy sleep in the room next door, in the yearning for life and death at once that breathed from every pore in my body.

Me, me, me. Unique, separate, different from every other living or dead creature in the world, from every bird or thing, from every woman, from every soul.

I closed the window.

I didn't know what to do with this searing existence inside me. If only I could sleep. Dream. But dreams, however spectacular, had never succeeded in telling me anything but themselves, eluding words, contexts, the pleasing clarity of insight.

What doesn't surrender to words isn't worth them. Its existence is accidental, unconnected.

What to do?

My experience, my memories, from them too I can conclude very little apart from the practical, the matter-of-fact. For every experience is so different from its fellows. How can anything be implied from the one to the other? How is it possible to learn anything at all, to formulate a method of conducting oneself under this high sky, this slow ceiling? I'd like to know what to do next. What to think. How to act. But everything I've ever thought was only itself. Without added value. Without hidden content. The thing itself and no more.

"I have to go away," I said out loud, "that's what I have to do."

The sound of my voice calmed me, giving an outline to reality, a hard edge. I said again, in a voice hoarse with the packet of cigarettes I'd smoked during the evening, "I'm going away."

I switched on the reading lamp and opened the book sent me by Armand. It contained a cycle of poems written by the poet during a stay on one of the islands in the Ionian Sea. One poem in particular attracted my attention. It was called "The Procession". In the footnotes it explained that this island, like all the other Greek islands, had a saint of its own. A Byzantine saint from the sixteenth century called Gerasimo. This Gerasimo was the patron saint of the mentally ill, the troubled in spirit, and ordinary people who were depressed or miserable. Once a year thousands of people came to the island from all over Greece and walked in procession from the church of the saint to a plane tree he had planted with his own hands, whose leaves brought succour to all the unhappy souls seeking relief from their suffering.

I closed my eyes. Where was the guest now? Was he all right? Was he happy, was life treating him well? I tried to concentrate with all my might and to send him my sheltering love. Perhaps it would be able to protect him, even a little, from all the troubles and predicaments that he was no doubt bringing on himself.

I imagined the procession. At the head marched a brass band, dazzling in the shining gold of its bugles and trombones. After the band came the dignitaries, the priests and the churchmen, and behind them broad-shouldered stalwarts with moustaches carrying flags, crosses and icons and the reliquary holding the saint himself. And bringing up the rear all the ordinary people who bore no office and whose only wish was to be saved and purged of their misery. Their tortured faces were illuminated with enthusiasm, their eyes touched by hope.

I saw the rocky hills round about, and at their feet a little village. Its white houses with their faded tiles surrounded by gardens full of brightly coloured flowers. I saw dusty olive trees and clumps of thorny bushes dotted among the rocks. I saw goats grazing in the distance, raising their eyes to stare in astonishment at the passing parade of human commotion and then going back to crop the low vegetation. Looking down, I saw the sea in its dazzling brilliance, its infinite expanses. Blue and flat, full of promise, as if it was the solid, stable element, and not the physical earth on which we led our lives.

And among the marchers I saw the faces of my mother, of

Nehama, of Armand, sweating under the burning sun. Armand was carrying my mother's bag and a bottle of mineral water, Nehama was grumbling, full of demands for him to pick a sprig of rosemary for her or give her his arm when the path grew suddenly steeper. I saw my mother striding forward resolutely, not allowing herself to be distracted by the spectacular view, concentrating on her goal.

I saw Katyusha carrying Arthur in her arms, stumbling over wayward stones, complaining in Russian to the child, who was wearing a straw hat with a round brim, his squinting eyes riveted on the golden trombone in the band. I saw Rivki climbing energetically, her hair wild, her eyes shining, wiping her face on her sleeve. I saw Gidi, panting in his elegant clothes, his white silk shirt sticking to his back. I saw Zara bounding about, stopping to sniff at the dry bones of a goat which had departed this world, causing a commotion in an anthill trampled by her heavy paw, chasing a butterfly. I saw Bat-Ami and Herb – Bat-Ami tottering on high heels and shaking her head over the difficult conditions of the journey and Herb leaning heavily on her arm, worn out by his illness. I saw my father stepping lightly, effortlessly, a stalk of grass in his mouth and in his hand a dry branch with which from time to time, like a restless child, he hit the rocks he encountered on his way and the trunks of the olive trees. I saw the guest, reflective behind his dark glasses, smoking as he walked, whistling occasionally, inspecting the surrounding landscape, and sinking into his thoughts again. I saw myself, looking exactly like one of the Greek virgins who had never known a man, in my dark clothes, with my Vladimir Madonna's face, in a motley crowd of other women – solitary widows, worried mothers, disreputable girls and demented old women.

Under the plane tree stands St Gerasimo. His face is the face of an aged Byzantine saint in the icons the guest liked so much, the cruder, stranger ones, where the expressive power overcomes the refinement of colour and line. And all of us, in turn, bend down and kiss his emaciated feet with their slender ankles, their distorted nails, calloused as the feet of a tramp, and he blesses us, lays his hands trembling with age on our dusty heads, our hair soaked in the Mediterranean sun, and instantly all the misery is released and departs from our weary souls. The sadness flies out of our hearts like a black bird soaring into the sky and disappearing behind the mountains, and the bitter taste of loss gives way to the sweetness of the saliva in our mouths.

And afterwards I saw each of us returning to his life, to his strange, unavoidable fate. I myself returned to my room, breathing in the smell of the paint, the smell of my childhood, the smell of passing time, and settle down to my work. And when the darkness rises and fills me, blocking my thoughts, burying every idea in its shapeless womb, suffocating me with incurable longings, I undo the knot in the crumpled handkerchief and breathe in the dry smell of the leaves plucked from the plane tree.

I switched on the overhead light. I looked at the unfinished work on the easel. I took it down and stretched a new canvas on the frame. I began to work, at first slowly, groping after that elusive concentration, courting it with the tricks of a practised suitor – with nonchalance, with mechanical, almost casual activity, with minimum effort, until it yielded and sucked me into it, making me forget the night, the room, the burden of my feeble body, my bitter soul, my mother and the guest and for a moment or two even myself, the strange Susannah Rabin, and who could wish for greater happiness than that?

I worked into the morning, sometimes sitting down for a few minutes, smoking or just staring into space, and then suddenly getting up and returning to the painting.

The daylight filtered in, paling and obliterating the electric light, the real star making her appearance on the stage and pushing the ambitious extra into a corner. I heard my mother's morning movements, water running, doors slamming, footsteps, dishes in the kitchen sink.

I wiped my hands on a turpentine-soaked rag.

I dipped the brush in black and wrote in clumsy letters in the bottom right-hand corner of the finished work "Susannah Rabin".

I was at peace.

When my mother came into my room she found me in bed with the blanket over my head and she tiptoed out. I waited until I heard the rattling of her keys and the slamming of the front door and raced to the telephone, stumbling and tripping over an out-of-place chair on the way. I dialled the number of the outpatients' clinic.

"Rivka Finkwasser," I said, "it's urgent."

"Impossible," I heard the indifferent voice of the switch-board operator, "she's got a full list today, she asked not to be disturbed."

"But I'm a client, I mean a patient of hers," I faltered over the definition of my relationship to my social worker.

"Sorry. She specifically said not to put through any calls to her." I could hear the vigorous chewing of her gum.

"Just tell her it's Susannah, and it's urgent."

"I've just told you, miss, it's impossible." I heard the bubble of her chewing gum bursting in my ear.

"Tell her Susannah, Susannah Rabin. You'll see that she'll take the call." By now I was almost begging.

"I'm sorry, miss."

"Just say Susannah Rabin. Just tell her," I yelled, trying desperately to stop her from hanging up.

"Susannah who?" The chewing stopped for a moment.

"Rabin. Susannah Rabin."

The silence on the other end of the line frightened me more than her obstinate refusal. Now she would hang up and cut me off.

"Rabin? Like Yitzhak Rabin? Are you any relation to?"

"Yes," I yelled, unable to restrain the excitement aroused in me by the intolerable ease of this solution to my problem. "Of course I'm a relation to. Of course I am. An aunt, I mean a cousin. A second cousin, that is."

A Frozen Moment Of The Present

> Beauty is momentary in the mind —
> The fitful tracing of a portal;
> But in the flesh it is immortal.
>
> The body dies; the body's beauty lives.
> So evenings die, in their green going,
> A wave, interminably flowing.
> So gardens die, their meek breath scenting
> The cowl of winter, done repenting.
> So maidens die, to the auroral
> Celebration of a maiden's choral.

Wallace Stevens

Surprisingly enough, the parting was emotional but not sad. They all came to say goodbye. Armand, Katyusha and Arthur, Rivki, Gidi Bochacho and of course Nehama, who was once more in a wheelchair, which my mother pushed with surprising skill. I refused all offers of lifts and insisted on going by taxi and alone, as befitted the guest's faithful disciple. After partaking of a festive breakfast everyone stood in front of the entrance to our building, waiting for the taxi that was to take me to Rosh Pinna. Their faces looked pale and vulnerable in the spring sunshine.

The street where I lived lay before my eyes, already organizing itself for its future role as one of the exhibits in the museum of memory, as if it had fenced itself off behind an invisible barrier with a little sign saying: "Please don't touch". Each detail stood out in sharp isolation: the rubbish bins, the ragged oleander and hibiscus bushes, a skinny cat which inspected us with eyes full of pus and scratched itself, the distant cries of a rag-and-bone man, a granny with a cellphone and a pram on the opposite pavement.

I went up to Armand, who was holding Arthur in his arms, and pressed my cheek to his, once on the left and then on the right and then on the left again, making a little kissing motion in the air, just like they do in France.

"A bientôt, Armand," I said.

"A bientôt, Susannah ma chère."

And perhaps, if my poor French had been up to it, I would have said other things too. I would have said: Look, I've caught up with you, I'm a thousand years old already with all my memories. And perhaps something different, human, simple, precise. But what did I know, apart from words of flattery and farewell?

I stroked the child's broad cheek with the back of my hand. "You're a great kid, Arthur," I said. He sniffed and gave me a squinting stare.

Katyusha, who in spite of the nip in the air was wearing the grey silk dress with the narrow straps in honour of the occasion, planted two smacking kisses on my cheek.

"Good luck, Suzy. I hope you won't regret giving me dress."

"Of course not, I'm too thin for it," I smiled.

Rivki was standing a little apart, holding Zara's leash while the dog sat pressed to her leg, panting quick, hot pants and taking a keen interest in what was happening.

"Goodbye for now, Rivki," I said. "Thank you for everything."

"Thank me? I should thank you, my dear. I can't tell you how happy I am with her. She's a fantastic dog. And it's terrific that you're going and everything. Believe me, there's nothing more important for a woman than to realize herself, nothing, I've finished with all that other nonsense too – self-realization is all that matters."

I put my arms round Zara's neck. She squirmed in excitement, wagging her amputated tail from side to side. "Hang in there, sweetheart." She licked my face, knocking my sunglasses sideways.

The taxi drew up next to us. "Rabin, special to Rosh Pinna, is that you?"

Everyone began moving round and looking for something to do, but I only had one suitcase and a small travelling bag with the logo of the bank on it.

"Yes, that's us," said Gidi Bochacho and went with the driver to put the suitcase in the boot. On the way he asked me, "Susannah, I can't decide: should I go and pick up the ticket first, or stop off at Sheinkin Street to buy shoes?"

"First the ticket, then the shoes," I pronounced.

I bent down to Nehama and hugged her as hard as I could, kissing her crumpled cheeks, which were covered with a mixture of face powder and tears.

"Take care of yourself, Nehamaleh, and of my mother too. I'll call and write. Just as we said."

"I will. And you look after yourself over there, in that institu . . ."

"Nehama!' My mother maintained a high level of alertness even at difficult moments like this.

"All right, all right, excuse me, that art centre. Once I used to go with Lieber to a spa up there in the Galilee, because – I told you – he had colitis and the vegetarian diet calmed his stomach, so I know the area round there very well, it's something outstanding, the Jezreel Valley, the Hula, the cranes in the autumn. Or is it the spring? By the way, Susannahleh, did you know that Ben Gurion, that *alte kakker*, dried the Hula swamps for nothing? To impress the Americans, as if he was eradicating malaria. And what did he eradicate – *gurnischt mit gurnischt*, nothing times nothing, people died there like flies. Here I have to agree with Armand, he was really off his rocker, maybe because of all that standing on his head. You know that . . ."

"Nehama!" my mother's call to order came just in time because the taxi driver was already sitting behind the wheel and grumbling about traffic jams on the way out of town.

Gidi shook my hand warmly.

"Well, I have to run. So the travel agency first and the shoes later?"

"Exactly, Gidi."

Nehama rolled herself in the direction of the taxi, afraid of missing an argument with the driver.

The taste of future, guessed-at longings.

The taste of peppermint cough mixture. The coldness of the thermometer under my tongue.

My eyes sought my mother's face. She stood to one side, grinding a cigarette she had only lit a minute ago under her heel. I looked at the movement of her slender ankle.

And I thought, here it is, it's happening.

A frozen moment of lucid present.

I stood opposite my mother, examining her face, trying to absorb it into myself, to engrave its every detail, down to the smallest wrinkle, on the slate of my future memory. The short distance between us was packed with emotion. I could sense the umbilical cord, cut by the careful hand of the midwife somewhere in the past, still continuing to live its secret life. A flexible organic tissue connecting my belly inseparably to hers. I could have gone on standing there for ever, paralysed, concentrated on her, attached to her with every fibre of my being. And perhaps I would have done just that, if she hadn't closed and opened her eyes in a soft, unequivocal command: Go on, child. Go now.